THE EMBERS OF HEAVEN

Alma Alexander was born in a town on the banks of an ancient river, in a country that no longer exists. She has lived in Zambia, Swaziland, South Africa and New Zealand, and now lives in Washington, USA, where she writes full-time and runs a monthly writing workshop with her husband. She has written one previous novel for HarperCollins, *The Secrets of Jin-Shei*. For more information about Alma Alexander and her books, please visit her website: www.almaalexander.com

Also by Alma Alexander

The Secrets of Jin-Shei

ALMA ALEXANDER

The Embers of Heaven

HARPER

Harper
An imprint of HarperCollins*Publishers*
77–85 Fulham Palace Road
Hammersmith, London W6 8JB

www.harpercollins.co.uk

This paperback edition 2006
1

First published in Great Britain by
HarperCollins*Publishers* 2006

A catalogue record for this book
is available from the British Library

ISBN-13 978 0 00 720407 6
ISBN-10 0 00 720407 8

Typeset in Sabon
by Palimpsest Book Production Limited,
Polmont, Stirlingshire

Printed and bound in Great Britain by
Clays Ltd, St Ives plc

ACKNOWLEDGMENTS

My thanks to my invaluable beta readers, whose input clarified many things for me – Neil, Sharyn, Nick, Glenda, Bil. You helped make my characters come alive for me, gave them an extra dimension, laughed with them and wept for them. I am grateful. Jerry gave me the inspiration to begin the book, and by virtue of that, began the thought process that created the whole storyline, by introducing me to the work of young artist Daniel Conway, and most specifically, the image called 'Her Silent Silhouette' (which can be seen at http://www.arcipello.com/site/viewpic.php?id=160).

My husband Deck, as always my first reader and a consummate editor without whose input this would have been quite a different and a diminished book, has a lot to put up with while I am in the throes of carving out a new novel. My eternal gratitude for his patience, his kindness, his unfailing optimism in the face of authorial despair, and for making me stop writing occasionally in order to eat lunch (which he also cooks!) or take a few moments to rest my soul by gazing out into the serenity of our cedar woods.

I owe a great debt to the writers of the numerous articles and more than twenty-five books which I read in order to be able to write this one. In order to recreate my fictional and fantastical counterpart of what we in our world know as China, I have devoured books on Chinese history and its many revolutions, biographies of many of the leading political figures as well as those of ordinary people caught up in the extraordinary events of the Chinese civil war and the Cultural Revolution; books on cultural history and on geography and on kinship and family in China. All of this was treasure which was carefully gathered in order to build up my own version of the land of which I wrote, the alternative fantasy China called Syai where the events of this novel take place.

Special thanks to Jill, without whom none of the miracles of the past few years would have happened, and to Katie and Susan, my British editors, who believed in *The Embers of Heaven* from a time before the beginning – when the entire story existed as nothing more than a synopsis and a writer's vision.

Alma Alexander

When Jill first asked if there was a sequel, I said no —
until it became impossible to keep saying that,
because I was holding it in my hand.

So this one is for Jill, with my thanks.

THE EMBERS OF
HEAVEN

Water. They were lost in a world of it, their ship slicing through the silky waters of the open ocean, prow pointed to where the sun rose out of the water every morning. The ocean was smooth, cobalt blue, reflecting only sky. Sometimes there would be porpoises racing the ship or playing in its spreading wake; sometimes, a long way away, something huge and dark broke surface with its fin, blowing spray – but days went by with nothing in the world but sun and sky and sea, and the days were long.

The nights were longer still; quiet, soundless except for the creaking of the ship and the splash and lap of water against the hull. Out on the prow there was a space where ropes were coiled. Empty barrels were tied up in a raft right up near the bow of the ship. It made a good, comfortable nest, and the hiss of parting waters as the ship cleaved through them made for a gentle, soothing lullaby.

It was there that the first dream came to Amais.

Curled up in a comfortable loop of thick twisted rope, she might have believed that the sounds of water lapping against something hard and solid actually came from the sea and the ship she was on – but the sound was wrong for that.

It was the sound of water breaking on something stationary, not a travelling ship's hull. And after that, when she blinked and looked around, it was easy to see that she had left the ship far behind and was in some strange and yet oddly familiar place.

There were two people in the dream, aside from the dreamer herself: a woman and a little girl, holding hands. They had their backs to the dreamer and she could not see their faces. She could not see the woman clearly at all, just the shape of her in silhouette through a translucent parasol which covered her slender body down to her waist. They were both wearing old-fashioned, almost antique gowns, court garb which existed only in paintings and in stories; the little girl wore her long dark hair loose except for a topknot high on her head, held by two black lacquer hairpins. Behind them, steps with a broken wooden hand-railing led down into dirty water splashing against the bottom step. Floating debris bobbed in the water and piled up against the rise of the stair. It was dark, but there was a soft light about, something that resembled the way the sky looked when it was reflecting a huge but distant fire.

That was all. The water, the stairs, the two incongruously clean and elegant women in their rich court gowns, as though waiting for death or for rescue, trapped on a high point while fire and flood raged around them. Just like on the ship – there was water everywhere, but this water was dark and bitter and lifeless and life-taking. It was the aftermath of something, a disaster beyond words. Only a little bit away from the edge of the lowest stair the water was black and opaque and somehow passively threatening, as though it were about to rise, engulf even this last little spot where they clung to survival and safety.

Water, lapping. Water, spilled, insistent, all-enveloping – like a primeval world, the world where the earth had yet to rise from the sea of creation. As though a world was ended . . . or was about to begin.

The little girl turned her head slightly – just enough to cast a glance back to the spot from where the dreamer watched, hovering like a transparent and incorporeal ghost behind the two figures on the platform at the top of the drowned stairs. The child's face was obscured by strands of wind-tousled hair, but she had huge dark eyes, enormous in her pale face, glittering with their own light, the light that might have been knowledge, or recognition, or pity.

Then she turned away again, her hair spilling back across her shoulders, falling to where a formal sash was tied in the ceremonial way, so that a long train of it fell over the knot at the back of her waist and flowed down the back of her gown. The train had writing on it, but it was not something that the dreamer could read – at least not here, not now, not in this half-light, not before the rest of the dream was made clear. The little girl held on to the older woman's free hand with an air that managed to be both terrified and protective at the same time.

The sky was pearl grey, streaked with improbable shades of cinnamon and apricot; the air was alive with breezes that whipped and collided and teased the waters below into an unquiet whispering sound.

It was the end of the world.

It was the beginning.

The Language of Lost Things

The old gods dwell in their abandoned temples in
your memory – sad places dusty with disuse, with
dark altars empty of offerings. But they endure the
weight of these with what power they may claim as
long as their names are remembered, until the hour
in which they are finally and irrevocably forgotten.
Then they blow away like dust in the wind, like the
cold ashes from the dead altars. On such ashes as
this our world is built. In it the footsteps of new
gods may one day leave traces of their passing, on
their way to their own cold oblivion.

The Book of Old Gods

One

There were only two questions that governed Amais's existence.

She would wander out of the house, still wearing some esoteric item of Syai clothing her mother, Vien, kept carefully folded away in a wooden chest, or proudly step out to the snickers and astonished stares of her peers with her hair in what she fondly believed was a good rendition of a hairstyle once worn by empresses at the Syai court. Her mother would strip off the offending garments or impatiently tug Amais's wealth of thick curly hair out of its badly pinned and unruly coils into a semblance of order with a wooden comb, and murmur despairingly,

'Why can't you be like everyone else?'

But when Amais rebelled at learning the long and ancient history of her ancestral land and her kinfolk, or refused to go hunting for incense or some out-of-season fruit required for sacrifice to the spirits of those ancestors in the small shrine set apart in what was in effect a larger shrine to Syai itself in her mother's childhood home – citing the fact that none of her friends had to do such outlandish things – the wind would change. Vien's face would assume an expression of martyred sorrow, and she would ask instead,

'Do you have to do what everyone else does?'

Perhaps it would have been easier if it hadn't been for the two grandmothers and the games they played for the souls of their bewildered granddaughters, Amais and, in her turn, Nika.

Vien's mother, the grandmother Amais knew as *baya*-Dan, hardly ever set foot outside the door to what, on the outside, was a perfectly ordinary whitewashed little house tucked away at the end of a village street behind what was almost a defensive barrier of ancient olive trees. Inside, its shutters usually closed to keep out the bright sunshine and shroud the rooms within in a permanent twilight, the place might have been transported from a different world. Candles and fragrant incense burned on little altars draped with scarlet silk; scroll paintings and poems written in the long elegant script of *jin-ashu*, the ancient secret tongue of the women of Syai, hung from the walls. A low table held all the paraphernalia needed for a proper tea ceremony, and it was at her grandmother's knee that Amais learned how to perform one properly. It was something that seemed to be a fit and useful thing for her to know while she was steeped in the dreamy atmosphere of what *baya*-Dan insisted on calling the True Country. It all seemed ludicrously silly when Amais stepped over this magic threshold and back into the real world, where the golden sunlight of Elaas glinted off the bluest water in the world and the white walls of the village houses clung to the hillside. But inside, in *baya*-Dan's enchanted house, it was the only thing that made any sense.

Baya-Dan had been born in Elaas, as had her own mother, and her mother's mother before her. Her forebears had lived out their own tranquil lives in the midst of an alien society. They married their own kind, from within the community, with the women keeping ancient traditions alive in the home while the menfolk pursued the work of trade and commerce

8

which had brought their ancestors out from Syai a long time ago – sailing trading ships, keeping ledgers, building fortunes.

But for *baya*-Dan it had been so much more than that.

When she was no more than sixteen, her path had crossed with the black-sheep scion of the Imperial family – a Third Prince, a 'spare' aristocrat from within the core of the Imperial family itself; one who professed to be bored with protocol and the puppet-play of Syai's ancient Imperial Court and who said he had chosen to leave it all behind and seek his fortune in the world. It was never mentioned that he might have sensed the winds of change that were about to scour his country and his family and had taken whatever steps he could to escape the storm. The young Dan had been reared properly in all required traditions, she was the right age, she was presentable, and her father had put enough aside for a generous dowry. Dan herself had been young enough to be impressed by the fact that she had married an Imperial prince, and she had somehow taken this elevation in status to mean that she was single-handedly and personally responsible for the safekeeping of the traditions of Syai, here in the alien lands so far from her ancestral shores. The conviction had deepened when she had allowed a particular festival and its sacrifices to slide one year, and the very next voyage that her husband had undertaken had been his last. Dan had taken the blame for the storm that had claimed the ship, with the loss of its cargo and all hands. The commercial blow to the family's fortunes had been considerable, but the personal loss was far more grievous to Dan, who had responded by retiring to a tiny house in a fishing village, on an island far from the commercial hub of the mainland, and withdrawing into her own small world where it was easy to pretend that the world outside – the Elaas of the sunlit seas and laughing, beautiful people – simply did not exist.

Her daughter, Vien, had been kept on a tight leash,

intensely protected and guarded, both sheltered and imprisoned deep within the shrine to Syai that her home had become. For her, the world outside was the free air outside a cage. The more Vien's mother wrapped her in Syai's soft but bitingly tight trammels of tradition and responsibility, the more she was cocooned in the shadows of her candlelight and incense, the louder the laughter outside her windows in the moonlit nights rang in her own soul.

Her mother had chosen to lead a life far more traditional than even her peers back in the True Country now led. Vien was taught everything that a high-ranking court lady should know. She was taught how to read and write *jin-ashu* script and the subtle nuances of the women's language; she memorised imperial lineages dusty with antiquity, learned about the secrets of her gender and her race. Far away from the real Syai, inexorably changing under the weight of its history, Vien learned how to lead a life rooted in fairytale and dream. She was presented with the vanished world of her ancestors as though it had been a living and vital thing, and was asked to accept the reality of things that either no longer existed or were fast fading away. But here on the island, isolated even from such news as filtered through from Syai to the expatriate community on the mainland, it was just as easy to believe that such things as the ancient and sacred sisterhood of *jin-shei* still governed the relationships of every woman in Syai, and that emperors were chosen on the basis of an empress-heir's prophetic dreams.

Vien endured this for long, weary years. Her childhood slipped away, fossilized in these ancestral halls. But the world outside was ever louder in calling to her, ever more insistent in its presence – and Vien finally chose to utterly rebel against her suffocating heritage. She became the first of her line since the family had left the shores of Syai, centuries before, to truly step outside of her world.

Somehow, in spite of her sequestered life and sheltered existence, she had managed to make the acquaintance of Nikos. He was three times forbidden to her – he was not of her kind or of her culture; he was a simple fisherman with no fortune; and he was younger than Vien, who was in her early twenties by the time their paths had crossed, by a handful of years.

They were married in the moonlight, in a temple of Nikos's people, by one of his priests.

Dan had simply disowned her daughter.

Nikos's widowed mother, Elena, had not been overjoyed either at her new daughter-in-law. But Nikos was her last surviving son, and after a short period of friction Elena had simply concluded that Vien was not so much disrespectful and recalcitrant as genuinely ignorant of any kind of life other than what she had known in her mother's house. So Elena put aside her pique, and turned instead to teaching Vien how to prepare fresh fish, how to use Elaas herbs in her cooking, how to bake the particular sticky sweets of which Nikos was so fond, and how to erase as much as possible of the sing-song accent with which she – even though she had been born in Elaas – spoke the language of the land outside her mother's makeshift temple to Syai.

All that changed when Amais was born.

In Dan's own inimitable and high-handed manner – she had been married to a prince, after all, and had never forgotten that she could claim the title and privileges of an Imperial princess if she so chose – Vien's mother had sent word that her granddaughter was to be presented to her in her home at a certain auspicious hour.

Elena had snorted in outrage but Vien had rocked her small newborn daughter in her arms, and had dropped her gaze in the face of her mother-in-law's sharp comments.

'She is my mother,' Vien had said, finally. 'I owe her my respect, at least. And this is her grandchild, after all.'

Elena had thrown her hands up in the air, in the expressive manner of her own culture, in a way that Dan would have considered a vulgar show of emotion in public and could not have ever conceived of doing. 'Mark my words,' Elena had said darkly, 'no good can come of it.'

Vien had offered up the child as she had been commanded, and Dan, holding her granddaughter in her arms after first wrapping her up in a scarlet birth-cloth taken from one of the many cedar chests in her house, had inspected the drowsing child's features closely.

'Her skin is too fair, and her eyes are too slanted, like a cat's . . . Oh well, I suppose that can't be helped, under the circumstances,' Dan said critically. She sniffed, giving the impression that she was holding back from saying far worse. 'Be that as it may. You will bring her to me every day. For an hour or so, while she is still in swaddling clothes. After . . . we will see.'

'Whatever for, Mother?' Vien said, looking startled and not a little trapped. Perhaps her mother-in-law's words were coming back to echo in her mind.

'So that I can start teaching her, of course,' Dan replied, in a tone of voice that indicated Vien was simple-minded not to know this already. 'She has unfortunate aspects to her lineage but she was born on an auspicious day. That means that her life will matter. She will be given in abundance, but whether joy or sorrow I cannot tell. It may matter how much she knows of her people and her past when the Gods come knocking at her door asking for her.'

'Ridiculous,' Elena had snapped when Vien, a little bewildered, returned to her husband's house with her daughter in her arms. 'The child is a helpless baby, not a scion of the Gods. What else did she have to say on the matter, your mother?'

'She named her,' Vien said. 'The child's name is Amais.'

'That's a mouthful,' Elena said trenchantly.

'It means "nightingale",' Vien added helpfully.

'Ridiculous,' Elena said.

But Nikos had, somewhat unexpectedly, taken Dan's side and had overruled his mother.

'This is all she has left,' he told Vien in the darkness of their room at night, with the contested child sleeping the sleep of the innocent in the crib he had made for her with his own hands. 'Let her have that much. Amais is a beautiful name, and it means a beautiful thing. We can give our daughter that gift.'

So Amais was taken dutifully to her maternal grandmother's house every day. She seemed content to be there, perhaps lulled by her grandmother's quiet, melodious lullabies, quite happy to kick her baby heels on the piles of cushions that Dan provided for her. Later, when she started to crawl and then to toddle, Dan placed no restrictions on her activities in the house, merely removing small grasping hands gently from draperies when they looked about ready to come down on the child in a heap. Amais grew up to the sound of her grandmother's voice, first the songs and then the poetry that was read to her while she listened, rapt, not understanding half the words but happy to be in the circle of *baya*-Dan's world. For a while she was too young to know how different her two worlds were, the world of twilight and old protocol where she was a sort of princess-heir wrapped in silks and scarlet, and the world of sunlight and sea where she ran gurgling with childish laughter from foam-tipped waves breaking from a sapphire-coloured sea as they lapped at her round heels.

Amais grew into a chubby, moon-faced toddler with round cheeks and what looked like far too much forehead. Dan had been right – Amais's fair skin was scorched into angry red blotches if she did not protect it from the sun, and her eyes had not been of the degree of roundness required of a princess of the Imperial blood. But the eyes in question had quickly turned from the guileless blue of babyhood into an improbable shade of golden brown flecked with green, and her hair, the despair and secret pride of both grandmothers, was a serendipitous mix of Vien's hip-length mane that fell thick and straight like a black waterfall and Nikos's riotous curls, and framed Amais's face in huge smooth waves.

On this, both grandmothers were in full agreement.

'She is not pretty . . .' Elena would say thoughtfully, looking on as the toddler laughed up at her father when Nikos would come home from a long day's work and sweep his small daughter up in his arms.

'. . . but one day she will be beautiful,' Dan would say, across the island in her own exotic house, watching the same toddler explore the texture of some ancient brocade, apparently in completion of the same thought.

'All I want her to be is happy,' Vien would sigh to both women.

Elena would smile at that, and spill a reassuring fairytale of how it would be for Amais when she grew up and reached out to claim her place in the world. But Dan was both more pragmatic and more frightening in her response.

'Beware of too much happiness,' she had murmured, and had turned away for a moment as if the laughter of her daughter's child had been a knife in her heart.

14

Two

Vien was eight and a half months pregnant with her second child, heavy and graceless and swollen with a baby that could have been born at any minute, when Nikos's boat went out one spring morning. The crew waved goodbye to such family as had gathered to see them off, as they had done hundreds of times before, and left together with a flotilla of other boats exactly the same as theirs, sailing off into the sweet newborn sunshine of a spring dawn glinting on the sapphire seas.

Seven-year-old Amais, who had woken early that morning from uneasy dreams, had been fretful and weepy, and Elena, in order to give heavily pregnant Vien some respite, had taken the child out to see her father off on his day's fishing.

'I will catch a mermaid for you, *korimou,* little darling!' Nikos called to his daughter as the sea widened between them. 'Now go home and be good for your mother!'

Amais had clung to that unlikely promise all day. When Elena readied herself to go to the wharf to meet the fishing boats at the end of the day, Amais insisted on going with her, wanting to be right there when her father brought the gift of that mermaid ashore for her.

One by one, the boats came back that night. All of them, except one.

Elena and Amais waited there as the other boats came in, exchanging smiles and the occasional word of congratulation or commiseration with the crews and their families as they straggled in and showed off their catch. But the sun rode lower and lower in the sky, and still Nikos's boat had not come. Elena grew quieter and quieter, standing there carved like a statue, her eyes fixed on the horizon, her lips moving ever so slightly in what might have been prayer. She already wore the black kerchief of the widow, and was no stranger to sea death. Neither were the others, the family members of the rest of the men on the lost boat, who also waited there on the wharf. They all wore the same expression, which was essentially no expression at all – their faces were stony, as though they were already bracing themselves for the grief that was to come. Amais was too young to completely understand, but her grandmother's hand on hers had turned into a cold and clutching claw made from marble, and the child's own heart was beating very fast as the beautiful spring day drew to a close.

The sunset was beautiful, perhaps the most beautiful that Amais could ever remember having seen. The sky was streaked with unlikely colours – something that resembled the rich red of the wine they made from the grapes grown on the hillside above the harbour, a deep violet-amethyst shade where the sky began to darken into twilight as the sun went down, and traces of dark gold . . . the exact shade that Amais had imagined of a mermaid's hair. Someone, without speaking, without asking, lit a lantern and hung it on an iron hook set into the wharf – a makeshift lighthouse, calling them home, the lost ones, the ones that most of the people on that wharf already knew would not return.

It was full dark when the first of the statues, another black-kerchiefed woman, finally moved, let her hands drop helplessly to her sides, let out her breath in a deep sigh that ended in a quiet sob, bowed her head, and walked slowly away from the sea, back to the hushed village. It was as though she broke the stasis. One by one they did the same thing, like a ritual, bowed their heads to the sea, walked away.

Elena was the last to go. Amais had been standing there with her on the wharf for hours, had grown stiff and uncomfortable, but not for anything would she have moved, would she have let go of the hand that clung to her own as though she were the last anchor in a storm-tossed world. But Elena was almost unaware of her. When she too opened her lips a crack and allowed a breath to escape – a sigh that sounded like she was letting her soul out of her body and sending it over the waves to search for her son's spirit – her hand relaxed for a moment, and it was only then that she looked down and blinked, seeming to have just realised that she was still holding her granddaughter's hand in her own.

'Let's go home, Nana,' Amais whispered, profoundly sad, not yet fully aware of all that this night would mean to her.

'Home,' Elena repeated through cracked lips, as though the word held no meaning.

'Mama has been alone all afternoon,' Amais said, her voice taking on a tone of urgency, 'and the baby . . . the baby is coming . . .'

'The baby,' Elena repeated again. It seemed as though repeating someone else's last words was all that she was capable of right then, as if her own mind had ground to a halt, unable to move past this moment, this loss. And then she shook her head once, sharply, as though to clear it from the cobwebs of sleep. 'The baby,' she said once more. 'Yes, you are right. There is the baby.'

They walked back to their house in silence, still holding hands.

There was a light in the window as they approached, a lamp lit by Vien the good wife and left to light the way home for her family. She herself was waiting inside, very pale, her hands folded protectively over her swollen belly.

She knew, long before she saw only Elena and Amais enter the house. She could hear the absence of Nikos's footsteps, the void which his voice and his laughter would have filled. Her world was emptier for his soul. Her face was stark, her eyes very bright, and when the door closed behind Elena, who had finally let go of Amais's hand, Vien let out a small whimper and folded over herself as though she had been stabbed in the heart.

The whimper became a moan, something that took all her breath, and it wasn't until that first spasm had passed that Vien could whisper two words:

'*The baby . . .*'

There was no time, after that, for going to get the midwife, for going to get any help at all. Vien's second child, another daughter, was born just before midnight on the same day that her father had died. Elena, who delivered her, held the tiny newborn infant in her arms and stared at the child's face. It would have been hard to find any resemblance to her son in that bright-red puckered face with its eyes tightly shut and its bud of a mouth opening and shutting like a baby bird's when demanding sustenance – but Elena was seeing things that only a mother who had just lost a child and been given another in his place could see.

'Her name is Nika,' she said softly, and there was no arguing with that. It was the prerogative of the grieving mother, of the grandmother – this child, at least, her daughter-in-law's culture would not swallow. This was her son's child, named for him, born to be his substitute. There had been something implacable in her voice.

But *baya*-Dan was not one to relinquish something she considered hers, not without a fight. This child, as Amais before her, was summoned to the house where the tiny enclave of shadowed Imperial Syai was being preserved in the Elaas sunshine. The second grandmother had looked the babe over, and smiled a small secret smile.

'This one,' she prophesied, tracing the contours of the child's face with one bony finger, 'is going to look like you, my daughter. Look at those eyes, look at the shape of her face. Her name is Aylun, little cricket.'

'Her name is Nika,' Vien said. 'Elena already named her for her father.'

'Her name is Aylun,' Dan repeated firmly. 'You will see. You will bring this one, too, as you have done with Amais.'

But Elena would have none of that. 'Not this child,' she said to Vien when she returned from her visit to her mother, the baby cradled in the crook of her arm. Elena all but snatched the child out of Vien's arms, inspecting her closely, as though there were traces of the Syai cobwebs still draped on her swaddling clothes or evil spells woven in the air above her small head. 'This is my Nika, my baby, the child that will carry the spirit of my son. *She* already has Amais.'

Almost overnight, Amais had been abandoned by her father's mother. She became almost invisible in her father's house, with her grandmother's attention wholly focused on her younger sister. *Baya*-Dan commanded her attendance daily as usual, but now Amais chafed at it, feeling as though she had been traded, one child for another, one granddaughter for each grandmother, forced to choose one of her two worlds and barred from the other.

The first year of Nika's life passed thus, in tension and frustration. A barrier developed between Vien and Elena, who appeared to consider her granddaughter's mother merely a necessary evil, basically handing the child over to be nursed and then snatching her back as though prolonged contact with her mother would infect her with an incurable disease. But as that first year passed, it began to become painfully obvious that fate had played a joke on the family.

Amais, the elder, the one who had been abandoned to whatever destiny her Syai heritage might have in store for her, grew into her father's image, gently made female by the curve of cheek or the slope of delicate shoulder inherited from her mother and with a captivating touch of the exotic. She had her father's wild black hair, gleaming with blue highlights, curling riotously around her face, setting off those beautiful and almost uncanny eyes – she was a melding of all that was beautiful from her two worlds, as though she had been a work of art that had had two bright and vivid colours mixed on a palette, and emerged with a shade that was unique and all her own. But at least she had that trace of her father's kin in her.

Nika was all Syai – tawny ivory skin, round eyes with eyelids draped in drowsy epicanthic folds over irises so dark that the pupil of her eyes could barely be seen. She had the rosebud mouth and the small-boned grace of a Syai empress. It was as though Nikos had had nothing to do with her at all. She was, as Dan had said she would be, far more Aylun than she could ever be Nika, the Elaas name sitting almost gracelessly on this tiny, alien person to whom it just did not seem to belong.

But it was this child that held the spirit of Elena's son. Somehow, she managed to ignore the incongruities in the physical appearance of the children. Vien sometimes smuggled Nika – or Aylun as she always was in her Syai grandmother's house – out of Elena's sight for a few hours, and Aylun too would drowse happily in the lilting tones of *baya*-Dan's lullabies.

As for Amais, her own education at her Syai grandmother's hands – and it had become painfully obvious that it was just that, an education, that Amais was being groomed for something – accelerated. Amais and her grandmother were now reading the classics together, accounts of Imperial life in old Syai, ancient poems inscribed in crumbling books carefully put away in wrappings of silk and waterproof oiled cloth, tales of travel and trade set down by generations of exiles, all hoarded and treasured for four hundred years and passed down the centuries from generation to generation until it came down to this – an old woman and a young child who only half-belonged to this lost world.

It was not as though Amais had no interest in the things that she was given to study – some part of her was held rapt and fascinated by it. But there was that other part of her, the same restless spirit that had made her own mother respond to the laughter she heard echoing from beyond the brooding walls of Dan's house, and there were days that she squirmed and sighed and cast longing glances at the shuttered windows, feeling in her bones that she should be out on the rocky shores of Elaas's blue seas, scooping out small crabs from their hidey-holes or gathering clams at low tide. It was in that year, aware that Amais's attention was slipping away, that Dan allowed Amais to actually hold in her hands a set of thirteen small notebooks bound in faded red leather. Amais recognised them: her grandmother had read from those books while she listened, rapt, to the tales of long ago. The diary of a girl who, Dan said, was not much older than Amais herself when she began writing down the days of her life.

'These belonged to Kito-Tai,' *baya*-Dan said, her voice edged very slightly with an odd sort of triumph, watching the many-times-great-granddaughter of the ancient poetess touch the worn covers with light, almost frightened fingers. Amais was wholly here now, completely caught in the moment; the childish games of the Elaas children out on the sunlit shore were not even a memory of temptation. 'They are yours now. Take care of them – they are very old. They are her journals, and there is a lot of her poetry in there, too. We've read some of them already, on the scrolls – but those were transcribed, for sale in the marketplaces. These, in here, are her originals. Written in our own language.'

'Our own language?' Amais questioned, looking up. 'You mean *jin-ashu*? The women's tongue?'

'Yes, and now you know enough of it to be able to read those,' *baya*-Dan said, laying a loving and possessive hand over her granddaughter's where it rested on the red leather of many centuries ago. 'I have already read some of this to you. But now they are yours, they are my gift to you. They will be here for you, whenever you want them.'

Amais took one of the books at random, opened it, ran her finger reverently down the ancient page that lay revealed. '*Jin-shei*,' Amais murmured. 'She was *jin-shei* to an empress. The empress listened when she talked, and did what she said. And Nhia's, too, her *jin-shei-bao*, her heart-sister . . . and then Nhia became a Blessed Sage and was given a shrine in the Great Temple in Linh-an . . .' The latter was catechism; Dan owned a book about the Great Temple, one that described its appearance, its Gods, and detailed biographies of all the emperors and sages whose niches had been dedicated in the Second Circle of the Great Temple. It had been brought over by one of the later waves of immigrants from Syai, and was not quite the age of Kito-Tai's journals, but it was old enough – sixty or seventy years at least. Amais knew about Nhia because she had been singled out by her grandmother, because they had read her biography together, because she had been mentioned by name in every one of Tai's journals that resided in the cedar box. Making the leap from Nhia's status of Tai's *jin-shei-bao* to that of Blessed Sage of the Temple, as though the one had naturally followed from the other, however, had been something that Amais had done entirely on her own. Her grandmother might have objected mildly, but before she had a chance to do so Amais fired another distracting question. '*Baya*-Dan . . . have *you* ever had a *jin-shei-bao*?'

'I was not so fortunate,' said her grandmother in a tone of noble sorrow.

22

'But back in Syai, every woman had them. At least one. Didn't they?'

'They still do, I am certain,' murmured *baya*-Dan. 'It is the women's country, where you could find a sister in a friend, could depend on her, believe in her and in your bond when everything else failed, know that she always stood between you and doom.'

'Did you ever keep a journal yourself, *baya*-Dan?'

'Not quite like this,' Dan said. 'She was special, Kito-Tai. She was a poet. She saw every day through a poet's eyes. She filled a book every year of her life, you know. These are just a handful of her journals. The rest were lost and scattered, or just gone. Four hundred years is a very long life for a book.'

'Four hundred years . . .' Amais breathed, the eyes her grandmother had thought too slanted now quite round with wonder.

'That is your heritage,' Dan said. 'That is what you came from, that stock.'

'My mother never told me about this,' Amais said.

Dan allowed herself an inelegant snort. 'Then it is just as well that you have me,' she said.

But the passing of the journals seemed to herald a new phase in Dan's life. Amais had always known her as what she considered to be old – *baya*-Dan was straight-backed and clean-limbed, but her hands had gnarled with age and her face was seamed with fine lines under the mass of carefully dressed silver hair. After the child she continued to stubbornly call Aylun was born, *baya*-Dan seemed to consider her task done, her life well spent. She withdrew even further from the reality that was her world. Elaas, the bright sunlight and the sapphire sea and the vines of ancient vineyards twisted with venerable age at least as respectable as Dan's own, all that simply ceased to exist for her at all. If Vien didn't come by to make sure she ate – and that the food was prepared properly according to Dan's own high standards of the lost world of

23

Syai as best as could be managed – the old woman would be just as likely to spend the time in a sort of waking dream, drifting through the days with her eyes wide open but her gaze bent more on the ephemeral glories of her past than on the physical surroundings of her current existence.

Elena had almost forbidden her treasured younger grand-daughter to go to what she had taken to calling 'that woman's little palace' when Vien brought the news that Dan was dying, and wanted to say farewell to her grandchildren. The words 'Good riddance!' were hovering on the tip of Elena's tongue, but they remained unspoken. In some ways the two old women were far more alike than they realised or might have wanted to know. Both had a reverence for the circle of life, for those who went before, and for those who came after. Nika, what-ever Elena might have wished, was of Dan's blood, and Elena could not find it in herself to forbid the child to go and receive the dying blessing of her mother's mother. She watched the three walking away from the house – Amais running ahead to pluck some flowering weed by the roadside to present to her grandmother upon arrival, Vien holding Nika's still toddler-chubby little hand – and had a sudden vivid premonition that she might not be seeing this for very long, this remnant of family that was hers, this shadow of her lost son.

She almost called them back, ran to snatch little Nika up in her arms, demand that the child renounce her divided blood, that she become her own laughing little boy all over again. But perhaps it was already too late for that.

Vien had brought the toddler into the shadowy room where Dan now lay under the embroidered coverlets on her bed. Sensitive to the solemn mood of the occasion, Nika approached her grandmother's bed when given a light push by her mother, and Dan lifted a hand over the child's head, letting it flutter down on her silky dark hair for a moment.

'My little cricket,' she whispered. 'You were born in such

an hour . . . I wish your life could have been easier . . . but you and I will meet in Cahan one day. May you have light and grace all your days.' She allowed her hand to stroke Nika's hair, and then sighed. 'Send me your sister.'

Vien snaked out an arm and whisked an almost hypnotised Nika, who would always be Aylun in this place, out of the way. Amais stepped into the space so vacated, and this time Dan's hand was not light, offered no stroking. She reached out and closed her fingers around Amais's wrist, stared into her eyes with a gaze that was suddenly too full of power and passion to belong to a dying woman.

'Take the journals,' she said. 'They are for you. You are the last of Kito-Tai's line. Take the journals, and don't let her name be forgotten. Or your own.' Her eyes fluttered, closed, all passion suddenly spent, as though she had been filled by some external spirit which had now left her. 'Or your own . . .' she whispered, releasing Amais's hand.

Amais turned her head, alarmed, and sought her mother with a gaze that was almost frightened. 'Mother . . .'

'Watch your sister,' Vien said in a whisper. She pulled Amais free of the dying woman's bedside, planting a swift kiss of reassurance on the top of her daughter's head. 'Wait for me in the sitting room. Go.'

Amais took Aylun into the other room and gave her one of *baya*-Dan's shawls to play with – she didn't think her grandmother would mind. For her own part, she went to the chest where she knew that Tai's journals were kept. She knelt on the floor beside it for the longest time, her mind curiously blank, and then opened the lid and carefully took out the small pile of red notebooks that were her legacy. They sat there in her lap, in apparent innocence – but they had changed for Amais. Before, they had been a fascinating if somewhat distant link to her ancestry and her past. Now they were heavy with portent. It was as though Amais had

25

been charged with something by her grandmother on her deathbed, and these journals were the only way to find out just exactly what it was that she had accepted as her life's work. Her grandmother had not *exactly* asked Amais to promise anything, and Amais hadn't *exactly* given her word, but it had been implicit in that last conversation.

Don't let her name be forgotten. Or your own . . .

When Vien came out to gather her children up, her eyes were red and swollen.

'*Baya*-Dan . . . ?' Amais asked, her voice quavering just a little.

'She is gone, Amais-*ban*. She is gone.'

Don't let her name be forgotten. Or your own. Those words her grandmother had uttered out loud. But now, as Amais remembered them, it seemed to her that there had been another phrase, unspoken, ephemeral, ghostly, hovering in the air and settling lightly in Amais's mind and memory: *Or mine.*

Or mine . . .

But was it Dan's name she had wanted made immortal . . . or that of the strange spirit that had possessed her just before death came to claim her?

'Come on,' Vien said, holding out her hand. 'There's things I need to do now. Let's go home.'

Amais got up obediently, gathering up the thirteen precious notebooks, wrapping them up in a secure little parcel and hugging them to her chest all the way back to Elena's house. Somewhere in between those two places, the shrine to Syai where *baya*-Dan's spirit now lived and the cheerful green-shuttered house that her still-living grandmother inhabited, walking in the sunshine of Elaas with the treasure of Syai clasped close to her heart, suspended in the empty air between two worlds, Amais realised for the first time in her life that she was no longer sure just where 'home' was or how her heart was supposed to find her way there.

Three

Amais kept her head down and herself out of the way in the months that followed, months in which everyone around her seemed fractious, annoyed, or outright furious at things that hovered just outside her comprehension. Vien let down her hair and donned the traditional Syai mourning attire for her mother, which led to Elena making somewhat acid comments about the propriety of wearing so much white with her mother newly dead and her husband not a year in his grave. Vien cast her eyes down and took the barbed remarks in pious silence, her hands folded before her in gracious eastern position, suddenly prominently and obviously alien in the house where she had tried so hard to fit in and where she had once been wholly accepted.

Amais had been dressed in like manner, and the small knot of village children who were her companions had been curious and blunt, as children often were.

'That's what we wear in mourning,' Amais had explained, plucking at her white dress with nervous fingers. Out here in the Elaas sunshine, in the bright light of Elaas customs, the white garb did seem outlandish and strange.

'So your people are happy when someone dies?' her friend

Ennea asked. 'White is a colour of joy, you wear it when you marry, not when you die.'

'But back in Syai . . .'

'Is that where you're really from?' asked Dia, the school-teacher's daughter, a slightly higher social caste than the rest of them and generally given to passing on oracular pronouncements from her exalted parent as though they were edicts handed down from the Gods on their mountain. 'My papa says that blood will tell.'

'I was born here,' Amais said fiercely. 'I am from here!'

'But your mother wore black like she should when your father died,' said Ennea, with a child's utter disregard for tact or feelings, intent on pursuing some fascinating nugget of information and oblivious to all else.

'That was different,' said Amais, conscious of a sharp pain as the scab over that older wound, unhealed yet, cracked a little to allow a trickle of pain like heart's-blood to escape. 'My father was of Elaas, and . . .'

'But so is your grandmother,' another girl, Evania, pointed out. '*My* grandmother says she was born on the mainland, in the city, before she came to live out here – but she was born here. So she was of Elaas, too.'

Amais remembered the silk-swathed rooms of her grand-mother's house, the scrolls of poetry in a foreign tongue, the scent of alien incense.

'I don't think so,' she said carefully, too young to analyse the thing completely, aware that she could not defend it in the face of the practical questions of her playmates because they simply could not understand it.

'My mother says you're strange,' Ennea said.

But she had still been willing to stay Amais's friend and companion for all that, and no more was said on the matter, at least for the time being.

Dan had been cremated, on Vien's insistence and with

28

considerable trouble – since the body had had to be removed from the island in order for this to be accomplished, and getting the necessary permits was not a totally straightforward matter. In this, the established Syai community in Elaas stepped in to offer a helping hand – and that might have compensated for much, being welcomed back into her own world after choosing to step out of it for Nikos's sake. But the relations between Vien and her own people remained formal and a little cool. It was as though Amais's dilemmas were projected onto her mother, written much larger than those plaguing her own small self. Amais was still a child, and therefore obliged only to obey the instructions of those older and wiser than her – but Vien was an adult, with an adult's decisions to make. Decisions that would affect not only her own life but those of the people who depended on her – her two daughters.

And it soon became apparent that there was yet another voice, perhaps the most forceful of all, that guided Vien's choices – the insistent ghost of her mother.

When Vien first said the word 'home' and meant something other than the small cottage by the sea where she lived with Elena and the children, Amais almost missed it – but there was something in Vien's face, a soft and yet steely determination that frightened her into paying much closer attention.

The wind of change started blowing quite softly, nearly imperceptibly.

'I must take Mother home.'

That had been the innocuous sentence that let the first breath of moving air into the cold, stagnant little house, which was thus demoted, without ceremony, into a temporary dwelling. No longer the 'home' that Amais had known – the only home that she had ever known.

Elena did miss it, that first time. She simply ignored it, like she ignored so many things in those days. She ignored Vien's views on how her younger daughter should be dressed, fed, disciplined. She ignored Vien's older daughter altogether. She tried hard to ignore Vien's white clothes and the white ribbon she wore woven into that incongruous glossy smooth black hair that now hung long and loose down Vien's back.

But it quickly became too big to ignore. Mysterious people with inscrutable faces and round dark eyes came to call on Vien at Elena's cottage, treating Elena herself with scrupulously correct if icy politeness. Vien herself would disappear for several days at a time to the mainland, her only word on her absence that she had 'arrangements' to make. When she returned to the island after her final visit to the mainland, she carried something in a large envelope, clutched to her breast as though the contents were more precious than jewels.

That time even Elena had to notice.

'What do you have there?' she asked in the voice she now customarily used with Vien when she spoke to her at all, clipped and brusque, as though she had judged her daughter-in-law of some crime and found her unforgivably guilty.

'Tickets,' Vien said. 'We're going home, the three of us and Mother. Back to Syai.'

Everyone looked up at that, Amais in stark astonishment and Elena with something indefinable that was equal parts fury and fear.

'It's a long, wasted journey for a baby to make,' Elena said at last after a moment of silence, riding her emotions on a tight rein. 'Really, Vien. Your mother lived on these shores all of her life. She can hardly object to being buried in those hills now.'

'Did she?' Vien questioned softly, and Amais began to pay much closer attention. This was starting to sound a lot like the frustrating conversations she had had with her friends out at the rock pools, dressed in her inconvenient white 'mourning' garb. 'I don't think she ever quite lived here. Not really.'

'She was born here,' Elena snapped. 'As far as I know, she never set foot in Syai.'

'Her body, no,' Vien said. 'But her spirit . . . I do not think her spirit ever left Syai. She was half a woman all of her days, yearning back to the things that made her who she was. She deserves to rest there, in peace at last.'

'Syai is a long way to take the child to a funeral,' Elena said crisply.

Amais bowed her head to hide the sudden tears that welled in her eyes. There was only one child in Elena's mind, and it was not herself.

Her little sister, untroubled by all this, slept in her crib, oblivious to the conflict around her and about her. She would never know, Amais thought. She was too young for any of this to have meaning. She had never known her father, could never remember him.

'It is a long way, yes,' Vien said, and lifted her head, meeting her mother-in-law's eyes. 'But it isn't just a funeral that we would go for, Mother-in-law. We go . . . to stay.'

Elena's eyes widened for a moment, in pure shock that she could not hide, and then narrowed again and hardened until they were chips of obsidian in her set face.

'I forbid it,' she said, dropping each word like a pebble. Amais could almost hear them rattle as they rolled around on the floor at the women's feet.

'I'm sorry,' Vien said, 'but you cannot. It is not your place.'

'This is my son's child,' Elena said, crossing the room and snatching up the sleeping toddler out of her crib. Nika woke up abruptly, knuckled her eyes with her hands and began to whimper softly as though Elena's hands were clutching claws locked around her, holding on tight.

'It is my child,' Vien said. 'And here she would always be *wangmei*, just like . . . just like I was.'

'What are you talking about? What is that? She is my

31

son's daughter, the last thing of his that I have on this earth. She is no *wing* . . . whatever that is.'

'*Wangmei*,' Vien repeated patiently, standing her ground. 'It means "stranger of the body", an outsider, someone who obviously does not belong in a community. Someone different. Look at her and tell me how she will fit in here in a few years' time, when she's grown enough to want playmates, friends.'

'Amais never had a problem,' Elena said defensively, bringing her other granddaughter into the discussion for the first time, but only out of desperation, sacrificing her as a pawn to keep her claim on the younger, the precious one, the now openly wailing toddler in her arms. Amais's eyes were wide, her mouth parted, her heart beating painfully fast.

'Amais, *korimou* . . .' Vien said, letting a quick and strangely soft glance rest on her oldest for a moment. She had used the word Amais's father had called her – it was hard to tell whether she had done it deliberately or instinctively, but either way it suddenly sounded strange to Amais, coming from her mother's lips. 'Would you let your grandmother and I talk alone? I'll come and find you in a few moments.'

'But, Mother . . .'

'Please, Amais-*ban*. It is important.'

Amais slipped off the chair where she had been perched trying very hard to be invisible and dragged herself outside with unwilling obedience. But this concerned her – this was her life they were discussing in there! – so she didn't go far. She merely turned the corner and crouched underneath the window. It was shuttered against the sun, but beyond the shutters the window was open and it was not hard to eavesdrop on the conversation within.

'Amais is just as much *wangmei* as anyone,' Vien said as the door closed after her daughter. 'But Aylun . . .'

'*Nika*,' said Elena fiercely.

'Aylun – for that is the name she takes with her to Syai,

not Nika,' Vien countered. 'She could be Nika only here, in this house, in your heart. But she can still be saved, Elena. She can have one world to choose from and she will never know different. Amais . . . it is already too late for Amais. She is already of two worlds, and will always be torn between them. My mother is probably to blame for that. Perhaps I was, too, for letting her take my child, so young, so malleable – but Amais is already lost here, in this place, because she already knows who she is, who her ancestors were. She is more than *wangmei* here, she is always going to be *xeimei*, stranger of the heart, someone who might well have the sense of belonging to this community but who will never be a real part of it. Just like I never really was.'

Amais suddenly felt hot tears welling in her eyes. *She will take me away . . .*

'You were,' Elena whispered fiercely, rocking her Nika in her arms. 'You *were*. When you chose to be.'

'Amais would have chosen to be, in these last months,' Vien said, and tears stood in her eyes. 'Why have you not let her, Elena?'

'No,' Elena said, and for the first time her voice broke, brittle with the weight of too much sorrow. 'Don't take her away from me, Vien.'

'You have already done that,' Vien said. 'I don't have to do anything – you have already pushed Amais away yourself.'

'Not Amais. This one. Go, if you have to – take your child – but leave me Nika. Nika has my son's eyes. She . . .'

'Elena,' Vien said quietly, 'she does not. Amais does. Nika *is* Aylun – she has my mother's face, her hair, her eyes, her mouth. She will never be Nikos, Elena. She can't be.'

Elena stared at her, shaking her head minutely, as though she found her words incomprehensible, as if Vien had suddenly started speaking in the language of her ancestors. Which she had, in a way. This had been the first time she had ever used a word of that language in her mother-in-law's house, and it seemed almost ironic that the words she used meant 'stranger'.

'Excuse me,' Vien said, her voice floating out of the shuttered window, quietly filled with the calm serenity of one who had fought hard battles but who had finally won a war that had been raging for a long time in her soul. 'I think I had better go and find Amais now, and talk to her.'

Amais, under the window, uncoiled like a whip and raced across the rocky slope behind the house, down the path that led to the cove. She knew the track, every stone and rut and bump on it, and she fled surefooted along the familiar route, around the first curve and out of sight of the house before her mother had had a chance to turn around and open the door.

She wasn't even aware that the tears that had gathered in her eyes had spilled down her cheeks until she came to a stop at the bottom of the path, leaping down onto the shallow beach of boulder and coarse sand, and had to wipe the back of her hand across her eyes in order to clear her blurred vision. It was only then that her mouth opened like a wound and she sobbed out loud, her whole body shaking with an unexpected and bottomless grief.

The ocean glittered in the sunlight, sparking memories, bringing out things that it was suddenly a white pain to think about. Amais covered her mouth with both hands, as though that could keep the memory from coming, as though she could simply banish it back down into the repository from which it had been called – but it was too late, already too late for that.

She had gone out in a small sailing boat with her father when she was maybe four or five years old, something that she thought of as her first real clear memory. She had already been able to swim like a fish, and there was no fear there – but the women in the household had put up a fight nonetheless and part of the joy of that memory was the way that her father had cut through the whole brouhaha with a simple, 'She'll be with me.' And she was, that was exactly what she was – they were out there together, father and daughter, the white sail furled and the boat bobbing on the sapphire waters with the two of them ducking and diving around it and each other in the warm sea. She had giggled with pure childhood joy, and shrieked with laughter when her father splashed her from behind the boat or dived under to tickle her feet as she kicked out in the water.

That alone would have been enough to hold the magic of the memory, but there had been more.

They had been joined in their games, quite suddenly and with startling gentleness, by three dolphins who came to investigate the noise and stayed to play. They did spectacular leaps and flips, dived back into the water, swam underneath their two human companions and around them, occasionally lifting their heads out of the water to gaze upon them with luminous, intelligent eyes. Amais dived under with them, fearless, and could hear the echo of their sounds in the water. They'd bob their heads to the surface, and so would she, and they'd nod at her as though in approval and utter small chattering noises. They came close enough for her to touch them and she did, running her small hands down the length of the huge animals, almost twice her size. She had finally taken courage and stopped in mid-caress, wrapping her arms around one dolphin's dorsal fin. It seemed to understand her intentions immediately, squirmed gently until she sat on its back with her feet dangling on either side, and then took off, cleaving the surface cleanly and leaving a white foamy wake behind. Amais was first too startled and then far too enchanted to be in any way afraid. By the time the dolphin circled back to where his companions and Amais's father waited, she kissed her ocean steed squarely on the nose, which he gave every impression of enjoying, and turned to her father, treading water, her face one huge exhilarated grin.

'Did you see me? Did you see me ride him?'

'I saw you,' Nikos said, his own face wearing an expression of matching joy.

And then they were suddenly gone, the dolphins, as though they had never been there at all, as though they had been just a dream.

'I hoped they would come,' Nikos had said, after he'd helped to hoist her back into the boat and had raised the sail for home. 'I wanted you to meet them. They're my friends, they often follow the boat; sometimes they will even lead it to where the best fish are. The littlest one is a baby. He was born last calving season, nearly grown now but I remember him when he was quite small, maybe only a few days old. They brought him, you see, they brought him for us to meet. I promised them I would show them my own child one day, when I had a chance.'

'Thank you, Papa!' Amais had exclaimed, her face still one huge grin after her experience.

Nikos had reached out and ruffled her wet hair. 'They're your friends too, now. They always will be. They never forget. You must never forget them, either.'

'I won't,' she had promised.

She had *promised*.

But she had also promised *baya*-Dan something else, something quite different.

Don't let her name be forgotten. Or your own.

She owed other debts, to long-gone ancestors, to people who had walked this earth centuries before her, and who had never seen a dolphin leap from the sea.

She wished that she didn't feel as though keeping one of those promises meant inevitably and permanently breaking the other.

Four

Aylun was asleep when the family boarded the small boat that would take them to the mainland, carried in her mother's arms. The bigger pieces of their luggage had been loaded already; the travellers perched on a couple of battered trunks in the midst of the boat, a number of smaller packages at their feet. Vien also wore a bag slung crosswise on her body, strap on one shoulder and the bag itself resting on the hip on which she was not balancing her sleeping toddler. In that bag were the most precious of the things they had brought with them – Dan's ashes in a small bronze urn, what there was of Dan's gold and valuables that was small enough to be carried by hand and that could be exchanged for the things they would need on their journey, tickets for the various conveyances that would take them all the way back to the shores of Syai, and necessities for Aylun's immediate needs.

Amais carried a similar bag. No concessions had been made for her size and on her the thing looked enormous, overwhelming, threatening to make her buckle under its weight. In hers she carried whatever her mother required but could not fit into her own luggage, as well as the thirteen precious red journals that had been left to her by Dan and

– smuggled in as a last-minute sentimental impulse but already starting to be a subject for second thoughts – a couple of pebbles from the cove where her father had taken her to swim with wild dolphins.

The family's break with the island seemed to be complete. Elena had not come to see them off at the wharf, and neither had any of Amais's erstwhile bosom friends and companions. Those people who did happen to be there as Vien and her daughters departed seemed reluctant to meet their eyes, to look at them, even to acknowledge that they saw them. Many found something to be busy with, keeping their heads down. Only a couple of women offered a wan half-smile, and one or two children, probably too young to know better, waved goodbye as the boat carrying Vien and the girls pushed off from the dock.

Vien kept her back to the shore, clutching Aylun, occasionally patting the bag she carried with one hand as though to make sure it was still there. It was Amais who sat facing the island they were abandoning, and it was only Amais who saw Elena finally come running all the way down the wharf and then back again to shore, taking an awkward, stumbling leap off it onto the pebbled beach, her customary headscarf clutched in one twisted hand revealing black hair streaked liberally with grey and falling in untidy strands about her face and neck. She was calling something, but either they were already too far to hear clearly or else her voice was very weak – it was impossible to make out what she was saying. Vien sat with her back straight, without turning her head. She must have heard that voice, must have recognised it, but she gave no reaction to it at all, and Amais could see nothing on her mother's face except a glint in her eye that might have been either determination or a concealed tear. But Amais, for her part, could not find it in herself to leave without a word, without a thought – even though she had been the despised and ignored one ever since her father had died and her sister had been born to take his place in Elena's heart. Amais had never forgotten the early years and the fact that her father's mother did love her, long ago, once upon a time. And Elena was the last link with that other world, the world with her father and his dolphins, the world where she had suddenly been put on trial and declared a stranger.

With a final glance at her mother, half guilty and half defiant, Amais lifted both hands and waved back to the grandmother she was losing, waved back hard, as though that single simple motion alone could convey all that now would never be said.

Elena had stopped stock-still as Amais's hands came up, and for the longest moment she stood frozen, immobilised by this farewell. And then she lifted one of her own hands, very slowly, and allowed the black kerchief she carried to be stirred by the breeze. They waved to each other, in silence, grandmother and granddaughter, for as long as they could see one another, until the boat slipped around a promontory and turned towards the mainland and blotted out the small beach and the woman standing alone upon it, with the memory of Amais's childhood dissolving in the white sea foam as waves lapped and whispered at her feet.

Everything was bigger on the mainland. It was the first time Amais, nine years old, had seen a human dwelling bigger than anything to be found in the village in which she had grown up, and where she had known every face, from the newest babies with eyes barely opened to the world to the wizened ancient widows who sat in the sun outside their houses and blinked at the cerulean Elaas sky all day, counting clouds like sheep. Amais watched round-eyed as the bigger pieces of their baggage were hauled onto the shoulders of burly men naked to the waist, burned bronze by the sun under which they toiled, and carried onto the larger ship on which they would continue their journey. She watched other passengers stream on board, people wearing strange clothes, the men in buttoned-down jackets and patent leather shoes and the women wearing white gloves and large lace-and-ribbon-trimmed hats that cast their features into alluring half-shadow. She thought they were all beautiful.

But their own accommodation was not shared with the beautiful people – Vien and her daughters had a tiny cramped inside cabin with no view and no air, just four bunks stuffed into the smallest space into which they could possibly fit and a platform that served as both table and nightstand screwed firmly to the wall in between them. The only other fixtures were a cubbyhole that was supposed to serve as a closet, into which one of their smaller trunks that still didn't quite fit inside had been crammed, and a small porcelain basin in one corner. They were to share a bathroom and toilet with five similar cabins that surrounded them.

Amais surveyed all this as she paused in the doorway, and her expression must have betrayed something of her appalled dismay, because Vien, pushing in behind her with the toddler she carried, now waking and fretful in her arms, clicked her tongue at her eldest daughter and schooled her face into a stern expression.

'We probably could have done better, yes,' she said, answering an unspoken question. 'But it's a lot more expensive, and our means are limited right now. We must save our gold for when we get home – we will need it there. Besides, it's ours – we don't even have to share that fourth bunk with some stranger. There's more room than you think.'

'Yes, Mother,' Amais murmured obediently, but her heart quailed at the prospect of spending weeks, possibly months – she had no idea how long the journey was going to take – in this claustrophobic space.

'You can take the top bunk,' Vien said, inspecting the accommodations. 'Aylun cannot sleep up there, and I must be where I can attend to her at night if I need to, so the two of us will sleep in the lower bunks. Now, help me sort this stuff out so that we have room to move. Some of it can go in the other top bunk, the one you aren't using; it will give us a bit of space.'

'May I go and see the ship, Mother?' Amais asked, anxious to escape the confines of the cabin, grasping at whatever excuse she could muster.

'Later,' Vien said implacably.

So Amais spent the best part of an hour soothing her fractious sister and playing finger-games with her, sorting out the stuff in the trunk and hauling out things her mother considered necessities so that they could be better accessed atop the free upper bunk, and then squashing the trunk in as best it would go between the basin stand and the foot of one of the lower bunks, allowing free space to stand up and turn around in the midst of the cabin. She had not even noticed that the ship had actually started to move until her mother, satisfied with the arrangements in the cabin as best they could be made, took Aylun in her arms again and told Amais to lead the way up to the deck.

They were already a couple of ship-lengths away from the shore. A crowd of people stood shouting and waving, and the railings on that side of the ship were thronged by passengers who were waving back. Vien, with nobody to bid farewell to, simply turned her back on them and took her children to the opposite side of the ship, where there were fewer people and the view of the sunlit sea was unimpeded.

'Look,' she said. 'Over there, somewhere, is Syai. We're on our way. We're going home.'

But it was her father's dolphins that Amais searched for in the waters that quickly turned from sapphire to deep cobalt blue, her father's dolphins and her father's spirit, wanting to say her farewells to them, wanting to assure them that she could not bid them goodbye because a part of her would never leave them. She thought she saw a silver fin break the surface of the water, once, a long way away – but she could not be sure, and, although she stayed at the railings for a long time after her mother grew bored and a little seasick and retired below with Aylun, she did not see the fin again.

And the sun rode across the cloudless sky, and dipped towards the horizon, and then beneath it; and the quiet stars came out; and the first day was over. Already Amais was alone and adrift upon the open sea; the land of her birth was lost behind her, the land of her ancestors only a secret promise far away in the night.

The shipboard days followed one another, monotonous and long, marked by persistent bouts of seasickness on the part of Vien and Aylun. Amais was apparently her father's daughter in more than one sense – she was remarkably un-affected, having got her sea legs within hours of boarding the big ship, and when she wasn't tending to her prostrate mother and sister she spent her time exploring. Frequently she was gently but firmly steered away from areas of special sensi-tivity or specific salons on the top deck which were exclu-sively reserved for the passengers travelling in spacious outside cabins with portholes, out of which one could see the sea and the sky. Amais didn't care, really – she hadn't wanted to join the ship's aristocracy, only to see the places they had claimed. Denied those, she found other spots that she made her own. One of her particular favourites – and one from which she would probably have been evicted had she been observed – was the very point of the ship's prow, where huge ropes and the anchor chain were coiled and stowed. The place, once rearranged just a little for her convenience, made a comfortable nest for Amais. On several occasions, when her family had been particularly violently ill and the cabin smelled overwhelmingly of sick, she had even escaped and slept out here in the open air, lulled by the hiss and lap of the ship's prow cleaving the waters beneath her. She'd take her journals out there with her, Tai's journals, and pore over them, immersing herself in Tai's world, deliberately turning her back on the sea and the dolphins and the call of her father's blood. Those were in the past, for now. There were things she needed to know, for her future.

She was troubled by dreams out there on that prow, she who had always slept soundly and deeply, and – as far as she had ever been aware – dreamlessly. If she had ever dreamed before, she had never remembered the dreams when she woke. But now she did, and they came thick and fast, and some were of the lost past and some were simply dreams, unknown, unexplainable, impossible to interpret or understand without context, which, as yet, she completely lacked. Sometimes there was nothing but voices – her grandmother's, for instance, reading some familiar passage from a poem or a genealogical line, or uttering those last words of hers that were so much a binding laid on Amais by a dying woman; or an unfamiliar voice, a woman's, calling, *I'm lost, I'm lost, come and find me, come and set me free* . . . There were weird dreams of almost frightening focus, sometimes a single phrase or even a single word written on scarlet pennants in gold calligraphy, things she could not quite read but knew were written in *jin-ashu*, the women's tongue her grandmother had taught her, and that they were very important, if only she could get close enough to see them clearly and understand them. And sometimes there were dreams that were almost complete stories in and of themselves – she dreamed of strange skies, as though something far away, something vast and distant, was on fire. Once she woke from a vivid dream where she stood under such skies with a child, a little girl, both of them dressed in a manner described by Tai in her journals, their hair in courtly style, standing on a shattered piece of stairwell with only a shattered city around her – and she thought she knew what was burning then, but that didn't seem quite right either.

It was then that she started keeping her own journal, not meticulously and neatly and every day like Tai had done all her life, but haphazardly, whenever the mood took her, using a half-filled notebook she had found abandoned on the deck after one of the beautiful people from the forbidden salon had passed that way. She had not believed that the precious notebook, with all those inviting blank pages waiting to be filled, had been simply dumped – and she had spent an entire morning stalking it, wandering around that part of the deck, waiting for somebody, anybody, to come and claim it. Nobody had done so, and Amais decided that the Gods of Syai must have sent her this gift, and took the notebook with a completely clear conscience. She wrote her journal half in the language of Elaas, which was the language of her father and her childhood, and half in graceful but oddly formed and unsteady characters of *jin-ashu*. Amais had been taught how to read the women's tongue, but the calligraphy of it, writing it herself, was something that *baya*-Dan had only begun to teach her in earnest a few years back. She was quickly beginning to realise that she had barely scratched the surface of *jin-ashu*, that there were so many more layers there than she had believed. She was using Tai's journals partly as inspiration and partly as a manual to teach herself more of the secret language, forcing herself to write it using the coarse lead of a broken pencil instead of the delicate brush and ink in which the characters ought to have been inscribed, finding it hard work but in general quite pleased with her progress.

44

But the journal proved to be a stepping stone for something quite different. She soon found that she was not as comfortable in the journal format as her ancestress had been. She started writing down her thoughts as long poems. Initially they were pastiche, no more than clumsy copies of the classical poems her grandmother had read to her and those she found in the pages of Tai's books, but even to her own untutored eye they improved with daily practice until she was quite proud of what she could do with the old and glowing words of the classical high language that had been her grandmother's gift to her. The poetry, however, turned out to be another stepping stone, to something else again. She started writing down stories, casting her own dreams into fiction, writing about her hopes and fears and expectations as though they were happening to someone removed from herself, finding it easier to conquer and understand them that way.

The notebook she had found on deck soon ran out of room to write in, thickly covered with what was a remarkably good calligraphy for having been produced by someone of Amais's age, without proper implements, and with the added constraint of having to be smaller and smaller as the space to write in grew more and more cramped and valuable. One of the ship's officers found her sitting cross-legged in the sun one morning, squinting morosely at her notebook, trying to find a margin she had not yet written in.

'Hey,' the man had said in a friendly manner, smiling at the picture of the intense little girl bent over her words. 'Much too nice a day for that long face. Looks like that's pretty much all your book will take – what are you doing, writing a diary? Could you use another of those?'

It was impolite to answer in the affirmative; one never asked for gifts. But Amais looked down at her notebook, and then up at the officer, and nodded mutely.

'Then I will see you get one. There are plenty of notebooks

in the back of the storage cabinet. I'll see what I can dig out.'

'Thank you, *sei*,' Amais said, using the old form of address. The officer wasn't even one of the higher ones, hardly a 'lord'. But he was offering a precious thing. That entitled him.

He didn't understand the honour, naturally, and merely smiled as he tipped his cap at her. 'I'll find you,' he said.

And he did. He came up with two partly filled and discarded notebooks and – the greatest treasure of all – a completely blank notebook of substantial proportions, bound in thin leather.

'The captain's log is far more boring than what you might want to use it for,' he said.

'This is the captain's book?' Amais demanded, too impressed to be polite.

'Yours now,' the officer said. 'He'll only think they forgot to load his usual quota. You'd better keep it out of sight, though. You know.' And he had winked at her in a conspiratorial manner.

She didn't know whether to believe him – taking one of the notebooks destined for the official log of the ship's journey sounded entirely too outrageous, but she did it anyway, keeping the book hidden even from her mother, no small achievement given their cramped and untidy cabin.

Vien and the girls changed ships after they crossed the big inland sea, and loaded themselves into another even bigger vessel sailing east, all the way to the Syai port of Chirinaa, familiar to both Vien and Amais only as a lost city of legend. On the first night of this, the last leg of their journey, Vien felt well enough to leave Aylun sleeping in the even more cramped cabin, if that were possible, than the one in which they had travelled on the first ship, and joined her older daughter on deck.

It was evening, and the sea breezes were cool. Vien wrapped her shawl tighter around her and leaned her elbows on the railing to look down into the water below.

'Soon,' she said to Amais. 'Soon we will be there.'

'What will we do there, Mother?'

'I will make proper arrangements for your grandmother,' Vien said. 'That is the first thing that I will do.'

'But where will we live?'

Vien hesitated. Just a little. 'I don't know yet, Amais-*ban*. But we will see how it is when we get there. All will be well.'

Amais tilted her head to the side, and regarded her mother with a sudden chill, a touch of fear. There had been a light in Vien's face just then, something that spoke of an exile's homecoming, a glow of joyous expectation which might not have been wholly unexpected in one of what *baya*-Dan had called *li-san*, the lost generations, the ones who went away, who left Syai behind. But that joy was drifting, ephemeral, rootless. Amais could quite clearly see her mother on this journey, see her wrapped completely in its expectations, its visions, its dreams. She could not, hard as she tried, imagine Vien at the journey's end, could not see what Vien planned to do with Syai when its soil was firm under her feet. Their lives seemed confined to the limbo of the ship, with quiet waters all around them, an eternal voyage fated never to end.

She did not know what scared her worse – the knowledge that her mother had no real idea of what to do next, or the nebulous thoughts that were forming in her own mind, a still shapeless and formless thing, something that had been born of her dreams and of the promise she had made *baya*-Dan on her deathbed. Something that was waiting in Syai for her hand to be laid upon it. Something that was for her alone, that nobody else in this world would be able to do.

47

Five

The port in Elaas where they had boarded their first ship had been a city, and Amais had thought it huge and full of people. The port across the Inner Sea where they had boarded their second ship had been even larger – a busy, exotic place that smelled strange across the waters a full day before they had caught sight of land – but Amais had not really had the chance or the inclination to explore it in the rush of changing ships, transferring luggage, finding a place to lay their heads, securing their cabin. They had been on their way almost before Amais had really had a chance to feel solid ground under her feet once more. The only thing left in her as she had climbed on deck to watch the ship leaving this ephemeral shore behind it was a faint regret that she hadn't had a chance to pay more attention to a place she was not likely to come back to.

But that passed. The transit port had not been either kind of home for Amais, and she had been too stretched between future and past to have time to feel anything that didn't have roots in either fear or impatience. She wanted to see Syai now, the Syai of her grandmother's tales, of the old poems, of Tai's journals – the glittering place where she thought she could find what she needed to glue together the mismatched halves of her spirit into something that resembled a whole. The captain's purloined notebook filled with stories, fairy-tales describing a world with ancient sages stepping down from their temple niches and walking the city offering blessings, with glittering empresses who were sisters-of-the-heart to little girls who sold fish in the marketplace and the great adventures they had together, with Imperial Guard phalanxes dressed in black and wielding magic daggers. It was a world woven from Tai's journals, from *baya*-Dan's stories, from Amais's own imagination – something she now anticipated with a feverish desire, waiting to step into those stories herself, become part of them and let them become a part of her.

When the ship's notices, pasted on the public notice-boards every day, finally started announcing their imminent arrival in Chirinaa, Amais was already exhausted with expectations, building the place up in her mind into a city whose walls would shine with gold, its streets paved with rubies, full of people dressed in bright silks and women whose hair dripped with jewels, with opulent teahouses on every corner serving fragrant mountain tea in white porcelain teapots painted with cranes and hummingbirds.

The reality was quite different – at least the reality that the ship disgorged the small family into on the quay. There might well have been ruby paving stones somewhere, but not here – not out in the busy working harbour, teeming with barrels, boxes wrapped in massive chains and secured with even larger double-lock puzzle padlocks, scraps of torn oilcloth and tarpaulin underfoot, vats that smelled achingly familiar with whiffs of new-caught fish and salty brine clinging to their sides, sloshing open tanks that contained heaving crabs and lobsters, bales bound with thick ropes, and, everywhere in between this chaos and confusion, scuttling

49

and quick-moving no-man's wharf-cats, and bare-chested and bronze-skinned dockworkers with shaved heads and hooded eyes. The place smelled of coal dust, of sweating bodies, of all the various scents, both pleasant and evil, of the ocean. There was even a very, very faint whiff of something oily and rotten, a miasma that was a reminder of the wide marshes that lay not too far away to the west of the city.

Vien shepherded her older daughter onto the dock, carrying her younger on her hip as she had done when they had departed Elaas in what now seemed to Amais to have been another age of the world, and then stood there surrounded with the luggage that had been unloaded at her feet, hesitating, unsure of what to do next.

'We should find an inn or a hostel or something,' Amais said at last, after a long silence.

'Yes,' Vien agreed, her tone conveying simple concurrence and a total loss as to how to start looking for such a place. The labourers hefting their loads passed back and forth, parting to flow around Vien and her daughters as though they were a rock in a stream. Some might have turned their heads marginally to glance at the solitary woman and the two children, apparently waiting for something that never came, but most simply ignored them other than as an acknowledged obstacle in their path.

Amais scanned the buildings beyond the wharf. Even to her young and inexperienced eyes they did not look promising at all. Some were no more than padlocked storage facilities, with their windows securely covered by wooden shutters. Others, those that had actual people going in and out of them, seemed to be evenly divided between two types. One consisted of a string of busy offices where men ducked in with bulging bags and armfuls of paperwork, re-emerging with sour faces and tight lips that betokened either their having sucked on a particularly sour lemon or having just paid large sums of money to people they considered undeserving for 'services' they resented being obliged to buy. The other, which she could smell all the way across the wharf, had quite different purposes, and the people coming out of these places wore expressions that, if not ecstatic at their lot in life, were at the very least tolerably content with it for the duration of the panacea doled out by rice wine or sorghum ale.

There was nothing visible that would remotely do for lodgings, and from what Amais could overhear from the conversations going on all around her, the language that was spoken here was different from the one she thought she knew, the one she had thought would be spoken by all of Syai – a different dialect, a different accent. It sounded harsh and foreign and she found herself close to tears of pure frustration and helplessness even while her mind was collecting these sounds and smells and images, sorting them, cataloguing them, filing them smartly away for future reference, for future stories. There were lots of stories here. Amais could feel them all around her, rubbing against her ankles like friendly cats, ducking into alleys just out of her line of sight and inviting her to follow.

But those were for later. Those were for when she was fed and housed. And Vien . . .

'*Nixi mei ma*?' The voice was soft, almost too soft to be heard over the hubbub of the harbour. Both Amais and Vien turned their heads, sure they had heard something but not certain of what. Their eyes met those of the man who had spoken, wiry and barely tall enough to be eye-level with Vien. He bowed to them, having got their attention, presenting them with a brief glimpse of a beaded round cap that fitted snugly around his head, and then straightened again, smiling.

Amais scratched around in her brain for the meaning of the words he had just uttered, and came up, incongruously perhaps, with, 'Have you eaten?'

'No,' she said helplessly, slanting the words in what she

thought might be comprehensible to the local speaker, staring at the man. 'Thank you,' she added, after a moment, and bowed back in the manner that he had done. It seemed to be called for, just basic politeness.

His eyes glittered as he offered a small smile. When he spoke again, it was slowly, enunciating his words, and Amais found she had little trouble understanding him.

'I apologise for intruding,' the man said, 'but I think that you are strangers in the city. Might you be looking for a place to stay tonight?'

Vien still looked a little confused. Amais glanced at her and translated. Vien blinked several times, quickly.

'But who is he?' she asked Amais, in the high-court language of old Syai that she had been taught by her mother.

The man obviously understood, because he bowed again, this time directly to Vien. 'Beautiful lady,' he said, in heavily accented but compatible dialect, 'my sister runs an inn not ten minutes from here by pedicab. It is safe, cheap – might I interest you in lodging there with her tonight?'

Amais found her heart thumping painfully, her eyes darting from the smiling tout to her apparently frozen mother. Aylun, in her mother's arms, was obviously being clutched at ferociously, but had caught the mood of the moment and didn't do more than let out a small soft whimper.

'We have to sleep somewhere, Mother,' Amais said, in the language of Elaas, something she knew that the man would not understand. His expression didn't change as she spoke, but she saw his glance sharpen as he tried to interpret her words.

'But how do I know we can trust him?' Vien said, thankfully in the same language. Amais had not been at all sure that she would take the hint. 'I mean, he could be anybody, taking us anywhere . . . I don't know this city . . .'

'We have to stay somewhere,' Amais repeated.

'Do you think we should take the chance?'

Aylun whimpered again, a little more loudly. Vien bent her head over her toddler to hush her, and Amais bit her lip.

'I don't think we have a choice,' she said.

She did not tell her mother, not ever, that she had heard the man give instructions to the lead pedicab that would convey them all to the inn at which they were to stay – and then, a few minutes into the ride, having watched the three lost returning souls staring around them with round eyes and open mouths since he had loaded them and their luggage into the pedicabs, change his instructions. At the very least she had thought she understood, 'No. *Not the other place. Go to . . .*' and what followed was incomprehensible, perhaps an address. Either way, it would have been imperceptible if she hadn't been paying attention. But the pedicabs suddenly turned away from the warren of steadily narrowing dirt streets into which they had been heading and emerged onto a busier thoroughfare, a still narrow but cobbled road in decent repair, choked with pedestrians, pedicabs, bicycles, horses, donkey-pulled carts, the occasional antiquated rickety-looking sedan chair that looked more affectation than a comfortable or even convenient form of transportation, sherbet and sweetmeat vendors, and children who appeared to be selling or giving out printed sheets of paper and who were darting in and out of the traffic in a manner that made Amais clutch the edges of her seat in fear for their lives. A couple of times she thought she saw a woman dressed in the silks she had originally envisaged, but the women in question were not out in the street exactly, but hovered in certain doorways, or were in the process of sashaying up narrow stairs that led into mysterious shadows of upstairs parlours.

A sharp bark by the leading pedicab operator brought them all to a halt outside a shabby hostelry. Vien paid the pedicabs, and then offered a handful of what she had been given in change to the man who had brought them here, and again it was only Amais who really paid attention to the reaction that the money produced. His face washed with ephemeral expressions of surprise, delight, and perhaps a faint tinge of regret. She knew that her mother had offered too much, that the man might have wondered how much more she had on her, if it wouldn't have been more lucrative to have delivered them to the first place he had had in mind, after all, and not to the one where they now found themselves, shabby and threadbare and with the turquoise paint peeling off the pillars outside the front door, but looking quite respectable for all that.

The proprietress, a hatchet-faced woman with a mouth that appeared to have forgotten how to smile if it had ever known it, showed them to a single small room on the third floor of this establishment – but after the cramped cabins on the ships the place looked like a palace to Amais. They would each have a pallet of their own, without the need to climb swaying ladders when ready for bed, with actual room to move between them. The windows were shuttered; the landlady crossed to them and flung the shutters open, letting in light, air, and all the smells of the city.

'There is a teahouse around the corner,' she said to Vien, 'if you want dinner. Rent is a week in advance.'

Vien dutifully counted out the rent money in gold – the only currency she actually had on her – and the landlady left with a raised eyebrow but without another word. Amais had the uncomfortable feeling that once again her mother had doled out too much. It was hard with gold – she made a mental note to find out if any of it could be exchanged for local money that could be better figured out.

Vien deposited Aylun on the nearest bed, and sank down beside her.

'I don't think I can go anywhere tonight. I need to rest, I need to think.'

'Aylun will be hungry.'

'I know,' said Vien, rummaging in her bag for more gold. 'Go to this teahouse. Bring us back something to eat.'

Amais opened her mouth to say something, and then changed her mind, taking the coins her mother had thrust into her hand and turning away. She closed the door very gently behind her, as though she feared that a slam might wake her mother up – for that was exactly what Vien was, dreamy, almost sleepwalking, buckling under the weight of this place and its impressions and all that it meant – and the memories that crowded around incongruously of a different life somewhere far away which now seemed no more than one of Amais's stories. Amais knew all this because she fought against the same shock herself. Part of her was whispering, *Welcome home*. The other part wanted nothing so much right at that moment than to hear her father's deep voice utter, in a language unknown in this strange land, words that would have made her instantly feel cocooned in the security and the power of his love: 'She is with me.'

Vien ventured out of her room only on the third day, and did not go far. The streets seemed to frighten her a little, and she looked lost and unhappy. She tried for days – she would take the urn with the ashes of her mother, as though that was a talisman against some unspeakable horror that awaited her in the city and which she was pitifully unable to understand, and venture forth with a clear intention of visiting the Chirinaa Temple and taking care of this, the most sacred and – as she had thought – the most pressing of the things she had sworn to do when she returned to Syai. But she never made it to any Temple. She avoided Temples as though she were afraid of them, of what she might find there. Chirinaa had been so very different from what Vien had thought it would be. Not that she had ever had any clear expectations, but the reality had been coldly inimical to all of the ones she might have begun to shape in her mind, and Vien instinctively shied from having this last illusion destroyed. What if the Temple was nothing like she expected? What if there too she was so inept, so inexperienced, so utterly lost? What if she did or said the wrong thing and her mother's spirit remained forever denied rest?

Amais had immersed herself in the world of Tai's journals and her own stories and had come to her own conclusions. She was watching her mother; she was watching the city, so different from the Imperial Syai she thought she knew, the one she had believed utterly that she would enter when she stepped onto the shores of Chirinaa. Instead of that, she found herself in an unquiet city seething with sulky rebellion and sometimes overt outrage – a city which had been one of the anvils on which Syai's revolutions had been forged over years and centuries, a city whose streets had run with blood as one side or another labelled some other group as dangerous and unleashed calamity upon them. It was a city that had risen in rebellion more than once, most recently, according to the street talk that Amais overheard, for a young man called Iloh, whose name was proscribed but was somehow whispered by every shadow. It was a city in which that particular rising had been bloodily and ruthlessly suppressed by the man in Syai's high seat, General Shenxiao. There was no grace here, no calm nobility of an ancient court, no rich and exotic heritage – nothing, in fact, of what Amais and her sister had been brought here expecting to find. Only bloodshed, only austerity, only fear.

All of this connected, somehow, and the answer to their difficulties became blindingly obvious to Amais.

'We don't *belong* here, Mother. That's why you won't even think about leaving *baya*-Dan here. We aren't from Chirinaa. We are . . . we are from Linh-an. We aren't home after all, Mother. We aren't home yet.'

Six

On such small things do fates turn.

There were three sons on the small farm in the fertile hills of the province of Syai known as Hian. Tradition said that one would be educated to take care of the ledgers and the accounting, one would work the land, and one would be responsible for the household and his aging parents, when the time came for them to be taken care of.

Tradition sent the eldest of the three sons, Iloh, into the tiny school in the village below, trudging down the hillside and joining a handful of other small boys in a classroom barely big enough to hold their growing bodies and way too small to confine their boisterous spirits. Every boy, inevitably, had his own interests and concerns – and in some of the pupils the enthusiasm was simply for doing the minimum expected of them and then escaping back into the glories of the real world, hiking into the hills to pick the sweet berries or trap small animals out in the woods. Iloh was one of the few whose passions were kindled for a different thing – for the power of the word.

The boys were taught simple, basic things – how to count, and enough of the *hacha-ashu* script to be able to produce a coherent sentence in clumsy calligraphy and to read at the very least the simple folk renditions of tales and songs that had been copied out onto scrolls and parchments and notebooks. But Iloh saw more, wanted more, and he was one of the few to whom the teacher showed the school's real treasures – a couple of scrolls of parchment with classical poetry inscribed on them, works of art in themselves, the calligraphy flowing and perfect and the ink unfaded over the years. Those, and a handful of books, mostly novels, printed on cheap paper with ink that sometimes smudged if you ran your finger over the page too fast. But to Iloh, both the magnificent scrolls and the cheap paperback books were equally valuable. Perhaps the latter even more so than the former, because the novels were written in a language closer to the contemporary vernacular than the poems, and were thus easier to understand.

'You might want to continue your education,' Iloh's teacher had told him when he was eight years old. 'There are other schools, better schools, bigger schools.'

'Perhaps Father might allow me,' Iloh said, but without conviction. His father was a patriarch of the ancient kind, autocratic, indifferent to all except his own will. Iloh had quickly got the idea that the education he received was not for his own sake, but the farm's, the family's, and that there would be no indulgences.

But even that small hope had vanished absolutely in the year that Iloh turned nine. A widowed sister of his father's had returned to her family home from a neighbouring province in the spring of that year with her own small son after the death of her husband. Iloh's father had taken them in, no questions asked – they were family, and there was nothing more to be said on the matter. But the three-year-old boy, Iloh's little cousin, arrived sallow, sickly, and coughing a lot. Before his fourth birthday came around, he was dead. Less than six months after that, so was his mother. And before her body was cold in its grave, it became obvious that she had left a deadly legacy behind. She and her son had not died of a broken heart, mourning her lost husband. They had died of a disease.

The disease, however, had not died with them.

In the autumn of that year, Iloh's middle brother, Guan, began to cough and then to waste away. His mother removed him from the rest of the family and stuffed up the gaps in the windows and doors of his room with rags, so that the evil disease could not come out and claim anybody else. Guan fought valiantly for months, isolated and lonely in his convalescent cell, but even his mother's devoted nursing did not save him. He was just over six years old when the final stages of the illness set in, starting to cough blood into the handkerchiefs his mother left by his bed.

The convalescent's father had initially vetoed the doctor being summoned to the house, because such visits cost a lot of money. He had suggested to his wife that they pack up Guan and take him to the doctor's rooms in the village themselves.

'He will not live through it,' Guan's mother had said, and had begged, pleaded, for the doctor to be allowed to come. The patriarch finally succumbed, and sent his oldest son to fetch the doctor from the village. Iloh had gone, his mother's desperate pleading voice echoing in his ears – but it had been a different voice, a sort of strange premonition, that made him pause beside the corner of his schoolhouse, three houses away from the doctor's home, and stand with his hand on the dirty wall, palm flat against it, oddly convinced that he was somehow saying farewell to the place.

It had seemed to be only an instant, a stolen moment in time, but it might have made all the difference in the world if Iloh had not stopped by the schoolhouse. By the time he got to the doctor's he was told that the healer had just gone out. Desperately asking for his destination so that he could follow him, Iloh was told curtly that the doctor was not an errant goat to be fetched from pasture, and to sit outside the house and wait for his return.

The doctor had taken an hour and a half to come back – from, as it turned out, a birthing in the aftermath of which the new father, a wealthy landlord who already had four daughters but whose first son this had been, had kept him aside for a small celebration. He was not drunk – precisely – but there was definitely a brightness in his eye and a looseness to his step that showed that he was not wholly sober either. Iloh had jumped up from his seat on the bench outside the back door and had waylaid the doctor as he approached his house – and had been rewarded with a small, almost disinterested frown.

'I don't really have time to do a house call,' the doctor said.

'But you just came from one,' Iloh replied.

'That's different. They promised me a suckling pig to be delivered in time for the festival days.'

Iloh thought quickly. 'My father has none to spare. But he could give a chicken . . .'

The doctor shook his head imperceptibly, and made as if to pass.

'Two chickens!' Iloh said desperately, heedless of promising such largesse in his father's name. 'Three, if you make him well!'

'Chickens,' the doctor said with an edge of annoyance. 'Everyone gives chickens. What am I to do with more chickens, boy? You can't afford to pay my fee.'

'Please, sir,' Iloh whispered, 'it's my brother.'

'I'm sorry, lad, but I need to get some sleep . . .' the doctor began.

Iloh drew himself up to his full height – which was not much at nine, but he was certainly tall for his age and had promise of more height to come. In any event, the expression on his face made it seem as though he had several extra inches on him.

'My brother is dying!' he said. 'And if I have to drag you all the way, you are coming to see him, tonight. My father sent me to fetch you, and I am not going back without you!'

For a moment, the doctor – taller and wider than his diminutive opponent – actually seemed to shrink in Iloh's presence, but then he reminded himself that this small person that threatened him was a nine-year-old child and had no real power over him.

'Sorry, lad,' he said. 'Bring coin, tomorrow. No chickens. Better still, bring the patient and we can see what can be done for him. But not tonight. Out of my way.'

He left Iloh standing there in the path with a hot coal of frustrated fury in his belly and eyes burning with something that was almost loathing. The boy actually went back to the house and banged open-palmed on the door, calling for the doctor to come out, but he was ignored and after a while he made his way back home, empty-handed and coldly angry, smouldering with the beginnings of an idea that would one day shape his whole existence. *To each according to his needs and from each according to his ability – my brother needed, and could not pay a suckling pig and was therefore not a priority. The world is not a fair place.*

They tried to take Guan down to the doctor the next day, as the doctor had demanded, but by the time they got to the village from their farm, the boy was dead.

Guan's little sister, Leihong, was next. Despite her mother's efforts to isolate her from her sick brother, she succumbed to the disease three days before her second birthday. That left the youngest son, Rubai, and the eldest, Iloh.

61

And, just like that, Iloh's schooldays were over.

If it had not been for his father's act of charity towards the widowed sister and her child, everything would have gone according to the original plans – but now the farm itself was in jeopardy, the family's very livelihood. Rubai was four, far too young to do any but the most rudimentary chores – and, even if he had been older, his mother had begun guarding him like a dragon, protecting him from every little thing that could bring him harm. Iloh was all that was left. His father's edict was pragmatic and uncompromising. The urgent need for an extra hand at the farm outweighed the potential future requirement for an educated farm manager.

The village teacher actually wept when Iloh came in to say goodbye.

'Of all the boys, why you?' the teacher said. 'You had the will and the energy and the enthusiasm. All the rest . . . they would not even miss it. But you . . .' He had been holding a couple of the novels that Iloh had been particularly fond of, and which he had borrowed from the teacher – for perhaps the fifth time – and which he had come here principally to return, since he would not have the opportunity to give them back to the lender any time soon. But the teacher seemed to have other ideas, because he suddenly put the two shabby books back into Iloh's hands and closed the boy's rigid fingers around them. 'No,' the teacher said, 'you keep them. In your hands they are a far greater treasure than they would ever be in mine. And if you ever have the chance . . .'

'Thank you!' breathed Iloh, staring down at the books as though he had been given gold. He would have loved one of the beautiful old poems, too, but he was practical enough to realise that he could not care for that as it should be cared for. He was grateful for what he was given.

The two books were all he had by way of reading matter. Very quickly he learned both books by heart, but he clung to them with a fanatical zeal, and read them and re-read them constantly. The stories were fiction, but both were based on some tenuous historical facts, and it was easy for Iloh to think of them as though they were real history, that the events they depicted really happened. One of them was a tale of ten thousand brigands, no more than a collection of episodic stories – but the other, a tale of an ancient kingdom of his own land, powerfully gripped his imagination. He was learning lessons from the tattered novel that its creator had never dreamed he had placed in there.

Iloh grew taller still as the next few years dragged by in endless farming chores, and so did his little brother. Some of Iloh's lighter chores around the house evolved to be his brother's duties before he had turned seven. That meant that greater duties, and field work, the tending of the rice paddies and the narrow sorghum fields cut into the hillsides, began to fall to Iloh.

One of the most important and perhaps the most onerous of the chores was the constant need for fertiliser – and fertiliser was no more than farm muck, the manure of the family's few animals and the nightsoil of the family themselves. By the time he turned twelve, Iloh was charged with carrying balanced buckets of this 'fertiliser' from its origins in the house and the farmyard to the paddy fields. It was hard, backbreaking work, and Iloh escaped from it into his own head, letting his body tread the well-worn paths it knew well while his mind roamed across the landscapes of his imagination, dwelling in the worlds of his novels, extrapolating his reality and weaving it with fiction and wondering what kind of a world that would make – even putting together tenuous poetical lines of his own while he shovelled the farm manure in the rice paddies.

The work was necessary, and Iloh understood this – but still he would often snatch a break from it, laying the wooden yoke he carried on his shoulders, on whose ends the two manure buckets were balanced, by the well-beaten path he trod between the house and the fields, and sneaking off into the welcoming shade of an ancient willow tree that trailed concealing tendrils on several crumbling tombstones belonging to forgotten ancestors, long scoured bare of any identifying marks by the years of exposure to the elements. The tombstones were strategically scattered in a way that concealed Iloh from anyone taking the path to the paddy fields. They provided the boy with a solitary and secret place to which he could retire and snatch the time to read a few pages of his precious books, which he always carried in a pouch at his waist, and he would escape for a few moments from the drudgery of his daily life into the glittering world of the history that never was.

The fact that his pair of malodorous buckets, abandoned by the side of the path, would be a telling clue to his whereabouts had not even occurred to him – but it was thus that his father, who had noted his son's frequent absences, discovered him happily poring over one of his beloved books.

'And do you think that the work will do itself?' Iloh's father demanded.

'But I have already carried some fertiliser to the fields this morning,' Iloh said, looking up, still half-lost in his other world, only barely registering his father's fury.

'How many? How many have you done?'

'Four, I think. Or perhaps even six. I don't recall.'

'And who is supposed to recall? I cannot stand over you every moment of every day. You are nearly twelve years old. You are practically a man. It should be your responsibility to take care of this job that you have been given to do! Four buckets! Pah! That is barely enough for a quarter of that field!'

'But the house is so far from the field, Father,' Iloh said, still dreamily.

'So I should move the house to the paddy fields so that it is more convenient for you?' his father demanded.

Iloh blinked several times, closed his book, and rose to his feet. Already he was as tall as his father, and showed signs of growing even taller – but somehow his father still managed to give the impression that he was talking down to the boy from a great height, the height of patriarchal authority. 'So how many buckets should I bring?' Iloh asked, his voice clipped and precise.

'I don't know! Ten buckets! Sixteen!' his father said, transported beyond the realm of the reasonable to the extremes of the ideal.

Without another word Iloh bowed his head a scrupulously measured fraction that denoted just enough of the respect due to a father from a son and not an ounce more. He stowed his book back into his pouch, and walked past his father without a backward look, to hoist his yoke and its two empty buckets onto his shoulders and head towards the farmhouse. Somehow curiously deflated, his son's immediate obedient response having taken the wind out of his sails, Iloh's father followed him out of the shelter of the old willow, shaking his head.

Towards the end of the day, with the sun already low and golden and almost ready to vanish behind the hills, Iloh was missed again. This time the father knew precisely where to look – and that was exactly where he found his wayward son, reading the same book he had been reading that morning.

'Once already I have spoken to you, and here I find you back again wasting your time!' his father shouted, standing before his son with his feet planted wide on the earth of his ancestors, his arms akimbo.

Iloh lifted his head, a lank strand of his straight black hair falling over his face. 'You said I should do my chores before enjoying my reading, Father,' he said quietly. 'I have done them.'

'What? What have you done?'

'Those sixteen buckets of fertiliser. They are at the paddy,' Iloh said. 'You can go and count them if you don't believe me.'

His father stared at him for a moment without a word, and then turned on his heel and stalked off down the path in the direction of the paddy field. He had nebulously intended to go there and catch the boy out in a flat lie – because the sixteen buckets he had named would have been a good day's work for a grown man twice Iloh's age. But instead he could only stand and stare at the field's edge as it became obvious that Iloh had spoken no more than the truth. It was also revealed as to how he had done it. The yoke used to carry the buckets had been left beside the field, perhaps as an unspoken but pointed comment – Iloh had rigged the yoke to carry four buckets instead of the usual two. He must have staggered under the load on the narrow path from the farmhouse to the field, the heavy buckets dragging barely above the ground; his shoulders must have been purple with bruises, his back must have been screaming from the strain. But there was enough strength left in his arms to hold the book he loved. For that, he would have moved mountains.

No more was said about the reading of books behind the ancestral tomb.

Seven

Perhaps it was his father's new silence on the matter of his reading habits that put the idea in Iloh's head, or perhaps it was the echo of the conversation he had once had with his village teacher.

Or perhaps it was the arrival in the household of a quiet woman carrying a small child in her arms, the widow of a man who had owned the fields abutting those belonging to Iloh's father, a man who appeared to have died from the same disease that had claimed Iloh's aunt and his cousin and his two siblings. The land had been for sale. Iloh's father lost no time in offering to buy it, with money he raised on loan. Part of the price was that he care for the widow and her baby, and so she moved into his house, and, in the time-honoured way of old Syai, she became his concubine.

It was another mouth to feed, but there was also more land with which to do so. More land meant more work. It became obvious that it was more work than Iloh's father could do, even with both his sons. He parcelled out a section of his newly gained land and rented it out to another family, in exchange for a third of their harvest.

The concubine changed everything. She was young enough

to be fertile, and in the year that Iloh turned thirteen the concubine produced a child, half-sister to Iloh, named Yingchi. A new woman was in the house, with a new baby, a child fathered by the family patriarch and therefore with its own place in the family hierarchy. The little girl was a concubine's child and tradition said that such children called the primary wife 'mother' – but this was a little girl who was not Iloh's mother's child, and whose cries and gurgles reminded the woman constantly of her own lost daughter. It made her sad-eyed and melancholy as she drifted about the place, mistress of the house in name but barely able to bring herself to care about anything at all any more. Rubai, the cherished and protected second son, was also lost to her – he was growing up fast, fast enough to start being assigned farming chores and able to acquit himself well in doing them.

Iloh was fiercely intelligent, aching for knowledge and understanding, and aware that he was never going to find them with his feet in the oozing mud of the paddy fields or bent over the grain with a harvesting sickle in his hand.

He simply announced to his father one morning that he was going away to school.

'There is a new school,' he said, 'in the city. The village schoolmaster tells me that they will take boarders. I will go there, and start from the beginning.'

'And who do you think will pay for such schooling?' his father said. 'I barely have enough money to scrape by as it is. And besides, you are too old. Look at you, strapping lad that you are. You practically have to shave in the mornings. Are you telling me that you will go into the same classroom as seven-year-old children? And endure it?'

'If that is what it takes then that is what I will do,' Iloh said. 'And do not worry about the money. I will manage somehow.'

'And what am I to do for help on the farm?' his father

said. 'Rubai is too young to replace you, and a labourer costs money I don't have.'

'I will study,' Iloh said, 'and I will work. When I have money, I will send it.'

'And when you do not have money you will starve, and so will we,' his father prophesied morosely.

His father complained and protested right up until the morning that Iloh packed up to leave his home for the school in the city. He took no more than his precious books, a change of clothes, and two pairs of new shoes that his mother, rousing herself out of her lethargy long enough to ensure her eldest son was at least well-shod on his journey, had made for him. She also handed him a package of sweet cakes for his journey, and managed a smile for him as he bade her farewell. She had not made the cakes. It had been the concubine who had done that – the silent woman who had taken over the running of the household when the primary wife abdicated responsibility. But she had no claim on the son that was leaving, and she had merely done what she had conceived to be her duty. As he left the house she had said nothing, waiting silently in the shadows as he passed by.

But Yingchi, Iloh's little half-sister, apparently could not allow him to leave without her blessing. She was lying on her back in a makeshift crib and raised both her chubby arms as Iloh passed, her hands spread out like a pair of small fat starfish as she waved them about. Iloh paused, glanced down at the child, who chose that moment to offer a guile-less and completely endearing toothless smile, baring her pink gums at him so widely that her eyes were practically screwed closed by the breadth of her grin.

Iloh reached out and offered a finger to one of those hands, betrayed into an answering smile. The starfish fingers closed around his finger, tightly, and Yingchi opened her eyes just a little, staring at him gravely, her lips still curved in an echo of the smile that had riveted her brother.

'You take care of things here,' he said to this tiny scrap of a sister. 'I'll be back soon.'

She gurgled at him, and a bubble of baby drool formed in the corner of her mouth. He gently disengaged his finger and wiped her face, stood staring at her for another long moment, and then turned and walked away without looking back.

Iloh could not afford a conveyance to take him to the city, so he slung his bundle over his shoulder and walked – every step of the way. It was a long and lonely journey; nearly four days passed before he could glimpse the outskirts of his destination, and it took another day to find his way in an unfamiliar warren of streets, asking directions of strangers who would shrug their shoulders and pass him by or point him to wrong addresses or dead-ends – but he finally found himself at the gate of the school he had chosen towards the end of that fifth day, a grubby, ragged boy with hungry eyes.

'I have come to learn,' he said to a gatekeeper who came to ask his business.

'How old are you?' the gatekeeper said, after a pause, looking him up and down.

'Twelve,' said Iloh. It was a lie, but not a huge one; being thought younger than he was might increase his chances of being accepted, and yet he could not shave too many years off his true age and be believed. Not with his height; not with a face that was fast losing the round curves of childhood, revealing the features that would belong to the grown man who was emerging from that chrysalis.

Some of the other pupils were clustered just inside the gate, sniggering and pointing. Iloh tried to ignore them, holding his chin high.

'You're too old,' the gatekeeper said after a moment,

dismissing the new 'pupil', and turned to go back inside.

'That is not your decision to make!' Iloh said, desperation making him insolent and discourteous. 'I have come a long way . . . and I would like to speak to a teacher, or the headmaster!'

'The headmaster is busy,' the gatekeeper said archly. 'He cannot see just any riffraff who walks in from the street.'

'And what riffraff would that be?' a serenely commanding voice interrupted.

The gatekeeper flinched, and then turned with a deep bow. 'I did not know you were there, Excellency.'

'I am where the will of heaven wishes me to be,' said the second voice. Its owner emerged from the shadows of the school's gate, miraculously emptied of sneering schoolboys. The voice had seemed entirely too strong and powerful to belong to the almost frail-looking white-haired gentleman, his back unbent by his years, his hands decorously tucked into the wide sleeves of the scholar's robe that he wore. His eyes were a dark slate-grey, luminous and serene; but Iloh did not have that much chance to observe any more than this. He bowed immediately, very low, and kept his head down until he heard that voice speak again. 'Do I understand you come seeking tuition, boy?'

'Sir . . . yes, please, sir. I want to learn.'

'And what is it that you wish to learn here, son?'

Iloh looked up at that, his own eyes blazing. 'I will take,' he said, 'whatever knowledge you are willing to give me.'

One of the headmaster's bushy white eyebrows rose a fraction. 'Oh? Tell me, if you had a cabbage, a rabbit and a stoat, no cage, a boat that only holds you and a single one of those things, and a raging river to cross and only the boat to do it with, how would you ferry your three treasures across and have them all safe at the end of the day?'

Iloh had heard that one before – the reply would be to

71

make the trip over with the rabbit, to return alone, to fetch the stoat over, take the rabbit back, take the cabbage over, return alone, bring over the rabbit – but that would take too long, and so he simply cut through it.

'I would sell the stoat and the rabbit at market on this side of the river, for the fur, and I'd make sure I got a good price,' he said. 'I'd eat the cabbage for my supper. Then I'd cross the river in my boat, sell the boat on the other side, and buy myself a stoat, a rabbit and a cabbage. You said the three treasures – you didn't say I had to keep the boat.'

The headmaster laughed. 'I think you had better come inside, young man.'

It might have been Iloh's obvious thirst for learning, his penchant for creative thinking, the glimpse that the head-master got of an empty chalice aching to be filled. It might have been the fact that one of the pupils in the school, Sihuai, was serendipitously from Iloh's own village – a few years older than Iloh himself, he had shared the same tiny village schoolhouse for a short while before Iloh was snatched from it to work his father's land, and vouched for his erstwhile younger colleague. It might have been simply the fact that Iloh said he would pay for his education in whatever way he could, including, farmer's son that he was, tending the school gardens. Whatever it was, after nearly two hours of being interrogated on his future plans and subtly tested for his abilities, the headmaster's verdict was positive. Iloh was in.

It was nearly a year before Iloh went back home again, a gruelling and sometimes soul-destroying year in which he started from the bottom, in a class of eight-year-olds, and found himself wanting in the most basic skills compared to these boys. They teased him mercilessly, knowing that he could not retaliate, knowing that anything he did to them in return would draw harsh official censure, him being so much bigger and stronger than them. It was a year that almost made Iloh doubt his choice to come here, doubt his very need to learn. But it was also a year that built his character, his spirit, his mind. When he did finally return to his boyhood home for a visit, he was wearing the invisible cloak of a young scholar, and the villagers deferred to it. Even the old doctor – now somehow shrunken and made impotent by Iloh's new and broader vision of the world – gave him a small bow when they passed in the village street. Sihuai had been back before him, and had talked of him. People knew who Iloh was, and respected him.

He never forgot that first homecoming.

After that first hard, horrible year, Iloh showed such rapid progress and such promise that the headmaster promoted him. His calligraphy would always be crude, because he had first learned it that way, but Iloh's essays showed that he was a thinker, even a poet. They began to be posted up on the walls of the classroom, examples for other students, an achievement which Iloh was vividly proud of. He still had few friends, but a surprising one turned out to be none other than Sihuai, who was the scion of a scholarly family and therefore, in the class-conscious society of Syai, vastly Iloh's social superior. Sihuai was another student whose essays found pride of place on classroom walls – but his refined and elegant calligraphy made them far more of a pleasure to look at than Iloh's attempts, and it was partly that that sent Iloh to his schoolmate, humbly begging for help to better his writing skills. From those small beginnings an unlikely friendship bloomed, with the two boys – nearly of an age and with a shared love of the hills and valleys where they had grown up in their own separate spheres – finding many things to talk about.

Sihuai was one of a small set of boys who were regularly

invited into the headmaster's own home for lessons and discussions on the classics and history. It was a combination of Iloh's losing his temper with one of his younger classmates while insisting that the version of events portrayed in his treasured novels was in fact actual history and not just a dramatic rehash of what really happened, and his friendship with Sihuai – who had been aware of that particular event and had spoken of it to the headmaster – that resulted in Iloh's invitation to join the headmaster's circle. There, his misconceptions were gently dealt with. He was given other books to read, true histories, biographical works on great leaders of past centuries, and then he was invited to talk about them with his companions in the headmaster's office.

'Histories were written by people who had power,' Iloh said once, in that circle.

'Histories always are,' the headmaster said. 'Histories are written after battles are over, by those victorious in those battles. There are other versions of history, known only to the losers. We might never hear anything about those at all. But what do you mean by power?'

'Money,' one of the other pupils said.

'Yes, rich people are respected and honoured,' said another.

'No matter how unworthy they might be,' Iloh said darkly.

'But there are other kinds of power,' murmured the headmaster.

'Military,' said a pupil.

'But that is bad,' said the headmaster's daughter, Yanzi, who was a part of these study sessions. Two years older than Iloh, she was a willowy teenager with lustrous black hair and huge bright eyes, and there wasn't a boy in the school who wasn't half in love with her from the first time he laid eyes on her. 'That means that the way to have power over people is simply to have a bigger bludgeon.'

'Power you can buy is bad,' Iloh said thoughtfully. 'It is *political* power that is good.'

'But political power is worse than all the others!' Yanzi objected. 'Because it already contains both money power and military power. It is impossible for anyone to get political power, or to hold on to it, without having either that bludgeon or the money to pay for someone else wielding it on your behalf.'

'Power corrupts,' Sihuai said. 'You can see that everywhere.'

'Of course it does,' Iloh said. 'That is its nature. But power is a tool, and needs to be applied properly. In the history that we are learning, in the books that we are reading, it is a tool that is often misused – but it is power and *circumstances* that dictate that. The power itself is not necessarily a bad thing, just the way it is wielded. And nowhere in the books does it say that giving a man the power to make change is bad in itself – it's just that when . . .'

'Of course not,' Sihuai interrupted. 'The people who wrote those books were the winners, and the winners do not write histories that put themselves in a bad light.'

'One of the ancient emperors,' the headmaster said, cupping his hands together serenely and interrupting the squabble without raising his voice, 'was helped to change the Mandate of Heaven and overthrow an old dynasty before establishing his own. Within a year of ascending the throne, he had had most of his erstwhile friends and allies killed or exiled. Why do you think he did this?'

Iloh gave the headmaster a long look of blank incomprehension. 'Those people knew the way to a throne,' he said, sounding almost astonished at the fact that this needed to be said at all. 'If he had not done so, the new emperor's throne would never have been secure.'

'You do not think he was a bad man to have done this?'

75

'It was the only thing he could have done,' Iloh said.

'He had gained power,' one of the other pupils, a sallow-faced boy named Tang, said slowly. 'And he could not afford to let those others go free. Power can be lost as easily as it can be gained. All it takes is a single betrayal . . .'

'Power corrupts,' Yanzi said, her eyes cast down.

'Corrupts what?' the headmaster asked.

'Principles,' Yanzi said. 'Ideals. Character. Power changes people.'

'Wait,' said Sihuai, 'wasn't that the Phoenix Emperor? Didn't he turn aside a famine? He gave from his own table, shared the Imperial reserves of grain when the country starved. He saved a lot of people.'

'But at what cost?' Yanzi said, her voice passionate. 'The principles . . .'

'High principles carry too high a price if people are starving,' Iloh said. 'The emperor did away with the threats that could have been a danger to his rule. He then . . . ruled. If he was a good ruler . . . if he fed a starving people . . . how then could this be bad?'

'He *bought* the people,' Yanzi said obstinately. 'They kiss the hand that feeds them, no matter how black the heart that rules it.'

'When people have nothing in the food bowl,' Iloh said, 'they are unlikely to think about morality. They do what they need to do. And power is given to those who are not afraid to use it.'

A silence descended at those words. It took Iloh a moment, and every ounce of the strength of his developing convictions, to lift his head and meet the eyes of everyone else in that class – ending with Yanzi herself, who did not hold his gaze long before letting her own luminous eyes fall back to rest on the gracefully folded hands in her lap.

'Very interesting,' the headmaster said, throwing the words

76

into the silence like pebbles into a still pond. 'I would like you all to write an essay on the use of power, please. By the end of the week. You may all go now.'

Iloh, his blood still stirred in the aftermath of the discussion, hesitated briefly at the door of the headmaster's study and turned once, briefly, to look back. He had just a glimpse of Yanzi standing there in the middle of the room, looking straight back at him, with eyes that were steady, sad, and perhaps a little afraid.

Eight

Iloh and Sihuai were sharing a room at the school before
Iloh's second year there came to a close. Sihuai was a particularly neat and almost obsessively tidy boy. Iloh, by contrast,
took up every inch of available – and sometimes even not
so available – space. When he worked at his desk it always
overflowed with papers, sheets of smudged calligraphy, trails
of spilled ink, glue, discarded pens, dog-eared books with
sometimes deeply outlandish objects used as bookmarks, and
half-eaten meals with remnants of rice that were acquiring
the consistency of cement or in the process of giving birth
to entirely new and hitherto unknown species of mould.
There was even the occasional broken shoe, bent belt-buckle
or torn quilted jacket that he had been in the process of
repairing, straightening or patching, and which had been
simply discarded as a fresh idea occurred to him and he swept
all else aside to set it down on paper.

'For someone who thinks that it's his fate to save the
world,' Sihuai would mutter in a long-suffering tone of voice
as he picked up three of Iloh's books off his bed or a sheaf
of Iloh's notes from his own immaculately tidy desk, 'you
can't seem to keep your own nest tidy.'

'The world needs saving, and how!' Iloh would reply, with a self-mocking grin. 'I wasn't really planning on doing anything about it until after graduation, Sihuai . . . but if I *were* to start thinking about cleaning up the universe, sweeping rooms seems an awfully parochial way of going about it.'

They were very different, but they got along well for all that – and they were quickly joined by Tang, who was a sort of bridge between the two of them, himself half Sihuai and half Iloh. He could understand both Sihuai's aristocratic dignity and Iloh's down-to-earth zeal with equal pragmatism – and it was he who launched the idea of a shared adventure in the summer of Iloh's third year at the school.

'A beggar's holiday,' he said. 'We take nothing except a change of clothes and a towel and a notebook to write a journal in. And we wander where the roads take us, and we live on what we are given by the people we meet.'

'But what would be the purpose of such a journey?' Sihuai asked, considering the idea with doubt and not a little distaste.

'Consider it a test of your ideas,' Tang said. 'You and Iloh, you have such different ideas about people. Why not prove which of you is right? And besides – it is a study of power. You know what the old saying is – only a beggar knows what true liberty is. Give a man a chance to live free of obligation or responsibility, and I suspect few would choose even to be emperor, after.'

'I'm in,' Iloh said, with his usual immediate and fiery enthusiasm at an idea that caught his imagination.

'So am I,' Sihuai said after a hesitation. He was still in two minds, but he could not allow himself to lose face by admitting his misgivings about the propriety of such an adventure to his friends.

The three of them met up at the school's gate the day

79

classes broke for the summer, dressed in old clothes and comfortable sandals, each carrying a bundle into which were folded the items that Tang had decreed they might bring. They wore their beggar's garb with a sense of shining pride as they set out – but, inevitably, they were young scholars and they could not quite leave school behind. The discussion about power and the essays that they had written on the subject were still on their minds.

'Remember the ancient poet – "I did not see those who came before me, and I will not know those who will follow" – a man can only be responsible for the days of his own life,' Sihuai argued as they walked, their bundles slung jauntily on their shoulders.

'If a man takes responsibility for others, then that is not true,' Iloh said. 'Then he needs to know those who will follow. Look at Shiqai. He held it all in the palm of his hand and then he let it all shatter.'

'But that was in times of turmoil,' Tang said.

'Not so *very* long ago,' Iloh replied thoughtfully. 'It was only a few years before I was born.'

'The problem is that he tried to make new things with old tools,' Sihuai said. 'He was part of the court, and then he went over to Baba Sung and his party when the republic was proclaimed and made the emperor resign, and then he made Baba Sung resign and tried to be emperor himself. And after that, there was none strong enough to be any kind of leader at all – not of the whole country. Even we, here, have a lord who rules with an iron fist over this single province – and raises taxes for himself and not for any government in Linhan. He took three times the usual annual taxes from my father last year, and there is nothing my father can do about it.'

'Mine, too,' Iloh murmured. There had been letters from home. Things were not going well on the ancestral farm.

'A new force is needed,' Tang said. 'Something to change each individual. Something strong enough to pass from one man to another, to spread through the people, like a thought, like a touch of the hand. To make them believe something. Together. And then the power of many people, believing that one thing . . . under a strong leader.'

'You are thinking people are like a flock of sheep,' Sihuai said.

'But that is right,' Iloh said. 'People *are* a flock of sheep. And a strong leader is like a shepherd.'

'If sheep are looked after by a shepherd they have already lost their freedom,' Sihuai said. 'They are locked in a paddock out of which they cannot move. They are at the shepherd's mercy and can be moved from one place to another or killed at his whim. They seek safety in numbers and simply obey orders. What, then, is there left to do except eat, work and sleep – and all for someone else's benefit?'

'But they are fed and sheltered and cared for,' Iloh argued. 'What else do they really need? They cannot all be scholars or philosophers.'

'Look,' Tang said, as they passed a cow pasture just in time to see a cowherd armed with a long whip enter the enclosure. The cows, up until then peacefully chewing their cud, got up and began edging away from the whip and its wielder, rolling their eyes. 'The people are not happy with having a shepherd . . .'

'That only means,' Iloh said trenchantly, 'that the shepherd is weak and flawed, not that the theory is unsound.'

They travelled on foot, stopping when hunger overtook them to knock on doors of village homes and scattered farmhouses and beg their supper. Sometimes, with a little bit of coin offered in lieu of food, they would go into a cheap roadside teahouse and pay for a large bowl of rice and vegetables or a meat broth which they shared between them. They came to no lasting political agreement but they did not seriously quarrel either – they squabbled about ideas until it got heated but Tang usually defused things by laughing evenhandedly at both Sihuai's frosty injured sulks and Iloh's eruptions of volcanic temper if things came to such a pass.

It was Tang, too, who helped a girl at a country teahouse where they had broken their travels. They had had a particularly good day, and were flush with coppers they had to get rid of fast under the rules of their journey. Tang laid their bowls down on the table before his friends, and then turned to help the girl with the pitcher. She was smiling, but her gaze was steady and distant, focused somewhere far beyond the three friends.

'She is blind,' Tang said conversationally, 'but she can read faces, you know.'

It was typical that he had been the one to charm the girl, to flirt with her, to gain all kinds of information about her in less than a few minutes' acquaintance.

'I heard about that,' Sihuai said. 'One of my great-uncles studied this art, many years ago. I still recall the stories they tell about how accurate and precise his predictions were, all on the basis of running his hands over the bones of people's faces. Can you truly do this?'

'Yes,' the girl said with a quiet serenity.

'Do mine,' Sihuai said.

'Oh, young sir!' she demurred, sweeping her long lashes down on her cheeks. 'Your voice is so strong and assured. I am certain your future is already known to you . . .'

'Here,' Tang said, folding their last copper into the girl's hand. 'It isn't much but it's all we have and that means we have paid you a treasure. Can you do all of us?'

For answer she reached out a hand, and Tang guided it to Sihuai's face. She ran long fingers across his features, and then pulled back. 'You have the face of a scholar, or a sage,' she said. 'You will write many scholarly books, and live far, far away from your home. But it will . . . it will be exile, of a sort. You will want to come back, but you won't be able to, because you will be proscribed in the land of your childhood. You will have fame, but no fortune, and little happiness . . . and you will have many regrets in your life. Sorry. This is not very nice to tell. But that is in your face.'

'What about me?' Tang said, thrusting his face forward into her hand and closing his eyes.

'You are a man who knows how to make friends and keep the peace, although you have no idea of how you do this,' the girl said, and smiled with what was real warmth and almost affection despite her short acquaintance with her subject. 'But the friends you make are often only on the surface, and the peace is dearly paid for. You will love a woman who will marry another, and that other man will be your friend, and it won't be the first woman he gets that you will covet. You will hide your envy well, though. Your abilities will make you valuable to men in power – but they will balance their need of you with their fear of you, and you will need to learn to do the same. Your life will be hard but you will always know how to find the treasure within it . . . although you might think in the end that you have paid too high a price for it.'

'You really tell it like it is,' Tang said. 'What about Iloh?'

'Wait, I don't think . . .' Iloh began, but Tang had already grabbed the girl's hand and laid it on his friend's face. Her fingertips were feather-light on his cheekbones, on his lips. And then she sat back and gave him a long, thoughtful look.

'You will become a great man,' she said, 'a prince, or a councillor . . . and if not that, then you will at least lead a band of outlaws from a mountaintop. You have ambition and patience. You know how to hold people in the palm of your hand.' She hesitated, snatched her hand back, stepped backwards as if she had second thoughts about the rest of her reading. But she had accepted the copper, and she owed it. 'But you will be stone-hearted,' she whispered. 'You would command a hundred thousand deaths, and it would mean nothing to you if that was the price of achieving a cherished goal. You . . .' she hesitated again, but took a deep breath and continued, although a faint blush had come onto her cheeks, '. . . you will have many women, but you will truly love only once – and that will be a songbird, a woman whose spirit is free, and one you can never truly have . . .'

She bit her lip, as though she was regretting her candour now that she had said all that, and then turned around and hurried back the way she had come with the sureness that only a blind person walking a familiar path could understand.

'Cheerful, isn't she,' Iloh said after a moment, staring after her.

The other two 'beggars' were still staring at Iloh's face.

Iloh glared at them. 'It wasn't my idea,' he growled. 'It's all a bunch of superstitious nonsense, anyway. Let's eat; I for one am starving.'

They went on, later, and spent the rest of the summer climbing hills and crossing valleys, sleeping by streams or in sheds offered by friendly farmers, sharing space with ploughs and shovels and sometimes, memorably, dogs, goats, or wandering pigs. But then summer was over, and they returned to school – and then the years started piling on, faster and faster, and things ran away from them all. Shiqai, the warlord whose rise and fall had been the topic of their discussions that summer, had stolen the vision of the venerated man who had become known throughout the land as Baba Sung – 'Father Sung' – the father of a new nation. Shiqai's death, something that seemed to come at the hands of the Gods themselves extracting payment for his many betrayals, had left a nation leaderless and fragmented, with a thousand petty tyrants leaping up to take his place, plunging the country into nearly a decade of misery and suffering at the hands of mercenary armies who took what they pleased from the people – money, livestock, men for labour and women for pleasure – and were answerable to nobody at all. But now, at last, things were moving again, and Baba Sung had gathered a new vision together – and for the first time since the Sun Emperor had been forced to step down from his throne, Syai found itself emerging from chaos into a semblance of calm and order.

Iloh followed all this with an eager curiosity. Back at the school, in the year following the beggars' holiday with his friends, he read more and more books in his headmaster's study – frequently proscribed material that access was granted to only on the basis of the unspoken understanding that its existence was not to be spoken of outside that room, often with Tang or Yanzi at his elbow to discuss the issues raised by what had been read. The whole churning mess of human endeavour as history unfolded – especially the turbulent times that he himself lived in – fascinated him. He had begun to eat, sleep and dream politics; he talked of little else.

'Baba Sung has all the right ideas,' he told Yanzi once, as they were both poring over the same broadsheet detailing some recent achievement or atrocity. 'But he has had no power to make them happen. No real power.'

'You mean enforce them,' Yanzi said, with some distaste. 'And you mean military power.'

It was an old argument between them. Iloh shrugged it off. 'But don't you think Baba Sung's ideas are good? Remember what he said – "The nation was just a sheet of loose sand, not solid like a rock" – the winds of change blow us all every which way and until we start pulling together – all the people – until we start believing in a single truth . . .'

'Truth can never be proved,' Yanzi said. 'Only suggested.'

'Well, then, let us suggest a truth!' Iloh said. 'Baba Sung himself has said it – there are the three principles that he has written about . . .'

'Hush!' Yanzi said instinctively, glancing around. 'You only know about those because you read it in the secret things that Father has received. Do not endanger us all by speaking of it yet. Baba Sung and his principles are far away and the warlord's armies are near.'

'But I have been thinking about it,' Iloh began.

She placed a finger on his lips. 'Keep thinking,' she said. 'There will come a time for talking.'

But Iloh was consumed by his own private fires. He had been exposed to Baba Sung's high but distant political ideals, and they had acted like grit in an oyster, irritating his mind until they began accreting a layer of his own ideas, reinterpretations, beliefs. By the time he was eighteen years old he was eager to leave the country behind and go to where the events that would shape his country's history would play themselves out – Linh-an, the capital. The headmaster wrote him a letter of introduction to the librarian at the university in the city, asking if some job could not be found for this student, for whom he had developed both affection and respect. A job was found – a menial one, to be sure, cataloguing the library scripts and books in the back rooms, with pay that was barely enough to scrape rent together in the small compound he shared with four other students, one of whom was his friend Tang. Often meals were barely more than hot water seasoned with a few vegetables or a scrap of meat once in a while. But Iloh did not care about the hardships. He was poor, he was almost always hungry – but he was at the centre, where he wanted to be, where the ideas were.

He came back to the school only once, accompanied by

Tang and another student from the university, an emissary from the librarian for whom Iloh worked. The librarian, a canny if covert politician, knew very well that he himself was a marked man, that his ideas – despite being, on the face of it, so very close to Baba Sung's own catechism – were viewed with deep suspicion by the authorities. He had been branded as a troublemaker years before, and his dossier bristled with terms such as 'anarchist' and 'radical'; the only reason he had been allowed to keep his job at the university library at all had been the authorities' belief that he could do little harm buried in the library stacks.

But he'd found a way to communicate his dreams and to light a spark in others. It only took a handful of people like Iloh, young and bright and full of fire. If the librarian, the sage in the tower, could not pass his message to the followers who waited to rise for him, his acolytes could. And the message itself was a heady one for free-spirited youth – a new order, a new kind of society, one based on equality and fairness, one where one law held for all. It was Baba Sung's ideas, distilled and crystallised into a vision – and Baba Sung had not been called a dreamer for nothing.

Iloh was twenty years old. The turning point of his life was just around the corner for him, and he knew it. He was ready. He had volunteered to come, but his mission was a commandment – he had never lost touch with a network of like-minded people with whom he had been friends while at school, and he had returned to enlist them in a new enterprise that would shake their world.

'There is always a beginning,' the librarian, Iloh's erstwhile employer and his political mentor, had said on the eve of Iloh's departure from Linh-an. His narrow ascetic face was alight, his eyes aglow with determination and zeal. 'And this is our beginning. I charge you today to take the torch and set the flame to the bonfire that is to come. I cannot go

87

– the authorities know my face and my name and the only reason they have not yet swooped down upon me is because they think they have me pinned here where they can keep an eye on what I do. But you, you are different – you are young, and you are going back to see your friends, and you have the freedom that I lack. Go, with my blessing. Take this out there, to the people.'

'A People's Party,' Iloh had murmured, his eyes alight.

The librarian had been right in that the authorities had not put any obstacles in Iloh's path as he journeyed back to his old school, contacted old friends, walked once again the streets he had walked as a boy. But he had been wrong about Iloh's activities going unremarked. The authorities may not have known Iloh personally – he was young and had not had a chance to establish the kind of reputation that would invoke any kind of government dossier for himself – but he was already known, if only around the university, as a young firebrand with new and sometimes dangerous ideas. He had been the library assistant for only a brief while before he had been reassigned elsewhere, but in that while he had forged a firm bond with the old librarian. As a recognised associate of a man whose own government dossier ran to quite a thick file, Iloh's comings and goings were not hindered, but neither was he left to pursue them unobserved.

'We are being followed,' Tang told him on the second day of their stay in their old school. 'I can see a tail on us, everywhere we go. They note who we meet, who we talk to. They note who we have bought food from. I've seen one fellow just after we left with two policemen at his elbows. We can't talk freely, not here. What are we going to do?'

'What did you want to talk about that is so secret?' Yanzi, who was with them, asked.

'There is . . .' Tang began, but Iloh lifted a hand.

'What?' Yanzi said. 'Don't you trust me?'

'With my life,' Iloh said. 'But I cannot do it with the lives of the people who are with me. Not to one who is not part of it.'

'But I want to be a part of it,' Yanzi said.

Iloh glanced back at Tang. 'I have an idea,' he said. 'We will all – separately, without really hanging together as a group – go on a sightseeing trip. We can rent a boat on the lake, and it will be easy to control who can get on that boat. We can talk freely at last.'

'If I come,' Yanzi said, 'they will only think you are taking a girl out on the lake.'

'You have a point,' Iloh replied, with a wolfish grin.

So Yanzi was with Iloh and Tang on the night that they pledged their lives to the new force, under a banner that would be their own vision of Baba Sung's ideas. The three of them along with a handful of others, all young, all full of plans and ideas and an unshakeable belief that they were building something that would last forever, lighting a flame that would lead the generations that followed straight into paradise.

It was Iloh who wrote the founding declaration, and it was perhaps not grammatically immaculate or calligraphically perfect, but he poured out so much of the poetry that was in his soul onto that piece of parchment that the thing rang with power. Others took the original away, to copy it, to distribute it, to gather others into the fold.

That was the night on which the People's Party was born, on the altar of which Iloh would lay his heart, his soul, and his life.

And then the wind of time swept through the pages of history, and years tumbled past like fallen leaves in an autumn storm. And the revolution was upon them.

Nine

'*Gaichi mei!*' Iloh swore violently as he snatched his feet back from where he had been resting them against the warmth of the stove. They actually smoked. He stomped on the packed earthen floor of the hut, putting out the burning leather, wincing a little as the dance jarred seared feet. The stool he had been sitting on overturned from the violence of his motion, and the battered notebook he had been writing in fell from his lap and landed upside-down on the floor. He reached to rescue it and then lifted his feet one by one for an inspection, ruefully contemplating the soles of his shoes.

Two holes, charred on the edges and still smouldering from where the hot stove had burned through, gaped in his soles. His toes, visible through the gap, smarted; there would probably be blisters there before long.

The door of the hut opened with a little too much force and Tang peered inside, his gaze sharp and suspicious above the scarf that wrapped his entire face from the eyes down. Outside, it was snowing.

'It was nothing,' Iloh said, in response to the unspoken question.

'It was something,' Tang replied, his words muffled

through the scarf. 'I distinctly heard you, right through the closed door. I brought you something to eat, Iloh – you *have* to eat, you are flesh and blood like the rest of us even if you can't admit that to yourself. When was it you last slept? What happened just now?'

By way of reply, Iloh lifted a foot and displayed one ruined shoe.

Tang stepped inside, nudged the ill-fitting door shut with his hip, and put the bowl he carried in both hands onto the nearest horizontal surface before unwrapping his nose and mouth and displaying what might have been an intimidating scowl. But he was Tang, and Iloh was Iloh, and they had too many years between them. The scowl twitched, one eyebrow went up, Tang's mouth quirked at the corners, and before long he could not help laughing out loud, a short sharp bark of a laugh that had as much wry resignation in it as humour.

'I suppose you're going to want new boots,' Tang said.

'Just patch these, as best you can,' Iloh replied. 'I have no need of luxury, only the bare necessities. I can even live with the . . .'

'The practical answer to that is that there is going to be a foot of snow outside by the morning, and it's likely to stay there until spring,' Tang interrupted. 'If you intend on leaving this place before the thaw I don't think that even you will want to do it barefoot. Eat the beans. They will get cold.'

'In a minute,' Iloh said, gesturing with the notebook. 'I need to get this . . .'

'Now,' Tang replied, straightening up and crossing his arms in a belligerent manner. 'Right now, while I'm watching. Just so that I know you have done it and not simply forgotten about it again like last time. Do you have any idea how much disrespect you are showing to Shao by simply wasting these hard-come-by meals?'

Iloh looked duly chastened. 'Give me the bowl,' he said, laying aside the notebook.

Tang picked the food bowl up and passed it into Iloh's hand with a satisfied nod. 'And after you eat,' he continued, pursuing his advantage, 'you're going to sleep. Two days, it's been.'

Iloh glanced at him over the rim of the bowl. His eyes were filled with the affection of one old friend for another, but also with the kind of determination that Tang, resigned, recognised at once as being futile to struggle against. His shoulders drooped.

'Fine,' he said. 'At least eat. If I were *ximin* Chen, you might listen . . .'

'My wife,' said Iloh mildly, 'does not nag me. It is not her sole task to see to my needs. She is my companion and my comrade. And yours, Tang. She is part of the revolution.'

'As we all are,' Tang retorted. 'But revolution or no, somebody's got to do it. Give me your shoes.'

Iloh obediently eased the burned-through shoes off his feet without relinquishing the bowl of beans. In spite of himself, he had been hungry; something that he would never have admitted or gone in hunt of sustenance to assuage, but the simply prepared beans tasted like a festival feast. He was scraping the bowl clean even before he had eased the second shoe off his heel with his other foot, clad only in a none-too-clean and now very definitely holed sock.

Tang sighed.

'There'll be a pair of socks in it too, when I come back. Iloh, I *wish* you would sleep. You could carry an entire company's gear in the bags under your eyes.'

Iloh shrugged. 'These lean days,' he said, 'that would not be hard to accomplish.'

'Iloh . . .'

'Yes,' Iloh said impatiently, 'yes, yes, yes. I cannot carry the revolution alone. You have no idea how much I *am* relying on the people. But there are some things . . .'

Tang was shaking his head, but there was a wry and admiring smile playing about his thin-lipped mouth. 'I don't know why that is true,' he said, 'but it is true nonetheless. Your words matter. The people will rally to the flag when the time comes, but they will come because you have called them. The right words and the right time, and there is magic made, right before your eyes . . .'

'So, then,' Iloh said.

'So,' Tang agreed. Without wasting further words, he stomped out of the hut hugging the empty bowl and a pair of still faintly smouldering shoes.

Iloh bent to retrieve his notebook and his writing implements and settled back down before the stove. Flipping back a few pages, he tried to recapture his train of thought.

A revolution is not a dance party, or a silk painting, or a comfortable chair, or pretty embroidery. A revolution is not pleasant like a summer's day. A revolution cannot by its very definition be kind, gentle, courteous, magnanimous. A revolution . . .

He had stopped there, mid-sentence, when his feet had caught fire. Like much of what he wrote, things that were copied and printed and passed out to the cadres and the soldiers and the people in the fields and the factories and the villages and towns, it was homespun wisdom – he was one of them, after all, a man of the people, born in the countryside with a family that was moderately well-off by the standards of the times, but which, like most people in Syai did sooner or later, knew what it meant to be on the edge of hunger.

He stared at his own words. What was revolution, really? He had been born into an era which fairly crackled with it, one wave after another, a society constantly in its death-

throes . . . or was it just trying to be properly born . . . ?
Iloh did not, in theory, believe in the Gods of his ancestors
or in the heaven they were supposed to inhabit, but there
were times he could see those Gods looking sceptically at
the newborn nation that emerged gasping for breath, again
and again, and waving their immortal hands over that hard-
won life with a celestial pronouncement that the thing was
not good enough, throw it back, start again. He had read
about it in the books and pamphlets that he had devoured
when he had become a young man with hot blood surging
in his veins, when he had begun to think, as all young men
do, about changing the world – he had read about it happening elsewhere, and how other peoples and nations had risen
to take their own destiny into their hands. And he had felt
some of it on his own skin, when he was a child, when he
was a youth. But there had been many like him, back then
– children born into times of struggle and blood. Many who
knew all about it, who could testify to it by their own scars.
But not that many who were able or willing to reach out
and grasp the nettle, to take the choice away from those
capricious Gods, to build a nation in the image of mortal
man, in the name of mortal man.

That revolution.

The revolution that changed everything, that changed the
very nature of the sky that arched above the world, the sky
that would deliver the rain to nourish crops in the fields and
no longer be sanctuary for the distant and removed deities
who cared nothing for the people so long as the temples were
swept, the incense lit and sweet, the offerings properly
presented. And under that sky, men would be the same, with
equal rights, equal privileges, no matter how much incense
they burned to the forgotten Gods.

There was a phrase that was the guiding idea for everything that Iloh had dreamed about, had founded, created, or

set in motion. It had been there with him from the very beginning, from the day he had been turned away by the village doctor because his dying brother had not been wealthy enough to rate a visit from the healer, from the night on the lake that he and Tang and Yanzi and a handful of other fire-brands had been guided into something strong and new, a banner to unite a nation under. It had been a mantra, an incantation, a guiding light. Now he scribbled it down in the margin of his book, to remind himself, to re-inspire himself:

To each according to his needs, from each according to his abilities.

That had been the principle of the thing. Iloh had not stopped thinking of people as a flock of sheep that needed a shepherd's hand to guide them – but it would be a different kind of shepherd. It would have to be one of the sheep themselves, raised to the high place. One of the people.

Baba Sung had learned his lesson from the first time he had tried to wage revolution – and the next time he had a warlord of his own to wage his battles. Shenxiao was a skull-faced, whippet-thin man who dreamed, ate, lived and breathed army. Shenxiao and Baba Sung, together, might have been a formidable force – but Baba Sung had burned his candle at both ends and it became tragically clear that his race was run. He died a relatively young man, perished on the burning flame of his own bright spirit, leaving behind a legacy that took root in the popular mind: *be a nation again*.

And it seemed that it might have been possible. But as with every prophet there were always many who came in his footsteps ready to interpret his words. Shenxiao was one. Iloh, although still very young, was another. For a while they had worked together, yoked under that last will and testament of the founder of the Republic. But then Shenxiao made a sharp turn to the right, the People's Party reacted by veering to the left, the traces broke and the alliance died hard.

In the beginning, the People's Party was small, and led by the young and the inexperienced, advised by a handful of older intellectuals who shared their ideals. But it was the youth and the vigour of it that swept it to power, its principles proselytised as only the young and idealistic could do, and the party's numbers swelled from hundreds to thousands, and then hundreds of thousands. With its plain principles, pure from the well of idealism and not yet tainted by the thin poison of politics, it quickly attracted a membership that ranged from university students and office workers to the stevedores and factory workers and tillers of soil. There appeared to be something of value in the party's manifesto to a plethora of different kinds of people, giving the seal of its name an odd authenticity. The People's Party quickly became a force to be reckoned with.

Iloh was one of many, in the beginning – a group of young cadres who had been given tasks instrumental to the birth of the People's Party. In a handful of short years the many were whittled down to a few, and Iloh, inevitably, was among them – even if he had not played a pivotal role in the founding of the Party, his passion and his dedication to his chosen cause would have set him apart. The first time he met General Shenxiao face to face, he was no more than a Party secretary – one of a delegation, keeping his eyes open and his mouth shut and learning the ropes. The second time, Iloh had been given a place at the discussion table – still a junior, but one who had been tapped for rapid advancement. The third time, some three years later and with an unbroken and unblemished record of service at government level under his belt, he was the delegation leader, in command, no longer just a silent participant.

'It was Baba Sung's own idea,' he said at one of the meetings on that third occasion, when the topic of discussion had been land reform. 'But equal distribution of land does not have strings. You are still pandering to the land-owners, and the workers at the very bottom, who work their way to an early grave, still get nothing except perhaps a tiny reduction in taxes – and even that is only on paper, and if their landlord wants to ignore it he can.'

'You are young,' Shenxiao said, his lips parting in a thin, skeletal smile. 'You have still to understand why we sit here today. Baba Sung never said that land should be taken from those who have worked so hard to gain it . . .'

'Their ancestors might have worked hard,' Iloh said. 'For many the land is simply inherited, a part of their patrimony, something they feel entitled to. Whether or not it's justifiable.'

'. . . and summarily handed over to the barefoot peasant who has done nothing to deserve it except exist,' Shenxiao finished, as though Iloh had not spoken at all.

'But you say in public that the barefoot peasant will get that land,' Iloh said. 'You promise this.'

'Yes, and so long as the promise hangs there, all golden and shining like a riddle-lantern at Lantern Festival, everything is peaceful and calm. If they can guess the riddle they can have the land, but in the meantime let those who know what to do with it have a hand in controlling it. We need a lot of people fed – that happens when there are large fields and large harvests. Not when every small landgrubber plants a few stalks of wheat for himself.'

'You are betraying the founder of your own party,' Iloh said passionately. 'Do you know what they are saying, out in the country? "The sky is high and Shenxiao is far away." They used to say that about the emperor. You are no different than that leech on society, and Baba Sung himself said that the Empire had to go.'

'Even Baba Sung knew better than that,' Shenxiao said. 'He too was young once, that is true, and some of his ideas were those of a young man – but he grew up, and he grew wiser. A man who does not in his youth believe that the world needs to be changed is heartless, and has no feelings. But if a man has not learned by the time he is forty that it is impossible to swap an old world for a new one like a lamp on New Year's Day, that it is only possible to change the shape of the world so that one can find a higher place to stand within it – that man is a brainless idiot.'

Iloh had said nothing out loud, but his eyes, resting on Shenxiao, were eloquent. *You are wrong.*

They had not met again, face-to-face. The relationship between the two parties continued to deteriorate. On the face of it, Shenxiao's people, known as the Nationalists, had put an end to the chaos of the warlord years and had placed a central government in power once again, giving the people somewhere to look up to, a familiar situation where right underneath the Gods there was a place for the man the Gods had chosen to lead the nation – and everyone else had only to follow where that chosen man led.

But the Nationalists ruled with force of arms – with war clubs and with guns. Accession to positions of power, promised on the basis of merit alone, quickly devolved into a corrupt system where family or cronies were installed in places where they would be useful to those who wielded real clout. The government that had been Baba Sung's legacy and which had been welcomed like the sunrise of a new day became endured, then disliked, then distrusted, and finally hated. The rich landowners and the city bankers and businessmen still had their weight behind Shenxiao and his clique. The rest of the people – the peasants in the countryside, the workers in industry and in service, the young intellectuals of the cities – had increasingly begun to put their faith not so much in the People's Party but in the hands of a young man called Iloh who travelled the country and who spoke to them of equality, and of power, and of peace.

But Shenxiao held the army, the weapons, the metaphorical high ground. When Iloh and his people became too dangerous for Shenxiao to continue to even pretend to work together with them, he manufactured an incident in the city of Chirinaa, where the unions were strong, where the People's Party was known to be winning the battle for the people's hearts and souls. Blood flowed in the streets of the city, and Shenxiao made certain that fingers were pointed away from him, straight at Iloh and his 'shadow cabinet'.

Those of the People's Party who had still held positions of relative power inside the government machinery of Shenxiao's party were summarily purged – arrested, imprisoned, executed. The alliance was over. Before the year was out, the People's Party had gone to ground, and into hiding. Their leaders were marked men, and hunted.

Iloh had been one of them. He had married Yanzi less than a year before, and now, with his wife pregnant with their first child, he had to flee into the hills or face prison – or worse.

Yanzi was adamant that she would stay behind, in the city.

'You can't stay down here alone! It's dangerous! They know who you are, where to find you . . .' Iloh had argued, pleaded, begged.

'What do you think they would do?' Yanzi said, her voice sweet reason. 'I am a pregnant woman. If they touched me they would have their own people turn on them – some things are sacred, and if you foul them you are tainted by it forever more. And here I can be of far greater use to you than dangling at your tail with this belly up there in the mountains.'

'It would be safer in the middle of nowhere than here in the middle of the hornet's nest. I don't think you realise how ugly it's going to get.'

'Trust me,' she said, laying her hand over his mouth. 'I will be better here. I will send word when I can.'

'Then I will stay,' he said.

'Don't be ridiculous,' Yanzi told him sharply. 'Your name is on a list of wanted men. You would not last a week in the city – you couldn't even be with me, you'd have to go into hiding. You're better off up there in the mountains, leading, than down here skulking in a rat trap.'

He had let her persuade him that she would be all right, that nobody would touch her.

But that was before Iloh had fully emerged as the leader of the leaderless men of the People's Party up in the pathless hills of the north. Before Shenxiao put a price on his head. Before someone delivered Yanzi and her small son into Shenxiao's hands. Before Shenxiao broke every rule, and executed Iloh's wife and child to prove a point – *with me or against me, and if against me then no quarter shall be given.*

When word of that came, Iloh had asked a single question.

'How?'

'They shot them,' the courier who had brought the news said brokenly. 'They stood them up against a wall, and a firing squad shot them both. The boy was in her arms.' He looked up, met Iloh's eyes, and felt his knees buckle. It was kneeling at Iloh's feet that he whispered the rest, the answer to the question that Iloh had really been asking. 'They . . . it was fast . . . they didn't suffer.'

Iloh had turned without another word and walked away into the hills, by himself, his face a battlefield. Nobody dared follow, not even Tang, his closest companion; that grief and guilt had been too heavy, too raw. If they thought they heard

100

a howl from out of the hills, later, a howl that sounded more like a wolf than a man – well, it might have been an animal, after all. Yanzi had been part of the People's Party from the beginning, she had been there at its birth, she had believed in it no less than anyone else out here – and it had been her choice, after all, to stay behind in the city. But they knew that none of that would weigh with Iloh so much as the fact that he had been her husband, he had been the father to that child, and he had abandoned them to their fate. His choice, in the end; his guilt. Something he would never lay down, for as long as he lived.

When Iloh returned, Tang had uttered a single sentence about the fate of Yanzi, whom he too had loved from afar for many years.

'You should have taken her with you,' he told the man who had been Yanzi's husband.

Iloh had stared at him from eyes that were suddenly darker and colder than Tang remembered them ever having been before. It was as though Shenxiao had killed a part of Iloh's own humanity when he raised a hand against his family. But he had said nothing. And Tang had bowed his head, having said what he had to say, and had wordlessly taken on himself the task of taking care of Iloh, even after Iloh entered into what they called a 'revolutionary marriage' with another girl in the People's Party, one of the cadres on the run in the hills.

Iloh's eyes had acquired a strange, hard glitter after the news of Yanzi's death – the gleam of ice, of cold stone. Not tears, never tears, at least not that anyone else had witnessed. Iloh had not had the luxury of giving in to grief – only, perhaps, the chance to work for revenge.

It was the revolution, and revolution exacted a high price. *A revolution* . . .

The unfinished sentence Iloh had left dangling in the cabin

in the hills, on that night years after the revolution had begun, on the eve of its being won, still sat there on the page of his notebook, incomplete, nagging at him. A revolution needed a definition. He knew what it was, he knew in his bones, but somehow the pattern of the words would not form in his head. He tried and discarded a few variants, mouthing them silently, tasting the words he might write on his tongue, finding them wanting. There was something vivid and vital that he needed, something that conveyed the necessity of the overthrow of all gods and monsters.

It was . . . it would be . . .

A revolution is an act of violence, he wrote at last, *by which the new overthrows the old, where the oppressed throws off the oppressor, by which all men are made equal in one another's sight.*

It was not perfect, but it would have to do.

Iloh was suddenly surprised by a huge yawn that Tang would have pounced on had he been there to witness it. He got up and stretched, hearing his joints pop as he did so, reflecting wryly on the side-effects that waging revolution could have on a man. He was thirty-two years old and some-times, in his fifth winter of exile, his bones ached with the arthritis of a greybeard three times that age.

Iloh crossed over to the door and eased it open a crack. It was still snowing outside, and few things moved in the white silence in the space between the huts – one or two muffled shapes hurried somewhere with an air of urgency that probably had less to do with the errand they were on than a desire to be under a roof again with the possibility of a hot stove to thaw out frozen feet and hands. None of them noticed Iloh, or the thin ribbon of yellow light that spilled from the open door.

It was these people, in the name of all the people in the plains down below and in the walled cities of the old empire, who had rallied to a dream of a new world, who had helped to raise the flag of Iloh's vision. The few, in the name of the many. The few who had endured so much.

But soon it would be over – soon . . . The mandate was changing in Syai. The skirmishes that Iloh's army had fought with the Nationalists who held the reins of power had turned into battles, and the battles had begun turning into victories. More and more of the enemy were throwing down their arms – or, better, crossing the great divide and coming to lay their allegiance at Iloh's feet. Too much was going wrong down there, too fast; their generals had been too complacent, too rushed, too afraid. They had committed everything to this one final push, and it was failing. Thousands of men, perhaps tens of thousands, had paid with their lives, but now the prize was near, and Iloh could see the things he had dreamed of, the things he had made others believe with a fervour bordering on fanaticism, starting to take shape before his eyes. This bitter winter of exile, this was the last. He knew that. He could sense it in the wind . . .

He shivered, suddenly – the wind he had invoked in his thoughts had reached through the door he had been holding open to touch him with icy fingers. He had seen enough. This day, he had done enough. Tang was right – it was time to sleep.

And yet it was a different Tang that he was hearing, the voice echoing in his mind that of a more innocent time, a time when everything had still been possible and the price had not yet been exacted. Iloh remembered, through a mist of memory, a night when he and Tang had sat by the fire and quoted poetry at each other, the scurrilous and the sublime, the mocking and the prophetic.

'"Oh, but it will be a brave new dance when the music starts to play",' Tang had quoted.

'But what music will it be?' Iloh had asked. 'Will we even know it for music?'

'We will know it,' Tang said. 'We will write it!'

'But who will be asked to play it?' Iloh had persisted, in a strange, introspective mood that night. It was as though he had been handed a shallow bowl of water, and saw in the mirror of its still surface a vision of the years that were to come. 'Who will be asked to pay for it? What ancient part of ourselves will we have to give up in order to be granted the music of this new world . . . ?'

Iloh shook his head, clearing his mind of the memories, and retired to the pile of thin quilts on the pallet he used for a bed. He closed his eyes, covering his face with his hand. As almost always when he started drifting off into sleep but now stirred into a particular fury by the memories he picked over, questions rose like a flock of disturbed crows and darkened his thoughts with a blackness of fluttering wings. *Could I have done it differently? Could I have done it better? Will it be worth all this struggle and sacrifice in the end? Is it worth the lives that have been spent to buy it? What have we lost, that we might gain this? Who will speak the language of the lost things? This thing that we have bled for, fought to give life and breath to, will it live, thrive, grow strong . . . ?*

And then, as usual, he would answer himself, just before he sighed and surrendered to deeper slumber.

The world is ours, the nation is ours, society is ours. If we do not speak, who will speak? If we do not act, who will act?

The light was somehow very wrong. The image that shimmered before her eyes was a memory, a recognisable memory, but it had a golden wash over it, a light that suggested something ethereal, something that had never quite happened, or was still to come . . . the light of dream.

Amais could see the two little girls clearly: herself and her sister, sitting with what they believed to be studied adult elegance and yet still managing to be, endearingly and obviously, thirteen and six years old, sometime in their second year in Linh-an. They wore what they imagined grown-up high society ladies would wear to such an occasion, which in the children's case meant a hodge-podge of discarded garments from Mama's closets dressed up with scraps of silk and a heap of cheap bazaar jewellery piled on every available limb. The style of dress was somewhat eclectic, because Amais at least remembered the women of Elaas very well, and more particularly recalled the paintings and the ancient statuary depicting the old goddesses of that land and their elegant draped gowns. She had also never forgotten her brief glimpses of more exotic women; veiled women who had travelled on the same ships as them. Of course they –

particularly Amais, the elder, but also Aylun who had been told the same tales – were well aware of the sartorial traditions of their own cultural legacy, those rooted in the fairytales of Imperial past. In play, they used whatever element of these cultures happened to please them at any given moment. Amais always set the stage, spinning one of her fictions and snaring her younger sister into the charms of 'might-have-been' and 'once-upon-a-time'. Although Aylun used to copy her almost precisely, she had quickly started rebelling and using her own ideas.

This particular dream-party was a specific occasion. Amais remembered it well. It had been one of the first times that Aylun had asserted her independence and had insisted on putting together her own costume. Amais recalled the smooth slide of her mother's red satin robe as its too-long sleeves whispered past her own bony, childish wrists, and the weight of the ropes of fake gold coins, bazaar treasures, that she wore over her hair. Aylun wore a strange mixture of a half-veil covering the lower part of her face – which she finally discarded because she had to keep pushing it aside in order to sip her tea – and something that she fondly imagined passed as a classical Elaas gown, a bedsheet in its former existence, wrapped around her chubby frame and tied at the waist with a daringly purloined belt which their mother still regularly wore and which was not really sanctioned as play-garb.

They were bent over a low table with a child-sized teapot filled with cold mint tea brewed for them by their mother who indulged them every time they announced one of their tea ceremonies. It was Aylun's turn to be hostess; she was pouring the tea into tiny cups, one for her, one for her sister, a third (as they knew was protocol for any real tea ceremony) for fragrance alone, so that the guests at the tea ceremony might inhale the scent of the carefully selected tea variety offered to them, enhancing the experience with the use of all the senses.

They made what they believed to be polite conversation in the adult world – Aylun inquired very seriously about the price of fish in today's market, and Amais countered with some totally unrelated scrap of poetry or song that she had happened to memorise or had produced herself and which she believed it was the duty of all fine ladies to know. They sipped at their cold mint tea with exaggerated protocol and carefully rehearsed ritual – and then, because they were children, they started laughing. First one, then the other, trying to stifle giggles behind silken veils or flowing satin sleeves, failing, catching one another's eye, dimpling around the rosebud lips still dewy with their childhood, and then screaming with the laughter that bubbled up from inside them, laughing at nothing at all, for the pure joy of being themselves, and being there, and being young.

But the light was quite wrong – the light of dream, not memory. And the laughter turned to echoes, faded and vanished as the children in the golden mists changed irrevocably into something else, someone else. Amais became aware that she dreamed, and that she knew these two figures kneeling at an inlaid tea ceremony table made of rosewood and mahogany. This was no game of pretend – the tea was real, not the childish mint substitute, and the scent that rose from the spout of the teapot as the honey-coloured liquid came steaming out of it into the fragrance-cup was rich and haunting.

It was still a child who was doing the pouring, however. A little girl, familiar from old dreams, remembered as standing dressed in old court garb on the edge of the apocalypse under a fiery sky.

'It is early spring tea,' the child was saying, handing a cup to her companion, the young woman who had stood with her on the same wind-blown wreckage, under the same sky, whose back was still turned to the one who dreamed this dream, whose face was still hidden. 'Can you not smell the sunshine of it in the cup?'

'Yes,' the young woman said, accepting her cup and inhaling deeply. 'You're right, of course. But how can you know such things?'

'I know,' the child said gravely, 'many, many things.'

The young woman's hands tightened imperceptibly around her cup, and then her fingers relaxed, as though she had made them do so by main force of will. 'I wish I could know the things I need to know,' she whispered.

The little girl who had filled her cup paused as she put the teapot away on its warming stove, and then lifted her eyes to her companion and the dreamer who hovered behind her like a ghost at the feast. 'But you do,' the child said. 'You will know if anything had happened to her. How could you not . . . ?'

The grammar and tense of the sentence made no sense, and the dreamer, to whom it was not directly addressed, wished she could understand why it filled her with such fear and foreboding – but this was a dream, after all, and all fears were permitted here.

'There is danger all around me,' the young woman holding the tea cup whispered, and the dreamer's own voice shaped the words, like an echo, like the echo of that laughter she had once shared with her sister over their childhood make-believe.

The little girl who was in the dream – not Amais's sister, ah, not her sister! – reached for the teapot again. Not to pour this time – she lifted it with both hands, heedless of the heat that the boiling water within must have seared her palms with – and then brought it down with full force on the beautiful inlaid table.

The teapot shattered, pieces of fragile porcelain scattering in all directions, hot water spurting from the remnants – but what was inside the pot, had not been the tea-leaves that had been so seductively suggested by the fragrance cup still steaming deceitfully to the side. What lay revealed inside the broken teapot was not tea but a small, wickedly sharp dagger, washed clean, washed almost sterile of memory.

It had held memory once. The memory was what had been in the tea that had been sipped from the porcelain cup, what still curled in the steam from the fragrance cup, and the memory was pungent, and poignant, and sharply painful. The young woman set her teacup down suddenly with a small cry, and reached for the knife – and then stopped, trembling, her shaking fingers barely above the blade. The hesitation was instinctive, a recoil born of pure supernatural awe – and then, the little girl, reached out with both hands and gently brought those hesitating fingers down until they touched the gleaming metal of the blade.

And Amais the dreamer touched it too, disembodied as she was, hovering behind and above everything – and yet she could feel it as if under her own fingertips, that cool-warm metal, a presence in her hand as it was pushed down on top of the dagger, flat, palm down.

'Yes, there is danger,' the little girl said. 'But you will always know. And you will always be able to feel it – because this is the truth of it, right here. And you will hold it all in the palm of your hand before you are done. You will bear witness.'

The little girl shaped the other's hand, curled it around the dagger's handle, made her hold it, lift it, turn it point-first into the wooden table. And then moved the hand that clutched the blade, gouging a symbol on the fine inlay, a symbol of a language that Amais herself was only just beginning to remember, to reclaim.

Her alter ego, the young woman who now held the dagger, suddenly seemed to wake from some sort of a trance. The little girl's hands fell away, and the other's fingers tightened around the dagger, shifted for a stronger grip, and she completed the symbol that the little girl had made her begin, and then stared at the thing she had made, at the ruin she had made of the ancient inlay of the old elegant tea table.

The echo of children's laughter, rippling with innocence and delight, was all around as the scene wrapped itself once again in the golden mists of memory and dream, the last clear image remaining that of a woman's hand holding what might have been a dagger, or a pen dipped into ink – the symbols beneath it changing from something etched into wood to something stark and black in dark ink on white page, and back again.

'Bear witness,' the young woman said as the dreamer shaped the words with her own voiceless lips. 'Speak the truth.'

And the water-washed and tempered metal gleamed its answer before it was swallowed by the mists.

Truth. Yes. Witness and testimony.

Paper Swords and
Iron Butterflies

**Sometimes the things that shatter at the first blow prove
strongest of all after a thousand years have gone by.**

The Book of Ancient Wisdom

One

Time had not stood still in Linh-an, despite all of Amais's dreams, or Vien's expectations.

Vien and her daughters had arrived in the city in early spring, after nearly seven months of planning, scrimping, saving, and then doling out gold to agents and officials in expenses, steep travel fares, and sometimes outright bribery. The journey itself had been the least of it, but even that had not been easy or cheap. It had taken almost as much – in terms of money, stress and nervous tension – for a family that had travelled to Syai from halfway across the world to now simply cross the country from one city to another.

The serene land that *baya*-Dan had dreamed about in her cocoon on a faraway island seemed to be gone, swept away, vanished without a trace.

It was impossible to arrange anything in a coherent way because there were so many circumstances beyond one's control. The only way to get from Chirinaa to Linh-an, two city-islands in a sea of countryside seething with discontent and often open revolt, was to travel light. Vien left the heavy luggage with the woman at whose hostelry the family had stayed, with very little hope of ever seeing any of it again, and they took only the bare minimum with them: what was left of *baya*-Dan's gold, the urn with her ashes, a couple of changes of clothes each, and the thirteen precious journals which Amais had flatly refused to leave behind in the face of discussions, pleas, and even direct orders from her mother. They travelled by ship again, up the river, watching the shores with their hearts in their mouths, waiting for some insurgent group to pick their particular vessel to make a point with. They waited to be stopped, searched, robbed, despoiled. But they made it to the hills around Linh-an, and then they found a way to slip into the city with a column of exhausted refugees to whom both the guerillas in the countryside and the soldiers guarding the city walls had turned a blind eye.

It had been harrowing. It had also, at least for Amais, been wildly exciting. But the initial excitement, the sense of finally having completed their journey, had quickly faded into a grey reality. They could not survive on their shrinking hoard of *baya*-Dan's gold forever, so the first order of business had been to try and find a means of earning a livelihood here in the city – and Vien's plans and dreams of what used to be, or what might have been, had withered in the face of a harsh reminder of what was. It might have been different only a handful of short years before, but Linh-an – like most cities in Syai these days – was a city under siege, with Shenxiao's Nationalists entrenched within and the guerillas of the People's Party controlling the surrounding countryside.

Vien shrank away from it all. They were here at last, in Linh-an, with the Temple – *the* Temple, the Great Temple of their family's heritage – a few city-blocks away from the lodgings they had found, but Vien laid *baya*-Dan's ashes into Amais's young hands and sent her to the Temple alone, a week after their arrival in the city.

'You go,' she said. 'Take the ashes, take some gold. Find out where we can bury her.'

'But Mother . . .' Amais had protested, her hands closed tight around the urn. She had hoped, indeed, that she could go and see the Temple for the first time on her own, unhampered by the presence of her melancholy mother and the little sister who needed supervision and attention – but she had not figured on being entrusted with this, with the thing that Vien had repeatedly said was the most important duty that she had in Syai; the reason for her return here.

'Just go,' Vien had said, closing her eyes and turning away. 'I am so tired, Amais. My head aches so . . .'

So Amais, bearing the ashes and some gold, had walked to the Great Temple alone. When she reached one of its massive gates she stood for a long moment, her heart beating wildly, her breath coming out in short sharp gasps, her eyes shining. This towering edifice, its complexities known to her from earliest childhood through *baya*-Dan's intercession, had been part of the fairytale from the very beginnings, haunted by its Gods and its sages and its dead emperors waiting patiently in their niches.

The First Circle was an odd and aching disappointment when Amais set foot into the Temple itself. Her fertile imagination had already been here, many times, and she had thought – had believed without a shade of doubt – that she would know the place when she finally stepped into the real thing, quite simply *recognise* it. But instead of the bustling commercial centre of Tai's journals, Amais found a slightly shabby, strangely forlorn place. It resembled nothing so much as an ancient trade city recently bypassed by a new road, beginning to wither quietly in what would very quickly become backwater country. There was space for hundreds of booths along the outer wall, but many of them were shrouded in tarpaulins or locked down tight under wooden shutters. Those that were open for business still seemed to be carrying on a brisk trade, however – for those who came to the

Temple, the requirement to make offerings to the Gods and lesser spirits whom they had come here to pray to was still mandatory, and there were plenty of people waiting patiently in queues to purchase bowls, rice, wine, tea, fruit, and incense. There was even a cluster of *ganshu* booths, with their own clientele clustered around them and patiently waiting their turn with the fortune-tellers – in fact, those seemed to have more customers than the rest. A sense of which way to jump in the current unsettled times was apparently a sought-after commodity in Linh-an.

Amais tried to orient herself according to Tai's account of this place, from journal entries she knew faithfully by heart – tried to figure out where the booth of the bead-carver had been, the bead-carver who had become Tai's father-in-law. But nothing was the same. Even the blue paint of the outer wall of the Second Circle that Tai had written about in her journals, the pale and delicate ghost-blue that she had once described as the colour of Linh-an's sky at the height of molten summer, seemed to have almost completely faded away into a wash of dingy greyish-white.

That, obscurely, was something that Amais sharply felt the loss of. She had read about that colour, about the colour of Linh-an's sky, and had dreamed about what shade it would be, had been looking forward to seeing it at last . . . because it would have been new and strange for her, for the child whose own childhood sky was so different. Elaas blue, the clear sky that gave its waters their sapphire hue, had been a strong, bright colour, almost garish in Amais's eyes when she had raised them to the heavens after reading of the delicate nuances of Syai – but it had been the only thing she knew. It had been the sky that had arched over her father and had spilled its sunshine on the day's catch, the fish thrashing and dancing in the hand-knotted nets, droplets of water flying like diamonds from glittering scales. It was the sky that smiled upon an ocean where dolphins played, a sky where very different Gods lived than those who watched over Syai. Tai had painted a world for Amais, and *baya*-Dan had made sure that Amais knew its colours – but they had all been just that, colours on a pretty painting, and it seemed that in the real Syai the hues and nuances of that vanished world would remain just the colours of a dream for Amais. The colour of the sky was different here, but, in a way, it hurt more to realise that it was different from the thing that Amais had expected it to be than to know that it was different from Elaas. The latter difference she had expected, had waited for, had even yearned to see. The one she found instead, the difference between past and present rather than between two vividly different places, made her feel disoriented and not a little afraid.

Linh-an had changed . . . the Temple had changed. Amais had a sudden sense of the Great Temple, and all it had once stood for, teetering on the edge of a chasm, a balancing act between true faith and a shoring-up of at least a semblance of belief. Times were tight – while the Temple had tradition-ally been the place where the people had flocked for succour during their fallow years and bitter days, it had found its road much rockier since the fall of the old Empire and all it signified. It had been centuries since yearwoods had been universally used as Syai's calendars and the bead-carvers had found a home on the First Circle, with Cahan's blessing on all the days that the beads they made would signify for those who came to buy them. The secular had increasingly replaced the religious, and even those who wanted to keep the old ways had to carefully weigh the material costs of that choice against its spiritual benefits.

Amais belatedly realised that she had no real idea of what to do next. Purchase an offering? An offering for which deity? And what kind of offering? Was that still required in order to gain admittance into the inner sanctums of the Temple? Where was she to look for anyone at all who would know what to do with the ashes of a woman whose spirit had dwelt in these halls long before her body had failed her, half the world away? She vaguely recalled that there had been funeral brokers in the First Circle once, but they seemed to belong to a lost age of the Temple, to the days when funerals were elaborate and complicated ceremonies requiring the manufacture of paper effigies of whatever the deceased might need in the afterlife. And even those had dealt with the actual dead, with a body that was to be sent to Cahan with all of its paper-rendered treasures. *Baya*-Dan was already ashes, and Amais didn't have any idea if the correct protocol had even been followed back in Elaas, in the small community of Syai four hundred years removed from its roots. What if the Temple refused to deal with her grandmother's ashes at all?

She looked around, almost furtively, not quite knowing what to expect but half bracing for armed guards should she break any Temple taboo – but nobody seemed to be paying any attention to her at all. Sparing a final glance for those phantom Temple guards, Amais slipped quietly past the gate and into the Second Circle.

There was a susurrus of sound around her, with kneeling supplicants, mostly older women but an incongruously large number of young men clad in some sort of military uniform, murmuring prayers at the stone statues that stood in their niches as they had done from time immemorial, gazing out over the heads of worshippers with blind stone eyes. In some ways the people were here to ask for the things that they had always asked for – the small miracles of everyday existence – and to give thanks for things that had gone right in increasingly complicated lives. Amais could glean words and phrases as she walked past the kneeling women: *Why is my husband so unhappy? . . . my child is getting married, her happiness . . . my baby is healthy now . . . I need a child . . . food, blessed spirit, we are hungry . . .* But the young men in uniform had come here on a far more urgent errand, and had a single simpler prayer that Amais heard over and over again as she walked past whispering petitioners on their knees below a deity wreathed in incense smoke. *Let me survive. Let the storm pass over my head. Let the sword, the bullet, with my name on it not have been made yet.*

Amais knew that her business here was important, but all that the Temple had meant in her life was stronger than even the sense of duty that brought her here – these walls of legend that now rose about her took her breath away. This was the Temple – she was in the Great Temple – people from the pages of Tai's journals had walked these paving stones four centuries before. But there was more than just an echo of ghostly footsteps. There was a solid link here. A particular niche. A woman raised first to a position of status and influence and then to a place in the Later Heaven, by the power of *jin-shei*.

For all the detail of their maps and descriptions and drawings, her grandmother's books were old and outdated and sometimes deliberately less than complete. Despite all that, despite even her inability to map the First Circle with the ancient vision she carried in her head, Amais's feet now took her, with an uncannily sure instinct, around the perimeter of the Second Circle until she reached the niches of the sages, and then to a particular niche on the wall where the sages had been placed.

The niche of a woman who had lived and laughed in the same bright days that Tai herself had been young. Nhia, Blessed Nhia, the sage who had been *jin-shei-bao* to a poet and an empress.

Somehow none of the supplicants crowding the Second

Circle, all gathered before the more popular niches with their constant and insistent murmur of prayer and invocation, had chosen to come to this part of the Circle on this day, and Amais found herself quite alone. Nhia's niche had a single incense stick burning in a holder, a thin trail of scented blue smoke curling around the carved image within. Amais stood before it, aware that she was staring but unable to do anything about it. And then her legs gave way, as though all the weight of the occasion had descended on her shoulders at once, and she fell to her knees on the stone paving slabs, settling back onto her heels, her eyes following the coils of smoke as they rose towards the ceiling. The urn with her grandmother's ashes had somehow ended up in front of her, between her and the niche.

Her mind was both blank and awash with so many thoughts at once that it all just added up to white noise. And then something caught her eye, a movement in the corridor, and she turned her head marginally to look. Her eyes blurred with an unexpected film of tears. She could initially make out no more than an approaching shape of a feminine form, someone who walked with a limp, leaning on a cane.

Leaning on a cane . . .

Nhia. Nhia had been a cripple. And now a ghostly figure with a limp approached as Amais knelt before Nhia's own shrine. A superstitious dread gripped Amais all of a sudden, and she scrambled to her feet, gathering up the urn with unseemly haste as she did so and almost spilling the contents.

'Do you wish to make an offering?' the limping 'ghost' asked Amais in a pleasant low alto voice.

Amais blinked, clearing her sight. It was no ghost – this was not Nhia. It was just a girl, perhaps only a few years older than Amais herself, garbed in Temple robes and leaning on a cane while favouring one bandaged foot.

Amais glanced down at the urn she held and then back at the other girl, trying to gather her scattered thoughts together.

120

'This is my grandmother,' she said incongruously. That bald fact seemed to be all that she could come up with. 'I need . . . I need to bury her.'

The girl who had spoken to Amais – and in fact she was little more than a girl, despite the oddly mature voice – was dressed in a dark blue silk gown, and wore her long hair in a single simple braid down her back. There was little to identify her as belonging to the Temple but somehow she gave the impression of being an indelible part of the place, as though the Temple itself had grown a human avatar in order to address, without frightening it to death, the lost soul that had found its way to the sacred portals. She inclined her head at Amais's words, without giving any indication that they had been startling or impolite in any way. Amais had an uncanny feeling that the acolyte's next words would be something like, *We have been expecting you.*

Instead, the other girl gave a slight bow. 'I am Jinlien, of the Fourth Circle,' she said. 'You can discuss funeral arrangements with me, if you wish.'

But Amais stood rooted to the spot, staring up at Nhia's shrine.

'I thought you were *her*,' she whispered. 'I thought you were a ghost . . .'

For the first time the priestess, Jinlien, looked a little startled. 'I beg your pardon?'

'She had a deformed foot,' Amais said softly, in the hypnotising singsong voice that *baya*-Dan would have recognised, the story-telling voice. 'The Blessed Nhia. She was born with a deformed foot, and she limped . . .' And then the voice broke, and Amais indicated the cane with a small helpless gesture. 'And then you came in . . .'

'Yes,' Jinlien said, surprised, but with dawning understanding. 'This? I twisted my ankle falling down some stairs. The cane is temporary. I am sorry I startled you.'

'I should make an offering,' Amais said, talking almost to herself. 'A proper offering, something fitting, something that I would do in Tai's name and my own . . .'

'Tai? Who is Tai?'

Amais turned wide eyes to her companion, almost ludicrously taken aback that she did not know this immediately, that everyone in Syai didn't know this immediately. 'Nhia . . . the Blessed Sage Nhia . . . was *jin-shei-bao* to Kito-Tai. The poet. I am her many-times-great-granddaughter . . .'

Jinlien conquered her astonishment, inclined her head again. '*Jin-shei*,' she said. She tasted the word as though it was something rich and strange . . . but not wholly unfamiliar. As though a hidden hoard of some precious spice had been discovered many years after it had been laid down, and was found to be still good. 'It's been a long time since an offering was made here in the name of *jin-shei*. If you have a mind to do a formal offering, I can tell you exactly what you would need. But in the meantime . . .' She fished in the folds of her robe, came up with two incense sticks, and offered both of them to Amais. 'In the meantime, you can consider this a promise of what is to come.'

Amais hesitated for a moment, and then slowly reached out to take the incense, bowing her head lightly in gratitude. 'Do you usually carry spare offerings around with you?' she asked, holding the two sticks like they were something very precious.

'Often,' Jinlien said, with a tight and enigmatic kind of smile. 'For the shrines where no other offering has been made. Or for those who need something to make an offering with . . . like yourself.'

Jinlien waited politely, a few steps back, as Amais approached the shrine and lit the incense with a strange awe, half offering the required reverence to a sacred being raised to godhood and residing in Later Heaven, only a step away from the blessed gardens of Cahan itself, and half with a mystified but genuine sense of coming home across the centuries to say hello to a long-lost friend. This had been a living, breathing woman once – Tai's own *jin-shei-bao* and the companion of her youth, someone whom Amais almost felt that she had met, immortalised as Nhia had been in Tai's journals. It was as though this shrine was a vindication, proof that everything Amais had believed in and dreamed of was true, could be true, *should* be true . . .

And at the same time a reminder of so many things that had not been.

Amais hadn't realised that she was quietly crying until Jinlien put a comforting hand on her shoulder.

'Come,' she said gently. 'I will have some tea brought to us in the gardens. Let us talk of your grandmother.'

Two

Weeks turned into months, and months began growing into years.

The maples were scarlet and gold, shedding leaves like blessings over the heads of the surging crowds thronging the streets around the marketplace and near the Great Temple. The Mid-Autumn Festival had come round again, a time full of poetic significance and mystical augury. In the busy marketplace, a customer would haggle happily over the very last of the festival mooncakes shaped like animals or Temple pagodas, and then bear them away in triumph even as the stall-owner brought out a brand-new tray from underneath the bench, at twice the price, for the next customer in line.

The skies were clear; the moon would be full and yellow that night, and it would hang in the heavens like a golden coin, pouring a rich shimmering glow over the piled offerings of peaches and pomegranates and those cannily bargained-for mooncakes.

It should have been perfect. This was supposed to be the end of a fairytale, the part where the Gods benevolently handed out happiness and contentment and belonging. This was the fairytale which Amais had gleaned from her many-

124

times-great-grandmother Tai's journals – those that she had and treasured, a collection far from complete, fragmented and broken. But there were gaps of lost years even between the individual journals in Amais's possession, never mind the chasm that yawned after the final one that she owned and the later ones, those that she knew had to have existed given the fact that Tai produced one every year of her life, but which Amais had never even seen. She knew of her poet-ancestress's official biography from second-hand sources, from things she had heard or read from other people, but the real end of Tai's story – as she herself wrote it – was never to be known. Amais almost preferred it that way – she had always been free to supply whatever ending she wished, sometimes simply making it up as she went along. But that had been the fairytale she had grown up with, had often taken refuge in when her real life had become too heartbreaking, when things had been too difficult to understand.

In her childish dreams it had looked like this – almost exactly like this. The ancient walls, the cobbles piled with burnished leaves, the smell of roasted nuts and fresh-baked pastries in the air, the noise of the crowd as it milled around her. Like this . . . except that in those dreams she had been part of it all, she had worn the same happy, excited smile, she had skipped over the leafy cobbles holding the friendly hand of someone – it might even have been Tai herself, in Amais's young mind – someone whose presence would ensure that she belonged to this time and this place absolutely, without question.

This was Linh-an, the city of what had been legend to Amais, the holy ground where the spirits of her ancient ancestors lingered in the narrow alleys and by the massive gates cut into a wall that seemed rooted in time itself.

But it was far from perfect.

Even the brightness of the Mid-Autumn Festival – something that the government threw to the people of the city like a bone to a starving dog, something good and glowing to play with, to make them forget about their daily lives – had been a veneer, almost awkward and fake, despite the mooncakes and the vivid autumn maples. For Amais, despite her initial enthusiasm for the festivals of Linh-an, the whole thing had quickly turned sour. The orderly and dutiful way in which the government trotted out all the ancient festivals in order to keep the populace happy had only served as window-dressing for Amais, a routine, a stage-set that promised continuity and safety, shelter against life's storms. But it had proved to be a false sense of security. Too many things in Amais's life were uncertain, unpleasant, slipping out of control.

Those first years in Linh-an had been lonely ones for Amais. An exotic-looking stranger speaking with an unusual outlander accent and wearing shabby clothes was less and less likely to be greeted with a smile and a kind word in the unsettled times of war and conflict. If she was lucky, she would get served in the market without her order being accompanied by a suspicious stare from the shopkeeper – whose shelves were increasingly bare – and half a dozen bystanders who appeared to be taking mental notes on what she bought and where she went. Vien's invoking of the concept of *wangmei* and *xeimei*, the state of being a stranger both of body and of heart, when she had told Elena she was taking her daughters away, now began to take on a cruel irony – for Amais could not have been more of a stranger in the city of her ancestors if she tried. She had wandered Linh-an's streets, taking in the buildings and the people, seeking some trace, somewhere, of the world that had been ruled by *jin-shei*, the world of the ancient and sacred vow in which Tai had once walked. But there seemed to be little else in the air around her but talk of war and unspoken fear. People kept to themselves. The thick walls around the city kept out undesirables, and it seemed to Amais that every inhabitant of Linh-an had taken a lesson from their city and raised equally impregnable walls around themselves.

She had made one friend – a somewhat unexpected one, perhaps, but it had been the one kind face, the one warm voice, that she had found in the whole of Linh-an. Jinlien, the young priestess, had been intrigued by Amais's invocation of *jin-shei*, and Amais had returned to the Temple again and again, even after her grandmother's remains had been suitably bestowed, just for the pleasure of seeing a smile on someone's face as she approached.

It was here that Amais came when her mother, apparently oblivious to everything that was going on around her, had been persuaded to finally exchange what was left of her gold hoard for paper money.

'It would be the patriotic thing to do,' Vien had been told by her neighbour, the wife of a junior Nationalist officer, who had ferreted out the existence of the gold from Vien in an unguarded moment. 'Our men fight for us. They are often not paid at all, for months – I would know, wouldn't I? And you – you've lived here long enough to see – my own children go hungry sometimes. All gold belongs rightfully to the government. They can use it to settle debts, pay their armies, make sure we can sleep safe at night. It is not right to have treasure and keep it to yourself.'

To give Vien her due, it was obvious to her that if she did not surrender the gold voluntarily the woman would go to the authorities and have them come and collect it – in which case she might have no compensation at all. So she had taken all but a last final handful of *baya*-Dan's gold, money she had hoped to use to set up some sort of business through which she could support herself and feed her two daughters, and had taken it to one of the city's banks. She was given so much paper money in exchange that she had to hire an extra pedicab to bring it all home. That second pedicab inexplicably lost its way and never arrived at Vien's lodgings at all, and the money that she had kept had halved in value almost before she had got it home, and continued to be worth less and less every day, every hour.

'There is rent,' Amais had told Jinlien, trying hard to hold back tears. 'Aylun is so little, she doesn't know, she cannot help – and Mother . . . Mother is at the end of her rope . . .'

'Do you know that they never printed denominations greater than ten thousand?' Jinlien said. 'To do so would have caused Shenxiao to lose face by admitting that a problem existed. Instead, now you need ten thousand notes of that denomination in order to buy yourself bread and milk . . . if you can find it.'

'I need to find a job,' Amais said.

'You are a child,' Jinlien protested. 'You're barely fourteen. What about your mother?'

'She has a good hand in calligraphy,' Amais said, 'and she can cook a decent meal, when she is given the ingredients to produce one, that is. There is very little else, Jinlien. She has never been anything except a dutiful daughter to my grandmother, and then a wife and mother. And she can't do the heavy work, the factory work, it would destroy her. She's been doing little things – taking in sewing, cooking for people, caring for a few of the neighbourhood children who are not too young to give her one of her headaches – but it's all so little, and there are still bills to be paid.'

'It may not be all bad,' Jinlien soothed. 'Let me ask my cousin, who works in the university library. It would not pay much, but it would be something – and a neat writing hand would help a lot there.'

'Library?' Amais said with interest. 'Do you know – would they have any *jin-ashu* writings there?'

'Why would they?' Jinlien said. 'It was never a public language, nothing that would have found its way into scholarly libraries. Nothing that would have been catalogued, anyway.'

'I was thinking of Tai's poems,' Amais said.

'They would probably have some of those,' Jinlien replied, 'but they would likely be the *hacha-ashu* versions that were actually published, that were sold to people in the marketplace. The originals . . . I don't know that anyone would have even known to save them if they had come across them in her possessions after she died. Not unless she had left them specifically to a library, or to family, or to friends, or even to a surviving *jin-shei* sister if there was one. Are you looking for these poems?'

'The language,' Amais said. 'I am looking for the language, and for all that it meant. Syai seems to be a much colder place than it used to be in Tai's day. At least according to the journals that I have.'

'You should count yourself lucky that you have that much,' Jinlien said.

'But is there nothing left . . . ?'

'Something, perhaps. There are traces of it here at the Temple, in some of the older books. Much of that is lost already for there are none who care to take the time to read it . . .'

'May I?' Amais interrupted eagerly.

'I don't think it would be allowed,' Jinlien said with regret. 'They probably would not wish any secrets to be inadvertently revealed to anyone who isn't already one of us – one of the Temple's people. But I know that the midwives still use *jin-ashu*, by tradition, when they write their patients up in their books. Not the newly trained doctors, though. Not the modern medicine. It doesn't seem to lend itself to the grace and the beauty of that lost language.'

'But it can't all be lost,' Amais said despondently.

'There are other places,' Jinlien said.

'Where?'

'Would you go look? Even if I told you that you might not like what you found . . . ?'

'Oh yes,' Amais breathed. 'Oh, *yes*, Jinlien. Sometimes I think if I could find another who knew that language, I would find another who could remember Tai's world with me. A kinder place. With no war, and no hunger.'

'Who told you there was no war and no hunger four hundred years ago?' Jinlien questioned. 'It's an incomplete history, then, that you know.'

'But there was always the women's country. There was always that,' Amais intoned. 'There was always the language of gentle things, the strength that comes from knowing that there was a sister of the heart out there for you in the moments that were the hardest, when you most needed a friend . . . History isn't just battles and famines, Jinlien. It's people. It's always been people.'

'Perhaps I can see if both of you can be found a place in the library,' Jinlien said, and she was only half-joking.

Jinlien was as good as her word, and had come herself to Amais's lodgings to escort Vien to her new place of work and introduce her to her employer. There had been only the possibility of one opening, and even that had been granted as a huge favour. Vien seemed happier for a while after that, leaving for work in the mornings, returning in the mid-afternoon, leaving Amais to supplement their income as best she could and to take care of Aylun.

Vien had been working in the library for nearly two years before Amais observed that she had begun to take a little

130

more care than usual over her appearance as she left for work, glancing in a looking-glass to make sure her hair was tidy, even using some of her hard-earned money to buy cosmetics rather than food. Amais noticed, but she had been so grateful that her mother's mood was good and that they were somehow keeping their heads above water even though they had to keep swimming hard just to stay afloat, that she had turned a blind eye to the possible causes of this state of affairs.

Until the hour in which Vien returned from work one day and announced that she was married.

Three

Lixao was nearly thirteen years older than Vien, and had been a widower for many years. If asked about his work at the university library, which happened rather less often than he would have liked or thought appropriate, he would give an impression of being the head librarian himself, an indispensable part of the library's workings, without whom the place would grind to a complete chaotic halt. In fact, he was no more than one of the four archivists in the library, answering to several senior officials at least three levels of authority above his head. But he was the supervisor of a clutch of copyists, one of whom was Vien.

It would have been hard to pinpoint a specific time at which they first became aware of one another as more than a superior and a lowly employee. Lixao might well have been interested in someone as a potential concubine rather than a wife – he was sufficiently of the old school to consider that as a real possibility – but times were changing. Concubinage might have still flourished behind closed doors, in existing arrangements, but it was considered increasingly inappropriate to initiate such a liaison with a woman, especially one who had been married before and was already a mother. So

Lixao, once he found his eye caught by his new copyist, had courted her in the traditional manner with a view to marriage, and Vien – lost, lovely Vien, who had been struggling to find her place in a world that had turned harsh and alien on her – surrendered with joy to the idea of belonging to someone again, of having someone who would be obliged to take care of her.

She did not consult her daughters. She did not feel it necessary. Lixao had asked *her* to marry him, not the children – they were merely baggage that came along with the deal. He himself had children, after all – a son and two daughters, all grown and with families of their own – and they were not consulted either. When introduced to their father's new wife, Lixao's children were polite but indifferent.

Vien's daughters were another story.

Aylun was now nine years old, a precocious and beautiful child, but she had been allowed to run wild, to grow up under such discipline as her older sister had been able to provide. She had been taken from Elena's early influence and the entire world of Elaas when she had been almost too young to remember it. She knew of its existence, and she sometimes talked about the journey that had brought her from there to Syai with an air of one who was claiming it for a real memory – but even that was doubtful, and might have just been a cobbled-together version manufactured from the things that Amais had told her. Aylun had grown up in a world where no adult had really taken charge of her, and she had come to accept the existence of such a world as her due. When Lixao came into her life, he tried to assert a father's authority over her, attempting to mete out discipline over what he saw as transgressions and childish tantrums. The only result of this was that Aylun became sullen, rebellious, and – because Vien, as a dutiful wife, always took Lixao's part – estranged from both her stepfather and her mother.

For Amais, it was quite different.

She had known her father, and had idolised him. For her, Lixao could never be anything other than a counterfeit copy of a shining original, the figure of legend who had taught the young Amais to swim, who had taken her to play with wild dolphins, who had been a titanic pillar of strength and unquestioning love. If Nikos had ever disciplined her harshly, she had forgotten it. The word 'father' had a specific meaning for her, and it was not associated in any way with Lixao's prematurely lined face, short-sighted dark eyes behind round spectacles, and primly pursed thin-lipped mouth. He wanted both Vien's girls to address him as Father. Aylun, although she avoided addressing him at all if she had any choice in the matter, complied, if sulkily, but Amais refused point-blank. She was sixteen years old, nearly adult, and Lixao could hardly exact obedience by corporal punishment. He tried stern reprimands, but neither those nor Vien's tearful requests brought any results. Amais was very polite, adhering to every point of protocol required of her except that one. When she had occasion to speak to her mother's new husband she found ways of doing so without invoking any form of direct address at all.

Aylun was too young and far too caught up in her own rebellion to talk this over with in any meaningful way. Vien had happily allowed herself to be subsumed by her new position in life – someone's wife again, sure of her status, secure in the fact that someone else was dealing with the practical aspects of day-to-day living. She had even been provided with a maidservant, hitherto part of Lixao's bachelor establishment, who had been retained to cook and clean in the new domestic set-up. Amais fled to the only person in Linh-an to whom she could pour out her troubles, the only person who would listen to her problems and who might give advice for seeking solutions.

The Great Temple had become a sanctuary for Amais, a place where she could pretend that the old days were real again and all around her. There was a vast and brooding magnificence about the Temple; it was no longer a young and vibrant thing but it wore its centuries with grace, like a dowager empress. If the air trapped in its Circles sometimes felt stuffy and stagnant, unstirred by any wind of change for many years, it was also loaded with the comforting and familiar scents and sounds that made it easier to bear the contemporary dramas that flourished outside these venerable walls. As Jinlien's friend, Amais had gained access to some of the inner gardens of the Temple, largely unchanged since Tai's time; she had witnessed the leaves turn and fall in the autumn, and had seen peach and cherry trees, descendants or replacements of those that might have blossomed for Tai centuries before, burst into extravagant bloom in springtime. She had been allowed to tag along as Jinlien did basic Temple housekeeping tasks, like feeding the giant golden carp that moved sluggishly in the ponds and pools of the Third Circle gardens, or, after supplicants had completed their devotions, lovingly restoring the shrines of the quiet and holy Fourth Circle back to the quiet tranquillity and perfect order that the next worshipper would expect to find there; or even helping with the clusters of incense-burners at the three gates to the Fourth Circle – no two alike, crafted from copper and gold and ground rubies, glowing in improbable shimmery shades of red and gold, speckled with crimson and dark green.

The burners had their own rituals and customs, requiring a composed and serene frame of mind. Somehow Jinlien contrived to have Amais helping with the burners whenever she turned up at the Temple particularly agitated about something, using the age-old Temple procedures to soothe and calm a distressed supplicant coming to seek peace and fulfilment at the feet of the Gods themselves.

'They are in your hands,' Jinlien said, handing a dull bronze pot full of smouldering embers to Amais. 'There must always be a fire in the heart of the incense-burners. These, as you see them, have not been allowed to cool for almost a thousand years.'

'What happens if you let it go out?' Amais asked, distracted from her own problems by the grandeur of a legacy that had kept the earthly fires burning for almost a millennium with little embers of heaven.

Jinlien had dug around the fine incense ashes that filled the burners with a tiny ivory-handled spade and had extracted the old ember she was replacing into a brass pot of her own, nodding to Amais to insert a fresh one into the cavity provided, burying it lightly with more ash, laying a curl of new incense on the surface.

'You're carrying it,' Jinlien said as she worked, indicating the brass pot in Amais's hand with a nod. 'When they go out, their light dies. They turn into dead, dull things, like your ember pot.'

'But it's full of embers,' Amais said. 'Shouldn't there be enough warmth to rekindle it?'

'They never come back to life,' Jinlien said. 'If the fire is allowed to die, the incense-burner dies – and it cannot be revived. These have not cooled since they came out of the fires in which they were born; no amount of embers can replace that first spark of life once it's gone. Once a burner is cold, it is dead, good for nothing – its only value as a container in which new embers are brought to these, their living brothers and sisters.'

'So these were incense-burners too? Just like those ones?' Amais asked, inspecting her ember pot with something like astonishment. There didn't seem to be anything in common between the plain bronze bowl she carried and the wonderful glowing things she was tending.

'Yes,' Jinlien said, 'once upon a time. But their embers were allowed to cool, to die, and the burner died with it.'

'What happens to the one who allows that to happen?' Amais asked, lifting round eyes to her friend's face.

'The sight of the dead burner,' Jinlien said quietly, 'has often been considered punishment enough. It's like a murderer being made to spend the rest of his life sharing the same house with the corpse of the person he has killed.'

After being entrusted with something like this, it seemed churlish to carp too much about the iniquities of a fleeting mortal life whose troubles were to the incense-burners as the lifespan of a gnat, flashing past, gone and forgotten almost before they had vanished. The incense-burners' message to Amais, with Jinlien as proxy, seemed to be a soothing litany of calm and serenity, a glimpse of the true Way, a chance to place these temporary annoyances in context and to realise that they would not last forever.

But it was Jinlien herself, independently of the incense-burners and aware of Amais's continuing interest in the vanishing *jin-ashu* language of the women of Syai, who had inadvertently set into motion events she could not possibly have foreseen when she encouraged Amais to use her new stepfather as a connection to the library, with its dusty back rooms filled to the rafters with unarchived and esoteric books and scrolls, some of which could well have proved to be remnants of the thoughts and prayers of the women who had lived in the lost women's country of Syai from many centuries ago.

The first time that Amais approached Lixao to discuss the matter, it was in general terms. She had merely asked, without going into details, about uncatalogued material in the library.

'There are rooms of it,' Lixao said. 'We could probably put those rooms to better use – but nobody knows if anything really valuable is lying at the bottom of those stacks. So they are left alone. Of course, it is not for me to say, but if it were up to me the matter would have been dealt with properly years ago. Yes, yes, there are rooms of uncatalogued material.'

'Perhaps I could help with sorting it out?' Amais suggested hopefully.

'It needs trained hands,' Lixao said. 'We can't let children do that kind of work. How would you *know* if something was important?'

It was entirely possible that he had never meant to sound supercilious or dismissive, but that was what Amais heard – a patronising pat on the head and an unspoken *Go away, little girl, and don't bother me now*. Quick-tempered, passionate and far more precocious than Lixao gave her credit for, Amais bit off the retort that came bubbling to her lips and retreated, for her mother's sake. But she tried again, some time later, after she had had a chance to cool down, and that time Lixao finally picked up on her earnestness.

'What is it that you hope to find there?' he asked in a perplexed manner, obviously trying to mentally thumb through the library holdings and discover why a sixteen-year-old girl would be so keen to bury herself in ancient dusty papers.

Amais had thrown caution to the wind and offered up the truth. 'I think there may be *jin-ashu* writings in there somewhere,' she said. 'I would like to find them, and read them, and learn the language all over again, from its roots, from the hands of the women who knew it from the cradle. And perhaps help other women learn it too.'

'*Jin-ashu*?' Lixao echoed. 'The women's language? Stuff and nonsense. Why would the university library hold on to recipes and letters about infants' birthday parties?'

'It was not recipes and birthday parties!' Amais retorted,

138

finally letting her temper get the better of her. 'Women wrote histories in that language. Poetry.'

'Poetry? What kind of poetry would that be? If it's poetry that you're interested in, we have that – we have many scrolls of classical poetry, beautiful work . . . except I don't know if they'd let a child . . .'

'I am not a child!' Amais flared. 'Tell me, do you have any of Kito-Tai's poetry?'

'Of course,' Lixao said. 'I think we do, that is. The name is familiar.'

'Well, those poems were written in *jin-ashu*,' Amais said. 'They were written in *jin-ashu* first, in the women's language, long before any man laid eyes on them.'

'Ridiculous,' Lixao said. 'Kito-Tai is a classical poet.'

'A woman who happened to be a poet. Do you have this one?' Amais had copied out an early version of one of Tai's poems that she had found in one of her later journals, a delicate work about life and love and spring, and now she threw that manuscript down before Lixao. He reached out to pick it up by one corner, adjusting his glasses with one hand, and scanned the first few lines; then he frowned, adjusted his glasses further, picked up the paper with both hands, and read the whole poem.

'I recognise this,' he said. 'Or at least I think I do. It's different from the version I know. But it's familiar . . .'

'That is Kito-Tai's original,' Amais said, unable to prevent a note of triumph coming into her voice. 'You see? Women wrote great things. And it's all being lost, and buried, and forgotten. *Jin-ashu* . . .'

'*Jin-ashu* is obsolete,' Lixao said, throwing the paper down on the table in front of him. 'It is simply archaic; it's a useless fossil. Nobody would have bothered to collect anything written in it, not for decades. The only place any of it is left is where it rightly belongs – in the back-streets where the women rule – and why on earth would you want to go learning a language in which worn-out whores write of their worn-out dreams?'

Amais could have taken a week to answer that particular calumny, or else reward it with no answer at all. Her face set, cold fury blazing in her eyes, she had turned and left the room – and then, that very night, her mother's house, and the city of Linh-an.

She had taken nothing but a bundle of clothes and Tai's journals, and left a short note for Vien to find the next morning on the undisturbed quilts that were Amais's bed. It said nothing about where she had gone, or why she had done so – in fact, it said very little, aside from 'goodbye'. But it said that in elegant and neatly lettered *jin-ashu* – proclaiming as living the language her stepfather had relegated to the scrapheap of history.

Four

Security was tight, and on the face of it entering or leaving the city should have been fraught with enough difficulty for Amais's enterprise to be frustrated from the very start. She ought, by rights, never to have got as far as beyond the radius of a couple of blocks of her home. There was a curfew hour, and there were patrols dedicated to enforcing it. They would have made short work of a young girl who was barely more than a child and who could not, if she wanted to, provide them with any rational reason for being out in the night on her own.

But perhaps it was a night on which the old Gods of Linh-an chose to stir themselves and cast a cloak of invisibility over this young seeker. It had been under their watchful eyes, after all, that Amais's nebulous plans had been hatched in the first place. The lost sisterhood of *jin-shei* was something she often talked about with Jinlien in the Temple, and it had been Jinlien who had furnished both the impetus and the means to Amais's escape.

Amais had balked at the idea that the women's language and all that it meant had survived only in narrow circles of midwives and courtesans. She had brought Tai's journals to the Temple, and had read passages from them to Jinlien while she was on a break from Temple duties.

'Yes,' Jinlien had said, stirring with a trailing hand the quiet surface of a pond in the Third Circle gardens as she sat listening to Amais read, 'it was real, and it was powerful . . . the vow that could not be broken, the bond between one heart and another in the name of which anything could be asked and had to be offered. But that was then, in the women's country of ancient times, and this is now – and I have not heard of a real *jin-shei* bond in my lifetime, not here in the city, not with any woman I have known. None that move in my circles, anyway. I know that the midwives use *jin-ashu* and have a guild – but that isn't the same thing. And then there's the Street, with a sisterhood of each House, but that's transient, as far as I know, and shifts if a woman changes Houses . . . And there is no real trace in the Temple annals any more – I know, Amais, because you actually made me go and look. It's been decades, if not longer, since the word has been even mentioned in any of the records we have kept here.'

'But I don't believe it could just disappear,' Amais had said stubbornly, sitting up and lifting her chin in an attitude of obstinate and absolute conviction that made her look far younger than her sixteen years.

'Perhaps not,' Jinlien had admitted. 'It is quite possible that out in the country it still flourishes as it always did. But in Linh-an – in the cities – times have changed. It has become dangerous and complicated to owe a bond of such absolute loyalty to anyone.'

'And when were times not dangerous and complicated?' Amais had retorted. 'You yourself told me that history is not a summer picnic. Why would it be more dangerous to have a *jin-shei-bao* now than it would have been while an emperor sat on the throne?'

'Because the Empire believed in the vow,' Jinlien had said. 'The Republic does not. It believes in loyalty to itself, not to individuals, not something that cannot be controlled – Baba Sung's vision itself was to make us into a nation, and a nation is one thing, a monolith, indivisible, responsible only to itself.'

'But out in the country . . .'

'There may still be places where the law of the Republic is an alien and faraway thing,' Jinlien had said thoughtfully. 'I have no doubt that ancient loyalties will die out much more slowly in places where the modern Republican writ does not run – or at least does not run *yet* . . . But there are still parts of Syai where nothing changes, no matter who rules in Linh-an. There is a temple in the mountains called Sian Sanqin, the Temple of Three Thousand Stairs – where the servants of the Gods are ancient bent crones and toothless old men who remember when the world was young and the stars were barely kindled, but they couldn't tell you what day it is on the current calendar, and they are at least two emperors behind if you ask them who is currently on the throne in Linh-an.'

'Where?' Amais had asked, at the time genuinely diverted by the idea of this temple, apparently outside the constraints of the passage of time and the three thousand steps that had given it its name.

'You plan on paying a visit?' Jinlien had asked, entertained.

She had not given directions – not precisely – but she had given Amais a good idea of where to seek Sian Sanqin.

It had also been Jinlien who had taken Amais to see the place where the waters from the Seven Jade Springs, clear glass-green streams from the hills that were channelled specifically for use in ornamental lakes and ponds and fountains and most particularly for the water features in the Great Temple itself, were gathered into a single wide tunnel just outside the great walls of Linh-an and then brought into the city underneath a massive buttress, with a heavy iron grating across the mouth of the tunnel where it entered the city. A short stretch of the canal was out in the open, close to the wall where there were few formal dwellings or streets, but the city quickly asserted its supremacy and need for every inch of available space and the canal dived underground, flowing in brick- and stone-lined channels underneath the cobbles of Linh-an's streets, directed to the places it needed to go by a network of smaller conduits built thousands of years before by the architects of the city. Amais had asked why the whole thing had not been simply buried underground, and Jinlien had not known the answer to that – the reasons as to why the system was built the way it was had been lost for many centuries. But the grating in the tunnel had been designed to keep foreign objects or bodies out of the city, not in – and it was an unguarded, if somewhat difficult, way to escape Linh-an if ordinary roads were closed or crawling with armed soldiers.

That was the place Amais made her way to on the night she left the city. She was young and slender enough to slip over the top of the iron grating, between its straight top edge and the curve of the round tunnel, and drop into the waters beyond. It was deeper than she had thought it would be, and colder. The channelled stream was chest-high, and flowed strongly against her, making every movement a battle between her will and the water's mindless push into the city. There was always just enough room between the roof of the tunnel and the stream itself for Amais to keep her head above water and her small pack, with its precious cargo of Tai's journals, dry.

It was dark there in the tunnel, after she had left behind the faint light of the mouth through which she had entered and before she could glimpse the other end, and unexpectedly loud with the sound of rushing water – and there were moments of doubt, of anxiety, even stirrings of abject terror. Sometimes she could have sworn that the sound of the water was the sound of someone breathing, that she was not alone in this place; and that the water, changed from the brilliant clear glass-green that it was in the light of day to a black and unseen thing that made its presence known by touch and sound alone, harboured more underneath it than Amais wanted to think about – things with teeth and claws that fed not on flesh and bones but on the very souls of those who dared to trespass in this place.

The worst moment, perhaps because it came right at the final moments of Amais's passage and seemed to make an end of all her plans, was the surge of absolute joy when she realised the tunnel was ending, when the stale air she breathed in short sharp gasps was unmistakably stirred and sharpened by a freshness that came from *outside*. Then she found that on this side the tunnel split into seven smaller tunnels, each bringing its own stream from the hills to be mixed into this one body of water, and that she could not hope to crawl her way into any one of those. But then she discovered that this mixing chamber had a grating that opened out above her, a part of the outside wall through which the pre-dawn light was filtering down into the gloom of the tunnels. However, there didn't appear to be a gap through which any creature larger than a small cat could pass, and it seemed high – way too high to reach. But after the initial moment of panic Amais stumbled against the first rung of what could only be a ladder – and realised that a ladder leading up to the grating must mean that the grating had to be a way out of this place. She tried the first few rungs, precariously dangling the pack from the fingers of one hand, still keeping it out of the water, and then shouldered it awkwardly halfway up the ladder and climbed the rest of the way up.

The grating resisted her pressure at first when she reached

it, but she braced herself against the wall and kicked it with one foot, again and again, until something creaked and then cracked and then the grating gapped on one side. She pushed it apart far enough for herself and her pack to pass through. And then, somehow, she was out, cowering against Linh-an's massive walls *on the outside,* with Linh-an's fields and orchards climbing the hillsides that rose against the rapidly lightening sky. She was wet and shivering, and the first order of business, heedless of who might have been watching, was to change into a set of dry clothes she had bundled into her pack for just this purpose. She looked back, once, sparing a guilty thought and perhaps a hurried, and unheard, plea for forgiveness for her abandonment of Aylun to the vagaries of the new life that Vien had chosen for them all. But that was a moment, a fraction of a second, and it was all she had to give right then. The unknown horizon beckoned, bright with an undiscovered future, and Amais turned and crept away from the walls, into the light of the dawn that had begun to pour itself over Linh-an hills.

Her midnight plunge into the Seven Jade Springs might have been considered desecration, seeing as that water was Temple-bound and could therefore be thought of as sacred – but Amais was in pursuit of a truth she considered to be holy in its own way. She had murmured her own prayers asking pardon before doing what she did, but not to any of the Gods whose statues she had seen in the niches of the Great Temple. Amais had her own holy thing to worship, and that was what she had prayed to – *In the name of jin-shei, I ask passage* . . . But a prayer was a prayer, and all prayers were heard in Cahan. If the water was indeed holy, as the Temple claimed, then it didn't matter one bit that Amais had invoked a spirit not of the pantheon, or that she had said her prayer at the mouth of the tunnel and not while burning incense at the Great Temple itself.

The city was not going to help Amais in the quest at whose feet, young as she was, she had now laid her life.

Jin-shei was a lost and abandoned thing, it seemed, buried under the heedless rush to progress. There didn't seem to be time for such grace and elegance in the modern world any more. The things embedded in the ancient vow, its joys and its responsibilities, appeared to have been superseded or re-invented. It used to be that a woman knew what her heritage was, taught from the cradle, observing her mother's *jin shei* circle – the secret smiles that passed between two *jin-shei-bao* who lived close enough to touch lives every day, and the warmth and candour and honesty that pervaded the letters exchanged between those separated by Syai's vast and piti-less miles. It was something as natural as the wind in the leaves of the silver bamboos in women's gardens on warm summer evenings, something that had hardly ever needed to be studied or explained or dissected. It was there, for every woman – the sense of belonging, the sense of being a part of another woman's life, the sense of owing trust and joy to that sister, of being responsible to her, and for her. All of that, it seemed, had almost entirely vanished away, falling through the sieve of years like fine sand.

The Temple, apparently, had had nothing to say on the subject of the women's language and its secrets for genera-tions – or so Jinlien had said, having consulted its records. Amais had approached a known neighbourhood midwife once and broached the subject of *jin-ashu* with her, but the woman was strangely reluctant to speak to her about it. As for the other sisterhood, the women of the Street of Red Lanterns, Amais may not have been born into wealth but she was still a girl of good family and she simply had no obvious means to contact such women. She did not know how. And if she did, the level of distrust, even if couched in terms of distant politeness, would be high enough for any meaningful communication to be extremely difficult. The midwives would not talk to Amais about *jin-ashu* because it was the language they kept their last secrets in, and the other sisterhood, the women of the city's teahouses who plied that other ancient trade, could not speak to her because of the social barriers that stood in their way. So if there was anything to be learned, anything to be saved, it was out there, in the country – out where the civil war was now heating up to an incandescent final push, where the People's Party forces were apparently, according to rumour, answering the prayers of those young men at the Temple and promising *After this, peace*. The truth that Amais sought was hidden in secret places like Sian Sanqin, and the memories locked in the minds of ancient acolytes still serving the Gods long toppled in Linh-an in the wake of the Empire's fall.

Amais, her mind full of *jin-shei* and her determination to rediscover its ancient secrets, had not even considered the political situation when she had left her mother's house. The civil war was peripheral, not part of her quest – it was as though there was a road of destiny before her, wide and straight, and Amais could see nothing else, nothing to distract herself with, to the left or the right of her. In some ways it was very like something Tai had once called the 'ghost road' in one of the journals, something deeply mystical and magical that she had apparently had so much trouble understanding that she had cast the whole idea in terms of high poetry. Amais could not be sure, four hundred years later, how much of it – if any – was based on reality and how much was pure dream, a vision seen through a poet's eyes, something not unlike the strange dreams that sometimes guided her own footsteps. But something seemed to be guarding her own path, because she had passed out of the city unseen, and then somehow drifted north and east across the country, skirting areas of particularly intense conflict by serendipity or by instinct, finding places to shelter and – out here in the countryside – more people who were willing to help a stranger, in a matter of weeks, than she had done in all the years she had spent in Linh-an.

When asked what her name was, she did not give her real one. She gave one that was close enough – Mai – but when she would offer to do something for her hosts in repayment for their hospitality it often turned out that they preferred to hear her sing some sweetly melodious and exotic song from her childhood in Elaas than have her do physical labour, and she remained nightingale in spirit if not in reality, her grandmother's name for her suddenly weighted with a sense of prophecy coming true.

It was true that most of the people who took Amais in could be of no more assistance in finding Jinlien's fabled Sian Sanqin than they might have been if she had asked which way the heavenly gardens of Cahan lay, but if she asked to be pointed in the direction of the mountains nearly everyone knew enough basic geography to be of that much assistance. And if there was a presence that guided her steps and kept her purpose, however nebulous and lacking in actual detail, it helped to bring her to the foot of the right mountains. As she got closer to her destination, she even began to find individuals who had heard of the Sian Sanqin Temple itself and were able to provide more and more accurate directions.

It was still with a sense of astonishment, after weeks of wandering, that she found herself at the foot of Jinlien's three thousand stairs – a place she might have thought was no more than a romantic exaggeration that people were often given to in bestowing place names. But it proved to be the truth, a wide, meandering staircase of ancient and uneven steps leading up to a high saddle between two peaks, where, from the bottom of the stairs, a pagoda-shaped roof tiled in vivid blue was barely discernible.

Amais took almost three and a half hours to climb all the way to the top. Sian Sanqin had none of the grandeur of the Great Temple in Linh-an – few places could – but its setting more than compensated for that. Every now and then she'd pause to nurse the stitch in her side and look down the way she had come, and find her breath taken away by the beauty of the vista – or else she'd look up at what she still had to climb and a new angle of the staircase would show her a new vision of the Temple on top, or hide it completely behind some looming rock so that it looked like she was climbing a stairway that led only to the clouds in the sky. Here and there at the edges of the stair, ancient images of Gods and spirits had been carved into the living rocks, often with niches obviously intended for offerings hollowed out within the images themselves and within arm's-reach of the staircase. Most of them had been there for so long that their faces, if they had ever had any distinguishable features at all, had faded to a softly rounded, indistinguishable blur, with only gentle hollows where eyes might have been. The effect on the supplicant climbing the tall stair, oddly enough, was to feel more watched rather than less so – and it was with a peculiar lack of surprise that Amais finally rounded the last corner, gasping for breath in the thin mountain air, and found a monk wrapped in loose brown robes waiting for her. He held a handful of incense sticks, some with smoke already gently curling from them and some brand-new and waiting to be lit, and his eyes were folded into what were almost twin horizontal slits by the breadth of the largely toothless smile he offered as he greeted Amais with a bow.

She returned the bow, gulping air, and accepted instinctively the handful of incense sticks he handed her. Seeing him waiting there had been oddly inevitable, as though he belonged with the three thousand stairs and the old blind Gods and the blue pagoda that rose at his back – but this welcome, complete with means of making an offering, did startle her a little.

'Were you expecting me?' she asked hesitantly, glancing behind her as though someone else might be following her, someone for whom this greeting might really have been meant.

'In a manner of speaking, young *sai'an*,' the monk said in a high, reedy voice, his language far closer to the classical high tongue that *baya*-Dan had spoken in far Elaas than the language used in the streets of contemporary Linh-an. 'When someone begins to climb the staircase of three thousand steps, we expect that they are heading for Sian Sanqin.'

'But how did you know when I . . . ?' Amais began, and by way of forestalling reply the monk gestured with his hand for her to turn and look down.

From the vantage point on which they stood, it was perfectly possible to see all the way down the fantastic staircase, every step of the way, to the floor of the valley – and even beyond, along the slopes of the foothills, the eye being led further and further until it seemed as though all of Syai lay open and waiting as though in the palm of one's hand. Amais could not suppress a small gasp, what breath she had managed to catch suddenly torn from her at the sheer beauty of it all, at the quiet power of this place.

'This way, young *sai'an*,' the monk said. 'We will show you to the Temple. After, there is food ready in the refectory, and there is a bed waiting in the guest house. We are told many answers come from the dreams that are dreamed in this place.'

Five

There was no order in Sian Sanqin as in the Great Temple, no hierarchy of the Gods and spirits. It was as though here, this high up, this much closer to Cahan, it didn't matter any more who was of Early Heaven and who was of Later Heaven – all that was holy was equally holy, equally worthy of worship and praise. Reared by her staunchly hierarchical, old-fashioned grandmother, and then having every such notion emphatically reinforced by the tiered Circles of the Great Temple, Amais initially found herself at a loss when she entered Sian Sanqin. Everything seemed random. She recognised some of the statues – they were not identical to the ones in Linh-an, but they were similar enough in their features and their offerings for their identity to be obvious – but there were others she could only stare at blankly and conjecture as to what they were meant to represent. In front of one particular and very unfamiliar faceless statue the body of a dead cat lay in state, whether as offering on behalf of a human supplicant or as a supplicant in its own right it was hard to tell.

Amais thought it would be prudent to cultivate a broad base of benevolence in Cahan, and distributed the incense sticks she had been given across the breadth of the God-spectrum at random, not allowing herself to make any difference between those she recognised and those she did not. If they were here, they were worthy of an incense stick. She even left one at the shrine with the cat. It could do no harm, for her own soul or the animal's.

When she came out it was already getting dark, the sun being taken early by one of the two peaks above the temple. Such warmth as the day had carried lingered like a brief memory in places where sunlight had but recently fled, but deeper shadows already carried the night's chill, and Amais, shivering lightly, picked up the pack she had left by the entrance of the Temple when she had gone inside, slipped her bare feet back into her shoes, and hurried towards the nearest building that showed a light in the hope that it would be the promised refectory.

There were only a handful of people in the long, low room when she pushed the door open and entered the place. It was furnished with a couple of tables nearly the length of the room itself, with backless benches flanking them on either side. Three men not wearing monkish robes, pilgrims like herself, perhaps, sat in a cluster at the far end of one of the tables, talking quietly among themselves. They lifted their heads as Amais came in, registered her presence, and then went back to their conversation, giving no sign that she would be welcome in their circle. At the other table a cluster of Temple acolytes bent over their own suppers. Amais had had a quick pang of misgiving when she had first seen the tooth-less monk who had greeted her – he had been male, and what she had come here to seek was a woman's secret. Indeed, she had come to this place because Jinlien had spoken of 'crones'. But, as she took a longer and more appraising look, Amais saw that there were a couple of ancient women in the Temple group, their heads shaven just like their male

153

counterparts, but unmistakable in their shape even underneath the drapery of their robes.

It was one of these who rose from the table and crossed the room to Amais.

'Be welcome,' the woman said. She was thin and reedy, with shapes of elongated dugs discernible through her robe, and looked ancient enough to have remembered the first pilgrim that ever set foot in this place, before even the statues by the stairs had been carved. But her voice belied the vessel from which it issued, because it was warm and rich, liquid and gold like honey, and seemed to belong rather more to a wealthy aristocratic dowager who had been well-fed and pampered all her life than to a woman whose life was pledged to serve others and who owned nothing, not even the clothes on her back. 'Would you like to join us for your meal?'

'I . . . yes, thank you,' Amais said.

'You can leave your things there in the corner,' the old woman told her. 'I will show you to your bed after supper.'

She was greeted with smiles and nods as she approached the table where the Temple people were sitting, but they all ate in companionable silence. Supper was simple enough, a thick vegetable stew and a hank of coarse brown bread, but Amais ate ravenously, not even having realised how hungry she was until the bowl was set in front of her with a heavenly aroma tickling her nose. She had barely paid attention to her companions other than to return their greetings as she sat down, and it was with some surprise that she realised, after she had sopped the last of the stew with her remaining piece of bread, that she and the old woman were the last people left in the refectory. The woman's eyes were enormous in her ascetic face, twin dark pools filled with a deep, quiet serenity and a sense that time had stopped, had ceased to be of any importance whatsoever. Amais's initial instinct had been a sudden urge to apologise for keeping the woman

154

from her duties at the Temple, such as they might be, but that was quickly smothered out of existence by the sheer weight of the other's presence in this place, as though she had been assigned to this and *had* no other duties except to be at Amais's side.

'Thank you,' Amais said at last, choosing the path of courtesy and simple good manners as she gathered up the detritus of her meal and took it to the washing-up bowl in the far corner of the refectory. 'It's been a long time since I've tasted a stew like that.'

'We are close to Cahan here,' the old woman said, 'and heaven is kind.'

'Where do you get . . . ?' Amais began, but the old woman lifted a hand to stop her.

'No questions are answered in this place,' she said, 'until the sun comes up over the mountains. Come, I will show you where you will sleep. Tomorrow, we can speak further.'

Amais, who had been about to inquire about nothing more pressing than the provenance of the vegetables, which did not seem likely to have been grown on this holy crag, swallowed the rest of the question and did not speak again. The old woman took up one of the handful of lanterns that had been hung around the refectory walls on iron hooks and beckoned Amais to follow. Gathering her pack from where she had left it by the door, Amais obeyed.

The dormitory was another long, low building, behind the refectory. The single room inside had been divided into two by a partition wall-screen of woven bamboo, providing a space for men and women on either side. Amais could hear the faint murmur of male voices from the other side of the partition, probably the other pilgrims from supper, but she appeared to be the only woman in residence at this time. Eight narrow pallets, unoccupied and neatly made with a small pillow and a rough blanket apiece, were ranged against

155

the far wall of the dormitory, and Amais's guide hung her lantern above one of them on another iron hook.

'We rise at dawn to worship in the Temple,' the old woman said, 'and you are welcome to join us, or go there yourself at a later time. We will speak in the morning.'

If Amais dreamed, she did not remember it the next day, woken by the sun and by chanting voices. There was a chill in the air. Amais breathed a prayer of apology to the Gods and stayed in her bed, pulling the blanket up over her head. She slept again, evidently, because the next time she became aware of her surroundings the sun was slanting at a different angle through the single window, pooling in a gentle wash at the foot of her pallet. Amais yawned, stretched, and swung her legs out of bed.

There were questions that had to be asked that day in Sian Sanqin.

By the time she made her way to the Temple – she felt an obligation somehow, here, to stop at the Temple before she went on to the refectory to see about breakfast – the place was deserted. Even the dead cat had gone. It was equally easy, in this rarefied mountain air where anything seemed possible, to believe that the cat had been removed as an unsuitable offering or that it had been granted access into Cahan. The humdrum and the miracle seemed so close in this strange Temple in the clouds that they might almost have been interchangeable.

The refectory was empty, too, and there seemed to be few places where one could go to actively seek the acolytes themselves – who apparently melted into the crags and the twisted mountainside trees when they were not required for Temple duties, because the place appeared utterly devoid of human life except for Amais herself. Amais found breakfast of sorts laid out – goat's cheese and more of that brown bread from the previous night, and a tiny oil-burner over which stood a cast-iron stand supporting a plump pottery teapot. She finished what had been provided – she was either in need of more sustenance than usual after her long climb to this place or else the food really tasted better in Sian Sanqin than any she had ever had before – and then wandered outside again into the mountain sunshine, breathing deeply of the crisp and clarifying air. A part of her was grateful that she was alone; this was the kind of place where solitude could be a gift, not a burden. And in any event Amais was never quite alone – not while she carried Tai's spirit with her in the shape of the journals. She was perfectly content to wait, if waiting seemed to be required. She found a sheltered spot on the far side of the Temple, where the mountains opened up into a view of an alpine valley and then more snow-bound peaks rising beyond it, and settled on a sun-warmed rock like a contented cat with one of Tai's journals in hand.

She might have thought that here, removed from the bustle of Linh-an in which the events in the journal had been rooted, Tai's world would seem somehow more distant from her own. But it seemed that one of the virtues of Sian Sanqin was indeed, as Jinlien had said, the tearing away of the barriers of time – and everything that could happen in the world had probably already happened, or was about to happen somewhere. All things were true, all things were possible, nothing was ever dead and gone or irretrievably lost because if it was gone from the place where it had been expected to be it would probably appear in another place, wholly unlooked for.

In this context, it did not seem surprising in the least for Amais, when she looked up from the pages of the journal she had been reading to rest her eyes on the distant mountaintops again, to find that she had company. The old woman from the previous night had made herself comfortable nearby, sitting against another sun-drenched rock, with her hands folded in her lap, her head resting against the rock wall at her back, and her eyes closed. She might have even been asleep, but there was a sense of being awake and aware that rested lightly on her, and that left Amais herself in no doubt of the truth.

'Have you ever,' Amais said, as though she was picking up a conversation they had already been having, something that had merely been interrupted by responsibility to everyday tasks and chores, 'had a *jin-shei-bao*?'

'Once,' the old woman replied in that rich honeyed voice, giving no sign that the question asked had been in any way unexpected or extraordinary. She might as well have been answering that first unfinished question that Amais had posed, about where the acolytes got the vegetables for their stew. 'I had two. A long time ago.'

Amais, who had not even been aware that she was holding her breath, let it out with a sigh. 'Where are they now?'

'One is dead; she has walked in the gardens of Cahan for many years,' the old woman said without emotion, with an air of merely imparting information. 'The other is down in the valley, there below us, with her family, with the responsibilities of her house and her kin.'

Sitting limned in the mountain sunshine, her eyes glowing, Amais had never felt so alive in her life. She felt the wind brushing the skin on her face and hands like a caress, she felt her blood rushing in her veins, her heart beating fast against her breast. For all her faith, for all the stubborn belief, this was the first time that she had touched the living thing and known it to be true.

'Can you tell me about it?' she asked, and her voice was full of passion, of quiet exhilaration, of the humility inherent in asking such a thing from one who shared that bond.

'Were it not for *jin-shei*,' the old woman said, 'it would

be her you would be speaking to now, here on the mountaintop, and I would be in a house in the valley with grandchildren around my feet. But perhaps it is better if she told you, for it is her story more than mine. You will pass her house when you come down the Great Stair and make your way out of the valley. I will give you a letter, and you can bear my greetings to her.'

'Thank you. I will. When was the last time you saw her?'

'Nigh on forty years,' the old woman said, her voice still full of serene tranquillity. 'What you come seeking, young *sai'an*, sometimes comes at a great price.'

Six

The promised letter materialised before the end of the day, an old-fashioned scroll sealed with red wax as though it had been an Imperial directive, its destination and the name of its recipient written on the outside in an ethereally graceful *jin-ashu* script. But it was not just the sheer beauty and virtuosity of the calligraphy that moved Amais almost to tears when the letter was first delivered into her hand. It was its mere existence – its matter-of-fact existence, here on the edge of the world, the only place in what had once been *baya*-Dan's beloved homeland where, apparently, the values she had cherished still flourished and were carefully tended and nurtured. Almost everywhere else in Syai the language and the secrets of the women had been trampled in the wake of wars, revolutions, the rush to apparent equality in status and education of men and women, the path of progress strewn with the wreckage of the grace and beauty that had gone before and that apparently could not stand against the weight of the march of years, fluttering underfoot like the broken wings of crushed butterflies. But here, in a lost Temple where time had stood still or had at least moved at a slower, more careful pace, things like *jin-ashu* and *jin-shei* not only still existed but they actually survived in their ancient state, accepted as part of contemporary reality, never thrown over for the shiny new baubles promised by progress and modern times, never dismissed, destroyed or defeated. The last refuge of something that was at the same time unutterably fragile and stronger than the granite in the mountains at Sian Sanqin's back, the Temple seemed to be one of the few places where those ancient butterflies still lived and thrived – iron butterflies, stronger than their peers in city and village where the tentacles of progress had reached, a shelter from where that which had been lost could begin to be found again.

Amais stayed at Sian Sanqin longer than she had thought she would. She did not wholly understand this place, not reared as she was in the city traditions of Linh-an, which had, in the four centuries of her family's exile from Syai, solidified into a monolithic slab of truth and the accepted way of doing things. It seemed to leave no room for addition or alteration but simply *was*, demanding acceptance in its entirety simply by virtue of its existence. But Amais was beginning to realise that a resurrection of all the things that she wanted to see return to the fabric of life in Syai would not only need changes to that ancient unalterable creed, it would depend on them. A melding of the old and the new would be the only way to restore that ancient secret language, and its power, to the women of Syai – and in mere days in Sian Sanqin, Amais was beginning to understand how much she still needed to learn about her land's past and its present before she could begin even contemplating a future, let alone attempting the daunting task of shaping one.

Without a word, Amais would rise at dawn and walk down to the Temple with the acolytes who tended its Gods; without a word, she laboured at their side at whatever task she was handed – and her presence had been accepted and unquestioned by the Temple and its folk, and tasks had been found.

She spent nearly two weeks on the mountaintop, attending dawn prayers, cleaning out old incense and offerings, which somehow magically appeared at various shrines and niches although it was impossible to ever actually catch anybody in the act of making them, sweeping the Temple floors, changing viscid and fouled old oil in the Temple lamps, lighting them when the sun went down and extinguishing them after dawn prayers. She sank into the Temple, became part of it, learning from its words of worship and its silences, dreaming strange dreams, none of which she ever seemed able to remember when she woke, as she slept in her assigned pallet.

But it was a dream, in the end, that made her leave the quiet holy mountaintop at last. It was nothing coherent or recognisable, just a series of images that she retained as her eyes flickered open one cool morning: *a knot of silent women standing together and staring at her mutely, some of them with their hair cropped short and just brushing their shoulders or else hacked off in uneven clumps so that they had the haunted and hunted look of fugitives or transgressors who had been on the receiving end of mob 'justice'; a pile of notebooks filled with fine* jin-ashu *characters, overflowing with a sense of something urgent and important; a flowering tree in a field above an ancient family cemetery whose markers had long been wiped clean by the centuries and which leaned at odd angles out of the soil where they had been planted; a woman's cry echoing as though uttered in a cavern or a dungeon deep beneath the earth . . . Herself, opening up her hands and releasing a cloud of brilliantly coloured butterflies into a cloudless blue sky.*

As urgently as she had been driven to find this place, so now she began to feel she needed to leave it. The dream images haunted her for a brace of days, and then she went to the old woman who had written her the letter of introduction and asked her blessing on the road ahead.

'Not my blessing but Cahan's be upon you, young seeker,' the old woman said with a small serene smile. 'We will give you bread and mountain water for your first day's journey.'

'Thank you, for everything,' Amais said, instinctively bowing her head as though to something holy.

'We are here to be found,' the old woman replied cryptically. 'Thank you for coming, for bringing the world up here with you, the world that turns outside our walls and leaves us in its wake. Sometimes we need to be reminded of it.'

Amais rose before the dawn light summoned the acolytes to another day of prayer and began descending the long staircase of Sian Sanqin while night was still upon it, in a wash of starlight, under a moon that was a pale sliver in the cold night sky. Sunrise caught her halfway down the stair, pouring down the mountainside, pooling into the valleys below, bright light of the Gods released from Cahan, changing the monochromatic silver and shadow of night into the many-hued brightness of day, and it was as if that was a sign. Sian Sanqin had been a gateway, and now she was walking from darkness into light, from ignorance into knowledge, from captivity into freedom, the thing sought hanging bright and beautiful close to the seeker's hand, like a ripe peach on a tree in the gardens of Cahan. All Amais had to do was reach out and pluck it.

She had been given directions as to where to seek the house of the surviving *jin-shei-bao* of the Sian Sanqin priestess. The road she needed to travel seemed to pick up from the foot of the staircase and led her straight down into the valley, past cultivated fields where, already, workers wearing clothes of undyed cotton and large conical hats of woven straw toiled in the furrows and the paddies under the new day's sun, straightening occasionally as Amais walked by to look at her and follow her with curious eyes until she passed out of sight.

The house that was her destination was an ancient country farmhouse, changed and added to over generations but retaining a sense of gracious harmony, its outside gate recently painted in a shade of deep brick-red, a narrow pagoda-style roof tiled in glazed dark-red tiles supported by two side pillars which sported *hacha-ashu* characters proclaiming prosperity, health and happiness within. There was space for a summoning gong that announced the arrival of visitors, but the gate was ajar, and the gong was missing. There was a sound of voices coming from within. Amais, hesitating, pushed the gate open a little wider and slipped inside.

The door was faced with a traditional screen, hiding the courts beyond from casual glances and opportunistic evil spirits. Amais stepped into the entry archway and cautiously peered around the screen. The source of the voices she had heard was just beyond – the cultivated formal garden of the outer courts, faced on two sides with colonnaded walkways with doorways opening from them, now filled with men and women in plain blue or grey uniforms, stepping in and out of the rooms, lounging on the edges of the stone fountain, lighting cigarettes and dropping used matches or grinding out spent cigarette butts underfoot on the once pristine walkways. A tidy stack of assorted weapons was piled close to the gate, where they could be quickly accessed in case of need. A white horse stood in one corner, resting one dainty hoof on its point with a dancer's grace, munching peacefully on a delicately blooming shrub. There was a lull in the various conversations as Amais stepped in, and many pairs of eyes turned in her direction, not all of them friendly.

Directly ahead, opposite the main gate, another gateway arched, providing access into the inner courts. This gate was firmly closed, and here was the small gong that Amais had missed at the front gate, with an accompanying striker made of polished wood hanging alongside.

Amais lifted her chin and crossed the yard full of uniformed troops without any impression of fear or haste. She struck the gong without hesitation as she arrived at the inner gate, and waited in the pool of silence, those watchful eyes still boring into her back. She was rewarded in a short span of time by a small window on the inner red gate opening to reveal the wizened face of what must have been a thoroughly ancient family retainer.

'I have a letter,' Amais said, 'for the Lady Xinmei.'

'If it would please you, give it to me,' the doorkeeper said in a reedy voice.

'It requires a response,' Amais told him.

'Very well. Wait here, then.'

The letter from the Temple on the mountaintop changed hands through the window in the gate, and the window was shut. Amais heard footsteps shuffling away. She waited with commendable patience and her face schooled into an expression of indifference as the minutes piled up. Behind her, the murmur of conversations interrupted by her arrival started up again, and although it was impossible to distinguish what was being said, Amais had an awful feeling that she herself was the subject of most of them. And then, thankfully, the same shuffling footstep returned, there was a rattling sound, and the gate swung open, revealing the complete person of the old gatekeeper who bowed low as he motioned Amais inside.

'My lady bids you enter,' he said. 'This way, *sai'an*, this way please, follow me.'

The gate was carefully closed and locked as Amais stepped through it at his invitation.

She was ushered into a graceful and beautiful place dominated by a large ancient cedar in the far corner and with walkways of white sand curving around flowerbeds, ponds, and stones and boulders of every colour, size and shape, which looked as though they had been brought here at great expense. Chief among them was a trio of upright stones of about Amais's own height, silver-grey, pointed up into the sky. A few steps from them rose a tiny, exquisite pavilion on which fluttered red ribbons with golden writing upon them. It was here that Amais was conducted, and then politely requested by the gatekeeper to wait.

There was a small table of inlaid rosewood in the middle of the pavilion, and on it the iron-burner and a green-glazed teapot, implements of the traditional tea ceremony, with several tiny handle-less cups laid ready. For a moment Amais was back in her grandmother's shadowy house, where she had learned how these ceremonies were properly conducted. The memory was so vivid, so strong, that for a moment she breathed the salt-laden air of Elaas once more, was almost the child that she had been, listening to *baya*-Dan's yearning, aristocratic voice reading the ancient poems of her race to the girl who would be the generation to carry on and preserve that legacy. *Baya*-Dan had been a strict old dragon when it came to things like this, but somehow Amais had not even realised just how much she missed her grandmother until she was faced with a reminder this potent, this familiar.

'*Huan-jie jin-shei*,' a melodious voice from behind Amais interrupted her musings. 'Be welcome in my house, in the name of the *jin-shei* vows of my past. How fares my *jin-shei-bao* in Sian Sanqin? I have not seen her in too many years.'

'Thank you for your hospitality,' Amais said, turning to accept this welcome and bowing to her hostess. 'She is well, your sister of the heart.'

'Is she happy?'

The tone of voice was almost plaintive, but there was more to it than this – allowing herself to take stock of her companion for the first time, Amais saw a lady who was well beyond what could be considered middle-age. At first sight she was still youthful in her looks, but the lines showing in her face, although few, were cut deep. Her hair was mostly grey, with a few stray strands remaining to show the brilliant black it had been in her youth, and carefully styled in the traditional manner with jewelled hair pins holding the heavy coils. She was clad in a robe of saffron-coloured silk with scarlet embroideries on the sleeves.

The *jin-shei* tie usually implied peers or contemporaries, but the old woman in the mountaintop Temple might have been the mother of the woman in the house in the valley. Life appeared to have weighed heavily on both the *jin-shei* sisters, but the more worldly of the two women had taken steps to hide those burdens from casual eyes and the other had allowed her life to show in her face and in her eyes. It was far harder to lie to Gods than to men.

But the question had made Amais cast her mind back to the Temple, and she suddenly had the vivid impression that the woman who had cast her lot with the Gods was somehow far happier than this sister of her heart, living in what was luxury and opulence compared to the frugal existence of Sian Sanqin.

'She is content,' Amais said carefully, after a pause. 'Or at least she seemed that way to me. Content and at peace with herself. But she said that there was a story behind your life and hers – and that it was your story to tell, Lady Xinmei. So I come to you from the Temple, as a supplicant.'

'What is it you were seeking at Sian Sanqin?'

'The women's country,' Amais said. 'The language that is lost, and the secrets it carried.'

Xinmei gazed at her for a long moment with glittering eyes, and then sighed, seeming to release a breath she had been holding against some unlooked-for evil thing. She

167

courteously indicated the small tea-table and the seating cushions piled around it. 'Will you sit?' she asked. 'We will talk. It has been a while since I have spoken on this with anyone . . . with another woman . . . with a woman so young. You have an unusual face, a strange accent. If I may ask, where do you come from, that your paths bring you to my door? Perhaps you will tell me your story, too, if you come asking to hear mine.'

It was the time-honoured trade, news and stories for hospitality. Amais was no stranger to it after her journey across Syai. So she told of her birth in a distant land, of a grandmother whose spirit had always dwelled in the Syai of old while her body lived out its days on a sunny island halfway across the world, of her own travels back to Syai with her mother and little sister, of the years in the city seeking answers to questions that had ceased to be asked a very long time ago.

'Have you been to the city? To Linh-an?' Amais asked. 'This . . . all this . . . this garden, the music of your fountains, the cut of your gown, it is all almost forgotten in Linh-an, I think, unless it is kept as a careful secret behind high walls and locked doors, hoarded against a stray glance of a stranger's eyes, against the coming of the night. Everything is so different from the world my grandmother told me about. I grew up believing in things that no longer exist.'

'It may be that it will soon be forgotten here, too,' Xinmei said, with a veiled glance towards the gate that led into the occupied outer courts.

'If I may be permitted to ask . . . who are they? What do they want here?'

'They are Iloh's people,' Xinmei told her. 'They are brave men and women, but they come with the winds of change, with talk of reform and what they call redistribution. Those of us who own property or collect rents are in danger for no other reason than being what we are – they call us land-lords, and evil. I think they are here because of three things – first, they wish to let us know that they are near, and they matter; second, they say they are here to protect us, the family and the retainers inside this house, from the mobs if such should rise against us, although if this happens it will have been the talk of these very soldiers which precipitates it; and, third, perhaps most obvious of all, they need a place to sleep and they would have had to evict the peasants from their homes if they chose to stay at their poor houses in the village. So far they've paid for their keep – but they've been here for nearly three weeks now, and I very much fear that the gardens of my father's house will never be the same again . . . They are everywhere, and it was brave of you, my dear, to even think about travelling across Syai at this time at all, let alone by yourself and with no protection. But let us not speak of them now. They are nothing to do with your own journey.'

'I had to go,' Amais said simply. 'I did not even think about this, about people like that, when I set out.'

'Brave,' Xinmei repeated. 'You have a courageous heart. If you come seeking the places where some trace of *jin-ashu* remains and it is still strong, you have found one right here. You do not know this, you are far too young and you have not lived in the land for long enough to have a memory of it – but in the days of Empire one of the daughters of this house was always sent out as a new emperor's concubine. I have letters, thousands of letters, some of them dating back four or five changes of emperors, from the women who were sent to the foot of the Imperial throne. All in *jin-ashu*, all written in a secret language that no man in the palace of their origin could understand if the letters were intercepted, and no man in the house of destination could understand until the women read it to their husbands by candlelight in the darkness before dawn. And then the letters going back

169

across the land, with quiet instructions as to what the concubine should tell her emperor in the nights she shared with him back in the city. For generations, my family has been the counsel in the shadows, the whisper that ruled the command that ruled the land . . . I myself would have been that woman in my generation, if it weren't for *jin-shei*. That is the story that you came to hear, I think.' She paused for a moment, her eyes veiled by dark lashes, and then lifted them to meet Amais's own. 'It is not,' she said, 'a story that I can be proud to tell. There are things in my past that I am not proud to have done. But my *jin-shei-bao* has asked me to do it in the letter that you brought, and it is a far, far lesser thing that she asks of me, so many years later, than I ever asked of her when we were both young. So I will do it. But first and foremost – you are a guest, and I have the hospitality of my house to offer you. Will you have tea?'

Seven

'What did I know?' Xinmei said, after the tea had been brewed, after the scent cup had been poured and set aside to flavour the air with the delicate aroma of fine tea picked in the mountains in springtime. 'I was fourteen, with all that age implies. I was selfish and ignorant and I thought – nay, I *knew* – precisely what I wanted and what my life owed me. And so I wronged two sisters, perhaps because of my own desires – one of my own blood and my family, the other my sister of the heart. You see, as I told you, it was I who was supposed to go to the emperor when the time came for my generation to offer up one of its daughters . . .'

The story was stark in its simplicity, in the end. Fourteen-year-old Xinmei was beautiful and wilful and precocious, all qualities that would have made her a natural choice for the emperor's concubine even if she had not been reared to the idea that this would be her fate. But that very precocious-ness came back to haunt her, because, young as she was, she had already chosen the sweetheart with whom she wanted to share her life. Being traded away to a man she did not love, even if he was the most powerful man in Syai, even if her role would be to guide and influence that power into the

171

channels her family wanted, became an appalling prospect for her, one she could scarcely bear to contemplate, and she recoiled from such a destiny. If she had been left alone to grow up at her own pace she would probably not have made the decisions that she did – but she was young, and desperate, and eloquent. And if truth be told her sweetheart was very young himself, and youthful passions did not need much convincing to come bursting out from behind the carefully constructed dams of protocol and decorum.

'I cannot go to the emperor,' Xinmei had told her mother, on the day before she was due to leave for Linh-an. 'I am not acceptable.'

'Whatever do you mean? You are the chosen one, you have been deemed suitable by your father and your entire elder kin!' her mother had protested.

'I cannot go,' Xinmei had replied. 'You cannot send the emperor a woman who is not a virgin.'

The implications of that calm, quiet statement struck Xinmei's household like lightning, leaving wreckage in its wake. Her father, summoning her into his presence, had been purple with rage. He had demanded to know who had spoiled her, but Xinmei, finding strength in the sure knowledge that such an admission would spell doom for the boy she had chosen to love, found surprising strength in refusing to name her lover. Her father had threatened to kill *her*, for bringing dishonour to the family name, for losing face to no less than the emperor himself; her mother had prostrated herself at her husband's feet and begged for her daughter's life. But, in the end, her father had been typically pragmatic about the matter. Xinmei would be allowed to live. Her younger half-sister Xuelian, thirteen at the time and assumed to be too young to have indulged in the kind of behaviour that had barred Xinmei from the Imperial bed, would be sent in her stead.

But Xinmei would not escape punishment. Her fate was

announced to her in a full family gathering the day after Xuelian left for Linh-an: if she was not to belong to the emperor of Syai, then she would belong to its Gods. Instead of entering a household where she would command servants, she would become one – she was to be sent off to Sian Sanqin, the Temple on the mountain, as a handmaiden herself, as one of the dedicated and celibate acolytes of the Gods of Cahan.

'I was to be punished,' Xinmei said to Amais, her gaze distant, focused somewhere on the long-gone years of her youth. 'My father could not send me to the emperor, and thus his plans were thwarted – and he was not going to be the one with whom it all ended, who failed to continue the traditions of our family's influence at the Court. Very well, he had dealt with that, he was lucky enough to have another daughter to send – although my heart broke for Xuelian at the time. She was a child, such a child . . .' Xinmei paused, dropped her eyes to the hands in her lap. Outwardly, she was calm, even serene – but as she told the tale of her life it was those hands that gave away her real feelings. They were tightly twined around one another, her fingers white with the pressure she was exerting. 'But there was still the matter of what I had done. And allowing me to marry my lover would have been condoning that. So he would make sure it did not happen. I would be locked away in the Temple . . . for the rest of my life.'

'And so you asked her to go,' Amais said with quiet conviction, putting the pieces together in her mind. She tried – and failed – to imagine the old woman she had left behind in Sian Sanqin as a young girl who was being asked in the name of the most holy of things to ascend that mountain and never come back down again as a free woman with her own life and dreams and hopes. Who was being asked to give herself, of her own free will, to the Gods of whom she had not thought of until that moment as having any say in how she lived her days. 'Your friend. Your *jin-shei-bao*.'

Xinmei looked up, and tears stood in her eyes. 'Yes,' she whispered. 'I asked her to go in my stead. In the name of *jin-shei*, I asked her. She was fifteen, a year older than me – but she was quiet, studious, meek, she had been leading precisely the kind of compliant and sequestered life that my father had demanded of me. She had no man that she loved; she was well past the age where a marriage might have been arranged, though, and I knew that she had refused one suitor when her family had brought him to her. She didn't *want* the life I wanted. She wanted something else, something different . . . even I did not know what. But she could find it in the solitude and the prayer up on that mountain. She could find it there far better than I.'

'But did she want to go?'

Xinmei shook her head slightly. 'I don't know,' she said. 'That, I never asked. All I did was write her a letter – I told her of my father's edict, of my love for the man to whom I knew my life belonged, even back then, even when I was such a child. And I also said that I thought I might already be carrying my lover's child.'

'Was it true?'

'Not then,' Xinmei said. 'I had hopes, but no evidence, no proof. But there was that to fight for – that life together. I wanted to be a mother. I wanted a family. I wanted an earthly life, full of earthly pain and pleasure . . . not the life of a priestess in a mystic Temple where people go to find the answers to riddles posed in their dreams.'

'Like I did,' Amais said, with a small and slightly sad smile.

'If it had been me that you had met up there instead of my *jin-shei-bao*,' Xinmei said, 'you would not have got your answers. If I were still alive, all these years later, I would have been a bitter and broken old woman. And you say . . . you say that she is not . . . ?'

It was a question again, a plea for reassurance, even for redemption. But Amais could not give it, not in the way that it had been asked for. As with Xinmei's phantom pregnancy of many years ago, where this lost *jin-shei-bao*'s state of mind was concerned Amais had only her own instincts and intuition and no evidence. She had not known any of this shared history while she was up in the Temple, or that this question would be asked, that an answer would be mutely pleaded for. 'I only knew her for a handful of days,' she said at last, choosing her words carefully, 'but in that time I never heard her say a harsh word – about anything, least of all herself.' She paused. 'Did you ever go and see her up there?'

'Twice,' Xinmei said. 'The first time was when that child I had told her I might be carrying was finally born – it might have been almost a year after she went to Sian Sanqin. And then, once more, years after that, but that time I did not make myself known to her. I was just one of the pilgrims. She probably never even knew I was there. But I needed . . . I needed to see.'

'And did you?' Amais asked. She felt as though she had reached back in time and brought forward something living and breathing – that she was looking into the eyes of an ancient truth, one that she knew she had been sent here to find. Her heart was beating hard, and her eyes shone with the light of someone with a mission. She had no idea of just how unutterably beautiful she looked as she sat in the tea pavilion, wrapped in the scent of the blooming garden and the fragrant tea.

'I thought that she was angry,' Xinmei murmured. 'I thought that she would rather not speak to me. Now . . . I am not so sure. Perhaps I should have said something then. But I did not, and I have not been back since. I asked for a hard, hard thing, and I knew it, and the canker of that guilt has been eating at my *jin-shei* vow ever since. I have never quite forgiven myself for it.'

'But what happened?' Amais said. 'How was your father convinced of this? How was it that you were not sent to Sian Sanqin anyway, despite the fact that someone else had agreed to go in your place?'

'The Temple took care of that,' Xinmei replied. 'They had been promised an acolyte, and they got one. My father had to be content with that – he could not rail against a Temple decree – that would have been flouting the Gods themselves. As for me, I was now someone else, another person altogether. I was no longer promised. I was free. And my father had run out of options.'

'He allowed you to marry?'

'He refused me a dowry, but he said nothing further on the subject,' Xinmei said. 'In fact, he never spoke to me again at all – until the time that he was on his deathbed, and he summoned me back to the house.'

'He wanted to say goodbye . . . ?' Amais murmured, finding herself oddly touched by this possibility.

Xinmei shook her head once. 'No. He was not a forgiving man, and he never forgave me. But Xuelian had worked out well instead, and he had no complaints on that score – and the Gods and the women's vow had thwarted him on the other project, and he had simply turned his back on it. But none of that meant that I was back in his favour.'

'Why did he wish to see you, then?'

'Because of one last act of malicious intent,' Xinmei replied. 'My husband – the lover of my youth – had been stricken down by a paralysis when he was barely into his middle-age, and it was my duty to care for him. He would have no servant do it. In a way, I guess that was expiation, after all.' She allowed herself a tiny grimace, the first time she had let her carefully schooled face show any sign of emotion. 'I was responsible to him, to that family; our daughter, the only child we had who survived to adulthood, had

176

married and moved away from our house and it was the two of us and a handful of old family retainers. But now my father summoned me back and told me that I was to inherit the farm, and take over from him.'

'This farm?'

'Yes, this place. This house, where I was born, where I rebelled, from which I was cast out once.'

'And he gave it back to you!' Amais said. 'How was that malicious?'

'Because it meant two things,' Xinmei explained. 'One was that he was disinheriting his rightful heir in my favour, which meant that my life would be filled for the rest of my days with the bitterness and the endless machinations of that rightful heir against me. In a way he sundered me from the very family I was to inherit. He knew that I would never have the cooperation of any of them in any decision I chose to make, and that I would be alone all my life.'

'But your husband . . .'

'My husband belonged to another family. I could not refuse my father and his deathbed edict. I could not take care of my husband in the manner that he demanded, and still accept that edict. So he tore me apart from him in the end, my father. He won, even if he did not live to see the fruits of his victory.'

'What . . . became of your husband?'

'He took a concubine, to care for him,' Xinmei told her, 'and after a while he forgot that he had had a wife . . . But he has been dead these many years now, and that is not the part of the story you came here to seek – it's what happened between the two of us, my *jin-shei-bao* and myself. The things that could be asked of a sister were sometimes impossible, but they could not be refused, they could never be refused, not if asked in the name of *jin-shei* itself. And look how that shaped all our lives.' She bowed her head. 'I still have it, you know.'

177

'You have what?'

'The letter that I wrote to her, to ask her. All the letters that we exchanged, in fact – all of them, mine to her, hers to me. She sent all of my letters back to me on the day she left for Sian Sanqin.'

'Is that why you thought she hated you for it?'

'No – at least, I don't think so. It was not an act of retribution; she was not vengeful or mean, it was not in her nature. It was simply itself – it was an act of farewell to the world she knew she would never return to. And yes, before you ask, before you even consider if you may ask, it has already been requested of me in the letter that you brought. The letters are yours to read, if you will.'

'I am grateful,' Amais whispered.

'It is the least I can do in payment of the debt I incurred when I asked what I had to ask of her,' Xinmei said.

'What happened to Xuelian?' Amais asked. That girl's fate, substitute for her sister in an emperor's bed, had not failed to make an impression on her, over and above the story of *jin-shei* that had followed in the wake of those events.

'She fulfilled all her duties,' Xinmei said, 'and far better than I might have done, perhaps. There are letters that she wrote home, also – would you like to see those? They are, after all, part of the story.'

'*Jin-ashu*?' Amais queried softly.

'Of course,' Xinmei said. 'That was our language. Tonight, you are my guest here. Tomorrow I will have the letters brought to you. You are welcome to stay in my house for as long as you need to.' She rose gracefully to her feet. '*Fang wodai fang nimen*,' she said softly. 'My house is your house. Be welcome in my home . . . in the name of lost *jin-shei*.'

Eight

The same aged retainer who had admitted Amais into the inner sanctuary of the Lady Xinmei on her arrival brought her a carved wooden box the next morning and handed it to her in silence with a small bow. If his pursed lips were to be any indication, he strongly disapproved of any of these 'family' things being handed out to all and sundry just like that, simply because they had thought to turn up at the gate and ask. Amais could only guess at how he felt towards the invaders in the outer courts, and how his gnarled hands must itch to usher every last one of the troops quartered in this house out of the gate, lock the doors behind them, and fumigate the quarters they had fouled by their presence in the ancient halls.

But she spared him little further thought. She had been offered the services of a bath-house by another aged crone of a female servitor, who escorted her into the facilities and provided her with a cake of home-made soap and a somewhat faded but still resplendent linen towel. Thankful at the opportunity, Amais luxuriated at the chance to get clean, even soaping and rinsing her long hair. She put on a pair of simple country cotton trousers, like a peasant hoyden, a short-sleeved tunic top, and coiled her damp hair under a large conical woven straw hat such as the fieldworkers had worn on the day she had arrived at the farmhouse. Despite the harsh reminder that the country was at war around her and the slightly ominous presence of dozens of uniformed men and women with cold eyes and lethal weapons with which to enforce their orders, however unpalatable they might turn out to be; despite the traces of tragedy which were waiting for her in the letters she had been handed to read, Amais felt young and free and vivid, and, in the manner of exuberant youth, particularly when it found itself in the shadow of danger, invulnerable. She decided on pure impulse that she would leave the farmhouse and find some pretty spot in the surrounding countryside where she could sit and read Xinmei's letter-hoard at her leisure.

A small postern gate turned out to exist in the back of the inner courts, right behind the giant cedar in the corner, and the old doorman, after its existence had been wrung from him, took her there jangling a handful of keys with every appearance of being resigned as to whether this guest of his mistress's came to bodily harm out there. It was all there in the square set of those lean shoulders – *If she wants to risk her neck by gallivanting across the fields it's no concern of mine*. There might have been a brief impulse to snatch at the family letters – if the guest wanted to venture out there she was welcome, but she should leave the family treasures behind – but it was scotched. There were too many years here, too many years of obedience and loyalty. The mistress had given the letters; he did not do it willingly or with a good grace but he was a servant and therefore he had to accept that the mistress must know best.

Released from the gilded cage of the farmhouse, Amais made her way along a narrow path bordered by long grass until she came to a gentle hillside, a long, low slope dominated by a gigantic yet gracefully symmetrical tree of a kind she did not recognise. At its foot and in its shade were the remnants of an ancient family graveyard, with headstones so old that some of them had almost completely sunk into the ground, following the bodies and the ashes of those whose resting places they marked. These old family plots were commonplace in Syai, and if properly planned, facing in the correct directions and on suitable ground, they were remarkably free of ghosts or lingering spirits. There was merely a feeling of peace here, of being at one with the past and the ancestors who had inhabited it – precisely the kind of atmosphere that would go perfectly with the letters Amais had come here to read.

It seemed to be deserted. Down-slope, a way away and to the left of her, a handful of people worked in a distant field, but there was no human presence anywhere within a stone's throw of where she was. Her only companions were the breeze that stirred the long grass by the wayside and the silvery leaves of the old tree, and the sound of birdsong coming from somewhere beyond the hill.

Amais took off her hat and shook her damp hair out, letting it fall about her shoulders and dry naturally in the sun and the summer breeze. She found a spot where a fold in the ground and a couple of old gravestones leaning towards one another made a perfectly comfortable cradle, sat down with a small contented sigh, and, offering a small prayer to those who rested in this place, nestled her back lightly against the stones, hauling out her box and its letters.

They had been sorted by date and carefully wrapped into individual silk parcels with *jin-ashu* script on the silk indicating the nature and the dates of the letters within. On one of these another note had been pinned, with a single line of calligraphy – Xinmei's hand, Amais supposed. It simply said, *These are the ones you want to see.*

They were the letters between Xinmei and her *jin-shei-bao*

181

sister, whose name, as Amais only found out now, was Lianqin. Xinmei's impassioned letter was there, the one in which she had begged Lianqin in the name of *jin-shei* to take her place in the Temple, but it was Lianqin's reply that riveted Amais's attention:

> *If you ask a bird to give up hope of the sky so that another might feel the wind on its wings; if you ask a man to give up his sight so that another might see; if you ask a peach blossom not to bloom so that its fellow on the branch might greet the bee and receive the blessings that allow it to turn, in the Gods' own time, into the peach – all of these things might seem hard to do, but if you ask any of them in the name of something that is bigger than they or you or I, then it can be done, anything can be done. If you ask me in the name of the vow that binds us, I will give you my space in the sky, my share of the light; I will let you be the blossom that bears the peach. I will climb the mountain and find the Gods that wait for me there and I will make that place the one where I was meant to be in this life and on this earth before Cahan calls me home. And I will learn to understand the blessings that the Gods choose to bestow upon me.*

Amais was so engrossed in this that it was some time before she became aware that she was being watched. When she finally tore her eyes away from the page, she found that she had to blink several times to clear the blur of tears from her vision – and then found herself staring into the eyes of a bare-footed man perhaps in his early thirties, dressed in simple peasant garb with a red kerchief around his neck, a barrel-sized pail on the ground at his feet as he stood looking at her with a slight smile on his face.

Amais's heart lurched, but it was not with fear. There was something in that smile that made her throat suddenly close, her breath coming in shallow little gasps through her parted lips.

They looked at one another for a long moment, and then Amais gathered what shreds of dignity she could after having been surprised thus and straightened, closing her mouth and tilting her head in a quizzical manner.

'Is there something you wanted?' she inquired, politely enough, pushing one unruly coil of almost-dry curly hair behind her ear.

'Ah . . . no,' the man said. His voice was pleasant, but not cultured. This was no etiolated aristocrat, the richness of the loamy earth of Syai was in his tone and his pronunciation. 'It's just . . . you reminded me somewhat of me. A very long time ago. Even the place . . .' He indicated the tilted gravestones with an economical nod of his head. 'When I was a boy, I used to escape to just such a spot as this, except that my tree was an ancient, twisted old willow. It was sanctuary, me and my books. And my father coming down upon me with the wrath of the righteous, chivvying me to do my chores. It's been a long time since I have thought of those days, but seeing you there . . . I do apologise if I startled you.' His smile broadened slightly, and he offered her a small courteous bow – and suddenly he was something else than Amais had thought he was. That bow was no sharecropper's gesture, but something civilised and full of hidden protocol, learned in halls and chambers of power. It was something that would have been worthy in *baya*-Dan's shadowy rooms, Imperial princess in exile that she was.

'And what was it,' Amais asked after a moment, 'that you were reading?'

'I owned two books at the time,' her companion said. 'If it wasn't one, then it was the other. I don't recall any more.

183

It's been wrapped in the shed skin of too many years, and put away deep.'

'You're a poet,' Amais said, in reluctant admiration.

He offered another light bow, this time of acknowledgement. 'It has been said of me,' he replied. 'It is not all I am.'

'Are you of these lands?'

'No. My home – and my willow tree – are far from here. It's been many years since I've been back there, and it will probably be more years before I return. Times are difficult right now . . . but better times are coming.'

'You know this? For certain?'

'Better times are always coming,' he said, and this time the smile was an outright grin. 'And you? Your looks alone make you a stranger in this place, to say nothing of that wonderful accent.'

'I am a visitor,' Amais said carefully, folding away Lianqin's letter. 'I am staying for a few days . . . with Lady Xinmei, at the big house.'

'Ah,' he said noncommittally, nodding his head. 'Then would you permit me, Lady Xinmei's guest, to rest from my work a while here among these stones and ask for your company?'

His eyes had come to rest on Amais's bare feet, and she suddenly blushed a violent pink, drawing her feet up and curling them under her.

'I . . . have no objection,' she said faintly.

He casually hoisted up the barrel he had been carrying as though it weighed nothing at all, although Amais could clearly hear liquid slopping in it and see that it was more than two-thirds full of water, and placed it out of harm's way by one of the gravestones. The strength it took to lift that thing must have been phenomenal. Amais, just from her one quick glance, was quite certain that she herself would not be able to shift it at all. Apparently quite unaware of the feat he had just accomplished, her companion selected another gravestone, right under the silver-leaved tree, and settled against it with a sigh.

The day was pure summer, warm and languid and full of contentment and a sense of being safe, secure, as though there was nothing wrong with the world and never would be, as though sorrow were a stranger and never an orphan or a widow had trod upon this blessed soil on which the two of them sat with a summer breeze stirring their hair; as though never an unhappy thought could cross the mind of any being who now drew breath and life. It was two people wrapped in summer and, somehow, in one another, their very presence in this place completing each other's existence.

Baya-Dan had had a word for something like this. Once, a long time ago, when Amais had been no more than a small child, *baya*-Dan had spoken about *yuan*, relationships that were meant to be, people who were meant to meet, who *had* to meet, who would unwittingly change the circumstances of the world they lived in just so that their path might cross with the path of this other person with whom they were born to share the same breath, the same light, the same summer's day.

They might have known one another for a century, or a thousand years, these two people who had only just met in an abandoned family graveyard that housed kin belonging to neither of them. Neutral ground.

Amais felt a strange, huge peace unfolding inside her, a great pool of quiet deep water beside which her spirit sighed and subsided in pure surrender.

'And what are you reading?' her companion asked. It was an oddly intimate question, for one who had not even asked her name – but then, names seemed oddly superfluous here. They already knew each other's names, or they did not need to know them. It was a simple, complicated thing . . .

185

'Letters,' she replied. 'From long ago. Letters from one *jin-shei-bao* to another.'

'Ah,' he said. 'Women's secrets.'

'They matter,' Amais said, rousing slightly. His tone had implied a gentle mockery of her reading material.

'Of course they matter,' he agreed, his expression serious again, almost apologetic. 'But we were two worlds, once, the men and the women of Syai. I would like to think that we are past that now, that we are all a part of something bigger, that we are all people and not just who our gender mandates we have to be. I would like to think that there is no more need for secret brotherhoods or sisterhoods, now that all people are brother and sister to one another.'

'You think that is true? Of our world?' Amais asked, turning a surprised gaze on him.

'Maybe not just yet,' he conceded. 'But that is the world I want to see. A world where all would look out for the good of the one, and one would do what is necessary for the good of all – and it would not matter at all if the one were a man or a woman so long as it were a human being.'

'It is a good dream,' Amais said.

He blinked, giving a strong impression that he was unused to people being so dismissively cavalier about his ideas. 'It is more than a dream,' he told her. 'It is the future. It is possibility. Your *jin-shei*, it is what used to be . . .'

'I came here to find the things that are lost,' Amais said. 'Do you have any idea at all about what *jin-shei* really was . . . ?'

Once again she had startled him, putting him in his place with a confidence and a passion that was rare in one her age. But this time he smiled. 'Educate me, then,' he replied, 'if you think it is something that I should know.'

'It was the thing in the name of which anything could be asked, anything could be possible,' Amais said. 'I can't . . .

I'm not *allowed* to speak of it, not to you! But I have journals which my ancestors have kept, and *jin-shei* shaped empires then – the vow between sisters, the things each asked of the other in the name of that vow. Oh, but it was a glory, and a responsibility . . .'

Her passion on this subject had brought colour to her cheeks again, a glow to her eyes. He was watching her with one eyebrow raised, a smile hovering on his face – but it was a smile of appreciation, even admiration. Amais, noticing his expression, dropped her eyes in sudden shyness.

'Sometimes it is a waste to destroy something good, even if it does not hold the power it once held,' she said after a pause, filling the silence between them because there was more to be said. '*Jin-shei* . . . meant something. Something deep. Something that a simple all-encompassing notion of all human beings being brother and sister to one another can never accomplish. There was a *choice*, you see. You would choose to be someone's sister, and know that you might be called on to pay the price of that choice. How precious can something be if you are handed it while you are still in swaddling clothes, simply by virtue of being the issue of a human father and mother?'

'A young philosopher,' he declared.

'Too ignorant,' Amais said with frank self-castigation. 'I would need to be old and grey before I could be that. There is still far more about this world that I don't know, that I'll never know, than there is of which I am certain.'

'But you are certain of this?' he questioned. 'This women's thing?'

'I am more certain of that than I am of anything else I have ever known,' Amais said.

And knew she lied.

Because there was one more thing in this world that she was certain of in that moment, and it was that she was meant to be here, in this place, with this man. Suddenly she could not lift her eyes to his at all, knowing that this would be written all over her face, knowing only that she was afraid of it.

She kept her eyes down with such ferocious determination that she utterly failed to notice that he had moved, and when his hand swam into her field of vision and reached out to cup her chin and tilt her face up to his she shivered, as though she had been touched by something not of this earth.

But he was of this earth. He was real, and solid, and very, very near. And when he made her look up into his face she saw there the same certainty that had been in her own heart, written on her own face, a moment before. *Yuan*. Destiny.

'Anything you believe in with the whole of your heart,' he said very softly against her lips, as if afraid of being overheard, as if he were not so much saying the words out loud but transferring them physically from his mouth to hers so that she could taste them, the sweetness of them, 'cannot help being true.'

Nine

For a moment – a wonderful, exhilarating moment – Amais had known nothing at all about her world except that *he* was in it, this still-nameless man, the mere brush of whose lips against hers made her feel as though she floated above the ground without touching it with her feet. But then the fear had come rushing in, and an absolute blank astonishment, as though she – that part of her that she knew and recognised – were standing somewhere outside her body and watching in a sort of appalled wonder as this man, this stranger, reached for her and touched her lips with his own and woke things in her that she had not known she possessed. She froze, and he felt it, and took that warm strong hand from her face – and she could have wept for the loss of it, and rejoiced that it was gone and did not by its very presence tempt her into thinking things she could not bear to be thinking about.

She fled, shamelessly, taking care only to gather the precious letters together with trembling hands and make sure they were safe – leaving behind her sandals, her hat, and the man who had kissed her, the poet, the dreamer, who watched her go without moving to stop her.

She ran all the way back to the house as though it were

a sanctuary, knocking on the postern door feverishly until the old servant opened it, practically falling into the house in her haste to be out of that perfect summer's day that had so treacherously trapped her in its honeyed webs. The old gatekeeper clicked his tongue at her breathless and dishevelled state. There was an unspoken *I knew she was going to come to no good* only barely being reined in from being spoken out loud, but it was there in his eyes and the expression on his face.

Amais retreated to the safe solitude of the room that had been given over to her use while she was a guest at this house. It took her almost an hour to stop trembling, to stop feeling the ghost of his kiss on her mouth – for the first time in her life she understood, rather than merely knew, what it would mean to have a real *jin-shei-bao* right now, someone to whom she could go, whom she could trust, who could give advice, and if not advice then at least offer a willing ear.

The truth of it was Amais was nearly seventeen years old – and she had never kissed a man before this day. And now, after she had, she could not conceive of ever doing so again if the man were not that stranger from the summer hillside.

Her hands were cold, and she lifted them to her face and laid her cool palms over burning cheeks.

'I don't even know his name,' she whispered out loud, more to hear her own voice and somehow convince herself that she was still the same person she had always been, that she still knew who she was and what her life was meant to be. But it didn't help. She still felt disembodied, as though her heart was somewhere out of her body and out of her control. It was ludicrous, but it was so.

She turned to the letters again, her heart still beating like a drum for a war dance, hoping to find solace or understanding in them.

It was Xuelian's letters that she found next, the letters

written home by what was at first an obviously homesick and very afraid child but which soon changed into something else. Xuelian may not have been the family's first choice for the emperor's concubine, but it quickly became apparent that she might have been born for the part. The Gods, as usual, had known very well what they were doing.

Xuelian was fifteen years old and had spent just under two years in the Imperial household when the Sun Emperor had been made to abdicate the throne of Syai. The Imperial family had been guaranteed their lives, and even some property – and the emperor, his empress and a small entourage were allowed to retire to a house in the country where they agreed to live lives of quiet seclusion. But not all of his household would go with him. There would have to be a price for the Imperial family's freedom to live without fetters after the emperor's abdication, and the price was negotiated by the cold and vengeful empress who had watched the growing affection between her royal husband and his child-concubine with a smouldering jealousy she could do nothing about – until that moment.

Xuelian had been offered to Shiqai, the one-time Imperial general and a powerful warlord in his own right, who had negotiated the emperor's surrender on Baba Sung's behalf when Empire first gave way to the dream of Republic. The same Shiqai who betrayed the Empire, then betrayed the Republic by seeking to reinstate the Empire but with himself at the helm. Even shattered and fragmented as it was in the wake of these upheavals, what was left of the land of Syai had rebelled, Shiqai's plans had been thwarted, and in less than three years the fearsome warlord himself was dead – some said from buckling under the sheer weight of his ambition.

In those three years he had not been kind to Xuelian. Although she did not say much in her letters, she was used harshly and it would have been impossible for her unhappiness not to filter through in what she wrote to her family, despite the fact that she never gave any details of her life. But that ended with Shiqai's death, and for a while Xuelian wrote nothing at all. Then, after a gap of nearly two years, she resumed her letters. She had been traded again, or rather another man had reached out and taken her for himself – no less than Shenxiao, Baba Sung's own protégé, the leader of the Nationalists. A tough man and a shrewd politician, he had understood the value of having access to all the insight and inside knowledge locked in the mind of a woman who had been close to the seat of power in Syai since she had been a young child. The fact that she was still young and beautiful enough to arouse his physical desire was just a bonus.

But times had changed, and Xuelian was no longer a concubine – she was merely a mistress, a woman kept by a man married to another in a house different from his marital home. It might have been better, on the face of it. Unlike a traditional concubine, she would never be subject to the whims and vagaries of the legal wife, to whom a concubine was traditionally subservient, and her experience in the Sun Emperor's household had given her bitter first-hand knowledge of how a wife who considered herself wronged or abandoned in a concubine's favour could lash out at the woman whom she thought of as having stolen her husband's affections. But the removal of this potential source of trouble from her life also meant a loss of privileges that were customarily accorded to a concubine. She had no rights, and could be simply discarded at will when her married lover tired of her.

But what else can I do? Xuelian wrote to her family, in a voice very similar to that of Lianqin when she had accepted the exile to the Temple and spoke of learning to appreciate whatever blessings the Gods had seen fit to bestow upon her life. Xuelian might have been sent out to become a quiet influence in the corridors of power on behalf of her family, but the fact remained that the only way she could do so was from the silken prison of a powerful man's bed. She was intelligent, and loyal, and keen-witted – but none of those things had been cultivated or given free rein to express themselves. She was only useful to anyone at all if she was, at least outwardly, a compliant sexual partner who would then be allowed the right of offering pillow-talk advice couched as deferential opinion, a kind of reward, a half-hearted permission to offer up her mind after the offer of her body had been accepted and consummated.

There were gaps in the letters. There seemed to have been a child, but that was fragmented and garbled; if there were more letters on the matter they had been lost, or had been deliberately removed from the box before Amais received it. And then the letters stopped altogether, petering out on an uncertain note, leaving it open for interpretation as to what happened next.

Amais read through the night by lamplight, drowning herself in these letters, in the life of a girl she had never known, whose troubles were so very different from hers. She hunted for missing letters in the remaining bundles in the box, but found none – and it was with a sense of astonishment that she realised it was getting light outside, her lamp an increasingly insubstantial ghost of itself as it competed against the dawn.

She gathered up the letters, carefully restored them to their original packaging, closed the carved box and – when she was done and the hour became a little more civilised – went in search of her hostess.

She found Xinmei in the garden.

'Good morning,' Xinmei greeted her. 'You look tired; did you not rest well?'

'I was reading all night,' Amais said, offering up the box. 'I thank you for these. I thought I knew all I needed to know about this world, but I realise now that I was mistaken – I have learned a lot from these letters. How did Xuelian die?'

Xinmei gave her a strange look. 'Whatever made you think,' she asked softly, 'that Xuelian is dead?'

It was Amais's turn to look startled. 'But the letters – they just stop, there is no real end to that story – I assumed they just stopped coming, that she was dead . . . ?'

Xinmei shook her head. 'Xuelian is alive,' she said. 'Very much alive. She is in Linh-an. She owns a teahouse called the House of the Silver Moon, the last house on the Street of Red Lanterns.'

'But how do you know of this? There are no letters . . .'

'She did not write that,' Xinmei said. 'I only know because I went to the city to look for her when her letters stopped, to see if she *was* dead, to give her a decent burial if she was, or at least a memorial from the family . . . but I found her, and she was quite alive and well, and it is a cause of great sorrow for me that she and I found very little to say to one another, in the end. I hear of her, every now and then, through other channels. But she hasn't written to me for years. I think she feels her duty to the family has been done – more than done; she owes us nothing any more.'

Amais, to whom these words were a shattering shock, was suddenly aware of a strong urge to go back to the city she had left behind – the city where a lot of her answers appeared to lie after all, even if she did have to cross the breadth of Syai to learn how to ask the right questions.

'I must get back to the city,' she said, voicing her thoughts.

'Right now?' Xinmei asked. 'That might be harder than you think. There is fighting near Linh-an. I think the war is drawing to a close at last, the Gods be praised – I do not pretend to know whether the right people will have won it, or if we will be better off under whoever comes out on top, but for better or worse the news that I hear seems to be that Iloh and his armies are well on the way to taking the city, and the land with it . . .'

Amais suddenly shivered. 'But my mother is in the city,' she said, an afterthought, but a sudden sharp fear that was quite real for all that. 'And my little sister. Xinmei, I have to go back – I have to find a way back . . .'

'You'd have to ask Iloh himself for a pass,' Xinmei said.

Amais looked stricken, and Xinmei allowed herself a small secret smile.

'But there is hope,' she told her. 'Did I not say that the troops in my courts are Iloh's men? And who do you think arrived just a couple of days ago to join them . . . ?' Amais's head came up sharply, and Xinmei nodded. 'Yes. Iloh himself is here. Come, over here – look . . .'

She laid a gentle hand on Amais's elbow and guided her to the wall dividing the outer courts from the inner. A pattern of blue and white tiles decorated the pillars on the inner side of the gate, and Xinmei tapped one of these lightly until it moved sideways, revealing a tiny spy-hole through which one could observe the outer courts. Xinmei peered through this herself for a moment, and then stepped away and motioned for Amais to take her place.

'He is there,' she said. 'You can see him. In the far corner, talking to three men.'

Amais stepped up to the spy-hole.

Perhaps she should have known, should have guessed . . . but she had not, and it was with an icy shock of recognition that she laid eyes on the face of the man called Iloh, the man who was leading the rebel armies in a bloody civil war that had already claimed thousands of lives, the man whose name had been swirling in the air ever since she had set foot in Syai years before, whose face she had even seen on badly printed posters in Linh-an which announced the price that had been put on his head. The man she had utterly failed to recognise when he had crossed her path in the old cemetery in the hills, only a day ago.

'You could ask him, if you wished,' Xinmei was saying behind Amais's back. 'I am told you have to go through channels, but he is quite willing to talk to people who come to ask a favour of him.' And then, as Amais backed away from the peephole, Xinmei reached out instinctively to steady her. 'My dear child! Are you all right? You look like you have seen a ghost!'

'I think . . . I need to be alone for a while,' Amais whispered. 'If I may, Lady Xinmei . . .'

'Of course,' Xinmei said. 'Please, the garden is yours. I will see that nobody disturbs you.'

Amais wandered in the inner courts for an hour or so, walking the carefully raked pathways with the staggering unsteady gait of the blind. She had deliberately chosen to immerse herself in that other world, the world of the letters, in the hope that she could make herself forget the encounter under the silver-leaf tree – and had thought that she had succeeded, right until the moment she had seen his face again and had known with a painful clarity that she had not, that she never could, that the sight of that face would always be a fire in her heart.

She retired to her room after a while, unable to bear even the thought of being that close to him, a courtyard away, divided only by a gate in a thin wall, both of them bareheaded under the same summer sky. Xinmei had her dinner sent in to her, together with a courteous note expressing her hopes that Amais should feel better soon. Night came, and with it a restlessness the likes of which Amais had never known. She tossed and turned, unable to find comfort, snatching fragments of fitful sleep and waking again with a start to stare with wide, bleak eyes into the empty shadows in the corners of her room. She finally gave up as the night was beginning to fade into the first pale light of dawn, and rose from her bed, putting on the same light peasant garb that she had worn on her previous foray into the countryside. She had seen where the old retainer left the keys to the little postern, and now she crept there in the pre-dawn half-light, took the postern key off the ring, unlocked the door with hands that did not seem to belong to her at all, and slipped outside. She hesitated for a moment – it was, at best, rude to unlock a locked door in a house not her own and leave it unsecured behind her, but if she locked it and kept the key she would effectively be locking in the inhabitants, which seemed worse. However, given the uncertain times, she decided to err on the side of caution and locked the postern behind her, pocketing the key.

The little cemetery seemed a lot further away than she remembered, and the land a lot more brooding and stark under the grey glow in the sky that faded out colours and cast everything as either shadow or light. But there were other things there, too – a sense of helpless excitement, something that was halfway between fear and exhilaration. And, once again, that thing her grandmother had called *yuan*. It was without a trace of surprise that she rounded the final corner of the path and saw that someone was already at the ancient cemetery, waiting.

Apparently Iloh was as aware of her as she was of him, because his head turned sharply in her direction even as she paused at the foot of the hill. They stood looking at one another for a long, silent moment, and then he spoke, his voice barely above a whisper.

'I hoped you would come.'

'Why did you not tell me who you were?' Amais asked, her own voice very low. They spoke as though there were spies in the long grass, in the leaf-concealed branches of the tree above them, behind or even below the sagging gravestones at their backs. 'Why were you doing farmyard chores at all . . . you, here, in this place which is not your own?'

'I sometimes do a chore or two for the peasants on whose land my people are quartered,' he said. 'It reminds me of who I am, of where I came from – these are people who could be

197

my own family. I spent my childhood working the earth with my two hands. It gives me roots, it ties me to the land. And if I had told you who I was . . . you would have done one of two things. You would have recoiled from me, or you would have bowed to me. I find that most people do one or another these days, as soon as I name myself. And you . . . you were just so beautiful and so passionate and so wise, sitting there in the sunlight with your hair blowing free . . . Perhaps I should have said something. But I was selfish. I wanted a few moments in which I was not the man you would have expected of the one named Iloh. I was simply . . . me.'

She appeared to have taken the few steps that had been required to close the space between them, and now stood less than a pace away from him, looking at him mutely with those improbable and astonishing eyes. Iloh found himself reaching out for her with a gesture of pure instinct, his fingers finding a strand of curling hair, twining themselves into it. They stared at each other, devouring one another's faces with their eyes, frozen by this moment, unable to do anything other than ache for things that appeared both irrevocably beyond their reach and painfully, vividly inevitable.

'Iloh,' she said softly, tasting the name.

His fingers tightened as she spoke, and then his hand followed the fall of her hair, dropped to her shoulder, rested there lightly.

'And what is *your* name,' he said, 'now that you know mine?'

She nearly gave him her travel alias – Mai – but something changed it in her mouth, and she gave him the truth. 'Amais,' she said.

He sucked in his breath sharply at that, as though he had been struck, and then, astonishingly, laughed. It was not a pleasant laugh; there was something harsh in it.

'Amais,' he repeated. 'Nightingale. Oh, by all that's holy in this world.'

'What is it?' she said, a little alarmed. 'What's wrong?'

'Many years ago,' Iloh told her, 'a blind girl read my face and forecast my destiny. Most of what she told me has come to pass exactly as she said. And one of the things she said was that I would truly love only one woman my whole life and that she would be a songbird, a free spirit, and someone I could never truly have . . . And I thought . . .' He paused, bit his lip, looked down – and then pulled his shoulders back, drawing himself up to his full height, lifting his eyes to meet hers squarely. 'There is something you should know,' he said, his voice suddenly changing, becoming rather more matter-of-fact. 'I am married. To a woman who is an artist – an actress – a woman whom I came to believe to be the soul mate that had been fore-cast for me when she chose her stage name – "Niaomai".'

'*Songbird*,' Amais translated softly.

'Yes, my nightingale,' Iloh replied. 'I should have waited. I should have known that you would come.'

The first shafts of true dawn had begun to creep over the hills, and glittered strangely in Amais's eyes as she reached out to lay her own hand lightly over Iloh's where it still rested on her shoulder.

'But I am here now,' she said.

With a sound that was almost a groan his hand tightened on her shoulder, and then moved to the back of her neck, down her spine, coming to rest on the small of her back and drawing her inexorably towards him. He burrowed his face into the mass of curly hair, nuzzled first the side of her neck and then the hollow of her throat, where a wild pulse beat in time with her heart as she gave herself to the embrace, moulding her body to his.

Iloh slept, after, under the silver-leaf tree – slept as though exhausted, or released. Amais did not. Instead, she watched him sleep as dawn broke and the sun began to climb into the summer sky – and then, finally, she carefully extricated herself from where she was lying with his arm around her and quietly dressed again, running her fingers through her tangled hair to give it some semblance of order and decorum. When she walked away from him, her bare feet made no sound on the soft grass, but he stirred in his sleep and sighed as though he knew she was leaving.

She turned around to look back, once, and it was as though she was watching something she had seen long ago in a dream. There was a single blossom in the silver-leaf tree that she could have sworn had not been there before, a golden flower, huge and bright, blooming right above where Iloh lay. Even as Amais watched, the golden petals began to fall. One came to rest on his face, on his brow, like a crown bestowed upon a king. One landed softly on his mouth and stayed there for barely a moment until his next exhaled breath made it skitter to the side and then fall away – but it had landed there, the portent of a king's eloquence. And a third had come to rest where one of his hands lay cupped over his heart, nestling into his palm – gold into the hands of a king.

It was only then that Amais recognised the tree.

She had seen it first in a dream that had come to her at Sian Sanqin, the dream that drove her from the Temple's tranquillity back into the seething and churning real world and its wars and upheavals. But she had not known what it was, what it signified, until she had found mention of it in the letters from Xinmei's box, letters she had been reading for two days now. It was the *wangqai* tree, the heirloom of Xinmei's family, the tree that bloomed only when a new emperor was crowned in Syai, a signal that a new concubine needed to be prepared and sent to the royal bed – and then with only a single flower. It was an announcement, a warning, a sign.

There was a man asleep under it now, covered with the petals from that one heraldic blossom.

A new emperor for Syai.

The journal looked old, worn, its leather covers faded with age from what had once been a bright vibrant red to a sort of dusty purplish shade, the colour of dead rose petals. The dreamer Amais was looking at this mysterious and yet disturbingly familiar object as though over someone's shoulder – it was the young woman from her dream again, holding the book in almost reverent hands, gazing at pages thickly covered with a graceful brush-and-ink script.

It had been a different world, back when these characters were inked onto the paper. A different time. A time of grace and gentleness, and subtle power that never really spoke its name but flowed like smoke into every crack and crevice of society, setting brick and mortar and heart and spirit, giving strength.

'So long ago,' the young woman who held the book whispered. 'So long ago. So fragile. So easy to forget.'

'Oh, no,' said the other voice from this dream-world, the little girl, who was sitting on cushions at the young woman's feet, a stack of red-covered books much like the journal her companion was holding piled around her. 'Nothing is ever really forgotten, you know. Time is a heavy thing, like ashes,

like snow; things just get buried in it, and by it. But then the ashes are swept away to make room for a new fire, and the snow melts in the spring, and there it is, the thing you buried, and it looks not a day older than when it was left there although a thousand years may have passed.'

'But I can only read some of this,' the young woman said, lifting her head, tearing her eyes away from the writing in the book.

'That only means,' said the child at her feet tranquilly, 'that there is still enough snow or ashes upon it for you not to be able to see it clearly yet.'

And she bent over her own task, something quite different from reading ancient script – she had a lap-board cradled across her knees where she sat cross-legged on her cushions, and the lap-board was covered by a piece of aged vellum paper, golden yellow and with the ragged edges that spoke of its having been lovingly hand-made. She had a pen in her hand, one with a flat metal nib usually used for calligraphy, but she was drawing something with it instead of writing. She had only just begun her task, and the shape taking form on the paper was still no more than a few bold straight lines, a mere ghost of itself.

'What are you doing?' asked Amais's alter-ego.

The child bent over her task, dipping the pen into a leather inkwell, drawing another careful, purposeful line.

'You will see,' the small artist said, 'when it is time.'

The young woman turned her attention back to the journal.

'This is poetry,' she said. 'I don't know this one. I've never seen this journal.'

'Can you read it?'

'I think so,' said the young woman carefully, and pointed her index finger at the lines she was perusing, following them while she pieced together their meaning, her finger hovering

202

just above the precious page. 'I think it says "Dreams are strong, when they are given leave to fly, when they are given wings. Dreams have never lived or breathed, and yet they are amongst the most immortal things.".'

'My poetry never rhymes,' the little girl replied, without lifting her eyes off her drawing.

'Your poetry?' repeated the other, nonplussed. 'This is ancient, more ancient than you can know. But you're right in one thing. In that era poems were pieces of exquisite verbal embroidery, they didn't need rhyme or metre to make them perfect.'

'Nothing is perfect,' the little girl said. 'Not the way you mean. Nothing can be that perfect. Things can be almost flawless, but they belong in their time and their age and what was thought without a blemish a moment ago or a hundred years ago is mottled with faults if you look at it again with a different pair of eyes. Dreams and ideas change, as the world changes. That poem was never in that journal – you just wrote it, made it from the words that are on the page and the thoughts that are in your own mind and the feelings in your heart. That's the way of poetry. You can never read it twice and have it be the same.'

'So young, and such a philosopher?' the young woman said, with a raised eyebrow and a smile.

'I remember,' the little girl said, looking up briefly before her eyes dropped down again, 'being young.'

The glimpse of that single short glance made Amais-the-dreamer shiver suddenly, because the eyes in that childish face were the eyes of a woman who carried the weight of worlds in her soul.

'There,' said the child, breaking that thought before it led to a conclusion, 'I am done. Look.'

What lay on the page, depicted in heart-stopping detail with only a few essential strokes and yet with a presence so

powerful that it stood out in three dimensions from the paper,
was a sword. It was an old-fashioned blade, one that might
have been used in the armies of an emperor from half a
millennium before – but its edge held its wicked gleam there
in the drawing, and it was easy to feel it slicing, chopping,
cleaving, going through bone and sinew and flowing with
blood.

The young woman reached for it instinctively, and her
fingers scrabbled for a moment on the paper. It was drawn
well enough for the simple fact that she could not touch it
to bring a startled small gasp to her lips.

'What does it mean?' the young woman whispered,
because this was a dream, and in dreams things always mean
something, carry messages and significance and an otherness
that belonged to worlds where every word was a prophecy
and every prophecy was true.

'Look again,' the child said, offering up the pen she had
used, wooden handle first.

The young woman took it automatically, staring at it, and
then did a double take as she realised that the metal nib with
which the drawing had been made was no longer at the end
of the wooden grip. Only a stub remained, something eerie
and half-melted, where the nib had been joined to the pen.

In the drawing, the blade of the sword in the drawing
gleamed with a light not its own.

'It is real,' the young woman whispered. 'You made it,
out of this thing. It's real, you turned the pen into the sword.'

'And yet you cannot hold it,' the child murmured. 'It
remains but a paper sword upon a painted page.'

'But I can feel it,' the young woman said. 'I can feel the
cold of it when I touch it.'

'The pen could make the sword,' the child said, 'but never
could the sword make the pen.' She blew on the drawing
gently, to dry it, and then removed the paper on which the

sword rested from its board backing and offered it up to her companion with both hands. 'Here, you keep that, and remember that the pen vanquished the blade, remember that when the time comes for you to believe it.'

'There will come such a time?' the young woman said, and tears stood in her eyes and in the eyes of Amais-the-ghost behind her, tears for which she could offer no reason or explanation, tears that were tribute to a pain yet to come.

'Times like that,' the little girl said, her voice a deep well of love and sympathy, 'will always come.'

She raised her hand, then, and something came to alight on it, like a trained hawk to its mistress. Except that this was no hawk – it was a butterfly, huge and yet somehow weightless, ethereal, its wings opening and closing gently as though moved by breath. It gleamed in the half-light of the dream with the gleam that should never have been – its wings were made of iron and copper and gold, razor-edged, glowing. The little girl on whose wrist it rested gazed upon the creature for a long moment, and then lifted her arm, flinging the creature into the sky. It flapped its huge wings and was gone, swallowed by the mists; so was the child; so was the young woman; everything was gone, except the golden mists and a voice that spoke out of it, like a prophecy.

'Poetry is remembered long after slogans are dust and ashes, dead offerings on the altars of lost gods. In the hour of destiny, remember the strength in fragile things.'

The Street of Red Lanterns

When you are worst beset by your troubles and
weighed down by your life's burdens – it is in the
arms of love that you will find the courage to
remember the things you must remember, the strength
to abandon the things you must forget, and the
wisdom to tell these things from one another.

The Courtesan's Journal

One

I must go back to the city.

Amais had told herself that it was this, something that smote her with the force of a command from the Gods themselves, that made her almost vanish from Xinmei's house on the morning that she had woken to see Iloh asleep under the *wangqai* tree. Xinmei had been astir when Amais returned to the house, and had been schooled in enough protocol not to ask about the reasons for her guest's sudden departure – but there was something in her face, something knowing in her eyes, something that was not censure and yet was not approval that made Amais certain that Xinmei knew precisely what had happened on the hillside at dawn.

It was not that Amais wanted to renounce anything she had said or done in those pearly pre-dawn hours – indeed, she hugged close the memories she had made, and knew that they would never fade from her heart – but as suddenly and powerfully as she had been compelled to keep the tryst that had taken her into Iloh's arms so she was now driven to put distance between them, between two people who had connected on such a deep and fundamental level but whose futures lay on such impossibly different and divergent paths.

She had made a silent vow to him as she turned to take her last look before she stole away that morning.

I will always be yours, if not always by your side.

But that was then. Reality had started creeping in almost as soon as she had left his powerful presence. Too many people were clamouring for supremacy in Amais's mind – there was the romantic heroine of a deathless love story, who had cast her lot with the one man to whom she belonged and now had to suffer the consequences of her choice; the pragmatic, practical fisherman's daughter from Elaas, who thought of the whole thing as an impossible dream and chided Amais to face the situation honestly, with the inevitable conclusion that it was all a fairytale that could not possibly have any basis in the real world; the child that she still was in so many ways, who had suddenly realised that she was adrift in a dangerous and unknown world and who only wanted the comfort of her mother – even such scant comfort as Vien had been able to provide in all the previous crises of Amais's life. It was the last that won, for the moment, control of her body. The uncertainty and the apprehension had been clear in her eyes as she had left Xinmei's house – and Xinmei would have been less shrewd than she was if she hadn't noticed them there, but it was hardly her place to detain her guest against her will. So Xinmei let Amais go, and then watched her for a long time from the postern gate with her mouth pursed into an expression that was half resignation and half genuine concern. Behind her, the expression on her aged gatekeeper's face had been much easier to read. *Not a moment too soon did that girl leave this house.*

As strongly as she had been driven to leave Linh-an, so now the city called to Amais like a lodestone, a homing beacon – both as the place where she needed to return in order to continue her quest for lost *jin-shei* that she had so vividly glimpsed in Xinmei's house, and as the only place in

Syai that she could think of which was home and safe, which would shelter her against the storms of her life. However, if the Gods had been keeping the war out of her way on her outward journey, they had decided to more than make up for that as she tried to return. The war now faced Amais at every turn, a barrier, a living and breathing enemy from whom it seemed impossible to hide.

On the second day out from the sanctuary of Xinmei's house, Amais was apprehended by a troop of the Nationalist army and questioned closely as to her intentions in that part of the country.

Iloh's enemies.

Amais had been taken by a two-man patrol of grunts to a tribunal of the three highest-ranking officers for disposal.

'Who are you? What are you doing here?' one of the lieutenants demanded, his eyes cold slits of suspicion.

Amais offered neither more nor less than the truth. 'I am from Linh-an. I came here on a pilgrimage.'

'Not with that accent,' muttered the other lieutenant.

'And where is the rest of your group? A pilgrimage to where?' the first man said, seemingly unable to communicate except by means of inquisition.

'I . . . no group. I came by myself. To Sian Sanqin. I came in search of . . .'

'Yes?' barked the lieutenant, leaning forward.

'I came to look for *jin-shei*,' Amais whispered.

'What?'

'Women's stuff,' said the commanding officer, his eyes resting on Amais with a mixture of wariness and calm appraisal.

'I never heard of . . .' began one of the men, but the commanding officer lifted a hand and cut him off in mid-sentence.

'You wouldn't have,' he replied, and it was more than the simple statement of the obvious, that a man would not have known of women's secrets – it was a judgement, however

211

subtle, of that particular man's ability to know or understand *anything* of importance. Amais, having lifted her eyes
for a moment, happened to catch the commanding officer's
eyes as his sardonic glance returned to herself from a swift,
impatient flicker towards his truculent lieutenant. They
looked at each other for a moment, the soldier and the
captive, and then Amais dropped her gaze. The officer said
nothing.

'Spy,' the first lieutenant summarised trenchantly.

The other lieutenant had laughed at the same instant, a
single dry chuckle, apparently seconding his fellow's judgement. 'A slip of a girl with a foreign accent, wandering around
sensitive strategic territory by herself?' he said, after the other
man had sat back and crossed his arms, his mind made up.
'A likely story. Who's your contact?'

'Please,' Amais begged, 'I'm just trying to get home . . .
to my family. To the city.'

'There's a People's Army between you and the city,' said
the first lieutenant. 'How did you hope to get past them?
Who's your contact? What information do you carry?'

It lasted for more than an hour, this interrogation. Amais
told them that she knew nobody at all who belonged to the
People's Party – and didn't lie, quite, because in a very real
way it was the Party that belonged to Iloh rather than the
other way around. But although she had answered their questions as honestly as she was able, her answers had apparently not been satisfactory enough for them to let her go;
neither had they been incriminating enough for them to kill
her out of hand. So when the commanding officer had had
enough of the cat-and-mouse game that the questioning had
turned into, he simply got up and said,

'Bring her.'

Amais was dragged in their wake as they made their way,
armed to the teeth and full of the desperate courage found

in men who already know their cause is lost, to one of the ongoing hotspots of the war.

A battle had been raging for weeks in and around one hapless and deeply strategic village, with skirmishes where victory was alternately tossed from foe to foe as though in a bizarre game of catch. The village was by this time a wasteland of rubble and ghostly burned outlines of what had once been houses and storage barns and pigsties. It had been overrun by one army or the other on a regular basis, its fields and hillsides won and lost and won again. Amais endured four of these confrontations, growing more and more terrified at every turn, fearing that she would be killed at any moment as she and a handful of other prisoners became too much of a burden for the fighting unit to worry about. Her captors lost no chance to tell her that if she had fallen into the hands of their opponents she would be dead by now.

'*They* take no prisoners,' one of the men had said, and spat out of the corner of his mouth with derision, to show his opinion of the guerilla forces his outfit was fighting. Iloh's men, those; something that Amais could not seem to make herself forget. 'They don't care about the people at all.'

Amais wanted to ask what had happened to the villagers who had once peacefully lived here with no thought except a prayer for a good harvest, but she could not scrape together the voice or the courage to even ask one of her fellow captives, all women except for two young boys who clung hollow-eyed to their mothers' tattered skirts. But her spirit quailed at this sudden explosion of noise and chaos and blood, and she was silent in the face of it all, silent and waiting only to die.

Amais and the other captives had been conscripted occasionally to change dressings and bandages on the wounds of some of the company. She herself had had to do it for the commanding officer, once. She tried to keep her head down and her hands from trembling, but all the time she was aware

213

of the eyes that rested upon her as she worked, aware of his gaze as though it were a physical weight on her skin. He had reached out with his good hand, after she was done, and cupped her chin, lifting her face so that she had to meet his eyes with her own; and she had braced herself for what might have followed. It was wartime, after all. People were fodder, one way or another. But he had done no more than that, had said nothing, had merely dropped his hand, sighed, walked away.

On another night not too long after that Amais had woken to the sound of stealthy motion, of grasping fingers groping for any reachable woman in the huddled pile in which they all slept – had known that others were awake around her, that all were holding their breath and muttering words resembling prayer, asking that this shadow might pass. They heard a smothered gasp as the exploring hand closed around somebody's wrist or ankle. And then there was another noise, a startled yelp, a scuffle. Amais had opened her eyes and seen the commanding officer hauling one of his men off the pile of cowering women by the scruff of his neck.

'They are prisoners,' the commanding officer had said, softly but firmly. 'They are not whores. Truth is the first thing that dies in any war; let not honour follow it.'

'You are no soldier,' Amais had whispered, her voice a bare breath between cracked lips. This was the man who had known what *jin-shei* was, someone who still clung, in small ways, to the kind of honour and high principles that had guided Syai's ancient society. Someone who pragmatically wore the Nationalist uniform, but underneath it still belonged, perhaps, to the vast and complex Empire that Syai once was.

He heard, turned his head marginally. 'I am now,' he said. 'If there was another life before this, count that, too, among the casualties.'

His authority held, still; the midnight groping by frustrated and angry soldiers had not been repeated. But even without that prospect hanging over the prisoners' heads, their captivity and their unwilling participation in this war was a brutal forge for the spirit. There was no trace of the women's country in any of this. There was no place for softness or gentleness or kindness – as Amais learned the hard way, when on the fourth skirmish the troop she was with lost badly. The captives had long since ceased to be guarded during these encounters, merely dumped in whatever hiding place their current handler thought most convenient and then picked up again when the skirmish was over. There was every confidence that the cowed women were still focused enough on survival not to do anything stupid like actually run into the crossfire to escape, and if they did then it was their own doing and not their captors' responsibility. That time, the fourth time, the man who came for them was not the Nationalist officer but someone wearing the same kind of uniform that Amais had seen not so long ago in the gardens of Xinmei's outer courts. Iloh's man stared at the terrified women with cold eyes that glittered like obsidian. After a long moment he lifted up the gun he was carrying without saying a word and aimed it at the group of dry-eyed captives, too spent even to flinch out of his way.

Perhaps Amais could have taken this as her fate, just as the others had apparently done – but the man had pointed his gun at one of the children, one of the little boys, who had found the sudden strength to turn and whimper, burying his face into his mother's ragged skirts. Something suddenly woke inside Amais – a resolve, a strength of heart, a quiet rage. Iloh, the Iloh she had loved with such a purity of spirit, would never have done this.

'The child has done nothing to you,' she said out loud, her voice, so long silent, sounding harsh to her own ears, like the cawing of a crow.

The man looked up at her, narrowing his eyes. 'What was that?' he said. 'Posh accent – you aren't from around here.

215

What are you doing with these dregs? Did they send you to spy on us?'

'Spy?' Amais actually found the memory of laughter bubbling to the surface of her mind, laughter that threatened to turn into hysteria if left unchecked. It had been that word, exactly the same word, which had been levelled at her from the other side when she had been taken. 'Spy? Look at us . . . look at *them*, for the love of Cahan. They are starving children, they are women too afraid to breathe. Their menfolk are probably dead. Who would they be spying for? And what possible use would any information be, gathered by the likes of them . . . the likes of us . . . You are the People's Party, you say – well, we are the people. What are you going to do with us?'

'Killing you would be kindest,' he said, his hands shifting on the gun.

'Do you have a mother?' Amais asked, very softly.

He gave her a long look and then spat sideways into a ruin, much like the Nationalist officer had done, and turned away.

'I never saw you,' he said, throwing the words over his shoulder like a bone to a starving dog as he picked his way across the remnants of a ruined wall towards a pocket of still sporadically chattering gunfire.

They were free at last – but these women had been taken beyond the point at which Amais had taken her stand. She tried to cajole, beg, even gently bully them into moving when night came and the gunfire fell silent, but they did not move from their safe spot. Perhaps they could not move. Amais finally gave up and crept away in tears, as the darkness of a moonless night fell around her and she knew that this was maybe the one chance she would get to find her way out of this hell. So she left them, the others, the children because of whom she had perhaps been willing to take a bullet with her own body, the tired and terrified women, the flotsam and jetsam of a war where both sides claimed to be 'of the people' and rode roughshod over whoever stood in the path of their progress.

She had seen the young Nationalist officer as she picked her way out of the churned-up battlefield, in the aftermath of the next battle, underneath a still-smouldering tree casting just enough light from its dying flames for her to recognise his face – abandoned on a battlefield as his men pulled out, his eyes dead and staring, his stubborn sense of honour now gone from the pack of men he had been commanding, leaving them prey to Gods alone knew what.

Amais remembered Iloh's dreams, the brotherhood that would bind one human being to another, that would make this land a single living, breathing giant. It was what Baba Sung had wanted, what he had left as his dying legacy – *be a nation again*. He could not have known how much blood would flow for that to become a reality.

The troop she had been with had crisscrossed the land so many times, gone this way and that, their only landmarks burned houses and ravaged fields, that Amais had completely lost her sense of direction. Now, alone again in a hostile land crawling with armed men, many of whom might shoot first this time, without bothering to saddle themselves with the burden of a prisoner, she watched the sun come up that morning in a quarter that made her blink at it with owlish surprise – but she decided to trust the wisdom of the Gods, after all, who knew which way east was better than she did right at that moment, and turned her face in the opposite direction. Linh-an had been south and west of Sian Sanqin and Xinmei's house. Amais had no idea where she was now, but south and west was still the only direction in which she knew to look for her home.

She starved, for a while. There were things to scavenge, but often there was danger involved in doing so, and if there was one thing that Amais knew in her sometimes lost and

217

drifting frame of mind it was that she must not fall into anyone's hands again. She had seen enough to realise that it was all coming to a head, and it would be her life next time, not just her liberty. And she had started to remember, however nebulously, through the fog of the experience of her captivity, that she still had much to live for.

Her family – the mother and sister to whom she was trying to return, back in Linh-an, and the vanished ones whose legacy she carried within her: Nikos, *baya*-Dan, Elena.

Her quest – taking a lost vow and the mysteries of a secret language from the obscurity into which they had been allowed to sink, back out into the light.

Iloh.

Iloh . . .

She dreamed of him when she slept, constantly, the way his smile curled his generous mouth, the way his eyes picked it up and glinted with mirth in the corners, the way his strong hands had curled around the handle of that barrel-pail of water he had carried on the day they had first met, the broad brown peasant's feet with which he stood rooted in the land from which his ancestors had come. He was everyman, in love with life – with its beggars and its monks and its robbers and its emperors, with the whole rich tapestry of it, the poetry of it, the love and the jealousy and the generosity and the wisdom and the folly of it. He embraced what came and did not shrink from anything. He was of Syai, deeply and completely, and believed that its future lay in his hands – and was willing to take any risk, submit to any torment, to grasp it.

Amais wondered, and wept while thinking of it, if he realised what was being done in his name out here – if the farmer's soul in him had spared a thought for the harvest that he was gathering, for the pain of the scythed corn as it fell under the blade, while he thought of the bread that would be made from the flour which was to be ground from it.

Two

The seasons were changing again as Amais crossed into Hian province – Iloh's home province, although she had no means of knowing that. She could smell autumn in the morning air and in the sudden chill that came on the land after the sun went down, and in the dreary grey rain that set in and would not cease for days leaving her either drenched and shivering as she pushed on through it or else cowering in some makeshift shelter, bleakly watching it fall, waiting for she did not know what. Sometime during this time her birthday came and went, unremarked, uncelebrated. She was seventeen. She felt a thousand years old.

Amais found shelter where she could, sometimes surreptitiously and alone in someone's barn or storage shack or byre, and sometimes invited in by people who looked barely above the edge of starvation themselves but who, in the manner of country folk everywhere, always found enough for a guest. There was more suspicion now than there had been in the years, the centuries, that had rolled over the land up until the latest war had been unleashed upon it. There had been conflicts before, to be sure, but nothing quite like this – not the squaring off of brother against brother, the

219

mistrust of a son belonging to one party of a father belonging to another. There were places where careful questions were asked before Amais was invited in, and there were places where whatever hospitality *was* gained appeared to be balanced on a knife-edge, its very existence depending on a single voice within the family. She spent anything from a few hours to a handful of weeks with people like this, confused and often mistrustful country folks who could not quite allow the distrust and suspicion that were a mark of the times to overthrow an ancient instinct of hospitality.

She paid her way as best she could, taking on any job, no matter how filthy or onerous or hard. She retched as she cleaned out a piggery ankle-deep in manure, bore in silence the bite from a whelping bitch that she helped deliver of a litter of no less than eleven mewling mongrel puppies, nursed without complaint the aches and pains and the runny nose and constant sneezes of a lingering cold caught while working out in the rain. And sometimes it really was better, and she would sing a child to sleep, or tell tales to the family after whatever poor meal had been cobbled together for them all. But all of it took its toll, weakened her in small ways she sometimes did not even recognise, exhausted her more and more with every step that she took, bled her mind and spirit dry of everything except pure survival.

Amais could not know, when she finally collapsed on the doorstep of a particular farmhouse badly in need of care and repair, just where it was that the Gods had delivered her – she only knew that she was weary beyond belief, lost, hungry, soaked to the skin in the aftermath of yet another of those endless drizzles that had dogged her footsteps for more than two days, and past caring what happened to her next. She could remember – or thought she could, by this stage she was finding it hard to tell the difference between what she dreamed and real memory – the shape of mist-wreathed hills, a sodden path worn by generations of feet that led her from the slopes of the hills down to the house, a shadowy figure of a woman bending over her. But the first coherent thing that she thought when next she opened her eyes and knew herself awake was the fact that she was tucked into a pile of quilts on the *qang*, the heated sleeping platform abutting the stove that was common in so many rural houses in Syai. She was in fact probably usurping her hosts' own bed. There seemed to be a good reason for it – she felt drained by malaise, emptied by either transcendent fatigue or some more physical condition like pneumonia. There was barely enough strength in her to speak in a voice that rose above a whisper.

'Hello . . . ?'

She had the sense that she was not alone in the room, but her greeting brought no response. She lifted herself up with some difficulty on her elbows, with every bone in her body aching as though she had been trampled by a herd of wild horses, and looked around.

There was another pile of quilts on the *qang*, not too far from where she lay, and she had allowed her gaze to skim it assuming it to be more unused bedding – but it stirred, ever so weakly, with life and breath. There was also a set of water pipes in the far corner, bubbling quietly, and somewhere in that pile of bedding the pipes' owner sighed and stirred, almost invisible under his coverings.

'Hello?' Amais tried again, struggling to sit up.

There was still no response, and now, sitting up and able to see better, she could understand why. The man wrapped in the other set of quilts looked asleep at first glance, with only a restless quivering of eyelids and a faint suckling noise coming from where his hand, infant-like, nudged the mouthpiece of the water pipe against his pursed lips. He was shrunken, his skin the colour and texture of aged parchment, his cheeks sunken and throwing his cheekbones into skull-like prominence. A few strands of thinning grey hair hung on to his scalp, straggling untidily from underneath a tight-fitting blue cap.

'You're awake,' said a new voice, a woman's voice, from the far side of the room.

Amais turned at the sound, and saw a woman whose age she could not guess at all, hollowed out and drained by the troubles of her life, dark circles underneath her eyes and her lips white and cracked. Her hands, where they curled around a basket she carried, were an old woman's hands, worked to the bone, red and chapped and with nails pared or bitten back into the quick.

'You were sick,' the woman said, after a beat of silence. 'You've been asleep for two days. I am Youmei. I have some broth simmering – it was the last but one of the chickens, but I thought you might wake today and you would need it. Will you have some?'

'You shouldn't have . . .' Amais said, honestly appalled that this struggling farm's last dregs of livestock were being slaughtered for her sake.

'It was time,' Youmei said, dismissing it. 'If that rooster had lived any longer he'd have been too stringy to eat anyway. No, don't get down from there. I'll get you a bowl.'

She set down the basket she carried, shook the rain off the threadbare shawl she had had wrapped around her head and draped it over the basket, and presently approached the *qang* with not one but two steaming bowls in her hands.

'I need to feed my master,' she said, handing one of the bowls to Amais and setting the other one down on the *qang* until she could patiently worry the water-pipe's mouthpiece free from the old man's spasmodic grip and settle him more comfortably in a more upright seated position so that she could spoon the broth into his mouth. The first few spoonfuls dribbled from the old man's half-closed mouth and Amais actually physically flinched at the sight of it. The broth was precious enough, it seemed, and seeing it wasted like this was almost too hard to bear. But then the old man seemed to recognise the taste of the thing as food, and began co-operating more fully. He folded his mouth around the bowl of the spoon and sucked greedily, like a child.

'How old . . . how old is he?' Amais asked diffidently, feeling as though she were transgressing the boundaries of courtesy and hospitality but somehow deeply moved by the loving devotion of this woman to the wreck of the man who lay cradled against her breast.

'It is not the age,' Youmei said, without looking up, spoon-ing another helping of broth into his mouth. If she had been offended, she gave no sign of it. 'It is the drug. And it is everything – everything . . . it is the way that life has ground him into dust and ashes and left him helpless. This was a good farm – but that was back then, before he lost every-thing. When I first came here it was after his middle son had died, but he still had two sons he believed he could entrust his old age to – but Iloh first went to school and then Rubai was killed by the Nationalists when Iloh became a wanted man . . .' She had finally glanced up, and then did a sharp double-take, straightening. 'Are you all right?'

Amais's hands had trembled as Iloh's name was uttered, and the spoon had rattled against the soup bowl. Under Youmei's gaze all colour had suddenly drained from her cheeks and she sat with her shoulders rigid, staring.

Youmei's own expression immediately changed, into one that was almost fear. The blood that had drained from Amais's face seemed to rush into Youmei's.

'Are you one of . . . ? Did you . . . ? Oh, please, don't let them harm him!' She folded protectively over the old man, as though she could physically shield him from attack. 'He's an old man who has lost his entire family . . . Let him live out the rest of his days in peace . . .'

'I'm sorry,' Amais said through stiff lips that didn't seem to belong to her. 'I mean him no harm, and I am deeply grateful to you . . . It's just that I never thought . . . *Iloh* . . . Is there an old willow tree by an ancient burial ground near here?'

It was Youmei's turn to stare. 'The willow died, some years ago,' she said slowly. 'We cut it down. It was firewood for two or three seasons. How did you know . . . ?'

There were tears in Amais's eyes. She herself did not know why she wanted to weep, but the tears were there, rushing in the back of her mind like water against a dam. It was the first time – the first time since that morning in Xinmei's house, since the days of captivity during the battles of her Nationalist captors' private little war against Iloh's guerillas – that she had felt the urge to give way to tears.

'I wish I could have seen it,' she whispered.

Youmei was looking at her with wide eyes. Her expression had graduated from the pure panic of a possibly lethal betrayal of a few moments ago into something more like complete bewilderment. 'But who told you about the willow tree?'

'Iloh did,' Amais said simply.

A single tear escaped, ran slowly down the curve of her cheek.

Youmei saw it, misinterpreted it. 'Oh, Gods,' she gasped. 'The teacher at the village school is out in Iloh's headquarters somewhere, and he makes sure we get to hear the news as soon as that is possible – but still, there are sometimes months without word . . . Is he . . . is he dead?'

'He was not the last time I set eyes on him,' Amais murmured. 'But that was . . . many weeks ago. Months ago. A lifetime ago.'

A new voice, quavering and trembling and thoroughly unexpected, joined the conversation. 'Iloh . . . ?' it said, demanded, a world of questions in a single word.

Both women looked down with surprise. The old man's eyes had opened. They were far from lucid or clear, and he stared somewhere into the middle distance, but somehow the name of his son had pierced the fog of his drug-soaked brain and he had responded.

'Shhh,' Youmei said automatically, soothing him as though he were a fractious child. 'It's okay . . .'

'Iloh . . . ?' the old man repeated, weakly but insistently.

'He is fine,' Youmei murmured, letting her fingers caress his temple lightly.

He subsided, closing his eyes again, drawing a deep and wheezing breath.

'I should go,' Amais said softly into the silence. 'I don't want to make things any worse. And you can't . . .'

She tried to struggle out of her quilts but discovered that her legs would not obey her – they felt like a pair of limp eels attached to her hips, without any bone or strength to them. Youmei made a small gesture with one hand.

'Stay,' she said. 'The Gods are wise. They have brought you here for a reason. If you have known him, then you are home. Where were you headed, that you came to this place?'

'Linh-an,' Amais said. 'I have family . . .'

'They said there was heavy fighting there, the last we heard,' Youmei said. 'I know, I wait for news of that place with fear and sorrow – my daughter is there.'

'In the city? But who is left here? Just you and . . . and Iloh's father?'

'I told you,' Youmei said. 'He lost everything. All his sons are gone – two dead, and one who will never return to this house. I bore him another, but the boy died before he was two years old. And he sold Yingchi, our daughter, a long time before that – to pay for *this*.' She indicated the pipe with an economical little tilt of her head that hid a world of pain.

'*Sold* her?' Amais repeated, astonished. 'Do men still sell their daughters . . . ? Does . . . Iloh know about this?'

Youmei blinked at her. 'You speak with an accent that is strange,' she said, 'and you are a stranger, indeed, that you do not know that. Children are often traded for life's necessities, out on the edge where life is hard.' She paused. 'No, I don't believe Iloh knows. He has not been here for many years. Certainly not since Yingchi has been gone.'

'Is she all right? Your daughter?'

'It is hard to say,' Youmei replied. 'She writes to me little of what her life is like – but it is in the things she does not say that I read the truth, and she has never given me a return address where I might write back to her. Her father did not intend for this when he sold her to a family who required a servant girl, but times were hard for everyone . . . it isn't anybody's fault that she ended up where she is now – it was the only thing she could do, probably, to survive . . .' She sighed. Too deeply.

'How old is she?' Amais asked gently. Somehow they were beyond the social graces; these were not questions that any guest could ask of their hosts and be considered well-mannered, but they were all, strangely, family here – the old man in his drug-blurred dream world, the woman who had borne him children and who now cared for him until such time as the ancient body followed the spirit that had already partly vanished into the realms of Cahan's Gods, and the girl who had last seen the first-born of this house asleep in her arms under a kingmaker tree.

'Yingchi . . . ? I have lost track,' Youmei admitted. 'She has been gone so long, and the years have been hard . . . I think she is twenty now. Maybe twenty-one.'

Perhaps Amais would not have been able to piece this together only a few short months before – but she had met Xinmei since that time, and read the letters in the cedar box. There were too many things left unsaid in Youmei's story, but there was more than enough there for Amais to be painfully certain of the address in Linh-an which Iloh's sister would not send home.

Xuelian and now Yingchi – emperor's concubine, and half-sister to the man who would become the new leader of Syai – their origins and their fates might have been very different but they had converged onto the same stream of destiny. There was more than one road that led to the Street of Red Lanterns.

Three

If, back at Xinmei's house, Amais had felt herself caught up in the urgent pull of main currents of history again, her unexpected washing up on its shores right in the heartland of Iloh's childhood country seemed to lull her into a strange, almost hypnotic calm. It was as though she was drawn aside from the mainstream, into a quiet eddy that was sheltered and serene and somehow outside of the relentless passage of time. Here the days followed one another like beads on a string, like the yearwood beads that Amais's ancestress Tai would have used to mark them. Perhaps, on the surface, it might have been a strangely unbalanced world. With only Youmei, Iloh's father, and an assortment of oddly compelling ghosts for company in the dilapidated farmhouse, and all kinds of new things now waiting for her back in the city, Amais might have expected to be itching to leave. But somehow she stayed, day after day, watching the autumn fade away, and a tough, lonely, often hungry winter come in its wake.

In the years that would follow, Amais would remember this time as the quiet calm before the storm, the season of gathering strength and courage and knowledge. She had once told Jinlien that history was built on people – and here, in this place, she was learning about the person who already had an iron hand on the future that would in its turn become the history of the war-weary land of Syai. Youmei had personally had only the barest glimpse into Iloh's childhood, but she had been privy to all that had happened in the years that had preceded her arrival into his home. And she had lived, after Iloh left, with the memories that his father had stored up of his eldest, vanished, famous son – memories that he had poured out lavishly to Youmei in the days before the Nationalists had crippled his farm by the heavy taxes he had to pay if he refused to grow the poppies that produced the drug which eventually claimed his land, his memories, and his mind. There was all that – there was a treasure trove of that. And in the company of the ghosts – Iloh's mother, too deeply wounded by her own early losses; Iloh's little sister, who had died so young; the two brothers who had also gone – there was the spirit of the old willow tree, brooding by the stump that remained, a place where Amais would walk on cold winter mornings and where she could almost feel Iloh's presence around her.

And even in the worst of the winter storms, somehow news trickled down to the three on the farm – it was a new age, and in the aftermath of the war's inevitable destruction of the infrastructure and day-to-day functioning of a nation, letters eventually found their way back into the hinterland. The bigger settlements around even had a smattering of radios, which spread news and rumours from the capital faster than ever before. They heard it all, the two women who would go without tea or rice themselves for days in order to offer some to someone bringing a fresh piece of news. They devoured the occasional letters that came from Yingchi in Linh-an, and the dated newspapers that percolated into the back-country. It was in the newspaper accounts that they first heard about Iloh's entry into Linh-an, bare-headed in the rain, riding a white stallion – with the gates thrown open for him and cheering people lining the streets as he made his way to the big square before the Emperor's Gate that led into the old city palace. There was even a picture – a fuzzy one, apparently taken from a distance, but Amais didn't need it to know what he must have looked like, the fire that must have been in his eyes as he rode in to claim his city, his country, his fate.

'I wish I could have been there, seen that,' she murmured, her eyes focused somewhere in the middle distance, playing the scene in her mind, wondering if Aylun had been there to watch Iloh ride in, if Jinlien had stood in the street outside the Great Temple in the rain, if the women of the Street of Red Lanterns had hung from their windows to see the white horse pass. It was the first time she had seen his title written down – not Emperor, despite the *wangqai* tree. Those days were over. This was Baba Sung's world, no longer an Empire but a Republic. The newspapers were calling him '*Shou Ximin* Iloh' – First Citizen Iloh – a word that would be taken by the nation and honed into something simpler and easier to remember, turning it into an extension of his name without which it quickly became unimaginable to think of him. He was never to be just Iloh again, he was Shou'min Iloh for the rest of his days, the anointed one, the first man of the people.

And so it began. Just when everyone thought it was all over, it began again – the morning of a new day, there in the rain in the Emperor's Square.

Without ever quite knowing how it came about, the two women had started sharing the responsibilities of caring for Iloh's father. It was Youmei who still took care of his basic physical needs, but he had consented without fuss to being fed by Amais, which allowed Youmei a precious few moments of respite a day. So when a man wearing the flat cap and blue uniform of Iloh's cadres trudged up to the farmhouse as the snows melted in the spring, it was Youmei who came to the door to greet the visitor. Amais was on the *qang*, in the back room, with Iloh's father cradled against her arm and a bowl of rice broth balanced on her knee.

The uniformed man had been formal to the point of stiffness.

'I am Tang,' he said, giving Youmei a tight little bow. 'I come from your son, Shou'min Iloh, in Linh-an. He has charged me to bring his family to the city. For celebrations on the occasion of the birth of the Republic.'

'I am afraid it might be too much for his father,' Youmei murmured.

'He is ill?'

'Iloh hasn't been home for many years,' Youmei said, 'and it was hardly possible to get word to him, after . . . after he had to disappear.' She spoke warily, keeping her eyes downcast. In the new world, during the war and in the triumphs and uncertainties of its aftermath, words could be sharp and dangerous things and had to be measured with care.

Tang said, in the clipped, precise manner of a man trained and toughened on the battlefield where clear communication was at a premium, 'What is the nature of this illness?'

'Come inside,' Youmei replied with a bow, ushering the visitor into the great room. 'Come and see.'

Amais was just finishing up with lunch, in the process of laying aside the bowl of broth and wiping the corners of the old man's mouth with one end of a faded cotton towel. That was the way Tang first saw her, bent over Iloh's father, her hair neatly braided into a thick rope that lay over her shoulder and on the crook of her arm, with stray curls escaping around her temples and brushing her cheeks. She looked up as he entered, and their eyes met.

She straightened.

He held her eyes for a moment, and then gave her a tight bow, taking his eyes from her and turning back to Youmei. 'I see,' he said. 'Will it be of any assistance if all of you were to move to the city? You are no longer working the farm, and it may be easier if there was access to a doctor who did not live half a day's ride away.'

'Leave?' Youmei said. 'But this is my home . . .' She had been shocked into what was almost rudeness but she quickly collected herself and remembered her duties. 'You will stay for supper? We will talk of it.'

Tang looked as though he had been about to say something, and then he appeared to think better of it and nodded sharply. 'I will be happy to help with any necessary provisions,' he told them.

'Thank you,' Amais responded, when Youmei hesitated. It would, again, have breached protocol to accept such an offer – it would have implied that the invited guest knew that the host was too poor to provide a meal, and that was an unforgivable thing for the host to admit. But times were hard, and this guest had come from what was now technically the head of this family. Youmei might never have brought herself to demean her offer of hospitality in this manner, but Amais had no such compunctions. She was at least partly a child of this new age – a new age where need took what it was offered, and refused to gnaw on empty pride instead of a freely given steaming bowl of chicken stew. She laid Iloh's father down gently on his nest of quilts. 'If you are willing to help us procure a chicken I will show you where you can find one for sale.'

Tang bowed his head in unspoken acquiescence. Youmei looked bewildered, aware of an undercurrent of something she did not understand going on here, but the situation was out of her hands. Amais climbed down from the *qang*, crossed

232

the room to the older woman, took both her hands in her own and squeezed them in reassurance. 'Don't worry about anything,' she said gently. 'We will return as quickly as we can.'

She reached out for a shawl to wrap around her shoulders against the chill that still lingered in the air, and walked out of the house without looking back. Tang followed her, and then fell into step beside her.

'I know who you are,' Tang said without preamble as the front door of Iloh's house closed behind them. 'He told nobody . . . except me. But he did tell me. And it took only a few words, and I knew I would recognise you at once if ever I laid eyes on you. I did not expect to do so in his house.'

The question was conspicuously unspoken, but loud in its absence. *What are you doing in Iloh's house? What do you want of him?*

'I did not know whose house this was when I came here,' Amais said quietly.

She told him something of her life since she had left Iloh's side in that other family graveyard, under that flowering tree – haltingly, because she could somehow both remember too much of it and too little. Tang did not interrupt until she had come to the end, to her arrival at the farmhouse, and Youmei's nursing her back to health at Iloh's own hearth.

'I did not want anything. I did not ask for anything. I myself don't know why I didn't leave long ago and go back to the city – that's where I was headed, that's where I wanted to go – all the family I still have is there and I have no idea if they are alive or dead right now. But I didn't go. Somehow, they needed me here, in this place. And somehow . . . I needed them.'

'Do you have papers?' Tang asked.

'Papers?' Amais echoed, turning to look at him blankly.

233

'How do you expect to enter the city without papers?' he said. 'They will want to know who you are.'

Amais stared at the ground at her feet, her face white. 'I did not even think,' she said, 'that this would be a problem. I have no such papers.'

'You will not be allowed in,' Tang told her. It was not a threat or in any way hostile – it was just a flat statement of fact.

Amais's head came up sharply. 'But my mother . . . my sister . . .'

He shook his head. 'That is nothing to do with the men who are at the gates,' he replied. 'You never left, as far as anyone knows – even if you did leave with all your papers intact it was during the old city, when everything was different. Now, the only people who are allowed to keep a domicile in Linh-an are those who can prove that they belong there. But they will have been issued papers after you left the city. And you do not have those papers.'

'Perhaps my family did it,' Amais said. 'Perhaps there is a record of me in the city.'

'But it does not show you left it,' Tang replied. 'And if you never left, how is it that you are trying to get back in?'

Amais squared her shoulders under the shawl. 'There has to be a way.'

'Where is Iloh's sister?' Tang asked unexpectedly.

Amais turned her head to stare at him. 'What?'

'He had a half-sister. Yingchi. She would be . . . maybe a few years older than you. The daughter of his father's concubine.'

'*She* is in the city,' Amais murmured. 'Youmei does not know exactly where, but we do know it's in Linh-an, because that's where her letters come from.'

'Linh-an? Yingchi is in Linh-an? How long has she been there? What does she do there?'

'She has not been living in that house for some years,' Amais said. 'When her father . . . took to the pipe . . . it was his daughter's purchase price as a bondservant that bought his habit. And after – her mother does not know. There is never a return address on the letters.' She left it at that. Youmei's suspicions, the possibility of Iloh's sister plying her trade in Linh-an's teahouses, was not her story to tell or to judge.

'But she has never officially *entered* the city,' Tang said after a thoughtful pause.

'Not with the new papers,' Amais affirmed, glancing up at him.

'This can be straightened out, in the city,' Tang said at last, coming to a decision. 'The real Yingchi is in the city, and she is supposed to be here. You are here, and you are supposed to be in the city. You are of an age, within a few years. If the family comes to Linh-an with me, we will show that Yingchi entered the city – and after that, the bureaucracy can untangle it.'

'Thank you,' Amais said. 'Yes, I will come to Linh-an with you. I will help you find Yingchi, even, and return the identity I am borrowing.'

Tang hesitated, avoided looking at her, his left hand closed around the wrist of his right on his back as he walked. 'Iloh . . . would want me to bring you to him, now that I have found you. He wanted to . . . *wants* to . . . ask you . . .'

'The answer to that question,' Amais said softly, 'he already knows. He has always known it.'

Four

In the end, it was only Tang and Amais who left for Linh-an. Youmei had too many reasons not to want to go. Here, on the old farm, she was surrounded by country she knew and understood and by people who knew and understood her. In the city she would be unknown, mistrusted, suspicious – a stranger, without friends or any kind of real support, saddled with the responsibility of caring for a sick old man and possibly with the heartbreak of finding out what had become of her daughter in the years that they had been apart.

They had talked of it, Amais and Youmei, one morning – very early, in the dark hours before the dawn broke, almost in whispers so that they would not wake the others.

'I do not need much,' Youmei said to Amais. 'You fixed the roof for me before the snows came, and so the house will be dry, and there will be just the two of us here, and even if I don't work the outer paddies I can make enough of a harvest to feed us – and anyway, when you and . . . Tang, is it? . . . went away to get one chicken for supper and came back with three that in itself is enough to keep me going for a while. And now that he knows about us . . . about his father . . . perhaps Iloh will send us food if times get tough again.'

'Tang will tell him,' Amais said. 'Perhaps now that he has done what he has set out to do, now that he has nothing more to prove to himself or to his father – perhaps he will come back and see you.'

'And you will write, and tell me what is going on in the city,' Youmei said, her eyes huge and eloquent.

'I will do my best to find her,' Amais replied, squeezing the other woman's hands, answering the unspoken question.

So they had gone, Tang and Amais, with Youmei watching from the doorway of the farmhouse until they were completely out of sight.

It had been over a year since Amais had last seen the walls of Linh-an. On the outside, nothing seemed to have changed – those walls were eternal, had always been there, would always stand. But within them, inside the city, the year that had passed had altered everything – and things were still changing.

The gates were guarded by men and women wearing Iloh's blue or grey uniforms and the ubiquitous flat caps worn low on their foreheads, and they were not window-dressing or decoration – they scrutinised everyone who passed the gates with narrowed eyes and tight lips, the first redoubt, the front-line soldiers on whose shoulders the security of the city rested. Because she was with Tang, whom they recognised and deferred to, Amais's passage was smooth – but she was very aware of how different things might have been if she had tried to return on her own, without papers, without identity. Tang had stopped a little way into the city, out of sight of the gates and their intense and devoted guardians, and had handed Amais a piece of paper with a red seal stamped on it.

'That will get you through to me,' he said. 'See what you can find out from your family, what they've done about you, and come and give me the paperwork. Do it soon.'

The words had been a warning. Paperwork mattered in

237

this new world. As with everything new, this newborn Republic was insecure enough to set tough rules and demand that everyone abide by them – thus continuing to prove and justify its own existence.

'What do I do with these?' Amais said, holding up the papers that identified her as Iloh's sister Yingchi. 'I promised her mother I would find her.'

'I will start a discreet inquiry,' Tang replied. 'Don't stir things up by blundering about by yourself. Given the situation, you might seriously endanger both of you. Hang on to the papers, keep them safe. I will send word.' He paused, took a moment to give her another long, appraising look. 'I will tell him that you are here,' he told her.

Amais dropped her eyes and bowed her head in a motion that was many things – gratitude, deference, pride. When she looked up, Tang was gone.

The city itself was different. It was as though even the air had changed – there had been little enough of old Syai in the atmosphere of Linh-an when Amais and her family had first got here, but now even that tiny whiff of it seemed to be gone. There was a new mood, an excitement tinged with fear. Huge banners filled with slogans were hung from windows and across walls. Amais detoured to walk by the Great Temple, and even that, in between two of its gates, had an enormous picture of Iloh draped on its outer wall. There seemed to be just as many people gathered in the street underneath the picture, gazing up at it, as there might have been inside the Temple itself, kneeling before the niche of any given deity. Amais shivered, ever so slightly, at the unbidden comparison of Iloh not with a mortal emperor but with an immortal, a God, something that had stepped out of Cahan itself and now strode the world like a giant, crushing things under its heels without even realising that anything had been there. She paused for a moment, staring at the suddenly unfamiliar place that the Temple had become with the addition of that poster, wondering if Jinlien was somewhere inside – if life went on as usual, with the carp needing to be fed, the burners needing to be tended and the niches cleaned of old offerings – but she did not go in, letting her step lengthen again, tearing her eyes away. The urgency that beat in her blood was for other things right now, for other people.

The building where her mother and stepfather lived had another poster on it, with a smaller Iloh portrait and underneath that the word *Xiqanin!* The calligraphy was crude – splashed on with huge brushes and paint rather than ink – but the word was an elegant relic from the Imperial age. *Xiqanin* – 'ten thousand years' – was the cry that the people had traditionally greeted their emperors with when they walked the city's streets. Amais's heart lurched with a sudden and painful memory of the *wangqai* tree and its golden flower.

Nobody was home. For one terrified moment Amais succumbed to an impulse of pure panic – *What if none of them are there any more? What if they are gone? What if they are all dead?* – and the spectres of those lifeless eyes she had seen on the battlefields rose to haunt her, set in the familiar faces of her mother and her little sister. And then she took herself in hand.

'They weren't *in* the war,' she muttered to herself, shaking off the icy touch of the dead. 'They were within the city. They are perfectly safe.'

They were just not *here*. She considered waiting until someone – anyone – showed up, but it was mid-morning and it could conceivably be hours before anybody did. She suddenly and painfully wanted her mother – wanted a chance to throw herself into her mother's arms, bury her face into Vien's shoulder, feel Vien's arms come around her and rock her like she had done when Amais was a child and some exaggerated childish calamity had exploded into her world. Or as Youmei might have done with her daughter. It was hard to remember, in the end, after watching Vien fade into a grey wraith that had needed protecting by her children rather than rousing to protect them against others. Had she ever, in fact, done what Amais now pictured in her mind, or was it just something that Amais had made up from scraps of other people's memories, from the fragments of stories that she herself had scribbled down in her notebooks when she was younger?

She could have gone straight to the university library, but something in her shrank from her first meeting with her mother being under the curious, watchful eyes of all the other people there – and particularly the weight of Lixao's resentment and disapproval. She needed privacy for that first meeting, needed . . . needed time to retrace some of her steps, to find her way back to the place she was before.

Time. Hesitating under the benign gaze of Iloh's portrait and its heartfelt wish for eternal life, Amais wondered a little bleakly if anyone would know if she took some of that surfeit of time wished on Shou'min Iloh on the poster, whether a couple of years siphoned off here or there would be noticed in that extravagant, monumental pile of ten thousand of them. But it seemed that the universe had already granted her what time it could, in those quiet months of learning how to breathe again in Iloh's house. Now, back in the city, time shook itself off like some creature waking from a deep sleep and launched itself forward in an almost unseemly rush.

Vien had taken Amais into her arms when she finally came home, and had held her for a long time, crying quietly, without saying a word. Lixao had been haughty but oddly quenched, as though he might at one time have demanded an apology from the wayward child before he would allow her to live under his roof again but had been forced by the new rules of the city and the land to question his own authority. Aylun, at first, would not speak to Amais at all. But it was with all of them that she was part of the crowd who thronged the streets and squares of Linh-an on the afternoon of that day in late Chanain, mid-summer, that Iloh had chosen for the official birthday of his Republic. With her family at her side, in the midst of the surging masses of the cheering people of Linh-an, Amais was just one of a multitude, another body in a thousand bodies, not even considered important enough to be given access to the front part of the great Emperor's Square, where the podium had been built on which Iloh and his high-ranking officers were to stand. She was almost all the way in the back, where parents hoisted small children onto their shoulders to let them glimpse the podium and Shou'min Iloh, blocking the view of those behind them, hauling the children back down again when the protests became too loud. There were thousands of lanterns, hundreds of thousands of voices raised in an endless echoing cry of 'Xiqanin! Xiqanin! Shou'min Iloh!'

To Iloh, the square beneath his benevolent gaze and waving hand was just a mass of upturned faces, a thunder of voices. To Amais it was as though all of that were in a different dimension, a background roar of noise, an overwhelming mass of flesh pressing against flesh. Through it all, even when her view was blocked by those pushing and shoving for better vantage positions in front of her, she could clearly see Iloh's face, the fire in his eyes, feel the surge of his triumph as he stood on this pinnacle of his achievement – at the helm of a new state he had fought and bled for, with his hand on the dream once given to Syai as a legacy by Baba Sung. *Be a nation again.*

And he had done it. He had achieved it. Amais could see the pride of it sit on him, like a crown.

Amais felt it surge through her, too, that pride – she could feel it beating in her blood as well, helplessly remembering little things from back on that lonely hillside near Xinmei's farm. *I was his; he was mine*, she caught herself thinking, fiercely, like a raptor bird claiming its prey. She knew she would never forget that night, she had always known it, but even she was taken by surprise by the strength of that memory, carried in her mind, her heart, her very skin that prickled as a random brush of another body against hers there in the crowd became reinterpreted as the remembered caress of Iloh's fingers. She had to wrap her arms around herself, suddenly clutching at her shoulders with her hands, to stop herself from trembling.

There were supposed to be fireworks that night, but the day that Iloh had chosen for the occasion had dawned hot and sultry and before it was half-over big thunderheads had gathered in from the north. Iloh's speech, the proclamation of the Republic, was delivered to the accompaniment of streaks of lightning and the ominous rumbling of thunder. The storm broke well before things had been concluded, and rain sluiced down onto the city as if poured down from the heavens in bucketfuls. It took only a moment for everyone to be drenched, wet hair plastered over people's faces, guttering lanterns succumbing to the downpour – but even with the prospect of a delay in the promised fireworks, none of it could dampen the fire of enthusiasm that glowed in the city on that day. People were celebrating. It was probably true that many of them were not clear as to exactly what, but at this point nobody cared. The next day they would have to deal with everything again, all the problems, all the niggling bureaucracies of a brand-new state, all the guards on the gates, all the wreckage of a long and bitter war that still had to be cleared up. Things would still cost too much in the markets and there would still be bad news in the newspapers, people would still die and be born, the normal workaday everyday world would return. But for now, at this moment, they had a new star in their heaven, and even if the people in those crowded streets did not know where it would lead them in the end, they were happy just to have something to follow.

Amais stood in the midst of this mass of surging emotion, in the rain, at once utterly a part of it all and completely isolated from everything. She watched it all, watched the people dance and sing and shout '*Xiqanin!*' until their throats were raw. She stayed as the crowds began to thin, as though in a trance, after Iloh had left, after the excitement began to dissolve in the rain and people began to drift off and away. She only came back to herself with a start at a small but insistent tug on her sleeve, and turned to blink owlishly at a young girl at her side for a moment before realising it was her sister.

'Come home,' Aylun said. 'Come on home. They're all gone. Amais . . . are you crying?'

'It's the rain,' Amais lied, smearing at her wet face with the back of an equally wet hand, doing very little good.

'I missed you,' Aylun said unexpectedly, and the brightness in her own eyes was quite definitely not the rain. 'I missed you so much . . .'

Aylun was ten years old. Later, much later, Amais would remember this moment, standing with her arms around her sister in the rain, staring over Aylun's head at the empty podium where Iloh had been not so long before, waving at the crowds. Aylun had still, at that moment, been a child – inasmuch as either of them, with Vien as their mother, had ever been allowed to be children. But they were all about to be swept up into a time and place, a crisis, with everything they knew about to tear itself apart and remake itself in a new image. In such a moment, when a world was newborn as this rain-washed evening was, nobody in it would be allowed to remain a child for long.

243

Five

The day after the annunciation of Iloh's Republic, Amais, driven by an odd premonition of doom, started keeping a journal again – one in which she wrote every day, much as Tai had done. This time, unlike the previous attempt she had made which had not lasted and had morphed into her fictional worlds, she stuck to it – she felt as though this was the only real way to steer a straight course through the chaos of the young Republic's growing pains.

There were many things she had wanted to do once she was back in the city – go to the Temple and talk to Jinlien, find Yingchi as she had promised that she would do and write back to Youmei, go in search of the House of the Silver Moon and the secrets of *jin-shei* that it held. But Iloh had big ideas and even bigger dreams, and it seemed that he could not wait for them to ripen in their own time. The edicts from the top came thick and fast, and Syai struggled to keep up with the changes that were mandated. Amais found herself just another cog in that wheel.

Baba Sung had talked about land reform, but had lacked the power and the means to ever push this through in the manner he might have wanted; Shenxiao had fudged the issue completely because he knew that his own support depended on the moneyed classes who would have taken it exceedingly amiss if their land had been summarily confiscated and redistributed to the poor peasants who had hitherto toiled on the landlords' fields. Iloh had no such compunctions. He came from the land; although his own family had been reasonably well-off by the standards of the countryside, he had seen enough of the way things really were to take on the idea of land redistribution head-first. It had been there, from among the poor and the dispossessed of the hinterlands, that *his* support had come from – and he had a debt to pay. There were those who grumbled – the ones who would have to foot the bill for Iloh's ideas, but Iloh proved to be remarkably ruthless in dealing with opposition. He demanded absolute honesty, and then he turned around and removed the people whose honesty spoke against him. Those who did side with him he rewarded with power, and they repaid him with utter loyalty. The result of this was the countryside seethed with reform and fundamental transformation, with the gift of land being offered at the cost of an ideological conversion. Huge tracts of land were parcelled out to individual peasants to work, but then these were reorganised further – first into small cooperatives of only a few households at a time and with families still occupying their own homes, and then larger communes, with private land-ownership to all intents and purposes abolished and land and tools being pooled and jointly owned by dozens of families, hundreds of people.

Loyalty to party and state was emphasised. Iloh's words, quickly blazoned on everything from big posters hung from every available wall to scrolls pinned to individual lapels, were simply 'Serve the people', and by people he meant everyone. No distinctions were to be made for family, friends, lovers.

245

Amais recognised this decree. It was the dream he had spoken of to her, back under the *wangqai* tree – the brotherhood between all the people. In Iloh's vision, everybody owed the same allegiance to everyone else, be it a complete stranger, a mother or a father. In the communes, families were split into compounds where women and men lived separately in dormitories, children were cared for in communal crèches, and married couples had their time together carefully doled out hour by hour according to how the commune leaders decided the place should be run. Family ties, for so long the basic fabric of society in Syai, began to unravel.

It may be that one day we will all understand it in the way he means it to be understood, Amais wrote in her journal, her heart torn by what she saw happening around her, what she heard whispered about in dark corners in marketplaces where people thought they would not be overheard, and her loyalty to the memory she clung to of the Iloh with whom she had felt so breathlessly connected that night under the *wangqai* tree. *It may be that we will all believe it. But that day is not yet, and he does not want to know that . . .*

Iloh had no time for social analysis. Having set in motion the reform of the country, he turned his attention to the cities, and Linh-an, the capital, became the laboratory in which social changes were experimented with and then exported as decrees to the rest of the land. In Iloh's opinion, individual peasants, left unsupervised, would quickly revert to the old feudal ways of doing things, because those established hierarchies were the only way of life they really understood. The city-dwellers were fundamentally no different, and required a re-education from the very bedrock of their existence so that they could be forged into Iloh's new army, who would take his ideas forward. Within the first year of the Republic, Iloh's thoughts had been gathered together and published in a tiny book, small enough to fit into the pocket of one of those uniforms that everyone now wore. Bound in bright yellow leather, it quickly gained the sobriquet of *The Golden Words*, and became ubiquitous. These were the words that people were expected to study, to know, to live by.

They included instructions on ways to learn, from one's own mistakes and from others, how to be a better citizen of the Republic.

'*Serve the people without thought to self,*' *The Golden Words* instructed. '*Problems are inevitable, but all problems can be solved if they are properly and correctly understood and analysed. Failure must not be allowed to exist. If at first you do not succeed, you must apply fresh determination.*'

In accordance with this dictum, mornings in many work units were devoted to meetings, which sometimes went on for hours, where individuals would stand up and offer up self-criticism of how they had failed to live up to Iloh's standards. Silence was no defence, because those who would not criticise themselves quickly became the targets of criticism by others.

Vien was bewildered by the new system, and rarely came up to the front of her work group to 'struggle' with her failings. She could also not understand the need to guard one's tongue, because chance utterances or gestures that, however innocuous, could be used to illustrate a particular 'transgression' were now pounced on and trotted out as evidence for an individual's veering away from the line of Iloh's thought.

It fell to Amais to try and deal with the situation. Lixao stayed silent and somehow withdrawn, on this as on most other subjects, and Aylun had sought oblivion in becoming utterly and fanatically devoted to Shou'min Iloh's word and deed, and had in fact turned spy for the State in her own family.

Vien had never thought to conceal any of her past, and now that came back to haunt her.

'She has always thought of herself as an aristocrat,' a co-worker accused in one of the struggle sessions. 'Better than everyone. Just because her mother married an Imperial Prince.'

'An exiled Imperial Prince,' another co-worker chimed in. 'She could not even get it right – she's the product of a marriage between a social climber and someone who had to leave the Empire in order to assert his Imperial stature. What, he couldn't be royal enough if he had stayed here? He had to go and impress exiles overseas?'

'But I do my work,' Vien had murmured, not even defensively, but in simple confusion – she could not wrap her head around the fact that she was being accused of being born to her own parents, as if she could have had any control over that.

Family members were encouraged to attend these criticism sessions, as if learning about the sins of their mothers or brothers or sons would teach the other members of the stricken family valuable lessons. Frequently such 'lessons' landed in fertile ground, and relatives became accusers and judges. It was Aylun, little Aylun, barely eleven, who jumped up in one of her mother's criticism sessions and cried out,

'I saw her sit on a pile of new-printed pamphlets once!'

'I was tired,' Vien murmured.

'And how was this wrong?' one of the leaders of the criticism circle said, turning to Aylun with a smile that Amais, who was also present at that session, felt stab her in the heart.

'The pamphlets had the picture of Shou'min Iloh on the cover!' Aylun declared passionately.

The people in the circle gasped and murmured, exchanging glances. There was something here – a crowning sin. It wasn't just that Vien had been observed actually sitting down right on top of Shou'min Iloh's face, but that was somehow the thing that proved beyond doubt that she was seditious and disloyal. If she hadn't been so, well, so *Imperial* in her attitudes, if she had really been one of the people, it would never have even occurred to her to sit on such a place.

Amais had her hand at her throat, staring at Aylun in disbelief. Her younger sister's face was alight with a zealot's fire, the lips of her fine rosebud mouth, inherited from the very grandmother whose existence was being held against Vien in this circle, parted a little as her breath came in quick, excited gasps. She had done her bit for Shou'min Iloh – the upper edge of a well-thumbed copy of *The Golden Words* showed above the edge of her pocket.

'The family will leave now, please,' the circle leader said, after a moment. 'The unit needs to confer on *ximin* Vien's punishment.'

Aylun stood up and bowed to the circle. 'Long live Shou'min Iloh!' she said, before turning smartly on her heel and marching out of the room.

Amais, wordless, half-astonished and half-terrified, followed her sister. In the corridor, Aylun stood waiting beside the door, her arms at her sides like a little soldier. Her hair, which she had recently cropped herself so that it now swung free just brushing the tops of her shoulders, made her oval face with its creamy ivory skin look harsh and somehow both much older than its years and like that of a very young child, one who had failed utterly to comprehend what she had done.

'They might send her to a labour camp,' Amais said.

'If they do that, then that is what is necessary,' replied Aylun sturdily.

'Aylun, don't you realise that would kill her?'

Aylun turned glittering obsidian eyes to her sister. 'And what would you rather do,' she demanded, 'shelter someone who doesn't care one whit about what Shou'min Iloh is trying to do?'

'Iloh . . .' Amais began hotly, and then caught herself as her sister's eyes widened slightly at the omission of the honorific. Amais allowed herself a moment of bitter reflection – if only Aylun knew just what Iloh had been to Amais! – but then corrected herself. There was no point in drawing Aylun's fire onto her own shortcomings. 'Shou'min Iloh is only a man . . .'

'He is a man we must all try to be like!' Aylun declared.

'We cannot all be like him,' Amais said.

'Those who cannot, make us weaker.'

'She is your *mother*,' Amais whispered.

'Shou'min Iloh is my leader,' Aylun retorted, without a trace of remorse.

They did nothing to Vien, not that time – she got no more than a sharp censure and a somewhat acerbic instruction to watch where she parked herself when she felt the urge to sit down. But the shadow of it remained over her.

'We will watch you,' her co-workers said. 'You must learn to criticise yourself more. You are not better than the rest of us.'

Amais watched them, too, her mother and her sister, and saw the distance between them widen as the water would widen between her father's boat and the shore when he cast off for a day on the ocean. And she had an awful premonition that, like her father's boat, Aylun would sail away to some strange destination and never come back to her family.

Amais went back to the Temple in the beginning, often, to talk to Jinlien – but even there the mood had changed and become ominous. It was as though the people in the Temple were always looking over their shoulder these days, wondering which of their companions in the First Circle, or the Second, or even the more exalted Third or Fourth, were there only to keep track of who was at the Temple wasting precious time that could better be spent working for Shou'min Iloh's dream.

Jinlien was distracted in those days, as though fighting some secret battle from whose arena Amais was barred. There were circles within circles in Syai now, and it was very hard to know which ones were safe to speak one's mind in.

Jinlien did point out, during one visit, a woman who stood out from the rest by the fact that she did not wear exclusively the dark blue or grey drab that seemed to have been adopted by male and female alike in Linh-an in those days. 'That's one you want to talk to, if you still have plans on seeking out the House of the Silver Moon,' Jinlien had said. 'The one with the orange scarf around her head. She's been coming here for years, she's one of the administrators of the House, I think.'

'Xuelian?' Amais had said, turning sharply to follow the woman as she passed by with a handful of incense offerings, her head down and her face partially obscured by the veil of the scarf.

'No, that's not Xuelian. Xuelian herself only comes on special occasions. Come to think of it, she hasn't really been in for months, maybe over a year . . .'

'You *know* her?' Amais had asked, distracted by the chagrined discovery that the answer to that particular question had always been this close to her, and she had never known it.

Jinlien had laughed. 'Not personally, but it is hard not to recognise her when she is here. You will see what I mean if you should find yourself in her presence. But it's that one you should talk to if you want to speak to Xuelian.'

Amais had waited for the woman with the orange scarf later, after she had completed her devotions and had come out into the First Circle again.

'They tell me,' she said to her, 'that I need to speak to you if I wish to come and see Xuelian of the House of the Silver Moon.'

251

The woman first looked a little surprised, and then appraising.

'You have not cut your hair,' she said approvingly, scrutinising Amais closely. 'And you have good skin. And your eyes are magnificent. What are your skills?'

'I beg your pardon?' Amais said, the eyes that had been called magnificent widening in astonishment.

The woman looked perplexed. 'You want to see Xuelian, no?'

Amais nodded mutely.

'You are *not* looking for work . . . ?' the woman from Xuelian's teahouse said after a small pause.

Amais actually blushed. 'I . . . no. I am not. I have had greetings to deliver to Xuelian, however, for months now . . . and I have to admit that I have simply not had the time or the strength to seek her out after I returned to the city from her sister Xinmei's house.'

The woman threw Amais a sharp glance. 'You know Xinmei?'

'Only as a guest,' Amais said. 'I stayed at her house while I was . . . on a pilgrimage to another Temple, in the mountains.'

'Well, there is no time like the present,' the woman said, with a half-smile that hid a lot of things she was leaving unsaid. 'Why don't you come with me? Or, if you'd rather not be seen walking with me, follow me, if you like. The House is on the far end of the street, the last one on your left. Go to the side door, the plain one; the other one, the red lacquered one that faces the street, is only unlocked after nightfall.'

There was a time that Amais would have replied that she had nothing against being seen in the company of anyone – but in those early days of Iloh's Republic caution was not just useful, it was sometimes necessary. So she accepted the alternative and walked a few paces behind the woman with the orange scarf until she turned into the street that Amais had first heard of in what now seemed to be another lifetime. She had not been telling a falsehood when she had said that life had run away with her, that she had not had the opportunity or the occasion to come to this place before, despite her best intentions to do so. All the social graces that had stood in her way now seemed somehow unimportant in this strange and plain new world that had been born of war and struggle. And there had been more at stake, too – it wasn't just Xuelian now. There was also Yingchi, whose whereabouts Tang had been supposed to ascertain and then get back to her, but who had never done so as the demands of the Republic distracted him from the unessential. It seemed that Tang had not been the only one so distracted. Walking down this street, with her head lowered in an unconscious attempt at the necessity to obscure the features of a woman of good family when driven by need or business into this quarter of the city, Amais found herself aghast at how she could have let things go for so long. The quest for *jin-shei*, for the women's country – the quest that had driven her across Syai to seek her answers – had seemed to wither in the past year, under the weight of all the things that had been piled on Amais's shoulders. Now, here, in the Street of Red Lanterns at last, she felt things stir again, that distant dream that had been hers, a memory of a sacred vow.

Amais did not really know what she expected Xuelian to be, not even after Jinlien's comments, but it was certainly not the tiny, regal old woman who finally came out to greet her after she had arrived at the House of the Silver Moon and had been invited to cool her heels in a sumptuously appointed waiting room for the better part of an hour. Her first glimpse of the lady of the House made her instantly understand why Xuelian had not been to the Temple for a year – had not been outside these walls, perhaps, for months. Xuelian would have looked sadly out of place in the drab colour and cut of the clothes that passed for acceptable on the city streets these days. She blazed in scarlet silks, her feet wrapped in embroidered slippers of yellow satin, her silver-white hair dressed in the old-fashioned way, held at the top, as though with a crown, by a rare and fragile-looking fan-shaped comb of blue kingfisher feathers in a filigree of gold. Her eyes were round and bright, like a bird's, and her hands, the skin on them no longer young but nonetheless meticulously cared for, glittered with jewels.

'You have been a long time coming with greetings from Xinmei,' she said by way of an introduction. 'You have not heard much news from the country, then?'

'No,' Amais said, offering the kind of bow her grandmother had once taught her was the polite way to greet a female senior to herself. 'I have been remiss, I know.'

'Xinmei is dead,' Xuelian said in a tranquil voice. 'When they came for the land of our fathers, she asked by what right they claimed it. The mob were not in the mood to offer reasons.'

The shock was a physical one; Amais's knees began to buckle.

'Do sit down,' Xuelian said, indicating a chair, and Amais managed a couple of staggering steps backwards before collapsing into it.

'I am so sorry,' she gasped. 'I had no idea . . .'

'As it happens,' Xuelian told her, 'she wrote to me of you, before she died. You *are* Amais, are you not? You are exactly as she has described you.'

'She never,' Amais said, 'described you.'

'She could not, not the way I look now,' Xuelian said. 'I haven't looked the way she remembered me for, oh, a very long time.' She reached up to brush the kingfisher comb with

254

the fingers of one hand. 'The memory she has of me,' she said softly, 'is much closer to what I was when my emperor gave me this, on the first night that I went to him.'

Amais stared at the comb with fascination; it was as though she had been offered something from Tai's time. The Empire, which this woman had known, had lived in, had been a part of, had been so comprehensively erased by the Republic that Amais had almost forgotten that it had still existed – just the same as in Tai's day – within living memory.

'The reason,' she began awkwardly, 'why I wanted to see you . . .'

'She wrote of that, too,' Xuelian replied. 'She said you were looking for what remained of *jin-ashu* and *jin-shei*, the women's mysteries. Sad, isn't it – to find them only here, at last . . .' She paused, staring at Amais for a long moment. 'But . . . yes. Yes.' It was as though she was talking to herself, having asked some esoteric question of herself, and had then provided an answer she found more than acceptable. 'You have a foreigner's face and a strange way of speaking,' she said, addressing Amais again, 'but you have a Syai soul. I can see it in your eyes, strange as they are to me. You will do.'

'I will do for what?'

'I will teach you,' Xuelian said. 'I will give you what I know. What you do with it, after, if there is an after . . .' She clicked her tongue against the roof of her mouth. 'Sometimes I wonder if the world hasn't already ended, and I just haven't stopped to notice it yet,' she said, another conversational aside apparently aimed at herself rather than her guest. 'Will you take tea?'

For a long moment, Amais hesitated. If this should leak out, if it was known that she had come here, if Vien's co-workers spied on how her children spent their time, it might go even harder with the family than it already had – this

255

was a blatant recidivism, backsliding into a time and place as Imperial as it was still possible to be. But there was, in the end, no choice.

'Yes, thank you. I will.'

Xuelian might have been reading her mind, because the smile she returned to that acceptance was a secretive, knowing one.

'Yes,' she murmured, 'you are already here, and the guilt is applied by association . . . but don't be afraid. You're probably far safer if they believe in your guilt without question. If I have learned anything in my day, it is that often only the innocent are punished.'

Six

Xuelian had said that she would teach Amais, but it had been an odd comment, and the education, if it could be called that, was even stranger. There were no pre-arranged meetings; Amais would simply turn up at the House of the Silver Moon at random times, whenever life released her for a few spare hours, and Xuelian would be there, as though she had been expecting the visit.

Xuelian, too, kept journals – and there were many of them, years of them, decades of them. Sometimes she brought out a double handful at a time, looking for specific things, and she and her pupil would both pore over the tomes covered in a fine *jin-ashu* calligraphy. Xuelian despised modern implements. Amais owned a second-hand fountain pen, and had even stolen a few moments to type up an entry or two, which she would then stick into her own journal (that in *hacha-ashu*, of course) on the typewriters in the office where her mother worked, but Xuelian had dismissed all that with a wave of one be-ringed hand.

'*Jin-ashu* is the language of a slower, more subtle time,' she said. 'You have to find the time and the grace to write in it. If you don't possess sufficient of either, you might as well be a *hacha-ashu* hack.'

'Can you actually write *hacha-ashu*?' Amais asked.

'Yes,' said Xuelian with faint distaste. 'I can read it, too. But I have never read anything in a newspaper that was worth repeating. They use day-old newspaper to wrap fish in. That's about all it is good for.'

'I read your letters,' Amais said. 'They said a lot more than you wrote.'

'*Jin-ashu* will do that,' Xuelian replied. 'Spend enough time on writing a sentence, as you have to with the women's language, and it grows depth and perception. You have to think about things, writing in *jin-ashu*.'

'But there were times you did not write anything,' Amais said.

'Who said I didn't write anything?' Xuelian exclaimed. 'I just didn't write it back home. They would never have understood. Not the Shiqai years. But I wrote – oh, I wrote. It's all in there.' She caressed the cover of one of her journals as if it were a pet.

And that was how it went. They would start talking about the language and the women who understood it, and it would unwind like a ball of yarn, and Amais would be handed the chronicles of Syai's history as seen through the eyes of one who had lived it and felt it leave scars on her own skin.

Xuelian had been a child when she had been packed up and delivered to the Imperial palace as a substitute for her wayward sister. More of a child than Xinmei would have been – Xinmei, who had been carefully brought up to this, reared with the idea planted in her mind from very early on, educated and schooled in what it would mean in both the physical and the psychological sense. Xuelian had been allowed to grow up innocent, or as innocent as any girl in that family had any right to be. Perhaps that was partly why the first thing she did when she first looked on the face of the man she came to think of as 'her' emperor was to wholly and completely fall in love with him.

It would have been hard for any man to resist the kind of open adoration that Xuelian brought to his life, and the Sun Emperor was even more susceptible to that than most – he was not a strong personality, and he had always been aware that he had come to Syai's throne in the time-honoured way, through his empress, without whom he would have been nothing. So his relationship with his status as emperor was ambivalent – on the one hand he knew himself to have power, and enjoyed using it, and on the other hand he was a lonely and insecure man. His royal-born wife might once have chosen him from a clutch of suitors, but she had turned, over the years, into a cold and glittering thing who resented the weakness she sensed in her husband and despised him for it.

The Sun Emperor, the most powerful man in Syai, had wept on the night Xuelian had first come to him. She was a concubine; she belonged to him, and in a traditional relationship he would have reached out, taken what was his, and never even thought about the consequences. But it was hard to keep up that sense of Imperial entitlement when the thing being taken was offering itself with the kind of open innocence which Xuelian brought to him. The romance that suddenly polluted what Xuelian's family had thought of as a simple business arrangement might have scuttled the whole thing there and then – but in a strange and twisted way it had wound up strengthening the relationship the family had been hoping for and not weakening it. The emperor had become attached to his child-concubine – would tell her things he would tell nobody else, not even the empress. Xuelian wrote of her pillow talks to her family, dutifully. And all worked well for three wonderful years.

But then Baba Sung had happened. And the dream of Republic was born – and was then smothered in its cradle by the treacherous warlord Shiqai.

'I have never been without this comb' Xuelian told Amais. 'Not since he gave it to me, not even when Shiqai came for me and I lost everything else.'

'You never wrote home about him,' Amais said. 'Not really. There was very little about Shiqai.'

'What was there to write?' Xuelian said pragmatically. 'That he was crude, and lecherous, and did not know or want to know the first thing about making anything easy or enjoyable for a woman? I was still barely more than a child when the empress traded me to Shiqai in exchange for the Imperial family's life and liberty – I was the price of my emperor's survival, and for that alone I would have gone willingly enough, but he never even knew about it – it was her, all her, and I never even said goodbye. All I had of him was the comb, and even that I barely managed to smuggle out with me when they came to take me.'

'Did you ever see him again? The emperor?' Amais asked.

Xuelian sat staring at her folded hands for a long, silent moment. 'No,' she said. 'I never saw him again. But I saw *her*, the serpent empress . . . But we'll get to that. Before anything else happened, there were the Shiqai years. And the only value I had to him, other than the fact that I was a body on which he could slake his lusts, was that I had been an emperor's woman – and being an emperor was all that he ever wanted.'

'But he was just a soldier,' Amais said. 'Nobody high-born.'

'High-born enough,' Xuelian replied. 'He was a general in the Imperial army, and then he abandoned that and became a warlord in his own right in those lawless years before Baba Sung came.'

'And Baba Sung trusted him?'

'Baba Sung had a dream,' Xuelian said softly. 'And he took what tools offered themselves – and when Shiqai came, all Baba Sung saw was a useful tool. But he never asked the price before he took what he thought had been offered. Baba Sung was a dreamer of great dreams, but such a political innocent . . .'

'Perhaps it was to him that you should have gone,' Amais said.

Xuelian gave her a sharp look. 'He would never have had me,' she said. 'He was such a pure-minded monk when it came to things like this. And besides . . . this was the man who destroyed my emperor, in the end.'

'But I thought Shiqai did *that*,' Amais murmured.

'Only as a part of Baba Sung's plans – it was Shiqai who brokered the Sun Emperor's abdication for Baba Sung, because he had the emperor's ear, because he could. And then he demanded as his reward – and here was the price that Baba Sung had never asked to know – that Baba Sung make him president of the new Republic. And once that was done, Shiqai dismissed the council that Baba Sung had brought together and manufactured a petition which asked him to become emperor.'

Amais blinked. 'But you just said . . . ?'

'Oh, Shiqai believed in Empire,' Xuelian told her. 'It was just that he saw a different emperor on the throne. Himself.'

'Baba Sung couldn't stop him?' Amais said softly. 'But he was this great man, they called him the father of the nation – and he could not make Shiqai stop?'

Xuelian bared her teeth in what was only barely a smile. 'Shiqai did refuse politely, when they first came to ask him. And the reasons he gave then were all that Baba Sung might have wished. So Baba Sung said nothing, until it was too late. But that was all part of the game – one had to refuse something three times, even when one wanted it, in order to be able to accept graciously in the end. In old Syai it would not do to show one's delight at an offered gift. That was considered unseemly.'

'But Shiqai did accept,' Amais said.

'Oh yes,' Xuelian agreed, 'naturally. And then, as though the Gods themselves had had enough of his treachery, he simply . . . died.'

'How?'

'Only Cahan knows. Some say it was an overdose of ambition or hubris. I don't know that I would disagree with that. But he had come to my bed that night, and had taken what he wanted, and had then rolled over and gone to sleep, as he always did. I didn't realise that he was dead until morning, when I tried to get out of bed without waking him . . . and realised that he would never wake again. I actually spared a moment to feel happy – before I realised what it would mean for me.'

'What?'

'Well, I was wrong, of course,' Xuelian said. 'But that you know. That I wrote about.'

'Shenxiao?'

'That . . . was unexpected,' Xuelian murmured. 'I never thought that he . . . but then, that's more than enough for now. Don't you have to be somewhere . . . ?'

'It's another rally,' Amais said. 'The podium is back up on Emperor's Square. There's to be an announcement, and everyone is to come.'

'Ah,' Xuelian said dryly. 'Everyone.'

Amais hid a quick smile. 'Almost everyone. I will come and tell you what is happening, after.'

'Another parade, eh. Take my advice – bring an umbrella,' Xuelian said.

'An umbrella?' Amais echoed, startled.

'Every time,' Xuelian explained, 'that Iloh has appeared to the people, it has rained. Do you remember Republic Day?'

'Oh yes,' Amais said softly, dropping her eyes.

'Eh. Well. You know what I mean then. It rained when he first came into Linh-an, and it has rained every time he has shown himself to the people since then. And I'm sure I know why, too.'

'Why?' Amais asked, diverted despite herself, even with the wraith of Iloh invoked in her presence.

Xuelian waved her hand. 'It is of no matter,' she said. 'Just a story. But it's a very tempting explanation.'

'Tell me!' Amais insisted. 'You said you were going to teach me.'

'Not this,' Xuelian replied. 'It's just an old wives' tale.'

'But I'll be an old wife one day,' Amais said. 'I might need to know. So tell me.'

'Oh, if you insist – it was more than two hundred years ago, back when the Phoenix Emperor was on the throne. His children were on the river, and he was watching from a pavilion on the shore as they sailed their boat – and then a storm came up. He saw the boat capsize, and he saw the water demons rise up out of the water, reaching for his children – and he was a new emperor, of a new dynasty, and he saw his future vanishing before his eyes. So he fell to his knees and he prayed to the water demons, and he made a bargain with them – if they let his children live and his dynasty continue, then in another quarter of a millennium they could come out into the bodies of men and become rulers of the land in their own right. And so they did.'

'They let the children live?'

'The storm died,' Xuelian shrugged. 'Or so the tale tells. And here we are, those two hundred and fifty years later, and it rains every time Iloh sets foot out in the Emperor's Square. What else am I supposed to think?'

263

'Iloh is not . . .' Amais began passionately.

Xuelian, having paused to give her story dramatic impact, spoke at the same instant: 'But we will speak of Iloh . . .'

They both paused.

'I'll be late,' Amais said. 'I am to meet my family before we go to the square.'

'So, go,' Xuelian told her. 'I will see you again, after.'

There was no great downpour as there had been on Republic Day, but it drizzled steadily as Iloh spoke from the podium at the gathering. He had a microphone, and his voice was amplified across the square, sounding thin and tinny as it was carried across the heads of the crowd.

'The time has come for you to speak,' Iloh was saying. 'Let a thousand flowers of thought bloom in the land. Look at the Republic – it is *your* Republic – is it doing the things that you wanted to see it do? Speak out, and let us all know. We will be listening.'

The words were high-flying, and brave. But Amais had kept her journals too well, and in them she had noted what had happened when people had spoken out against Iloh in the past. When she wrote of the latest gathering in her journal on the night she came home from it, she flipped back to an old notebook and read what she had written before, about the men who had tried to stem land reforms they had thought too harsh.

'*I wonder*,' she wrote now, '*how much of this comes from Tang. Iloh has never needed people in the past to give his truth vindication. And I wish*,' she added despondently after a short pause, '*that it had not rained this time. Xuelian and her stories! I cannot seem to get rid of the image of Iloh and Tang drowning children of a long-dead emperor in river waters that lost themselves in the deep ocean hundreds of years ago . . .*'

'It will not last,' Xuelian had predicted, when Amais went

back with a report of the proceedings. 'Or, rather, let us say that it will last precisely as long as it takes for one person too many to say something Iloh does not like. Oh well – if there is anything I've learned in my days it is that every dog has his day.'

'That is not fair,' Amais said.

Xuelian lifted a quizzical eyebrow in her direction. 'Nothing,' she replied, 'is ever fair.'

'You hate him,' said Amais. 'Don't you?'

'I don't think I hate anybody,' Xuelian said. 'I spent all my hate a long time ago. I am too old now to waste my time on hating, it takes far too much of my energy and my time. But you have to admit, these days there are only two ways to feel about Shou'min Iloh – you either worship him, or you loathe him.'

'"*You would have recoiled from me, or you would have bowed to me*",' Amais murmured, very softly.

'What was that?' Xuelian said. 'My dear, my hearing isn't what it used to be. You need to stop muttering into your chin.'

'It was just . . . something he said once.'

'Who did?'

'Iloh. *Shou'min* Iloh,' Amais replied, laying ironic emphasis on the title.

'Was that in *The Golden Words*?' Xuelian asked. 'I don't remember it.'

'You've read *The Golden Words*?'

'And so has every one of my girls,' Xuelian said. 'It would not do to be caught out not knowing them. But where was it that he said that people would either bow or recoil?'

'Your hearing is better than you think,' Amais told her, unable to stop herself.

Xuelian's mouth quirked.

'He knows exactly what he is,' Amais said, with a touch

of passion she wasn't even aware of colouring her words. She herself had questioned whether this directive had come from Iloh, but that was in the secret places of her journal, and out here, in the real world, she could not help rousing herself in his defence if someone else uttered the exact same sentiments. 'He has always believed in what he knows to be true. He has never needed anyone's praise or approbation to do what he believes is right. Look how far he has come . . .'

'He really did get inside you, didn't he,' Xuelian said, looking at her pupil with sudden interest.

Amais dropped her gaze, bringing up both hands with fingers that had gone icy, to cover and cool the hot blush that had leaped to her cheeks. 'Oh, *Cahan*,' she whispered despairingly. 'Is it that obvious?'

'I did not mean it in that sense,' Xuelian said slowly, 'but *now* it is. Some adore him, some hate him . . . and then there's one who loves him.' She reached out and tipped Amais's chin back with one imperious hand so that Amais had to look at her through eyes swimming in tears. 'I've been doing all the talking,' Xuelian said, 'perhaps too much talking. The best education always goes both ways, with the teacher learning from the pupil. We both know how I came to be in the place that I am, but you will have to tell me just how a girl like you could have stumbled into being Shou'min Iloh's lover.'

Seven

There were just voices, in the beginning – voices in the darkness, familiar voices both, raised in argument.

'But speaking out is what you asked them to do,' said the first voice, and it was Tang, with his unmistakable crisp clipped tones. '"*It is your Republic*", you said.'

'I did,' said the second voice, and it was Iloh's – not the tinny, almost artificial voice familiar to thousands as transmitted through the microphones on the podium in the Emperor's Square or broadcast through cheap radios, but the real voice, that rich, full, loamy dark voice that Amais had first heard in the ancestral burial ground near dead Xinmei's house. 'I asked for *help*, Tang, I asked for opinions, for visions of a way forward. Not an outcry in favour of returning to all those Imperial iniquities that we have done away with! Not a concerted front against every idea we've ever put forward!'

'*You* put forward,' Tang said, and the darkness was dissipating a little – he was visible, in his stark blue-grey uniform, a slight frown on his face. 'Almost everything we've done has been your vision – there's *The Golden Words* out there, you can read the story of the Republic in them. Iloh . . . you asked them to tell you what they thought.'

'This is not what I had in mind,' Iloh said, waving a thick sheaf of papers in Tang's face. 'I said constructive opinion, I wanted input on building up, not just cavils and complaints and ideas on how to tear down what we've achieved and go back to things that most people who propose them haven't an inkling of what they would mean to society.'

'Perhaps you've been too harsh with them,' Tang suggested. 'From the day you declared the Republic to now, they've had to live very different lives than those they had known before.'

'Baba Sung proposed most of these ideas before I did,' Iloh replied stubbornly. 'The only difference is that I've actually worked to make them a reality.'

'Still,' Tang said, 'your primary directive is *serve the people*. You yourself said that every kind of service is noble. When they ask you for certain things and you refuse to even consider them, you are not living up to your own words, Iloh.'

'Do you *agree* with all those people?' Iloh asked.

'Not all of them,' Tang said, and his voice was careful. 'But some of them . . .'

'No, you're right,' Iloh agreed. 'It's been useful, in some ways.'

'That's something, at least,' Tang replied.

'I know who is against me now,' Iloh continued, and his voice was low and dangerous, almost fey. 'I know who I have to deal with to make sure that the edifice of the Republic is not undermined even as it is being built. I have already made plans – people need to be educated.'

'Iloh . . .' Tang had a hand out, palm open towards Iloh, as though he was trying to ward off a premonition.

'Here,' Iloh said, snatching another file off the desk beside him and thrusting it at Tang. 'This is what we are going to do . . .'

But the voices were fading. A glimpse of faces, one determined, one almost inscrutable with a hint of appalled astonishment, and then the veil of darkness came down again, and it was all gone.

And Amais woke with a start, alone in her room, with her heart beating very fast, the dream still clinging to her inner eyelids as though it had been painted there, the voices still echoing in her ears.

She had not always been blessed with the facility to remember her dreams, but ever since the journey from Elaas to Syai, the endless days and nights on the ship upon the open ocean, she could recall some, the important ones, when she woke. It had become almost a problem-solving device for her over the years, one she had grown to rely on – because the remembered dreams often held solutions to current problems and impasses in her life, couched in the usual exaggerated and sometimes deeply odd dream-metaphor, something she had had to work at learning how to interpret.

Some of the dreams had been vivid but unexplained and possibly unexplainable – visions about things that were yet to come in her life, perhaps, preparing her for something, showing her the way. But she had never yet had the kind of dream from which she had just woken, something so real and so clear, so much as though she had been there, physically present, rather than asleep in a bed across the city from where that conversation might have been taking place. But she had absolutely no doubt that she had somehow 'heard' something that had really been said. It was as though that connection she had had with Iloh from the very beginning had suddenly been sharpened to something new and keen-edged, the kind of blade that sliced through the fabric of space and time and made a bridge out of air and darkness between two people so linked.

Perhaps that had been brought into focus by the simple

fact that she had been talking truthfully about Iloh with somebody else for the first time since she had met him, trying to come to terms with his presence in her life. She had tried to explain to Xuelian, when the subject had come up – tried, and failed, because she herself was completely unable to rationalise her feelings for Iloh and the way they had been consummated. She constantly found herself surprised that the events of which she told had happened barely a year before. Sometimes it felt like centuries had gone by.

'You were sixteen years old,' Xuelian had said, 'and he was a charismatic and powerful man in the prime of his life. It happens . . .'

'I did not know who he was when I first saw him,' Amais replied. 'And it didn't matter, not in the least. I first thought he was just a local peasant, doing his chores.'

'But you found out that he was not,' Xuelian said. 'Be honest – would you have gone back that night to meet that peasant, if that was who you still believed him to be?'

Amais hesitated, searching herself, wanting more than anything to give Xuelian nothing less than the truth. Xuelian noted the pause and – unusually, for the sharply observant woman that she was – misinterpreted it completely.

'See?' she said, while Amais was still trying to find the right words. 'It mattered – even if only just a little, but it mattered.'

'No, you're wrong,' Amais said. 'The only moment in which his true identity really made a difference was not the one in which I came to him. It was the one in which I left him.'

'How so?'

'Xuelian . . . this was not my fairytale,' Amais said. 'I stumbled into it, and it held me – more of a trap than a dream . . .'

'A honeyed one,' Xuelian murmured.

'However sweet,' Amais said, managing to dredge up a

270

smile. But behind it her eyelashes glittered with tears as though they had been strung with tiny diamonds. 'He was not mine and could not be mine. He was just . . . *mine*.'

'Child,' Xuelian said, 'you are making no sense at all.'

'Did you ever believe that one day you could marry your emperor?' Amais asked softly.

Xuelian reached up to caress the kingfisher comb in her hair, a motion that was totally instinctive, beyond any conscious intention or control, and when she realised where her hand had strayed she snatched it away as though caught in the act of doing something indecent.

'No,' she said, too quickly. And then looked down at her silk-clad lap, where both hands now lay with their fingers tightly laced, as though one hand was preventing the other from further betraying motion. 'Yes,' she said, after a pause. 'There are times . . . I still do.'

'But you knew . . .'

'Yes. Oh, yes. I knew.' Xuelian lifted her head again and skewered her pupil with a gaze that was at once savage and somehow astonished. 'Child, how did you get to be so wise, so young?'

They had spoken of it many times, after – but it was not until some time later that Amais had mentioned her stay at Iloh's farm, his concubine 'stepmother', and the half-sister who had vanished into the city.

'When Tang came to get the family, just before Republic Day, he hardly realised that it was going to be only a stranger masquerading as Iloh's sister with whom he would return to Linh-an,' Amais said. 'I promised her mother, you know – I promised her I would find her daughter and send word. And then Tang said that he would take care of that, and things happened, and I never did anything – but perhaps you would know . . . Youmei said her letters came from the city but with no return address, and I thought . . .'

271

'You thought that she might be here, on the Street,' Xuelian said. 'Not impossible, but I doubt that anyone knows her real identity if she is Iloh's sister. There would be few houses brave enough to take that on.'

'She might not have said anything,' Amais said.

'What was the name?'

'Yingchi.'

Xuelian blinked, and then inclined her head in a quizzical manner, like some bright-hued bird of paradise. 'Oh, my,' she said.

'What is it?'

'I thought she might have changed her name, at least,' Xuelian said. 'But I *do* have a girl here . . . How old did you say she would be?'

'I'm not sure, but I think in her early twenties. Something like that. Iloh was thirteen or so when she was born.'

'Oh, my,' Xuelian said again. She reached out with one glittering hand and rang a small silver bell that had been left within her reach on a side table lacquered in bright scarlet. A girl dressed in saffron-coloured silk popped her head around the door.

'Xuelian-*lama*?'

'Is Qiying with anybody right now?' Xuelian asked, and Amais sat up as though she'd been stung. 'No . . . ? Then bring her to me.'

'Qiying?' Amais queried softly.

'It's possible,' Xuelian said. 'It's a direct inversion. She might just have thought that was enough. We shall soon see.'

'You mean,' Amais exclaimed, almost stuttering in disbelief, 'that . . . all the time . . . right here . . . ?'

Xuelian turned back to Amais, and actually laughed out loud.

'You never asked for her by name,' Xuelian said. 'And I certainly had no reason to think anything of it, under the circumstances – *she* certainly never said anything, not a word. She was a country girl from a farming family – that much I knew. But when you come to this place, what you were ceases to matter very much. If you want to shroud your past, nobody will ask questions – but should it prove to be dangerous for the house you become a part of, and endanger you or your *jin-shei-kwan*, your house-sisters, you will be held accountable.' She paused. 'And women have been. Make no mistake. We have our own code of honour here on the Street, and our own justice.'

There was a soft knock on the door, and Xuelian called out permission to enter. A girl with wide bright eyes and two coiled braids of long, lustrous black hair pinned so that they framed her face slipped into the room.

'You called for me, Xuelian-*lama*?' said Iloh's sister.

'Why did you not tell me who you were, Yingchi?' Xuelian said calmly, without preamble.

Yingchi flinched as though she had been struck, and then dropped her eyes to where the toes of her embroidered slippers peeped out from under the hem of her silk gown. 'Xuelian-*lama*, there are times I myself do not know who I am,' she said.

'But you do know who your family is,' Xuelian replied. 'That might not have mattered, had you been no more than the country girl you said you were when you came here. But you must realise that knowing what I know now changes everything.'

Both Amais and Yingchi looked at Xuelian in pure consternation – the one because she had hardly wanted to be responsible for turning Iloh's sister out into the streets, and the other because women plying this particular trade as independents, with no House behind them to protect them should things turn ugly, usually led short and brutal lives.

Xuelian noticed both looks, and understood perfectly

where each was coming from. She smiled, and motioned for Yingchi, standing frozen by the door, to come inside.

'Don't worry,' she said, 'I did not know until now, and nobody else outside this room knows – and as far as I am concerned nobody needs to know. I could have wished that you'd thought to change your name, Yingchi-*mai*, if only to protect the rest of us. I do wonder, though – now that he is here, and that he is powerful, why did you make no attempt at all to contact him?'

'He does not know me, or anything about me,' Yingchi said, moving as though her legs were made of glass and then collapsing on a seat very suddenly, as though the glass had turned to jelly. She glanced at Amais, warily, but she had been asked a question by the highest authority in her life, and she had an obligation to answer it. The presence of the stranger in the room was sanctioned by Xuelian and there-fore could not have a bearing on Yingchi's own conduct under the circumstances. 'And . . . and he scares me, Xuelian-*lama*. I did not know if he would even see me, and if he did, what he would do to me. What I am doing . . .' She ground to a mortified halt, glancing up at Xuelian, aware that she was passing judgement not only on her own lifestyle but on that of the woman who controlled her daily bowl of rice, the roof over her head, and such security as could be hoped for in this particular trade.

'What you are doing might reflect poorly on him?' Xuelian said coolly, finishing the unspoken thought, apparently less than troubled by the concept. 'It might, in his mind, at that. Men have such a twisted vision of women – they will come here, and to the other Houses, and they will make no secret of the fact that they enjoy the attention that they pay good money for, and the accomplishments of all the women in the Street. Did you know that some of the girls I have known could sing better than the professionals in the theatres and the operas, that some of them were better poets than the ones being published and winning acclaim . . . ? These things mean nothing, they are just taken for granted, these things are not what the men come here for. They come to find women who can hold sparkling conversations on any subject from raising pigs and growing tea to the latest political situation in the land, to find women who dress exquisitely in bright colours and wear jewels in their hair, to find women who can pour tea like the highest unattainable society lady and then turn into a tigress in bed – and they are quite happy that such women are to be found. But let one of their own try to step from their world into this one – and we are all monsters, every one of the women they come here to worship. The Houses suddenly exist for no other purpose than to lure virtuous young maidens into a life of sin and iniquity.' She laughed, and the laugh was short and harsh, a sardonic comment rather than mirth. 'I am not entirely displeased that you kept this a secret, child. Let it stay one. Amais, you had a message . . . ?'

'I spent a winter in your mother's house,' Amais said, unable to take her eyes off Yingchi's face, looking for Iloh's features there, seeking his voice in her inflections. 'I promised her . . . I would find you.'

'My mother . . . ?' Yingchi's eyes were wide, suddenly very bright, full of eager curiosity and anxiety, mutely pleading for news. 'You saw my mother . . . ? How is she?'

'She was well, when I left her, but she was tired and somehow . . . somehow defeated by it all, despite being dignified and brave. Your father . . . is not well.'

'I know of my father's . . . *illness*,' Yingchi said, with a trace of sarcasm so faint that Amais almost missed it, veiling her eyes with her long eyelashes.

'Your mother waits for your letters,' Amais told her. 'It would be a kindness to let her write back to you.'

'I cannot,' Yingchi said, looking up – and there it was, that echo of Iloh that Amais had been searching for, the steely resolve in her eyes. It was mixed with a lot of pain, but it was unshakeable. 'You write to her. Tell her I love her. Tell her you found me, and I am doing fine. She is another who does not need to know exactly where I am.'

'Are you that ashamed of your life?' Xuelian questioned softly.

'Others . . . might be,' Yingchi said, hesitating, picking her words with care. 'It would hurt my mother, and my father. It is possible they would lose face in the community, even the little dignity that is left to them after my father . . . after what happened to him. And I honestly don't know what it would mean to Iloh.'

'Xuelian,' Amais said suddenly, 'has he ever been here?'

'Here, in my House? No, thank Cahan, because right now I would be thinking back as to which girls he was with and praying that Yingchi had not been one of them.'

'No . . . on the Street,' Amais persisted, and there was colour in her cheeks.

Xuelian gazed at her steadily for a long moment. 'You are determined to hurt yourself with this as best you know how, aren't you?' she said softly. 'Yes, he has been to the Street. Few men in power resist its lure for long.' She lowered her eyelashes, breaking eye-contact, and when she looked up again it was at Yingchi. 'You and I,' she said, 'will talk more later.'

It was a dismissal, and Yingchi understood it immediately as such. She rose to her feet and bowed, turning to depart.

'Wait,' Amais said.

Yingchi hesitated at the door, glancing back at her lady for permission, then waited for Amais to continue speaking.

'I have something for you,' Amais said. 'I've been carrying the packet with *your* papers for a long time. I was you;

276

that's how I got into the city, after . . . after Iloh sent for you all.'

'He sent for us?' Yingchi questioned, and for a moment there was something else in her face – a hope, a fierce longing. 'You mean my mother and father are here?'

'No, they stayed at the farm,' Amais said. 'But I . . .'

'You have my permission,' Xuelian interrupted, 'to speak further when you are free, Yingchi. I think . . . the pair of you might have a lot to say to one another.'

It was another dismissal, and this time it was sharper. The quick flash of hope and joy that Yingchi had allowed herself to show vanished behind a carefully schooled expression. She bowed her head, opened the door a crack, and slipped out of the room.

'*Two*,' Xuelian said pensively, 'who love him. And both of them in my circle. How the noose tightens . . .'

'What do you mean?' Amais said, suddenly and irrationally afraid.

'I think you will find out soon enough,' Xuelian replied, cryptic as usual.

Two days after that conversation, Amais had woken from the dream in which Iloh and Tang had been talking of the Republic and what was to be done about the campaign of free thought and criticism that Iloh had rashly, as he thought now, loosed upon the people of Syai.

There would be a price to pay for that freedom.

Less than two weeks after that dream, Amais knew just how high the price was going to be.

Everyone who had said anything against Iloh's thoughts and ideas, anyone who had had the courage to propose solutions different from the ones that Iloh's *Golden Words* implied, anyone at all who could be found to have thought, spoken or acted in a manner that could be called treason,

277

now felt the full weight of retribution descend upon them. People were judged and condemned in intense 'trials', and punishments were instant and harsh – and if the accused did not submit and accept the guilt that had been forced upon them, the punishments could be made even harsher. There was much to do in Syai, Iloh had decreed, and he was going to see it done. Those who could be dangerous – the educated, the eloquent, the people who had criticised some of Iloh's earlier and more precipitous decisions and who were now being called reactionaries and recidivists – were given days, sometimes hours, to pack a few meagre belongings into a small backpack and then marched off to labour camps where they would 'rebuild the nation', where they could be re-educated and re-moulded to fit the new Republic.

It happened almost that fast in Amais's household.

Aylun had left home not too long before this announcement, to live in a dormitory with a dozen like-minded young people, most of them several years older than herself and of a better 'class' of revolutionary who were quite at ease with using Aylun as an errand girl and unpaid servant – but she was fiercely proud of that, in her own way, and did whatever was asked of her without demur, hoping to earn her own admittance into the higher ranks. Vien and Lixao went to work every day like automatons, came back, said very little – to their co-workers, to one another, to Amais. Speaking one's thoughts out loud could be a deadly danger in these days.

And then, one day, Amais left the two of them at home while she went out to buy food for the family. By the time she returned, Vien was gone – taken by a brace of taciturn guards (so Lixao told Amais later, shaking with the strength of his reaction) to a destination unknown.

Eight

Lixao knew – or would say – no more than what he had seen happen before his eyes. The men who had come for Vien did not say where they were taking her. Lixao had been too terrified – and Vien herself far too deep in shock – to even ask what would happen to her. When Amais began to try and find out where her mother had been taken, she initially met a stone wall of silence. It was with a sense of something approaching horror that she finally stopped haunting offices of tight-lipped cadres who would not or could not tell her anything, and went in search of her sister.

Aylun, at first, was defiant – and every bit as uncooperative as the officials had been.

'She is our mother,' Amais said. 'You have to know what she is, what she has always been. She will fall at the first sign of harshness. She has done nothing *wrong*, Aylun!'

'She must have,' Aylun said, 'else they would not have taken her. Shou'min Iloh does not make unjust accusations.'

'At least find out where she is,' Amais said. 'No more than that. Please, Aylun.'

She was pleading with an eleven-year-old, and somehow, in the twisted reality of their world, that didn't seem incongruous. But it was not until Amais tried a different tack – pointed out that Vien's conviction for treason, if not reversed, might detrimentally affect Aylun's own chances of getting into the People's Party hierarchy, which now ruled society with an iron fist – that Aylun reluctantly caved in and promised to see what she could find out.

Her information was accurate, but late in coming. Vien, and others like her, had been held for at least a month in a compound on the outskirts of the city – but by the time Amais found that out and went there the place had already been emptied. A sweeper working in one of the courtyards volunteered that she remembered the women had been transported to a larger camp. She wasn't sure of the exact location, but she thought it wasn't far, somewhere just outside the city walls, in the low hills flanking Linh-an. Amais scoured the countryside on that flimsy information, sometimes with her own papers and sometimes with false papers that gave a fake name and let her travel further than the daughter of a convicted traitor might have been allowed, but her timing continued to be bad. By the time she had located the farm that had been converted as a holding centre for the women destined for various labour camps in the country, the women were gone, and the paperwork, as usual, was labyrinthine.

Weeks and then months went by. Spring turned into summer, and began to slide into autumn again. Amais continued searching, taking desperate and hurried day-trips to places where she heard rumours of convicted women, but her mother was never among them. Aylun remained aloof, more so than ever, required by her own cadre supervisors to 'draw a line' between herself and her contentious family lest their guilt taint her own pure revolutionary record. Lixao stumbled through life in a sort of daze, reminding Amais forcefully of Iloh's own father, lost in his drugged stupor. It would not have surprised her to find out that Lixao had taken to the water pipe himself in order to take his overloaded mind and his exhausted spirit away from the harshness of the reality that faced him every day – but there was no evidence of that, and in a way that was far worse. At least, had it been the case, his lethargy and almost childlike dependence on Amais for a soothing word and a square meal would have weighed less heavily on her.

Taking care of her stepfather was something she felt she owed to her mother, but he was often needy, even clingy, taking time she could have used for other, more useful things. She could not find enough hours in a day to work at her own job – her family's work unit at the university had employed her too, but it made little or no allowances for her personal life or her need to find her lost mother. If anything, the circumstances of her mother's departure meant Amais was required to do the work she was employed to do and then more on top of that, even if it involved working late or working double shifts with only an hour or two snatched for sleep. In a better world she would have actually enjoyed the access she had to the library now – but she was given no time and no opportunity to delve too deeply into its resources. Her job was simply to catalogue and then remove, if necessary, books judged to be unsuitable for the current ideological climate. New books were being churned out all the time, and handed to her to catalogue and display – but she found nothing of redeeming value in any of these new works, apparently produced only to show the glories of the Republic and the villainy of all that went before. It was as though, in order for Iloh's shiny new world to be born, the old one had to be comprehensively denied and abjured, its very existence wiped from people's minds, its treasures destroyed along with its blunders and its mistakes.

Her visits to the Street were severely curtailed. Her initial contact with Yingchi and that side of Iloh and his family subsumed into the greater anxiety of her own family's disintegration. Xuelian was only present as a sort of bejewelled guardian angel to whom she occasionally fled to remind herself of the existence of another world, to read a few pages of journals, written in *jin-ashu*, from a lost and lovely time which seemed doomed to vanish forever from the minds of the very women who once cherished and nurtured it.

That autumn, just after Amais's nineteenth birthday, Iloh announced another new initiative.

'We are a great nation,' he said, during another rainy gathering on the Emperor's Square. 'We can and we must take our place among the other great nations of the world. But we cannot do it as we are. For too long we have had our face turned inwards, worried only about our land and our crops and our harvests. We are pastoral, agrarian, farmers instead of workers and builders. The land is important – that will never cease to be important – but there are greater things at stake than just our survival. We must take a giant step forward, we must take a chance, we must catch up to all the realms who have the advantage of having the world's respect and admiration. Our farms are organised now, and are worked by their communities – we need to turn our attention to other things, to factories, and self-sufficiency in our needs. To commerce. To industry. And this is how we will achieve it!' He brandished something in his hand, something that only those in the first ranks of the crowd pressed around him could see was a length of steel piping. 'Steel! Steel will give us strength! Steel will give us the beginning of a new Syai! This is the year that we will turn our minds to making steel – and we are many, and determined, and what we set out to do we will achieve. Build your own furnaces, in your backyards, in your farmyards, in your courtyards – rip out the useless old ornamental fountains and raise foundries in their stead! Make steel! We will take iron and forge a bridge into the future!'

Amais had stared up at the podium, trying to understand, knowing what Iloh's dreams were but failing utterly to comprehend how he thought this latest scheme would do anything to make them true.

But by this time anything that Shou'min Iloh said or asked to be done was treated by the people – half of them fanatically devoted to him in what was almost a cult of worship, the other half cowed into submission – as a direct command. Backyard foundries popped up like mushrooms, just like Iloh had demanded. They were fed with anything that came to hand – iron fences, ploughshares, even great cast-iron family cooking pots common in every village house. After all, the peasants were told, they would no longer need those – they would be fed at the communal kitchen, with communal food, and there would be no further use for those heavy, ancient monstrosities that their families had used for generations to cook the meals in.

Fields were neglected in a frantic search for iron. In the countryside, fieldhands raided yards and paddies, taking what iron was offered and often what iron was not, taking the hidden and the hoarded with just as much sense of entitlement as that which had been freely and avidly thrust into their hands. Men, women and even children abandoned chores and school and stumped purposefully along sleepy country lanes, laying hands on iron implements, iron spades and shovels, iron skillets, tearing iron grilles from windows. In the city, Aylun and her friends went on scrap-iron drives, lugging back whatever they found to the headquarters of the group where a backyard foundry, kept stoked to a red-hot glow, hungrily ate whatever was fed to it. Even the great grating over the channel of the Seven Jade Springs was ripped from its ancient hinges.

Youmei wrote to Amais about it, letters full of delicate detail and possibly dangerous secrets wrapped in the outwardly innocuous and endlessly subtle syllables of *jin-ashu*.

They came and took the great cooking pot, and the big iron plough, and anything else they could lay their hands on. I buried the other pot – the smaller one – out where the pigs used to be kept – the ground is still all churned up there and they would not notice it had been freshly dug. Perhaps this was unpatriotic of me – me, of all people, Iloh's own family! – but I could not give that up. It is all I have of my own home, all that I have of my mother's house. Even if I am never to cook in it again, I want to know it still exists. There is a part of me that would have died in the fires with that pot if it had been taken. Someday perhaps I will have the opportunity to tell Iloh why I did it, to explain, to apologise if I need to. I fully realise that if everyone held back their own sentimental objects nothing would ever get achieved . . . but it seems so little. I hope he would understand . . .

But Iloh's steel pipe was no more than a dream.

What was produced by a developed industrial base could not be matched by the simple enthusiasm of cottage industry, untaught, ignorant, without the necessary underpinnings to produce either the quantity or the quality of the steel that Iloh had dreamed about. That much became obvious fairly quickly. But the vision was pursued with dogged determination – after all, *The Golden Words* spoke of failure not being an option; that a solution to any problem lay simply in approaching it correctly and applying enough determination to ensure success. So the people fed their furnaces, with more and more fury as raw material became scarcer, and turned from the care of the land.

And then the rains failed.

Youmei wrote of that, too, in the aftermath.

It was late, far too late, when the rains did not come, to plant and expect harvest – but people suddenly started desperately ploughing their fields all around us, with the ox-drawn wooden ploughs of ancient days, old and rotten with their years, sometimes breaking in the traces. They tried everything – precious seed stock of winter wheat raided to keep famine at bay. But it is useless to try to shut the door in the face of a spectre that is already half inside the house. I have seen hunger before, but now I have seen people starving, children digging broken roots out of the ground with their bare hands and gnawing on them with their teeth loose in their gums, eating them mud and all. I gave my share to my master, sometimes, and there were days that I too tasted mud in my mouth . . . but we are surviving. Somehow. I might have known this was coming; I have a little put by, safely hidden, and I feel guilty sometimes just knowing I have it and knowing that others do not. There are times I want to walk out with my pitiful little hoard and hand it out to the children who sit by the dry irrigation ditches with their souls barely connected to their bodies, waiting for a breath of wind to rip them away and take them to Cahan . . . ah, Gods, what is it that we have done to transgress, to deserve this punishment? How long must we endure . . . ?

That winter was harsh and dry. The spring rains were late. The summer was hot and the sky hung over the land like an accusation. Autumn came again, and with it a sudden deluge of rain that flooded riverbanks and swept away the dusty topsoil from parched farmlands, taking what little was left behind by the drought.

Another winter came, and a mass famine stalked the land.

In the spring, it was Tang who came out to the Emperor's Square, in a mournful drizzle, to talk to the people. Iloh was not on the podium. Amais, in the crowd, tried to scan through narrowed eyes the people who stood behind Tang, their expressions carefully constructed masks, impossible to read – but Iloh himself was not there. She felt a stab of what was almost fear, so powerful that she almost completely failed to hear most of Tang's speech – but she took in the gist of it. A recantation. A turning away, to ideas that were no longer Iloh's own.

'Back,' he said. 'Back to the land. We will regroup – remember that failure is impossible, that all we need to do is remember how to focus our dreams and our determination. But for now, we will look to providing food for those who have none – take back the land your ancestors tilled; take it, and make it yield its sustenance. We need to care for the land again as though it were our child and the child were sick and we are nursing it back to health and vigour. Back to the land. Under this blessed soaking rain, back to the land. We need to return to our roots . . .'

It was only later, when she read the accounts of the rally in the newspapers the next day, that she realised what Iloh's absence had meant.

He had stepped down as the head of the country. He would remain, would always be Shou'min Iloh, the titular head of the People's Party – but the new leader of the land, the one responsible for the day-to-day practical running of the country, was *ximin* Tang. Iloh remained, even in the shadows, the most powerful presence in Syai – it was still his ideology that was the guiding light, his thoughts that were the basis on which society and the new Republic were built. But it was Tang's hand now on the tiller, his touch on the controls, and the people began to look around, see familiar ideas and visions re-emerge from the past where Iloh had sequestered them in his headlong rush to the new, to the better, to the improved and the enlightened. The old things had always stood in Iloh's way, and he had had no compunction of removing them if they became obstacles. Tang, more pragmatic, less visionary, knew how to incorporate them into the daily lives of people. There was a subtle release of breath, which people had been holding without even being aware of doing so. Amais, seeing it happen all around her, felt it like a physical pain – the sense of relief with which Iloh's absence filled the city hurt her, as though she were personally wounded by it. And yet . . . this was the man under whose orders her sister had turned into a stranger Amais no longer knew, under whose orders her mother had vanished without a trace.

She did not give up her quest for Vien, although she had a sinking feeling that urgency was no longer necessary, that there was no way Vien could have survived the harshness of a labour camp in the wilderness. But then, finally, she did get some solid information – from Xuelian, of all people, on one of her increasingly rare visits to the Street.

'For what it is worth,' Xuelian had said, handing over a piece of paper with an address written on it – the paper was a scrap torn from the edge of another sheet, with something about iron in a snatch of typewritten text on the other side of the page, but the writing was still *jin-ashu*, elegant and neat. 'I don't know how old this information is. I know it's true. Your mother was mentioned by name and by provenance – the presence of a Vien from Linh-an must mean something.'

'Thank you!' Amais breathed, her eyes full of tears. She

might have had the urge to throw her arms around the older woman, but Xuelian threw up her hand to forestall any untoward expression of affection or enthusiasm.

'Go,' she said, 'go on and find her, and return.'

'If this were the old country, the women's country, the Syai that my grandmother spoke of and that my mother came here expecting to find . . . if *jin-shei* still existed . . . someone would have known, Xuelian. Someone would have known long before now, and got word to me. What if it is too late? What if I am too late already . . . ?'

'You are right,' Xuelian said, 'we have lost our connection to our land. There used to be a connection between Syai and her women. Now . . . I am not so sure. But go, go quickly, go find that which must be found. And return safe. There are still things, even in this new world – especially in this new world, with all that has been lost from it – that we can talk about.'

Amais left the next day, defying warnings from her work unit that her absence would not be tolerated. Nearly five hours on a train took her to a small town consisting of little more than a clutch of houses around a large – and apparently mostly abandoned – factory; from there, she hitched a ride the following morning with a supply truck that went further into the countryside, to the address supplied on Xuelian's piece of scrap paper.

The labour camp that was her destination was a depressing, dingy place. After passing a checkpoint on the outer perimeter – Amais had had to buy, bribe and beg her way into the paperwork required to visit a camp such as this one – the truck stopped in a central square, which was mostly churned mud. The square was surrounded on three sides by barrack-like buildings, one apparently a dormitory for women, one for men, and one a mixture of administrative offices and a mess hall. Thin, hollow-eyed inmates stood listlessly in the mud in the square waiting for the truck and its supplies. Others could be seen trudging slowly in from some distant field or other place of labour, or peering through almost opaque glass panes in the narrow windows of the barrack houses.

'Someone will be here to sign for the supplies,' the truck driver told her. 'You'd better wait and speak to whoever's in charge these days.'

That sounded vaguely ominous, as though things were not really under control out here. The advice, to speak to an official of some description and gain permission to talk to the camp inmates, was good, especially in the political climate of the times. But Amais had waited too long, had come too far, to be able to waste her time in waiting for cadres of any stripe. She was here. There was a good chance, for once, that she had caught up with her mother. Amais thanked the truck driver politely, and walked away from the truck. He clicked his tongue against his teeth in an obvious indication of disapproval, but in the end it was none of his business and he made no further attempt to stop her.

Amais had a photograph of Vien. It had been taken when she had married Lixao, and on it she looked almost happy, her hair neatly dressed with a red flower in it, a small smile revealing white, even teeth behind barely parted lips. She showed the photograph to the women in the square, meeting mostly a dead-eyed stare of blank stupor – along with an inability or an unwillingness to give any information. It was a thin, mean-faced cook who finally came up with the information that Amais sought – an inmate herself, but one with more signs of life than most, and one who looked as though the hatchet clutched in her right hand might have been used on more than one previous occasion to slice more than the occasional side of mutton or pork.

The cook came out of the back door of the refectory just as Amais rounded the corner of the building.

'Excuse me,' Amais said, her desperation making her bold, trying hard not to focus on that hatchet, 'I am looking for a woman.'

The cook sniffed. 'I would not have taken you for one of those,' she said. 'Besides, there are probably better-looking women to be found somewhere other than this midden. This is the scrap heap, this is where all the rejects have landed – what makes you come here?'

'My mother,' Amais said in a thin voice. 'I am looking for my mother?'

'Ah,' the cook said, entirely unapologetic. 'I dare say there are a few mothers here. When did she get here?'

'I don't know. I have no idea how long she might have been here. I've been searching for months and always I'm one step behind. I'm hoping . . .'

'There haven't been any fresh inmates for a while,' the cook said. 'When I first came, it was right when they started this place, and women came in every day – almost every hour, in the first few weeks. Particularly the politicals.'

'I thought they were all . . . you were all . . . that it was a political offence that brought you to this place . . .' Amais said, startled into speaking her thought out loud.

'Cahan, no. I'm here for murder,' the cook said calmly. 'But the rest – the poor political sheep – in ones and twos and in huddled groups, they came. Most of them too cowed to know what's what. That's how I climbed up over their backs – I got into kitchen work and I had food when others were starving. But there hasn't been any new blood for some time. The cadres who run this place, they've changed a few times. Some better, some worse. The current crop is confused, I think. What news from outside, then? Things must be changing, if you can walk in here like this. When I first came here you would have already had your hair cut and you'd have been assigned a bunk to share with some other late-come convict – they slept three to a bunk at one time, although it's a little more . . . commodious . . . these days. What was her name, then?'

'Vien,' Amais said. 'She came here from Linh-an, from the city. Political prisoner. Here, I have a picture.'

The cook took the photograph in her left hand and stared at it for a long moment. She finally sniffed loudly, handing the photo back with a curt gesture. 'I know her,' she said. 'You might try the Field.'

'Which one?' Amais asked. She had not heard the capital letter – not until the cook gave her a strange look and thinned her lips into an almost invisible line of nebulous disapproval.

'There is,' the cook said, 'only one Field.'

She gestured at the mess hall, pointing to the muddy square beyond it, and the women's dormitory at the far end of that, implying there was something behind it worth investigating.

Amais had realised that a specific field had been meant – but she had still to make the real connection, and it was not until she rounded the corner of the women's barrack and saw the raw wooden planks with names carved on them, rising from a crudely fenced parcel of bare earth filled with barrow mounds, that she realised what the Field was.

She fell to her knees at the Field's gateway, as though her legs had been chopped out from underneath her by the cook's hatchet. Her eyes were dry and hot, like Syai had been over that last drought-stricken summer, her soul as barren and empty as Syai's parched land. Somewhere deep inside her an ocean moved, an ocean full of light, the sea where her father had been lost many years ago. It seemed to be in a different world than this piece of empty ground and its impersonal graves. She caught herself wondering with an almost academic detachment if her parents would find one another in the gardens of Cahan, and then thought, in an equally emotionless way, that it was unlikely that her father, being

291

from Elaas, would have made it there anyway. They might have been thrown together by the strangeness and the wonder of the world, but they did not share a heaven, or a hereafter.

There was nothing here of her father's land of life and laughter. Only fear. Only silence. Only loss.

It was a long time before she found the courage to get to her feet and stagger forward, slowly, leaning on individual planks at each grave as though she were a very old woman. And then she paused by one of them, staring down at it, her hand resting above the scanty information carved into the wood. A city. A woman's name.

Amais remembered her mother's insistence that *baya*-Dan be properly buried, in accordance with custom and tradition, by no less than the priests of the Great Temple itself. It was only at that thought, as she stared down at the plain burial mound bereft of any rite or ceremony, that something which might have been the memory of tears began to sting behind her eyes.

Nine

The first person Amais walked into as she stumbled back into the square, numb and staggering a little on legs which did not seem to quite belong to her, was the cadre in charge of the camp – a middle-aged woman with greying hair cut short to just above her jaw-line and the narrowed suspicious eyes of someone who had been a jailor for so long that the concept of freedom was beyond her comprehension. There was a moment or two when Amais, part of whom was still utterly detached from what was happening, was almost convinced that the cook's prediction would come all too true and that she would simply take her mother's place in the women's barracks, a pair of hands to replace a pair of hands, much as she had already done in the work unit back in Linh-an. Happily, the cook was also correct in that the current leadership were less than secure in their positions, and that news from the outside world had been hard to come by in the camp of late. The warden decided that Amais did not belong in the camp after all.

Her solution was to evict this possibly pernicious outside influence immediately. The truck was long gone by the time Amais had emerged from the Field, and the day was quickly drawing to a close – but neither of those factors were of any concern to the warden, who told Amais to leave straight away.

Amais walked out of the camp, into the gathering twilight, alone, feeling the weight of many pairs of hopeless eyes on her back as she left. At her mother's graveside she had reached a kind of nebulous intention to seek out the authorities at the camp, to ask for her mother's bones, to take her remains back to the city somehow and bury them next to where *baya*-Dan had been buried, with Jinlien's help and with all the correct ceremonies. It seemed agonisingly unfair that Vien had come home to this riteless, unmarked burial in a shallow grave in a muddy country field. Somehow Amais had never found the words to ask such a thing of the cold-eyed warden, and had had no reason to believe that such a request would be met with anything other than derision at best.

The drive up in the truck had been an uncomfortable one, with that ancient conveyance bouncing and jouncing its way along the unpaved and rutted country road – however, on foot, and in the country darkness, the road was a treacherous mass of furrows and holes, snatching at Amais's feet and twisting her ankles. There were few alternatives, lined as the road was with ditches on either side, and beyond that unfamiliar and even more rugged terrain. Amais struggled along, concentrating on putting one foot in front of the other. She must have walked for hours, her body on that endless road, her mind adrift in memories and dreams.

Vien had had a wonderful, lilting laugh. It had been years since Amais had properly heard it – but it was that, now, which returned to haunt her, like a recording of her mother's soul being played over and over again in her mind. Vien, who had been very young once, and brave, and ready to renounce all that she was by birth and by upbringing because she had fallen in love with a pair of dark dancing eyes that belonged to one not of her kind – who had been courageous enough to re-embrace all of it, in the end, in order to do what she saw as her duty by her dead mother and her living children. She had faced choices, and had made them; often they had shattered her and broken her and left her helpless in their turbulent wake, but much of that wasn't even her fault. It was not her doing that Syai had become what it had become. If she and her girls had returned to the kind of Syai that *baya*-Dan had preached at them all their days, everything might have turned out very different indeed – but they had not, and it was not, and everything changed in the moment when they had first found that out. Amais knew that in a lot of ways her mother had simply given up, abdicated responsibility, drifted where the tides took her, leaving Amais to be the strong one in the family and the one who took on the burden of Aylun. Aylun was on both their consciences, Vien's and Amais's – the one because she had not the strength to cling to her own survival and be a mother to a demanding child at the same time, and the other because she had been a child herself, scared and ignorant, and had only done what she could under circumstances wildly beyond her control. But Amais could not blame her mother for that. Not now, not here, not on this dark road on a moonless night with the ghostly echo of her mother's laughter inside her.

It was summer, late summer, but there was a sharp hint of cool air in the deepening night. Autumn was not far away.

A stray thought insinuated itself into Amais's mind, crept through it on tiptoe, vanished into nothingness again.

In a few weeks, I will be twenty-one . . .

That fact did not seem to matter, could find nothing to connect with in her scattered wits. It was thought without emotion, without making any connection to a possible future. It might as well have been, *In a few weeks I will be dead.*

She did not remember stopping, or lying down on a bank by the side of the road on ground that already struck cold through her clothes, or going to sleep. The first inkling she had that any of that had taken place was when she found herself opening her eyes, with her head pillowed on the crook of her arm, and it was day.

Her feet and the abused muscles of her calves throbbed with pain. She must have walked most of the night – and further than she had thought, as she realised that the shape she could make out through her still sleep-clouded eyes was the gigantic factory in the town in which the train from Linhan had deposited her on her arrival on the outward-bound leg of her journey. She sighed, stirred, sat up and rubbed at her eyes, clearing the sleep cobwebs.

On the road, a way away, she could see someone else walking slowly, head bowed, hands swinging free by his sides, as though lost in deep thought. Thinking that perhaps this was a local who might know how best to find the railway station from here, Amais uncurled from her bank, patted down her tousled hair and brushed down her clothes in an unconscious attempt to tidy her appearance, and stepped onto the road.

And froze, as the other walker lifted his head, and likewise halted in mid-step, looking at her.

The moment was brittle, sharp, a glittering shard of ice. Amais might have thought a hundred things at once, or she might have thought nothing at all – his simple presence, here, now, overwhelmed her, held her perfectly still, too full of feeling, too empty of it. And then the ice broke, with a sound in her mind that might have been just as sharp as the snapping of an icicle, and it all rushed back in – his voice, the strength of his arms around her, the memory of his sleeping face under the *wangqai* tree, the appearances she had witnessed in the rain on the Emperor's Square, the heavy hand and the firm ideas which had guided Syai to the brink of catastrophe, his shining visions of serving the people and his blunders in implementing them – Iloh, Shou'min Iloh, the man to whom she had once given all that she was and who had taken her heart, her body, her spirit, and now . . . her family.

That was what came bubbling to the surface first – perhaps not unexpectedly, given the place from which she had just come. Those were the first words she spoke to him after the years of their separation.

'*You killed my mother.*'

She saw Iloh physically flinch at that, and was glad of it, glad that she had hurt him, that she had stabbed at the heart of him, that she had been able to inflict on him the barest fraction of the pain that raged within her. They moved, then, both of them – towards each other, instinctively, with intentions far from clear, but when she was close enough to him to touch him Amais raised her arms, her hands tightly clenched into fists, and hammered his chest with blows even as his arms came around her to hold her.

'You killed my mother,' she said again, her voice breaking at last into the tears that would not quite come before. The fists that had been pummelling Iloh's chest uncurled instinctively, and she clutched at the fabric of the grey uniform he wore, burying her face into his chest, feeling a button on his jacket digging sharply into her cheek but welcoming the pain and weeping in the shelter of his arms in a paroxysm of released grief that threatened to go on forever.

'Not here,' he murmured into her hair, his hand moving gently, helplessly, across her back in a small tender gesture. 'Come.'

But she could not move, stood rooted there in that road, until he finally reached down with another whispered word and slid an arm under her knees, lifting her up with an easy

sweeping motion and stepping off the road into the shelter-
ing thicket of trees above the bank, the place where she had
just stepped out of, where she had spent the night.

He settled back into the V-split of a small tree, Amais half
beside him and half across his lap, and simply held her in
silence, gazing into the distance somewhere across the top
of her head, until she cried herself out and finally lay quies-
cent in his arms, her eyes closed.

'Why are you here?' he asked at last, gently, as she drew
a deep shuddering breath and fought to steady her resolve
– which had melted away, just like that, as soon as he had
been close enough to touch.

It took her several tries to speak; her voice kept breaking,
thick with tears yet unwept, threatening to drown in them.
She sketched out, very briefly, the events of the past few
months – the 'crimes' Vien had been accused of, her indictment, her disappearance, her lonely and unmourned death.

'They were your idea,' she said. 'The camps. "*The people
need to be educated*," you said. "*I know who I have to deal
with to make sure that the edifice of the Republic is not
undermined even as it is being built*." I cannot begin to imagine what she must have gone through in those last months
of her life . . . oh, *why* can't I hate you?'

'How do you know what I said?' Iloh asked sharply.

'I heard you say it,' she said, wiping at her face with the
back of her hand like a child.

'When? I said that to Tang . . .'

'Yes,' she said.

'But you weren't . . . nobody else was . . .'

'I heard it,' she told him. 'I don't know. In a dream. I
know I heard it. What were you thinking? For that matter,
what are you doing out here anyway?'

'They all turned against me,' Iloh said, with a tinge of
defensiveness. 'You know that much, you must have seen it

298

happen. I am still head of the Party, always that – they could not take that away from me – but Tang is now in my place as head of the country. Apparently my ideas were fine for running a guerilla revolution, but when it came to running a country I was finally judged, I don't know, too idealistic. Or too revolutionary. Too something.' His mouth twisted a little at that. It was something that had come from Tang, and that had hurt him – Tang had been with him for so long, since the beginning of it all, and now Tang had taken against him. 'But they all turned against me,' he said. It had not been only Tang, after all. 'It was their idea, the open forum for ideas, and they convinced me – and then all that the people had to say was that everything was wrong . . .'

'Iloh . . .'

'That's what I'm doing out here,' Iloh said. 'I needed time . . . to think. To figure it all out. Tang is backsliding, damn him. He can destroy it all yet, if he goes too far . . .'

'But you are still Shou'min Iloh,' Amais murmured. 'What are you doing walking a deserted country road alone at daybreak? I thought you would never again be out of sight of someone willing to take a bullet for you.'

'A man can feel suffocated,' Iloh said abruptly, 'with too much protection. Sometimes I need to be alone with my thoughts if I am to hear myself think.'

'And alone with your conscience,' Amais said.

'There is nothing that burdens my conscience!' Iloh snapped. 'I . . . *we* . . . needed people to work this land until we got to the place I know we can be. But for that I needed people who believed, who knew, who understood. The camps – they were meant to provide a focus for that work, and to be a place where such understanding could be gained . . .' His voice cracked with passion. These were things he believed in, even if he had gone about achieving them in questionable ways. Amais could feel the power of that vision in the sudden tightening of his arms, in the way his heart beat powerfully against her temple where her head leaned against his chest. 'Think about it! In less than a handful of years we achieved what Baba Sung's revolution couldn't accomplish in nearly four decades! Once you get the masses of the people moving, believing, anything can be done. Anything! Oh, I had such dreams . . .'

'But you destroy,' Amais whispered. 'You destroy all that came before. You cannot create a garden in a place which you first make into a desert.'

'Yes,' Iloh said emphatically. 'You can. You *have* to. If you do not root out the poisons that have grown in the good earth before, they will keep sprouting, and they will suffocate the new things that you are trying to grow. But you are using the wrong vision. You yourself tell me you heard me say it – and I still don't understand how, damn it! Dreams – superstitions – I have never believed in any of that . . .'

'Yes, you have,' Amais whispered. 'At least once in your life, you have. Or you would never have married your wife for the reasons you once gave me, you would never have recognised my name.'

Iloh, aware that he was staring at her with his mouth open, shut it with a snap. 'There was that,' he admitted at last, after a beat of silence.

'But you are still wrong,' Amais said.

'I am never wrong,' he replied, and his tone was amused, self-deprecating . . . and completely convinced of the truth of those words.

'Once a desert, always a desert,' Amais murmured. 'There are certain things that you can never get back, if you annihilate them. And then the garden . . .'

'But this isn't a garden, it's a house, and you cannot build a new house until you clear away all the rubble of the old. You have to have a clear foundation, if what you want to build is going to stand!'

300

'People aren't bricks, Iloh!' Amais said, rearing away from him, pushing at his chest with open palms of both hands. 'You cannot use them this way. If they do not agree with you or they do not understand your dream, that doesn't mean they are simply obstacles to remove from your path. There is a *choice* . . . !'

'There is a choice in peacetime. But we are still at war, Amais.'

'With what?' she demanded passionately. 'With whom? Why? Iloh, if there is war here, then you are the one fanning its flames!'

'I am not!' he responded with equal fire. 'Amais, I did not invent any of this – I set out the seed of the idea and then I watch it bloom . . .'

'You see,' she said, returning to her metaphor. 'A garden.'

He made a swift chopping motion with one hand. 'False analogy,' he said. 'Maybe that is my fault. But I didn't start this war, Amais – people were more than ready to rise to a new world, to tear off the trammels of the centuries that have been binding them and keeping generations of them poor and subservient and "in their place" – and they were supposed to know their place, and to stay there. Back in the days of Empire, people who tried to break out of their social stratum and their class were not put in camps for a re-education – they were executed without any further question! Why is what I tried to do so wrong? It is the people, Amais, the people! They will rise like a mighty wind and they will sweep all before them – the Imperial aristocrats, the corrupt warlords, all will break before that storm and fall like the dust they are into their graves! You speak of choice? Yes, there is a choice – what do I do with this force that I have seen gathering, that I have seeded with my dreams? Do I step in front of it and let it crush me like it will crush everything else that stands in its way? Do I trot in its wake, criticising and whining? Or do I, if I am given that chance, march at the head of this army of enlightenment and lead them as best I know how?'

'But things were done in your name . . . will be done in your name . . .'

'Yes, and I will use them,' Iloh said. 'If I do not, I fail at my task. I did not ask for the title – but they still call me that, Shou'min Iloh, the first citizen. And I have to live up to that standard. What I ask my people to do, I am always willing to do myself. Only history can judge me . . .'

Their eyes locked, fire with fire, both passionate believers, both willing to spend mind and spirit in the pursuit of a higher goal – but all of a sudden the one thing that mattered was that she was still cradled in the circle of his arms, and that her hands, still flat against his chest, were suddenly tingling with the pulse of the heartbeat she could feel beneath them. She drew a small gasping breath and moved instinctively, shifting one leg down so that it lined up with his thigh, the knee of the other creeping up towards his hipbone. His hand knotted in her hair.

'You were in the city,' he said hoarsely. 'You never came to me.'

'You never sent for me,' she whispered, against his lips, closing her eyes, surrendering to something stronger than herself. She felt his hand slide down, his palm hard against the curve of her breast, and then fumble with her jacket, slip in through an opening, find bare skin and sear it with his touch. 'Oh, *Cahan* . . .' she whispered, her lips against his ear. As his weight shifted, she yielded to it, and then her own hands were helplessly inside his clothes, needing skin under her fingertips, needing to find and remember the shape of him against her, around her, within her.

Her mind didn't understand this, did not even want it – not now, not after the things she had just seen and endured, not with this man of all men – but her heart and her body

302

understood, and for now that was enough, more than enough. Nothing had changed between them – he was still not hers, not, as she had said to Xuelian, her fairytale. But somehow, somehow, he was in her destiny. And she was powerless to change that.

This time it was Iloh who had gone. Not, as she had once done, leaving her asleep in the aftermath of love – they had talked, later, in each other's arms; they had whispered words that were a breathless, heady mix of love, and dreams, and politics. Then they had stopped talking, for a while, lost in each other again, limbs twined, skin straining against skin. And then he had sat up, and had said he had to go.

'I know now,' he told her, 'what I need to do. When next we meet, remember that – I *need* to do it. Remember that, if you find it hard to forgive me.'

He had asked if he could take her back to the city, or arrange transportation to any other place she wanted to go – but Amais had hesitated, and declined. There would be too many questions asked that could not be answered. She had somehow managed to pull her mind and body together, after he was gone, and find her own way back to the city – following, perhaps, in Iloh's wake, she had no way of knowing. When she alighted from the train in Linh-an's crowded, busy station, she realised that she could not face going home, not to that empty house with Vien imprinted on it, not yet – so she made her way to the Street of Red Lanterns, and Xuelian. She wept in that ornate lacquered room, into Xuelian's silk-clad lap, the old woman's hand on her hair like a grandmother's.

'Oh, sweet child,' Xuelian had said. 'How I wish I had an answer for you. But if I have learned anything in my days, it is that sometimes love is simply not enough.'

Amais looked up, her face tear-streaked, her eyes framed by eyelashes spiked with tears. 'You always say that,' she said, her voice trembling a little.

303

'Say what?'

'"If I've learned anything in my days" – as though it were only one thing, the ultimate lesson. But you keep on saying it. Whatever is necessary, that's the one thing you have learned.'

Xuelian smiled, and it was a smile of love. 'Child,' she said, 'and I do not use the words lightly, this time – if I have learned anything in my days . . .'

Amais hiccoughed, a sound halfway between a laugh and a groan. Xuelian smoothed her hair back from her face and gently laid her head back onto her lap, heedless of the wreck that Amais's tears were making of her silk gown.

'If I have learned,' she said quietly, 'anything at all in my days, it is that I will never know enough about life to understand it. That doesn't mean that I will ever stop trying. Just remember one thing, in the storm that is to come – men are like mountains, and they will raise the earth to do their bidding; but women are like water, and the more barriers they place in our path the more we will find a way to flow around and through and underneath them. That is power. Nothing can stand against it. And you . . . you carry the soul of Syai within you.'

She was whittling. And this time it was different. It was she, herself, who was doing it – there was no sense of separation, no sense of looking over someone else's shoulder, no sense of being a dreaming disembodied ghost. It was as though she had found an anchor, and the anchor was what she had always known it had to be – in the body of the young woman in her dream. In all the time she had dreamed of her, over and over again in dream after dream, Amais had never been able to see the young woman's face – and now it seemed blindingly obvious why. It would have been her own. She could not have seen her own face, not without the mirror that the dreams never seemed to provide. She was the one looking out from within it.

As now she looked down onto a pair of hands that were very familiar, and held a piece of soft wood and a curved carving blade.

The wood was still a shapeless burl, with no hint of what it was supposed to emerge as after its transformation. Dream-Amais appeared to have known this, however, before the dreamer-Amais woke inside her body and stilled her hands with her own ignorance and incomprehension.

She turned the piece of wood over in her hands, pondering.

'Time was,' someone said softly, 'everyone would recognise a yearwood bead.'

Amais looked up, and met the serene eyes of the little girl

who had always been her dream-companion. She wore her hair in two braided pigtails now, tied with lengths of scarlet ribbon, and had changed her high-court garb for the kind of plain robe an ordinary child might wear, if it hadn't been touched with gold embroidery and images of stylised water buffaloes worked in yellow silk didn't twine around the edges of her wide sleeves.

'I've never seen a real yearwood,' Amais said.

'I kept one all my life,' said the child incongruously, giving every indication that she meant decades and not just a childish handful of years.

'But weren't they supposed to be made of material that matched the reign?' Amais queried, fingering her wood burl.

'Jade for the Jade Emperor. Ivory for the Ivory emperor. Yes, if the reign rested on something rare and precious, that was what the yearwood was carved from – but even then there were those who could not afford to buy a jade bead every day of their lives. Wood has always been used as a substitute. Cherry wood and bone and soapstone, the poor man's ebony and ivory and jade. And besides . . .'

'Besides,' whispered Amais, 'there is a Wood Emperor on the throne. It is right and fitting. But I don't know how to do this. What am I making?'

'Not many keep them any more, but there are still some who have a yearwood in their home, counting their days,' the little girl said. 'And almost everyone still has the special beads made for the special occasions, like they had always done. For births and deaths and weddings and for Xat-Wau. It is necessary to mark the passage of those times in one's life, after all.'

'I have a birth bead,' Amais said. 'My mother had one made for both of us, my sister and me. But none of the others.'

'You had your Xat-Wau, didn't you?'

'Well, yes. The occasion, not the ceremony. I don't think my mother had the red pin to put in our hair, either Aylun or myself.'

The child reached out and closed Amais's restless fingers around the burl of wood that she was turning over in her palm like a worry bead. 'There is more than one kind of coming of age,' she said. 'There is more than one Xat-Wau in the lives of some people. You might need a bead to mark the passage.'

'But even back in the old days there were people who made these things.' Amais said. 'I cannot do this by myself! If it is that important . . .'

'Anything important it is best to do with your own hand,' the little girl said. She frowned delicately, reaching for the wood bead. 'But perhaps you're right. Perhaps you need to learn how to make it from the beginning. From small seeds do big things grow.'

She rubbed the piece of wood between her small palms, and dropped it to the ground at her feet. It sank into the soil, and the child smoothed the surface of the earth after it with the toe of her shoe, leaving no trace of its passage.

Amais looked up, confused. 'What am I supposed to do now?'

'Watch and wait,' came the reply. The voice was disembodied and drifting; there was mist all around, except for the place where the wood had been dropped. On that spot, a white light shone as if from heaven and, even as Amais gazed, a small fragile stem broke the ground and raised two pale green leaves towards the sky. The plantlet seemed to sigh, and shudder, and then it burst forth, growing, shooting out of the ground, its girth increasing, its skin growing from soft green to smooth young bark and then the gnarled carapace of a mature tree. Branches flung out from the tree trunk, separated into smaller boughs, twigs, leaf whorls.

307

Acorn-like seeds budded, ripened, fell like bounty – and where each fell another tree sprang, like the first, a grove, a small wood, a forest. Shadows spread on the ground. Wind began to whisper in the crowns of trees.

'What am I meant to do now?' Amais whispered, alone under the dim eaves of the murmuring trees, lost in the pathless wilderness.

'Follow,' the voice that guided her said, and it sounded like it came from every one of the trees, a woody whisper laced with susurrations of wind-blown leaves. 'Find. Make a bead to mark your passage.'

'But which way do I go?'

'The way your heart takes you,' the voice whispered, and Amais realised that she had said the words out loud too, answering her own question.

'The way your heart takes you,' she repeated, closing her eyes.

And then took a step, and vanished into the shadows of the wood.

The Golden Rising

Where there is debt, someone owes it and someone is owed, in turn. And there is always a debt between the future and the past.

The Annals of the Golden Rising

One

Amais did not go home on her first night back in the city. She had cried herself to sleep, her head pillowed on Xuelian's hospitable lap, and had then been removed to a comfortable bed – Xuelian's own, seeing as no other in that house could be trusted to leave its occupant unmolested for the duration of the night. Xuelian had offered what she could in those first few anguished hours, trying to lead Amais through the thorny thickets of love and all that it meant in the real world – but in the cold clear light of the morning, after all that could be said had been said, Xuelian had offered practical advice about things that needed to be done once the talking was over.

'You have to think about it, Amais-*ban*,' Xuelian said to Amais, sitting on the edge of the bed beside the younger woman, smoothing back the sleep-tangled hair with tender fingers, calling her by the name a mother might use with her child. 'For all things, there are consequences. You have lain with a man, and if what you told me last night was right, you were in the right phase of your cycles. Once is all it takes – and you have to think about the possibility of pregnancy. One of our kind, a very long time ago, wrote a book that became known as *The Courtesan's Journal*, and it has been copied by hand over generations, passed down from hand to hand, until all of us know it by heart . . .'

'The first time . . .' Amais began, hoisting herself up on one elbow in bed, her hair falling all around her like a black silk veil. Xuelian smoothed it back again.

'The first time,' she said, 'you were lucky. Think about what might have happened to you if you had walked away carrying his child then.'

'I did think about it,' Amais said reluctantly. 'In the very beginning, I thought about it – but then the soldiers . . . and the constant running . . . and the rain . . .'

'Well,' Xuelian said soothingly, 'at least you have none of those problems now. You're here. You're home. You're safe. But the situation is not much different in its fundamentals. Amais, you are alone. Your mother is gone, your sister is far too young, and even if that wasn't the case she is all but lost to you as a support of any kind – even if you told her who the father of your unborn child was, and perhaps especially not then. You cannot count on your stepfather for much assistance. You know that my House will be here for you if you need us – but you may not want to choose this life.'

Amais roused as if to speak, but Xuelian raised a hand to forestall her. 'No, I talk, you listen. I know very well that it is not the kind of life that many women would voluntarily choose to embrace. It has its pleasures but it also has plenty of drawbacks, and for someone like you . . .' She shook her head slightly. 'You have the looks, but that means very little. You might be sought-after . . . but you have no idea how to protect that inner core of yourself. Look at you now, after *one* . . . You would give too much away with every encounter, and die a little every time.'

'But you . . .'

'You and I are very different,' Xuelian said. 'And besides,

I did not set out on my life's journey in the House of the Silver Moon. I travelled a long road before I got here. I learned survival along the way, and sometimes the price of that knowledge was very high.'

'Xuelian . . .' Amais began, strangely moved by this odd confession. But once again Xuelian stopped her, laying her fingers on Amais's mouth.

'Hush,' she said. 'It is this way. That old courtesan's journal tells us that it is only in the arms of love that you will find the things to remember the things you have to remember, the strength to abandon the things you must forget, and the wisdom to tell these things apart. But sometimes, like I told you, love is not enough – and you have to think about the rest of your life. By yourself.' She thrust a hand into the folds of her robe, into some secret pocket, and came out with a twist of red silk tied with scarlet satin ribbon – that was the way things were in this house, even the smallest things were lush and luxuriant, as though everything was a challenge flung at the austere grey world outside their walls. Xuelian closed one of Amais's hands around the tiny scarlet package. '*Sochuan*,' she said softly. 'It is bitter herbs. But if you want to be sure . . . it is here for you.'

Amais knew very well what *sochuan* was. She stared bleakly at the red package, fighting to get her thoughts and emotions under control.

'If I am not with child, then I'll take it and that will be that,' she whispered. 'But if I am . . . ?'

'There are consequences, of course,' Xuelian said. 'As with everything. We will take care of you, here, until it is over. If that is what you choose.'

Amais looked up, and a single tear overflowed from her eyes and ran down her cheek as she lifted those brimming eyes to Xuelian's face. 'Xuelian,' she whispered, 'there is just this part of me that . . . that *understands* him. That knows him so well.

313

It's like sometimes I think what he's thinking, feel what he is feeling. Like I carry part of his soul within me . . .'

Even as she spoke, she was aware she uttered far deeper truth than she knew. It should not have been possible to know such things this fast, and even Xuelian would have demurred at Amais's sudden certainty that she *did* carry part of Iloh within her, right at that moment . . . but Xuelian was saying something, and Amais struggled to focus, to listen, to sort the liquid syllables into language and meaning.

'Who knows why we are moved to love whom we love?' Xuelian murmured, a wry half-smile on her lips. 'There are those who might say that the Gods are wiser than us mortals, and there are those who think that the Gods are just having their sport with us, a celestial game in which our lives are but pawns on a board . . .'

Amais turned her head away, closing her eyes against tears.

'I do not doubt your *yuan*,' Xuelian said. 'I do not doubt at all that what you have with Iloh is strong, and real. But how can you know that you will *ever* see him again . . . ? What lies between you was strong enough to ensure that you and he were the only people on a cold morning on a country road empty of other souls – but you cannot trust that to happen again, to keep happening. You then have two choices – to throw yourself in its path and *make* it happen, or to turn your back on it for good. You have not said to me what you want to do – but from what I have gathered, from things that you have not said, you will never claim him openly.'

'No,' Amais replied, her hand clenching around the twist of herbs. 'I cannot do that.'

'Then consider the alternatives,' Xuelian said gently. 'Oh, my sweet child. I wish I could give you a softer choice to make . . .'

She had left Amais alone with the *sochuan*. After a long time in which she simply lay back and let herself remember

314

everything, every detail, every texture, scent, sound of Iloh that she had ever been granted, Amais hesitated for a final moment before unwrapping the herbs from the scarlet silk and stirring them into a cup of green tea that had been left beside the bed.

It had been Yingchi who sat with her, after, when the herb started to take effect, when the pain came for her – for it proved that she had indeed been carrying Iloh's child. Yingchi nursed the woman who had been her brother's lover, changing sheets soaked in blood and perspiration, laying cloths of cool water over Amais's brow and holding her hand when the pain twisted her body and the regrets came to haunt her in between breaths drawn harshly through dry and cracked lips – *I was wrong . . . what if I was wrong? . . . ah, what have I done . . . ?*

'I know what it's like,' Yingchi whispered gently, older sister, holding cups of cool water or herbal tea to Amais's lips, smoothing sweat-plastered hair from her face.

'You know?' Amais had whispered back, her eyes dulled with both agony and anguish. 'How could you know?'

'We have all been through it,' Yingchi said. 'In the Street, we all know the bitter taste of *sochuan*.'

Amais recovered in a few days, enough for Xuelian to permit her to go home.

'If anything out of the ordinary happens,' she cautioned, 'anything at all – come back at once. We have healers who know how to deal with this sort of thing. Be well, my child. Come and see me again. Soon.'

So Amais had gone from the House of the Silver Moon, taking her ghosts and her yearnings with her. She tried to keep an ear to the ground, to hear something, anything, about what Iloh had done after he had left her on that country road. But if she had thought that Iloh had returned to the city, she found out she was wrong.

Or at least that was what the rumours seemed to imply, and rumours flew thick and fast. Some sources said that Iloh was still in Linh-an, but that his duties as the chairman of the People's Party were lighter than those he had been expected to shoulder as the leader of Syai's government – and that he had thus retreated from the public eye and was in effect 'retired'. Others said that he was not in fact in the city, but had retreated to a different base of operations, from which he was planning on returning to take his rightful place in the government as soon as circumstances allowed. Still others spoke of his being ill, and that his non-appearance in public meant that he was at death's door, or well on the way to it. Tang turned up several times on the podium in the Emperor's Square during the winter and the following spring, but always alone, or with other high-ranking cadres. Iloh was simply . . . not there.

There weren't even any photographs, not for months. Once the most photographed man in Syai, Iloh seemed to have dropped off the face of the world. Newspapers tried to steer clear of unsubstantiated gossip but they had been printing what they had been told to print by the Party for so long that they essentially said nothing on this subject – because the Party was saying nothing.

Until the day that Iloh, ready at last, chose to break the silence.

The first that the public knew of his return to the halls of power was an almost arbitrary photograph, not even on page one of the daily papers, but tucked away somewhere quietly on page three or four – Iloh, in swimming trunks and wearing a loose robe that hung open to reveal a lean and muscled torso of a man in his physical prime, standing on the banks of the great river that wound from Linh-an down to the sea harbour of Chirinaa. Near its mouth the river was wide, muddy and dangerous – its deep middle channel, fast-flowing and full of deadly eddies and whirlpools, was navigable by the big ships that plied their trade between two of Syai's bigger cities, but nearer to shore it ran to treacherous shifting mud banks and deep, sucking quicksands. It was not a playground, not in any sense at all, but Iloh had chosen it to make a point about his state of mind and body – to prove that he was not by any stretch of the imagination an old revolutionary who had been turned out to pasture and was no longer useful or powerful or dangerous. He had swum across the river at one of its widest, most treacherous points. The picture in the papers was of him after his swim, standing triumphant on the other side. There had been no further caption on the photograph, other than identifying the time and place where it was taken.

Amais had her hands full in her daily life, dealing with her mother's death and the ramifications of the circumstances of it, both in personal and work spheres. There had been fallout from her unsanctioned departure from her work unit, with stern reprimands and even certain sanctions being issued, leaving her in no doubt that if she stepped out of line again there would be a far harsher reckoning with the ultimate sanction, her expulsion from her work unit, not ruled out. In the city, in those days, that meant unemployment – or worse, becoming unemployable. She would starve.

Wrestling with all of that, she hadn't been paying much attention to the newspapers. She would have probably missed the photograph altogether had Aylun not come to the house on the day the newspapers carried the picture, triumphantly waving the papers, folded open to the page on which the image appeared, in her sister's face.

'Look! Shou'min Iloh swam the river!' Aylun declared, thrusting the newspapers at Amais.

Amais took the paper reflexively, and then stood for a moment holding it, gazing at the grainy newspaper picture, running a thumb almost without being aware of her actions across the edge of the photo and brushing the image of Iloh's hand, feeling – just for a moment – warm skin rather than rough, bad quality newsprint paper.

'Indeed,' she murmured, aware that Aylun required some sort of response.

Her attention, however, was focused not so much on Iloh himself – the picture was not a particularly good one, and Amais did not need it to conjure up the man's image in her mind – but on the small knot of people who stood behind and to the right of him, almost out of frame. One of them was a tiny, bird-boned woman with her dark hair pulled starkly back from her face from an uncompromising centre parting, whose features were no more than a blur in the photograph. Amais had never met this woman, had never even seen her – but she knew who it was. The actress who had called herself Songbird, of whom she had first heard Iloh speak in the family cemetery on the country hillside years before. His wife.

Not mine. Not mine . . .

Aylun had babbled happily about Shou'min Iloh and his power and his prowess and how he was coming back to the people, any day now, any day . . . Amais barely listened, except to braid her own thoughts into the possibilities that Aylun raised, weave her own questions into the fabric of unravelling history, and realise that she possessed no answers whatsoever. *You did not come to me*, Iloh had accused, the last time they had met.

Now, her thumb still covering the image of Iloh's hand, she found herself wondering, *And if you come back to Linh-an, do I come to you then? Or is she going to be with you?*

Do I tell you of the child . . . ?

Aylun left, at last, to go back to her compound and share her excitement and enthusiasm with a more receptive audience. There had been no gushing paean of praise attached to the photograph, it had been left to stand pretty much without any editorial comment at all, but its very existence, and what it signified, spoke for itself. Syai responded by a renewed surge of adoration for its Shou'min Iloh. All Tang's initiatives and reforms were suddenly rendered irrelevant and ridiculous. He was not, could not be, Shou'min Iloh. And Iloh now drove that point home, by returning to Linh-an in a very public fashion and calling for a People's Party Congress.

The results of that meeting were all over the city in a matter of days. A document of five points, a revolutionary manifesto, a clear signpost to the road ahead.

1. *It is necessary to clear away the old before the new can be achieved. The outlook of the whole society must be changed – education, art, literature, anything that does not correspond to our new order. Let the winds of change blow, let it clear away the cobwebs of old ideas, old culture, old customs and habits! Let not old and outdated ideas in philosophy, history or political science hold sway in your hearts and minds. Reactionary views and those who hold them should be strongly criticised!*

2. *We are all the people – workers, students, soldiers, revolutionary thinkers. All must unite. The revolutionary youth must become courageous fighters against the inevitable resistance to the revolution. Remember, there will be obstacles in our path – but they are there to temper our ideas and strengthen our resolve!*

3. *Let the people learn how to draw a line between enemy and friend – for sometimes an enemy is*

closer to their hearts than they believe and a friend may be one who speaks against them and in whose words they can then find vindication of their own ideas! Let the line of the Party be followed, and let none steer you away from that path – even though the other road might look smooth and easy and your road may be strewn with thorns and stones!

4. *It is normal and fitting that people should hold different views – but a difference of opinion with a friend is different from that with an enemy. Within the ranks of the people themselves there will always be those who hold opinions that are wrong, but unless someone has become irredeemable they should always be given the opportunity to learn from their mistakes. And even those whom you think are beyond deliverance should be given the same chance.*

5. *Remember that in all things it is necessary to grasp both revolution and production. They are twin hammers, one for each hand. We will use our revolutionary ideas to achieve better, faster, grander results in every field of human endeavour! Stand with both feet on the ground, let not thoughts of anything greater than us prevent us from becoming all that we can be – that we were born to be. Let Shou'min Iloh's Golden Words be our guide in all that we do!*

It took only another week or so before the storm gathered by those fighting words broke upon the city.

Two

It took a single night – but it was a night during which many hands must have worked themselves raw in order to achieve what Shou'min Iloh's manifesto said needed to be done. Linh-an had already known its fair share of posters and huge photographs of Shou'min Iloh, which adorned any building with space enough to support one – these were workaday, familiar. But overnight another kind of poster bloomed throughout the city. Written in crude, hasty calligraphy on enormous sheets of paper, they were plastered on every wall, every pole, every conceivable surface. Initially they were just reiterations and rephrasings of the five-point manifesto from the Party Congress – they screamed things like:

TO REBEL IS GOOD!
DRAW A LINE BETWEEN YOU AND YOUR ENEMIES!
CRITICISE REACTIONARY VIEWS AND THE PEOPLE WHO HOLD THEM!
LET THE WINDS OF CHANGE BLOW AWAY OLD IDEAS, OLD CULTURE, OLD CUSTOMS!

SHOU'MIN ILOH'S GOLDEN WORDS ARE OUR GUIDE!

They were particularly plentiful in the university district, where students had taken it upon themselves to suspend classes – until such time, one young girl told Amais passionately as Amais hesitated at the doors of the library in the morning, new things could be taught in a proper way.

'We need to educate the teachers,' the girl said, 'before they are allowed to educate us! We *are* the Wind of Change!'

That was the first time Amais had heard the name. The Wind of Change. Those who named themselves thus quickly changed it into something subtly different, something that combined the idea of that wind with their devotion to Shou'min Iloh and his ideas. Before the day was out the youth had adopted another banner, the Golden Wind. The next day's posters were all signed with that name.

It might have petered out if the students had been given no overt support, but another poster appeared on the walls of Linh-an on the morning of the third day, and it was signed '*Shou'min Iloh*'. Its wording and tone was not cast in the form of a command – but with that signature below it, it instantly became one – a single sentence, interpreted and misinterpreted in a hundred different ways within the first hour of its appearance, pouring oil onto the flames: *Attack the core.*

It was a blessing laid on what the students had started. A vindication. A rallying cry, and a pointing finger giving them direction and purpose.

Amais found it hard to sleep, her whole being attuned to noises in the night, wondering what kind of posters, what kind of protests, would be on the streets the next day. She knew that Iloh was savvy enough to know what those few words of his would do to the situation – and she found herself recalling his earnest voice, back by the side of that country road many weeks ago: '*I know now what I need to do. I need to do it. Remember that, if you find it hard to forgive me.*'

Units of the Golden Wind began springing up everywhere, like poisonous mushrooms; and it quickly became obvious that Iloh's dream of all his people being equal *was* just a dream. Social class had always mattered in Syai, but those boundaries were supposedly one of the things that the revolution had been intent on erasing. However, in the new and zealously revolutionary hierarchies, class now became paramount – a different kind of class, to be sure, but one that ruled society with every bit of the iron hand that the old Imperial strata had used in their day. A prospective member of any of the Golden Wind units had to show an impeccable political pedigree – a pure bloodline, descended from one of the so-called Golden Lines, the offspring of peasants, workers, martyrs of the revolution or revolutionary officials. Those who sprang from the loins of parents from Grey Lines – secretaries and clerks, shop assistants – would be considered, on merit, for 'promotion' into the more desirable ranks. But if one's parents ranked somewhere in the Black Lines – landlords or land-owners, counterrevolutionaries (and that meant anything and everything, including expressing discontent with the price of eggs in the market on any given day), former aristocracy and other miscellaneous 'bad elements' – one was effectively branded, removed from the circle of the blessed, deemed unsuitable to be one of the defenders of Iloh's *Golden Words*.

Amais was on the cusp, just too old to be part of the student movement on campus, to be in the thick of things – the main thrust of the movement appeared to centre on children still in school and the younger university students – but Aylun, who had turned thirteen that spring, found that the years she had put into the system as a devoted disciple of

323

The Golden Words suddenly counted for nothing in the light of the fact of her parentage. Aylun's mother was not only the offspring of an Imperial prince of the blood – something established beyond doubt in Vien's criticism sessions at her work unit – but Vien had been tried as a counterrevolutionary, a reactionary, a rightist, and she had been convicted of that crime, punished for it, she had even died in the correctional camp to which her sentence had sent her. And Aylun herself, to exacerbate matters, was foreign-born. When she stepped up to ask to join the Golden Wind, full of fire and fervour for her cause, the senior officers in her unit suddenly turned icy and dismissed her as unfit.

Devastated, she crept back to Amais and sat dry-eyed and shivering in the middle of the cramped living room of the quarters that Amais and her stepfather still shared.

'It isn't the end of the world,' Amais said to her little sister. 'Before this is over, it is quite possible that *not* having been a part of it will be . . .'

'You don't understand,' Aylun replied bleakly. 'I want to live my life in the service of the people, just like Shou'min Iloh said. I have always wanted that, just that. It isn't fair . . . If I could renounce my father and the tainted blood in my veins, I would . . .'

'Never say that again!' Amais rebuked her sister, her voice sharp. 'You never even knew him. He is worth eight times what you are sitting here whining after. He was brave and true-hearted, and he loved us.'

'What use is that?' Aylun asked, staring at her. 'He's gone, and we're here, and what matters *here*, now, is impossible because he existed. I want to give my whole life to Shou'min Iloh, and he won't have me . . .'

Amais flinched as though she had been struck. *I need to do this. Remember that, if you find it hard to forgive me* . . . His voice, in her ear. His hands warm on her skin.

His words, his ideas, wrapping Aylun into a cloud of ideological fury.

Yes, she was struggling to forgive this.

'Perhaps,' Amais murmured, 'you misinterpreted his words . . .'

Aylun reacted as though that was purest heresy, told Amais tartly once again that she did not, *could* not, understand, and left to find a more receptive audience for her grief.

In the meantime, the Golden Wind had done its own interpretation of Iloh's words, and was starting to put them into action. Groups of them roamed the streets of Linh-an, acting on informants' tip-offs, and would smash into the houses of people accused of having counterrevolutionary ideas or active ties to anti-Iloh factions. Whether or not any of these accusations were true was rendered increasingly irrelevant as the Golden Wind took on the responsibility of annihilating those four old things that Iloh had decried – old ideas, old culture, old customs, old habits. They were to die, and they were to die hard.

Amais just heard of this, at first, from whispered conversations, from frantic warnings passed between people in hushed whispers or scribbled notes passed from hand to hand in corridors or streets. People would be dragged out of their houses, sometimes out of bed in the middle of the night. Everything that had a connection to the history or culture of Syai – books, letters, statues, paintings, clothes that had an ounce of silk or a thread of embroidery on them – was hauled out and piled into triumphant mounds of 'evidence' for crimes that, if they had not actually been committed or were impossible to prove, were taken as being inevitable and simply treated as though they were already history. Often people's belongings were confiscated outright and packed up into boxes or crates that would be sealed and then left in the compound – and woe to the original owners if the seal was shown to be tampered with when a member of the Golden Wind came back to check on it. Sometimes the 'evidence' was taken in to be 'processed' somewhere, but often it would simply be left in a pile, doused with something flammable, and torched.

In a way it was like those ancient funerals of old Syai, where all the paraphernalia of the deceased would be burned with the body in the same funeral pyre for his or her use in Cahan in the hereafter. In their zeal to destroy everything old, the Golden Wind was using one of the oldest customs of all.

But all of that was just hearsay, rumour, the chatter of frightened women in the marketplace. It was different when it struck close to home.

The first time it was a family who lived next door to Amais. She had known them for years, and their only possible crime was that they owned two of the housing units in that block, and most of their income, their bread and butter, came from renting out the second unit to another family. It had been that very family who had denounced them, their tenants – Amais knew them, too, and could see some of them peering around corners as their landlords were hauled out into the courtyard by three or four Golden Wind cadres.

'Decadent lifestyle!' one of their captors jeered, holding up a white silk robe.

'It was a mourning robe for my grandmother,' the wife of the targeted family said hopelessly, her eyes cast down.

One of the Golden Wind backhanded her across the face, hard enough to snap her head back on her neck. 'Quiet, you.'

'And this,' the original cataloguer of 'evidence' was saying, weighing a handful of books in both hands. 'All of this. Look at it! Just look at it!'

'Please,' the husband began, rousing, and then cringed as

a blow was aimed at him, too. It never landed, and the youth who was holding him laughed, the laugh loud and ugly in the night.

'Not just a counterrevolutionary, but a cowardly dog of a one, too,' the youth jeered. 'Look at him cringing there at my feet!'

'And what are these?' the first youth asked, flipping through a different book.

'It's my journal,' said the daughter of the old couple, her voice the texture of cold ashes.

The youth snorted, throwing the journal carelessly onto the heap of other belongings already at his feet.

Amais felt a cold wind of terror blow through her. *Journals*. Tai's precious journals, which had survived so much for so long. Would this be their fate, too . . . ?

There were four of them there, the two old people, their widowed daughter, and the daughter's daughter, a child about Aylun's age. The granddaughter wore her hair in two long pigtails, tied up with a length of ribbon. When the Golden Wind people had finally had enough of torturing the family in that unit and put the mound of their belongings to the match, one of the other Golden Wind cadres, a young girl herself, grabbed hold of the child's braids and severed them close to her head with a single sweep of a sharp serrated knife.

'This is an imperialist hairstyle,' the Golden Wind girl said severely. 'It is not permitted any more!'

She tossed the hair into the burning pyre, and the young granddaughter's heartbroken wail tore through Amais's heart like a dagger.

Amais spent a couple of sleepless nights trying to decide what to do with Tai's journals, where a safe place could be found for them – if a safe place even existed in the madness of those days. And then, a few days later, she saw Lixao standing in their quarters, his hands helplessly hanging at his sides, his head bowed.

'It is my turn,' he said to Amais when she came into the room.

'What do you mean, it's your turn? Your turn for what?'

'They needed to find someone to blame.'

'To blame for what?'

He simply shrugged. 'I have had to write criticism after criticism,' Lixao said, 'pointing out all the bad things I have done, that I have thought. I even admitted that my marriage to your mother was a mistake. But nothing would satisfy them. My final criticism session . . . my trial . . . is tonight. Please don't come.'

Amais suddenly felt a surge of quite unexpected affection for this man, who had outlived his time in much the same way that Vien had done. The only difference was that he had been better at hiding it.

'Would it help if I was there?' she asked gently.

'I wouldn't want you . . . to see . . .' He cleared his throat. 'The truth is, they asked me to draw a line between myself and her family. Vien's children. If you were there . . .'

'Do I need to leave your house?' Amais asked.

'I don't think that would matter any more,' Lixao replied. 'It's tonight. Don't come.'

But Amais did go. She herself did not know why – she felt as though she owed it to herself, to her mother. Owed a debt – she had to go, to do something . . . but in the end, she did nothing, only sitting in the back of the room, a quiet witness with tears pouring down her cheeks as the young people put her stepfather through a chain of indignities and then through pain. They shaved his head, and then poured ink down his pitiful bald pate until it ran down his face and dripped off his chin giving him the theatrical visage of a traditional opera demon. They made him kneel on his ancient creaky knees, reach out behind his back until he could grab hold of one wrist with the fingers of his other hand, and hold out his arms as high as he could over his back, twisting his shoulders, trembling with no support as he knelt there – and if he wavered or lurched they said that the time he had already spent in the position 'did not count' and he had to start over. They took his glasses and made him smash them and grind them to dust with the heel of his foot. They made him stand on one leg like a heron, stripped down to a loincloth, his saggy old body bared to the laughing world. And then they took him away, after hours of this, and another man was brought out in his place.

Amais did not know if she would ever see him again.

A week after Lixao's 'trial', another big rally was called for the Emperor's Square – a Golden Wind rally, called by Iloh himself. Amais, despite herself, went – standing on the outskirts, too far away to even see the podium, but driven to be present, to be there, to bear witness.

'The Golden Wind is the flower of the revolution!' she heard Iloh's voice say over the microphone, floating above the heads of the cheering crowds. 'I am here today to tell you so! I am here to tell you – to show you – that I wear your colours proudly!'

A roar swept the crowd. Amais could not see, but the word came back like quicksilver through the ranks until it reached the outer edges of the crowd. 'Did you see? Did you see? He wore the yellow armband – Shou'min Iloh wore the yellow armband – he said he was one of us – one of the Golden Wind!'

Numbed with foreboding, Amais returned home from the rally to find two notes left for her while she was gone: one in her sister's hand, tucked in between the door and the door-jamb, and the other slipped under the door and lying, sealed

329

and addressed in an unfamiliar hand, just inside the entrance. Amais opened Aylun's first.

'*They accepted me tonight, there on the square!*' The note had a breathless quality, as though Aylun had scribbled it in a rush, probably on the way to some important meeting. '*I am to join one of the units of Shou'min Iloh's Thought Guard. It isn't the Golden Wind but it's the next circle. Goodbye – Aylun.*' It was in *hacha-ashu*, written with what looked like it must have been a pencil stub that badly needed sharpening, little of grace or style in it, only the essential, only the news. *Baya*-Dan would have wept at the sight of it.

The second note was unsigned, but written in a hurried although nevertheless still graceful *jin-ashu* script.

'*They are coming for you,*' it said, '*tomorrow. Be warned.*'

Three

Amais was to remember with some envy some of the letters she had received from Youmei – oh, for a pen where pigs once used to be kept, already dug up and riven, the perfect hiding place for an old cooking pot! But she lived in the city, and there were no pigpens here, no convenient hiding places for treasure about to be burned on the altars of 'progress' and revolution. Tai's journals, which had survived four hundred years of history and exile and strife, were never in such peril as this.

But taking the time to think about the problem of those journals – to figure out how to keep them safe, somewhere where they could not come to harm, and doing it before, as the cryptic second note said, the Golden Wind 'came for her' – was time torn from the problem of Aylun, and what her sister could be moulded into becoming. Amais had already seen the results of Golden Wind raids. The idea of Aylun being involved in something like that, of Aylun being the girl who had it in her to shear off the braids of a child and immolate them on a pyre before that child's own eyes, of Aylun's being the hand that would toss her own ancestress's journals into that same pyre, burned Amais's soul like acid. But she

331

had no idea where to even begin looking for Aylun – and she knew it would tear her heart out if she were forced to watch the destruction of those journals she had carried back to Syai across the oceans of exile.

She did think, briefly, of running – she was no more than human, after all, and she had seen enough of the handiwork of the Golden Wind to be afraid. *I could take the journals and go – somewhere safe, somewhere they will never find me, where they can't touch me* . . . But there were the ghosts of Lixao and Vien, who did not run. Could not run. And then there was Aylun, whom she could not abandon. Not yet.

I could go to Iloh . . .

Iloh could protect her. But what would the price of that be? She would owe a life of debt, she would never be free again, not to think her own thoughts, not to pursue her own dreams. He might never put her in a physical cage, but if she asked him for protection she would be in a cage nonetheless – a songbird in a cage, where her spirit would die slowly, a day at a time.

No. Not that. Whatever Iloh was to her, it was not a benevolently tyrannical protector. They had nothing on her, really – *nothing*. It was not for herself that she feared, but for her legacy, for that which she had dreamed of trying to win back, to protect, to cherish. Something of which Tai's journals were only a symbol – but, for Amais, a potent one, an irreplaceable one.

So. That first. Make sure the journals are safe – in the night, while the darkness was still her friend. In the morning, Aylun.

She wrapped the books in a length of yellow silk, not unaware of the irony of wrapping her treasure in the colours of The Golden Rising from which she was trying to save it, and then a layer of waterproof material, and then the whole package went into a canvas sack and another waterproof

332

layer around that. It still felt inadequate for what the packaging enclosed, but it would have to do – and if she had to return to her cache later and amend her arrangements, then so be it.

She slipped out of her apartments in the dead of night, scurrying from shadow to shadow in the street like a thief, scouring her environment for a place where the journals would be safe – at least temporarily safe, taken from the reach of those who might harm them. Nothing obvious presented itself. Amais was frustrated, frightened, aware that time was slipping away. Perhaps it was a combination of all those things that made her careless in the end.

To her credit, she hardly expected to meet another person on the streets this late – unless, of course, it was members of the Golden Wind out with a new set of posters and banners to drape the city walls with. But those, the noisy, busy people who were not out to hide themselves or their work, she would have noticed, would have known of their presence, would have given them a wide berth. Another scurrying shadow like herself, out, perhaps, on a similar errand and just as intent on passing unseen as she herself was, proved to be another matter. They practically ran each other down at a corner of an empty midnight street, colliding with a force that spun Amais back against the wall of the house behind her and sent the other staggering into the road flailing for balance.

They froze, then, both of them, holding their breath.

'I am not Golden Wind,' the other shadow spoke, breaking the silence first. It was a male voice. Not old.

'I am not either,' Amais replied, some part of her aware of the incongruity of this meeting, of this conversation. She knew that she should be running for her life, for the life of the things that she carried – but something held her, held them both. They were co-conspirators, out on clandestine missions. This was the trust between thieves, knowing that they had it in their power to betray each other if either said or did anything that might be taken as endangering their respective tasks.

In the silence of the night, the only sound was their breathing . . . and then there was something else, a murmur of conversation, raised voices. Amais instinctively shrank back into the shadows, discovered that there was an archway behind her, and in it an unlocked door that opened to her touch and which gave into a quiet courtyard. She reached a decision in an instant.

'Quickly! Over here!' she hissed at her companion.

He hesitated, but only for a moment; the voices were getting closer. Amais heard him draw in his breath sharply and then he took the few steps between them and flattened himself into the concealing shadows beside her. Amais closed the outer courtyard door behind them very quietly. They waited there, side by side, tense, aware that the door was their protection and their worst liability both, hiding them from the sight of whoever it had been in the street but also hiding those people from the two of them. Amais and her companion had no idea whether the voices they had heard belonged to people aiming for this very courtyard, which meant certain discovery . . . and very unpleasant consequences.

The voices did come closer, and soon they could hear actual footsteps, people approaching.

'Oh, Cahan!' Amais's companion murmured despairingly.

She did not trust herself to make a sound. She merely reached out and covered his mouth with her fingers, an oddly intimate thing to do to a stranger – but it was that or risk discovery.

The indistinct mix of voices resolved into several muffled but distinct ones, and it was possible to snatch at a passing conversation.

'. . . leave that one there,' a young woman was saying,

'and then we have four more to do in the next street. Come on, hurry up – we are meeting with Huiyan's group . . .'

'. . . the photo – leave the photo – it will be good right there . . .'

Someone tried the door behind which the two fugitives crouched, but Amais had her entire body weight pressed against it, holding it closed.

'That'll do,' a young male voice said, after some scratching noises on the outside of the door, and a rustle of paper, and then a muffled fastening of packs, more indistinct conversation; then footsteps, fading away.

For a long time neither Amais nor her companion moved at all, and then Amais allowed her body to relax and sag away from the door, letting herself gulp a long breath of air.

'That was fast thinking,' the young man said in a low voice. 'Are they gone?'

'I don't know. I think so.'

'My turn, then. Let me look.'

He pushed past her, found the door handle, pressed it lightly. There was a slight resistance to the opening of the door, and then a soft sound of ripping paper. They both froze again, the door ajar, but there was no further noise and the young man furtively eased the door open a little more. It gave without any further resistance at all.

The street was empty.

And then Amais realised what the tearing sound had been and made a small sound of dismay.

'Oh, for the love of Cahan,' she said softly, covering her face with her hand. 'We might have brought death into this place . . .'

He looked, too.

The passing poster-pasters of the Golden Wind had stuck a portrait of Shou'min Iloh on the door of the courtyard in which the two fugitives had been hiding. Unfortunately they had pasted the picture right across the middle of the door, and opening it had ripped the portrait precisely in half. Defacing pictures of Shou'min Iloh was a punishable offence. If this one was left here like this – with his face shredded – there would be trouble – but if the two of them took it down, the people in the courtyard beyond might be accused of removing the picture if any one of the group who had placed it here happened to pass by and notice it was missing.

'They could not know the door would be opened,' said the young man.

'Or they meant to seal this place,' Amais said. 'If they knew there was a portrait across their door nobody would dare open it, for fear that exactly this would happen . . .'

'Take it,' he said, stripping off the half-portrait on his side of the door with swift, economical motions. 'It can't be worse to take it than to leave it here like this.'

He was right, and Amais made short work of removing the remnant of the picture from her own side of the door. There was barely enough light to make out the features on the photograph, but Amais felt Iloh's remaining eye fix her with a gimlet stare, almost accusing.

'Give it to me,' her companion-in-crime said, holding out his hand. 'I'll take care of it.'

'We never met?' she said, the sentence a question.

'That would probably be for the best.'

'Do you know,' Amais said, taking a risk, but desperate enough for that, 'of a safe hiding place?'

He turned his head towards her sharply. He was wearing a hood that hid his face in shadow, but from within it his eyes glinted oddly as he looked at her. 'For you or something precious?' he asked softly. 'Is that what you are doing out here at this hour?' And then he lifted a hand in a swift motion, forestalling her reply. 'No, don't tell me. It's best I don't know, I guess. It's odd, though . . . I was looking for a hiding place myself. Perhaps we could hide each other's treasures. They might not find things if they were hidden in places they might not think to look.'

She stared at him, astonished. It made a perfect, twisted kind of sense when she thought it through – *let a stranger hide something you deem precious and those who might be looking for that thing which you treasure would only look in places where they thought* you *might hide it. It might be in plain sight in someone else's house but because it was not sought there it would not be found . . .*

'What is it,' she said carefully, 'that you are trying to hide?'

'Don't be afraid,' he said, an apparent non-sequitur until he pulled a long blade carved with *hacha-ashu* symbols from a scabbard secured to his back. Amais gasped anyway, took an inadvertent step back. 'No, don't be afraid. This is my treasure. My great-grandfather's sword. He was in the Imperial Guard once, when they still had an Imperial Guard, and the sword has been passed down from him to his son, and then to his son, and then to me. I cannot bear the thought of it being dishonoured in any way – not this, with so much honour upon it. I know they will take it if they come, the Golden Wind. But there are very few places you can hide a sword . . .'

On impulse, Amais held out her own package. 'My many-times-great-grandmother's journals,' she said. 'Four hundred years old. Doomed by simply being what they are – old ideas, old customs, an historical relic written in the language that no woman in Syai seems to speak any more . . .' She was surprised to find tears spring to her eyes. 'She was Kito-Tai. The poet . . .'

'They are in *jin-ashu*?' he asked.

Surprised, Amais nodded, and then realised he could barely see her in the dark. 'Yes. Yes, they are.'

'Then they would be safe from my prying eyes,' he said. 'I will make you a deal. Take the sword, I will take the books.

337

When this is over, and if we both live to see the day, we will return the treasures of our families. Until then, they are safer where strangers do not know to look for them.'

She hesitated for a very long moment, and then nodded. 'That is wise.'

He fumbled with the scabbard, let it down from his back, slid the sword back into it with a hiss of metal against tooled leather, and then offered it to her – freely, but with a reluctance she could plainly sense because she shared it, because it was present in the way her own hands clung to the precious journals she was entrusting to a stranger she did not even know the name of.

As though her thought had leaped straight into his head, he relinquished the sword, grasped her package of notebooks firmly, and pushed back the cowl of his hood.

'I am Xuan,' he said. 'I live in Siqaluan Street, at the back of the Temple. It is the house with the blue roof.'

She pushed back her own concealing scarf. 'I am Amais. Lichan Street, by the university.'

They stared at each other, their features indistinct in the dim street-lighting but instantly memorable in that moment. And then he lifted his free hand in farewell.

'Until we meet again, then,' he said, 'Amais.'

He turned, and let the shadows of the street swallow him. Amais watched him go, motionless, holding the Imperial sword with both hands.

There was a *yuan* in this too – fate – a meeting meant to be. It was not the fire from the heart of a sun that had burned in the hour of her first meeting with Iloh – but it was something, nonetheless, a quiet wash of starlight, an odd sense of living a memory of a love yet to come.

Cradling the sword against her body, Amais turned and retraced her steps, back through the empty streets of Linhan in the night.

338

Four

Amais did not go home after her midnight rendezvous, after all. Walking back to the rooms she shared with her step-father – who was now gone – she was seized by the same fear that had gripped her before. *What if they do come? And they tear the place apart? Where am I supposed to hide a sword that they won't find it? It is not a needle! And it is not mine to lose. I must find a safe place – a place they would never think of looking for a sword . . .*

In the end, the choice was obvious, but when she detoured via the back-streets until she found her way to what she knew as the Street of Red Lanterns it was with a sense of real shock that she halted and stared at the place where the street name had been scoured away with a dagger and a new name daubed onto the wall with sloppy calligraphy, presumably until such time as a more permanent marker could be installed – *the Street of the Rising Sun of the Revolution.*

'Ah, *Cahan* . . .' Amais breathed. 'Am I too late . . . ?'

But nothing else appeared to have changed in the quiet street – yet – unless the quietness of it was a change, at this time of day, during the hours of darkness in which it usually came alive plying its trade. There were lights in the houses, but the doors were closed, not open as they customarily were; the lights spilled almost shyly, from half-shuttered windows, from chinks in drawn drapes. The Street of Red Lanterns had turned furtive, afraid, the glittering courtesan turned back into the basest incarnation of her art, the street harlot pulling a concealing hood over her face even as she beckoned into the shadows.

Amais made her way carefully down the sidewalk. She saw muffled figures slipping in and out of various houses, but they kept their heads down and their footsteps quick and light, and if they had to pass anywhere close to her they averted their faces, instinctively, just as she averted hers. She might have been worried that somebody would notice that she was armed, in a manner of speaking, and raise the alarm – but tonight all that mattered was anonymity and obscurity.

The side door of the House of the Silver Moon was locked, unusually, which as and of itself was enough to give Amais a bad feeling – but the lacquered red main door that gave onto the street was ajar, just a little. A thin sliver of light lined it along one side. Muffling her sword as best she could in her wrap, Amais crept to the door and pushed it open just wide enough for her to slip through, restoring it to its previous condition behind her.

Candles burned in the reception room as usual, and there were two couples engaged in whispered conversations in shadowed corners. A slightly unsteady customer, apparently a little too deep into his cups, suddenly lurched up from a seat. Amais, who had taken him for a pile of robes carelessly dumped on the chair, stifled a small cry as he staggered towards her, both arms outstretched.

'Ah! Beauty!' he slurred, his eyes unfocused and a little crossed. 'Come to me! I've been waiting for you all night!'

Another form, slighter, steadier, sheathed in a body-hugging blue silk gown slit to the thigh, intercepted him before he could grab hold of Amais. One of Xuelian's girls; they all knew Amais by sight.

'Over here, my sweet one, you've been promised tonight,' she murmured. She glanced over her shoulder at where Amais still stood rooted to the spot, and then made a swift, economical little gesture with her head in the direction of the stairs. 'Up,' she hissed, 'quickly, before someone else assumes the wrong thing. It's a bit late for you to be here, isn't it?'

'Is she awake?' Amais asked, breaking stasis and taking long, urgent strides towards the stairs.

'Is she ever asleep?' the other girl responded softly as she allowed her male companion to subside back onto his seat. 'Go. Quick.'

Amais took the stairs two at a time and gave only the most perfunctory of knocks on Xuelian's door before she pushed it open and slipped into the old courtesan's room.

Xuelian, sitting at her make-up table, turned her head a regal fraction.

'Is it day?' she inquired, with a touch of theatrical surprise.

'You know it is not,' Amais said.

'You are not a guest in this house at this hour, usually, Amais-*ban*.'

'I have,' Amais explained, 'a favour to ask of you . . .'

The story came tumbling out, in all its strangeness – Aylun's note, the *jin-ashu* warning, the helpless terror of what might happen to the things that Amais considered her most precious treasures, the rush into the Linh-an night in search of a hiding place, the strange meeting with the young man bearing a sword. And the need to have the sword hidden.

'I have questions,' Xuelian said.

'There seems to be very little time for them,' Amais replied. 'Did you know they renamed the Street tonight?'

'Child,' Xuelian said, 'the fact that they scrawled a

341

different name on an arbitrary wall means nothing. It is not in the power of the Golden Wind to rename *this* street. You will see. As for time . . . time is what we make of it. As I said, I have questions. Why did you not simply bring the journals here in the first place if you thought they needed a safe sanctuary?'

'Because they are . . .' Amais began, and then stopped. She had no real idea, at that. It had seemed to her that she needed to hide the journals somewhere . . . somewhere *else*, somewhere *other*, somewhere that had no connection with her life, a place where nobody would ever think of looking for them. And besides . . . there was . . .

Amais looked up, met Xuelian's eyes. 'They were *jin-ashu*,' she said. 'If they came here and searched *this* place, they would be looking for women's things. It was not safe. Not for them, not here, where I knew the last roots of *jin-shei* lived – where everything could be destroyed at once, when they . . . when . . .'

She suddenly realised that she spoke of certainties – that she had switched from *if* to *when*, that she knew the Golden Wind were coming, that time was running out.

'You did not think,' Xuelian said, 'that they would look for a sword in a house of pleasure.'

Amais stared at her mutely. Instinct had brought her here, now; as to why the same instinct had not driven her to the same place before, with the other treasure, she could only guess at.

'All right, you may be right, at that,' Xuelian relented. 'Give me the sword.'

Amais fumbled with the unwieldy thing, handed it to Xuelian hilt first. She opened her mouth to speak as Xuelian drew the blade out of the scabbard – not all the way, just a little, enough for candlelight to glitter on the flat of it.

'Old,' she said, inspecting the blade with an educated eye.

'Valuable. Even without the legacy of which you speak. Very well, I will have it hidden under the floor of the cellar of this house. But that brings me to my sharpest question. What are you thinking of doing next?'

'What do you mean?'

'An anonymous warning told you that they were coming for you – and you plan on doing what? Going back to your quarters and waiting for them like a sacrificial lamb?'

'I have to go and find Aylun,' Amais whispered.

'No,' Xuelian said, with infinite gentleness, infinite sadness, 'you don't.'

'What? Why? What do you know?'

'I know of what happened tonight, while you were out in the streets of the city trying to find a place to hide your treasure,' Xuelian began, and her eyes were suddenly full of tears. 'These "special units" – the outsiders – the ones to whom your sister has chosen to belong – they were given a choice tonight. They were given a chance to prove their loyalty, to do a task that nobody else wanted to sully their hands with – and if they did that then they would be pure again, ready to be Golden Wind, to belong fully and completely and without question.'

Amais felt as though a fist had suddenly been driven into her solar plexus. She found it hard to breathe, and took a couple of shaky steps backwards to collapse into the nearest chair. 'What happened?' she asked, through suddenly bloodless lips.

'They sent them in,' Xuelian said, turning her head away marginally so that her aristocratic profile was turned to Amais, 'to kill the emperor and his family. They thought a signal needed to be sent, the point made that there would be no going back, no return. Tang had the family brought back to the city – back from the years of comfortable exile, out in the country house – Cahan knows what his plans for them were. But they were here, now, tonight . . . helpless. And Iloh seized the chance.'

'Iloh would not have . . .' Amais began.

Xuelian shook her head, a tiny gesture, barely noticeable, but it was enough to make Amais bite down on whatever she had been about to say.

'Iloh, or Iloh's minions,' Xuelian said. 'It did not have to be his hand, it was his word. The rest is semantics. The important thing is . . . they are dead. All of them, all the Imperial family. At the hands of the outsiders whose job it was to prove their loyalty to the cause before they could be considered good enough to join the ranks of the true revolutionaries. Your sister was among them.'

'How can you know that?' Amais whispered, holding both hands against her stomach as though it hurt there, as though she had been stabbed and was trying to keep the life from oozing out of her.

Xuelian lifted a piece of paper from her desk, let it flutter back down. 'I had word,' she said. 'I still had friends in that family. Did I ever tell you that she sent for me again, the empress who gave me away – she sent for me, years later, when her son was twelve years old, so that I could be his first, so that I could initiate him into the way of a woman's body? I, his father's concubine. She thought it would be . . . wise. I already belonged to them, after all.'

'And you did it?' Amais asked, her own eyes suddenly brimming with tears.

'She commanded. She was my empress. And that little boy . . . was my emperor's blood,' Xuelian said.

There was a pounding in Amais's temples, as though twin anvils had been set up there and a pair of blacksmiths were in full swing. 'Oh, Cahan, what a night,' she said despairingly.

'So,' Xuelian continued, turning back to her protégée. 'I repeat my question. What do you intend to do next?'

344

'I did not think that far,' Amais admitted.

'For what it is worth, here is my advice – do not let the sunrise find you in your house. If the warning was true, you are damned in their eyes in too many ways to count. You are foreign-born, your mother was found guilty of sufficient crimes to die in a reform camp, you have no idea what happened to your stepfather who was also accused, and for all I know they may be aware of your visits here and use that against you in any number of ways. Go to ground, until the madness passes. Unless you can get your Iloh to . . .'

'No,' Amais said.

Xuelian raised an eloquent eyebrow.

'No,' Amais repeated. 'I already considered that. I can't do it. It would be a death of a different kind.'

'Ah,' Xuelian said softly.

There was a silence, a heavy sense of time passing, too swift, too slow, quicksilver and molasses all at the same time, and they caught upon its flow like flotsam, unable to find anchor or peace.

Xuelian sighed at last, and reached out to pat Amais on the cheek tenderly as though she were a child.

'Then I cannot advise further,' she said. 'I will keep the sword safe.'

It was a sort of dismissal, gentle but nonetheless perfectly firm. Xuelian had work of her own to do before the night was over.

On impulse, Amais leaned over and hugged the old woman, wrapping both arms around her, leaning her cheek against Xuelian's shoulder – held her for a brief but eloquent moment – let go, stood up, smoothed down the legs of her cotton trousers.

'What was that for?' Xuelian asked, patting her carefully dressed hair back into place as though annoyed, but her eyes were bright under the lowered lashes.

'Good night, *baya*-Xuelian,' Amais said.

'Oh, get on with you, I am nobody's grandmother,' Xuelian replied. 'Child . . . stay safe. However you choose to do that. Find shelter from this Wind.' She groped on the make-up table with one hand until it closed – with a painful instinct, with a need – on the kingfisher comb that lay there. The last link with a man who died that night, whose entire seed was now ghost and memory.

She was there, with him, in that memory – in happier times. Not here. Not now. Not waiting for the axe to fall.

Amais backed out of the room quietly, so as not to disturb her, leaving her the solace of that dream – for however long she could still hold on to it.

She managed to get out of the House without further mishap with any of its clientele, and slipped into the Street. Hesitating for a moment in a deep shadow by the House, she weighed her options. Xuelian might have been right: if Amais's visits to this place had been noted it might be inviting further disaster if she were observed here tonight, especially in the light of the treasure she had left for the House to guard. But the shortest way home lay down the Street, and then across the mercantile quarter, back into the university neighbourhood. If she went the other way out of the Street, she would only be treading deeper into the warrens – where the Beggars' Guild still held sway, where danger lurked even without the chance of a stray Golden Wind cadre stepping in her path. The hesitation was brief, and she turned into the Street, hurrying past brooding Houses, aware that the sky was starting to lighten, however imperceptibly, in the eastern sky above the rooftops.

But there was something different about the Street than when she had come here not so long ago. Then it had been full of furtive silence, of waiting, of tense expectation. But that was then. It seemed, during her brief visit to the House

346

of the Silver Moon, that the waiting had come to an end.

At the far end of the street, between her and safety, Amais could see lights and commotion. There were shouts, screams, scuffles – people spilled on the front steps of houses and in the road, some dressed in the bright colours of the courtesans, others dressed in the drab grey or blue of uniforms.

With yellow bands on their sleeves.

'Oh no,' Amais whispered, freezing into immobility behind a set of steps leading into a nearby House. Even as she did so the lights in the house were doused; its windows sank into a brooding darkness, in a hope, perhaps futile, that it might look dead and abandoned and that the avengers might pass it by.

But they were being thorough. That much was obvious even from Amais's hiding place. They had gone from house to house, on both sides of the street, emptying them out, guns pointed at cringing men who had had the bad luck to be caught within, the occasional Golden Wind cadre in the process of removing the wide army-issue belt they all wore and starting to whip the screaming, cowering women with it, buckle-end down.

'Oh, Cahan, *no*,' Amais said, bleak, unbelieving.

And then the stasis broke, and she turned and raced back the way she had come. Back – back to the House of the Silver Moon, and the woman who had been one of the few people in this world whom she had loved, who had truly loved her.

Five

A tiny red lantern hung on the hook by Xuelian's door, the time-honoured signal for privacy, although Xuelian herself had long since ceased to require it for the purposes to which it was usually put. But she had her own needs, and it was the easiest, most obvious sign for her girls to leave her alone.

But the time for courtesy and manners was long past. Amais spared the lantern the barest of glances – it had not been there when she had left these rooms, not that long ago – as she flung the door aside and all but fell into the room, cheeks flushed, gasping for every breath as fear closed her throat.

'They're coming!' she managed to gasp out, staggering into the room, reaching for the dressing table to steady herself. 'I am barely ahead of them! There are torches in the Street! They're already in half a dozen Houses!'

'Of course they're coming,' Xuelian replied, very calmly.

'Xuelian, you don't understand! They're maybe two doors away! You have to get out of here now, before they . . . Aren't you *afraid*?'

'Child,' said Xuelian gently, and her voice trembled only a little bit, 'of course I am afraid. But there is nothing I can do to stop what's coming. I live in a house of silk and paper and it was never built to withstand a storm. I go where the storm blows me.'

'But they will . . .' Amais finally paused to take stock, and closed her mouth with a snap. She had looked at Xuelian, really looked at her for the first time since she raced into her room, and she suddenly realised that the old courtesan was dressed in her best finery. Her face was made up in the traditional way, with her magnificent eyes touched with kohl and her lips with rouge; her hair, silver-white, was looped and coiled in a complicated court style that had gone out of fashion decades before, and glittered with gems – and, set high like a crown, she wore the kingfisher comb. Its jewelled edges caught the light, and the delicate blue feathers, wrought into the shape of a flower, trembled as though with life itself when Xuelian turned her head.

Which she did, now, favouring her young protégée with a serene smile. It almost, but not quite, reached her eyes. Those were serious, fully aware of what was coming, touched with an edge of apprehension, but not enough of it to be real fear.

'You knew they were coming?' Amais whispered.

'I've been waiting for them. Every night for weeks. It was only a matter of time.'

'But you are . . .'

'I am one of the ones they will most particularly wish to gather into their net,' Xuelian said. 'I stand for too much that is now forbidden, rejected or despised. I would be an excellent figurehead.'

'For what?' Amais whispered, suddenly choked with tears.

'Well, but time will tell,' Xuelian said. She rose from where she had been sitting at her dressing table and crossed over to a rosewood writing desk set against the window. There were several leather-bound books on it. The journals. Amais recognised them: Xuelian had taken them out for Amais any

349

number of times, reading from their elegantly calligraphed pages as though she were passing on myths and legends from a time long gone, the woman who had once been a passionate emperor's concubine turned into an icon of peace and serenity.

'I want you to take care of these,' Xuelian said.

Amais stared at them blankly. There had been another set of journals that she had barely managed to save – if she had done it at all – Cahan alone knew what the man named Xuan would do with them. And here, now there was another legacy, another treasure to protect.

'But if you hide them in the strongbox . . .' she said. 'Or . . . or . . . with the sword . . . ?'

'They will look in the strongbox,' Xuelian replied. 'That is the first place they will go . . . after they are done here, in this room. And you don't want to draw attention to that sword, do you?'

'But they can't . . .' Amais said desperately, trying to force herself to believe in a place that would be inviolate, safe from harm. 'They would not know where to look . . . they . . .'

'But they will know that a safe place exists, and if they have to tear this house down around our ears, they will find it,' Xuelian said. 'There is always someone who thinks they know where the treasures lie and who will offer up the keys to the kingdom of Heaven itself if it will spare them a moment of pain or the merest thought of suffering. Besides, I've already taken care of that – I have put your sword in its secret place myself, and none of the girls can be forced to give it up, and most of the gold that was in the strongbox is already gone. So are most of the older journals, in fact. Only these are left here now, and I give them to you. I have written in here where I have left the sword . . . and where the treasure of the House of the Silver Moon is to be found. If you can get there, after the storm, take them.'

'But what about you . . . ?' Amais wailed, a child again in that moment, her hands closing reflexively around the leather books that Xuelian had folded her fingers over.

'My time is done, my life lived,' Xuelian whispered. 'My era has been over for a very long time. Now go, while you still can.' She touched a carving on a windowsill, and a wall panel beside the window suddenly clicked and sprang a little way open – a secret door, into a secret passage. 'Hurry,' Xuelian said, one hand tugging the panel open, the other on Amais's back, pushing her gently but firmly into the yawning opening. 'The stairs are steep and I am afraid it will be dark in there. Be very careful – perhaps it would be better to stay very quiet until you are sure that everyone has left. You will come out into the alley behind the Street, and a few sharp turns will take you into the Beggars' Quarter. Lie low for a while, and then try and get out of the city. I am afraid this madness that is about to take us . . . it's only just beginning. Now go.' She drew the girl to her and kissed her on the brow, gently, like a grandmother would have done. 'Go, and be careful.'

Amais stumbled forward, clutching the books, almost blinded by tears.

Xuelian's voice stopped her. 'Wait. Just a moment.'

Amais blinked her eyes clear, turned around. The old courtesan had crossed back to her dressing table and had picked up a square of white silk, embroidered with red poppies and a single tiny golden butterfly hovering just above one of the blooms. It was something that Xuelian herself had made when she had been one of the Imperial women, many years ago, and her hands had still been agile enough to ply an artist's needle, and scarlet and gold embroidery silks, now scorned as decadent luxuries, were her accepted due.

'Take this, too,' Xuelian said, holding out the square of silk. 'I would hate to see it . . . spoiled, or damaged. Take

351

it and . . . and keep it safe for me. And remember me by it, always.'

Amais reached for the silk, brushed for an instant the papery, aged skin on the other woman's hand, and felt her soul crying out with a knowledge that she could not deny. This was farewell.

'Go,' said Xuelian. 'In the name of that *jin-shei* that you would like to believe binds all of us together, over the centuries. Go – I can hear them coming.'

She gave Amais a final gentle push, and snicked the panel shut behind her.

Darkness folded around Amais's slender body, an apt physical echo of the way a similar darkness had wrapped her mind. Xuelian's words kept her frozen in place for a moment after the panel closed – now, in this hour, when everything seemed to be ending, she had been handed the words she had been chasing all across Syai, that she had wanted to hear for nearly all of her life – she had been asked something, as the women of ancient Syai had once been asked, in the name of *jin-shei*. It was that which paralysed her, held her perfectly still with the aching wonder of it – that, before the agonising stabs of fear and pain and loss laid clawed hands on her and raked across her soul.

And then she heard a crash, and harsh voices, and knew that she had escaped with barely a breath to spare.

She also realised that there was a tiny spyhole, a mere pinhole, in the panel. There was little in this world that she would have wanted to witness less willingly than what was unfolding in Xuelian's room – but it was beyond her not to look. She leaned forward, careful not to make a sound, and put her eye to the spyhole.

Four of the Golden Wind cadres stood in the room, dressed in identical nondescript high-necked coats and boots, which, Amais noted dispassionately, badly needed polishing. They were bristling with weaponry. One of them – by the looks of him the youngest, only barely older than Aylun, perhaps – wore only one knife at his belt. The others had two or even three blades apiece, long, serrated butcher knives and paring daggers, mismatched and casually gathered from any available source without regard to possible previous ownership or use, and impersonally lethal. Two of them had rifles, one wore a handgun next to a wickedly gleaming curved knife. One even had a couple of antique throwing stars tucked into the wide sash of his belt.

Not one of them looked to be over twenty years old.

Facing the old woman in the room, they looked like dangerously fey children, scions of the future turned viciously on their past, and particularly savage, almost feral, when contrasted with the quiet serenity of the victim they had come here to take.

Amais had thought they would demand the money of the House, tainted and illicit as it was, gathered by such heinous means – to be redistributed to the more 'deserving' in the eyes of the Golden Wind. But that was secondary for these four who were sent. They were here for the woman, and the money that had to be here was merely something that sweetened the pot. It was theirs for the taking and it would still be theirs – poured proudly into the hungry maw of the revolution, but theirs, their own contribution – afterwards, after their real work was done.

And the real work was only just beginning.

'Look at you,' spat out the oldest of the four, a young man, his eyes two slits of disgust and righteous outrage that Xuelian's existence had ever even been sanctioned. 'Sitting here like an old spider, in your silks and your jewels, while good people starve and die around you.'

'Nobody has ever starved that I had a chance to help,' Xuelian replied, and was rewarded by a stinging slap that snapped her head back on her neck. Amais stifled a cry.

'You don't speak, you with that voice of honey who has led so many astray into this decadent morass of luxury and indulgence,' Xuelian's nemesis hissed through clenched teeth. 'Do you have any idea how many could be fed and sheltered using just one of these?'

He reached out and snatched a jewelled pin from Xuelian's hair, brandished it as if it were a weapon every bit as lethal as the knives in his belt. Amais saw the old woman wince, and a long strand of hair hung from the despoiler's fingers. He had not been gentle about it.

His action seemed to be a signal for the others. Hands reached out, poked, prodded, ripped, snatched, pulled. Amais heard silk tear, things drop on the floor as more enticing targets were noticed by the attackers. She did not hear Xuelian cry out, or see her fall.

When the four men stepped back from Xuelian, breathing hard, Amais had to stuff her hand into her mouth to prevent herself from crying out aloud. Xuelian was still standing, but swaying gently on her feet. Her careful make-up was smeared across her face, which was red and swollen and looked like bruises were ready to bloom on every part of it. There was blood at the corner of her mouth, and on her arms, bare, with the sleeves of the silk gown ripped away at the shoulders and long scratches running from shoulder to wrist. The dress itself was slashed into ribbons, only a proud memory of what it had been only moments before. Xuelian's hair was mostly down, a cloud of silver white, sometimes streaked with blood; the rest was held up only barely by a few stray pins that had been missed in the assault.

And one of her assailants was standing a few paces away from her, holding the kingfisher comb in his hand.

Amais could not quite see Xuelian's face from where she

stood, but from the position of her head, her eyes rested on the comb, not the man who held it.

'And this pretty?' the comb's captor was saying, rubbing his stubby fingers with their short, dirty nails across the beautiful fragile kingfisher blue.

'A gift,' Xuelian said, her voice apparently coming from a place full of pain but still filled with a quiet calm that wrenched at Amais's heart. 'I have had it . . . for many years. It was a gift from the Kingfisher Emperor.'

'There was never any such emperor,' said the cadre sharply.

'Perhaps not in the history books,' Xuelian replied. 'But that was what I always called him.'

Amais could see *his* expression, if not Xuelian's – he was facing directly into the point-of-view of her peephole. And she saw it in his face – the wash of emotion – the merest dash of envy, followed by anger, a pious righteousness in the face of defiant and unrepentant iniquity, cold fury, contempt, and finally a strange, savage little flash of triumph.

She knew what he was going to do the instant before he did it, and closed her eyes so that she did not have to see it. But she heard it, the quiet snap of destruction as he crushed the fragile comb, broke it, rendered it trivial, a piece of garbage, before he tossed it onto the dressing table where it landed with a soft, ominous clatter.

She heard the defiler bark, 'Bring her!' – and there were sounds of dragging, a thud as a body met a solid object or two, another soft rip as a piece of silk got in the way . . . and then silence.

Amais turned away from the peephole before opening her eyes. Somehow she just could not bear to see that broken comb on the defiled dressing table. No matter what happened to Xuelian after this night, this was the place where at least a part of her had died. Amais knew that, because she knew what the kingfisher comb had meant to Xuelian, a last link with a past now so long gone as to be almost legend even in her own mind. Without that, without the memory to support her, she was empty – a husk that would take the pain or the humiliation that her captors would visit on her, and would barely know it was happening.

Amais probed yawning darkness in front of her with the toe of her foot, testing the ground. She felt the edge of a step. Shifting her grip on the precious journals, the white silk kerchief folded inside the cover of one of them, she let her free hand trail on the invisible wall at her right and took small, careful, precarious steps into the void.

Six

The sun was closer to rising than Amais had realised. That, or the rest of that sleepless night, walking the back-streets of Linh-an, wildly swinging between feeling sharply stabbed by pieces of a broken heart every time she drew breath or simply numb with grief, had passed in a grey blur of mindless wandering. She did not know where she was going or what she was going to do next, but it appeared that her subconscious had taken over and had come up with at least a temporary plan. The first light of the summer morning caught Amais in a street that, although it had also been roughly renamed, looked at least vaguely familiar. A street that led round the back of the Great Temple – not one of the three massive gates through which the faithful were expected to enter, but to the wall that stretched out behind the Temple circles, enclosing the gardens and storage sheds and sparse, monastic apartments of those who served its Gods.

Amais knew this place.

She could not hope to gain entry by herself, a stranger who did not belong to the Temple and knew none of the passwords or protocols required for access into these inner sanctums – but she knew someone who did know them.

Jinlien . . . if I could find Jinlien . . .

She circled the Temple wall until she reached one of the main gates, pawing at her pockets, looking for whatever money she had on her so that she might buy her offering and thus her way into the Circles. Perhaps, as she had so often done before, she would find Jinlien inside, busy with some housekeeping chore or talking to other seekers in the colonnaded walkways before the niches of the silent Gods. But the pickings were slim – she had a handful of loose change and one very soiled and crumpled small-denomination paper note that would not buy much more than a thimbleful of rice wine and perhaps a single incense stick.

She spared a brief yearning thought for the jar that stood on the dresser in her bedroom, which she kept full of 'Temple money' and fed with coins whenever she had any to spare – but if someone had asked Amais barely moments before that if she had missed anything that had been left behind in Lixao's rooms, she would have given the questioner a blank look in reply. There had been nothing that she felt bereft without – perhaps, at a push, one or two sentimental items that had belonged to her mother, but even those were afterthoughts.

In a way, it was a scathing indictment of her life: she was twenty-one years old and too many of those years had now been lived from day to day, from week to week, from month to month, waiting for things to happen or to stop happening, swept along by the whims of the adults in her life or by the winds of war.

The only decision she had ever made for herself had been the spontaneous and imponderable urge to go off in search of a strange Temple on a pilgrimage of redemption for *jinshei* and *jin-ashu*, the women's vow and the women's language. Even Iloh, the meeting heavy with *yuan* that had shaped her life, had been a part of that quest. If she had never gone on that journey, she would never have spoken to an old priestess at the ancient temple, never have come down from the mountain to seek the priestess's *jin-shei-bao*, never crossed the threshold of Xinmei's house. She would have had neither Iloh nor Xuelian.

Both lost, now – Xuelian swept away by the Golden Wind to the Gods alone knew what fate, and Iloh . . . Iloh might as well have been on a different plane of existence from her own. Amais tried to remember the feel of his skin, the sound of his voice, and all she could call to mind were the rough texture of the newsprint of his photographs and the tinny, crackling voice that carried across the Emperor's Square at his rallies. There was a glass wall between them – she could see him clearly through it, but could not bring herself to believe that this man had ever been her lover.

It was very early in the morning, and the stall-owners were barely beginning to set up their wares in the First Circle as Amais arrived at one of the three gates and slipped into the Temple. She waited just inside the arch of the doorway, watching, waiting for the merchants to get organised, for the customers to start arriving. But apparently it was a slow day, or else the events of the night before had made most people think it was more prudent not to venture out that day, not even to pray. Only a trickle of people came wandering into the Temple, less than half a dozen of them through the gate by which she stood.

It was a small child hanging on to a haggard-faced woman's hand who began to shed some light on the situation.

'Will the parade pass by here, Mother?' the child asked, skipping a little as it walked, happy in the blissfully ignorant way of the very young. 'Will we be able to see?'

'I hope not,' the mother muttered, just as the pair passed Amais. And then, more loudly, for the benefit of her offspring, added, 'Maybe. We will see when we are done here.'

Made reckless by the night that she had just endured, Amais turned her head as the woman passed. 'What parade?'

The woman paused for a moment, startled, wary, gripping the hand of her child a little tighter. But the child was too young to fear: the world, even this frightening world that they were all living in, was still merely exciting.

'The whores' parade,' the little girl explained eagerly, obviously aping something she had overheard her elders say. Her mother dragged her away with an abrupt tug, sparing Amais another sharp, suspicious glance. But the child, who was loath to lose her audience, turned her head towards Amais as she was being dragged forcefully down the corridor of the First Circle, and repeated her words more loudly, just in case Amais had not heard her properly the first time. 'The whores' . . . parade. The *whores'* parade!'

'Hush!' her mother hissed, giving the child's arm a rough yank to make her point. The little girl whimpered, stumbled, and then, chastened, fell into step beside her mother.

The night's work, it would seem, was not over yet for the Golden Wind.

Amais bought what offerings she could with her meagre hoard of money, keeping only a few coppers in her pockets, and wandered into the curiously empty and echoing Second Circle. The atmosphere was tense, the air almost crackling with it, as though the ancient place itself knew something that it was not yet telling those who walked its hallways and corridors. Nhia's niche was cold and incenseless when Amais came to it; so were most of the rest of them, the brooding figures of the holy sages carved from stone staring into empty air and pondering, perhaps, the fickleness of people caught in the turning wheels of time. Perhaps it would have been better, more expedient, to have sought out some other God – some deity more concerned with lives and fates and with what would happen to her next – but in one sense that would be abandoning herself to the ebb and flow of the tides yet again, bonelessly, doing nothing but bobbing in the oceans of history as no more than a piece of flotsam waiting to be deposited at some other transient anchor of her days.

Nhia – Nhia *was* an anchor. Nhia was part of the old days that Amais had grown up treasuring, had tried so hard to look for when she had first set foot back in the land in which they had flowered so long ago. Nhia was a sage, with answers, not just a silent and distant God who would counsel nothing more or less than a blind adherence to faith.

Nhia was a friend to the woman whose blood, so many generations later, ran in Amais's own veins. And Amais, now, could use a friend.

She lit her incense stick from the smouldering head of one of the few that were left alight in this wing, and carried it carefully back to Nhia's niche, wedging the incense stick in its holder, bowing her head before the statue.

'I am so lost,' she murmured. 'Tell me. Help me. Where should I go? What should I do . . . ?'

Her eyes closed, her shoulders folded inwards, her mind opening for any word of advice that Cahan chose to pass down.

Trust the people who love you.

The words echoed inside her as though they had been spoken out loud, into her ear, from right beside her. Amais looked sharply left and right, but she was still alone in the corridor. She lifted her head to Nhia's statue, staring.

'But who is there left,' she whispered, 'who loves me . . . ?'

We who are your jin-shei . . . we will always be with you.

'I don't understand,' Amais said, sinking to her knees. 'Amais . . . ?'

In a peculiar replay of a scene which had already taken place at this very niche once before – oh, it seemed to be a lifetime ago now! – Amais turned her head slowly to encounter a pair of Temple sandals, the edge of a blue robe, and then upwards to the familiar face of the person she had come here to find.

'Jinlien,' she whispered.

'Are you all right?' Jinlien said, coming down on one knee beside Amais and laying a gentle hand on her shoulder.

'I think so,' Amais said. 'I will be. But Jinlien . . . I cannot go home. There are people who might be looking for me. I need to leave the city – but I can't do it yet, not right now, not while the place is still in such an uproar from last night . . .'

'The emperor?' Jinlien said softly. 'We heard. Someone has been praying for the souls of the emperor and his family since before dawn in the shrine of the Lord of Heaven. But how are you involved . . . ?'

'I think my sister is,' Amais said bleakly. 'But that is not why they are looking for *me*.'

'Who is? And how do you know this is true?'

'There was a note,' Amais told her. 'In *jin-ashu*. I still don't know who wrote it but it was a warning – and – it's a long story . . . Do you have a hole I can crawl into, at least until tonight?'

'There are the second-tier teaching rooms,' Jinlien said after a small hesitation. 'Nobody has been in those for decades. Nobody is likely to in the next few days. Come with me – but later, you must tell me more. I can give you shelter but I cannot give you sanctuary, not without the permission of my seniors, and I cannot go to them without good reason.'

'Thank you,' Amais said. And then looked back up, at the stone statue in Nhia's niche. *And thank you. I don't understand yet. But I will try.*

Seven

The 'whores' parade' turned out to be rather less than the
child in the First Circle had made it out to be. Jinlien brought
Amais a copy of the newspaper the next day, and there were
a couple of photographs in it – all that had happened, apparently, was that a handful of the women caught up in the
sweep of the Street of Red Lanterns had been shown off by
their Golden Wind captors, some with half their heads shaved
to show their shame, others with exaggerated make-up
applied until they looked like frightening caricatures who
would have made any self-respecting male whimper and run
for cover rather than approach them for his pleasure. Amais
had almost not wanted to look at all, too afraid that she
would see Xuelian in some deeply undignified pose or, worse,
in pain – but if she had been among the haul she had not
made it into the papers.

Another familiar face, however, did – just at the edge of
the last photograph, her lips painted halfway up her cheeks
by lip rouge and her eyes roughly outlined with kohl until
they looked like two black holes in her face. Amais recognised Yingchi, Iloh's sister. The expression on her face was
more one of surprise than one of terror, but Amais's own

heart skipped a beat at the sight. Did her captors even know who she was? Would that identity work for her or against her . . . ? Amais pored over the short article beside the pictures but it did not say much – merely that the younger of the women would be packed off to 're-education camps' in the countryside, where hard work in the fields and diligent study of Shou'min Iloh's *Golden Words* would show them the way to a better future. There was no word as to what had happened to those judged to be too old to 're-educate'.

A far grimmer story, and one made more frightening by all the things that it did not say, occupied the first couple of pages of the broadsheet – the killing of the ex-emperor and his family, and the ramifications of that.

Sensitised as everyone had been to political tone and innuendo, the way that the articles in question spoke of Tang, Iloh's long-time friend and ally and until recently the head of state in Syai, indicated that his perceived sins and misdemeanours had been deemed to outweigh his usefulness to the powers who now ruled the land. There was a definite undercurrent that Tang would be thrown to the wolves if the wolves bayed for him loudly enough – but until they did, he would be kept close but helpless and disarmed. Iloh knew Tang to be a superior administrator and he would not waste that lightly – but Tang had done too many things against Iloh's writ, and that would be neither forgotten nor forgiven. But even given the ominous implications of all that, what was even more clear, and somehow more terrifying to Amais, was the sense that Iloh had won his battle but lost his war. He had launched the revolution in order to clear the decks and climb back into the high seat himself, because he had thought he was seeing the land sliding back into a morass of antiquated ideas that would only trammel it and tie it down, take it back into the dark ages from which he saw

Baba Sung, and then himself, deliver it. But the revolution had taken over, had sparked with a life of its own, had done far more than Iloh had ever bargained for it to do – and he had lost control of it. The slayings of the emperor and his family had not been sanctioned by him. He had said that it was good to rebel, but he had also said that everyone should be given a chance for redemption. What had happened instead was that the Golden Wind had heard only what it needed to hear, and had ridden roughshod over the rest.

There was mention, for the first time since the storm had broken, of the army. The army – Iloh's veterans of the civil war – had been conspicuously absent as the youth of the Golden Wind had rampaged and pillaged and burned; they had apparently been ordered to stay well out of it, were being saved for if and when they would be needed as a last resort to put out the flames of the Golden Rising. Iloh was not quite there, yet; the newspapers carried several quotes from him addressed to the Golden Wind, still praising their revolutionary zeal – but they were definitely aimed at cooling the hot blood of some of the more out-of-control cadres.

'You can stay a few days,' Jinlien had told Amais when she had brought the newspaper and some sesame buns for breakfast. 'Nobody knows you're here and nobody will ask questions. But, Amais . . . I'll be back, later, after my duties in the Temple end. You need to tell me what's happening. Let me help, if I can.'

Trust the people who love you.

Amais didn't know if Jinlien really fitted into that vision, but she was a friend, a friend who cared, a friend who might have good advice to give.

'I'll be here,' she said, rolling her eyes at the bare walls of the teaching room Jinlien had taken her to.

Jinlien smiled. 'Stay safe,' she told her. 'I'll come as soon as I can.'

Amais, left alone, took Xuelian's embroidered handkerchief from between the covers of the journal in which she had laid it and sat for a long time holding the piece of cloth against her cheek, remembering her friend and teacher. Then she tucked that carefully away, inside her own clothing, and leafed through the handful of journals that Xuelian had handed her just before the Golden Wind had come. One of the last entries, as she had said, was a set of instructions – both on how to find the whereabouts of a certain sword, carefully secreted in the basement of the House of the Silver Moon, and, more astonishingly, the way to find the cache of the House treasure, the bulk of which Xuelian, with almost preternatural foresight, had caused to be taken to a safe hiding place outside the city.

To the province of Hian – and a place very close, as it turned out, to Iloh's own ancestral farm, buried near the very land that he had ploughed and fertilised in his boyhood. Now that soil would be made to bring forth a very different harvest.

'Let it be used, if that is possible,' Xuelian instructed in her journal, 'to find and succour the women from the Street of Red Lanterns – and help them begin new lives, if they come out of this storm able to pursue them. Many of them are young enough to start again, with families, perhaps, and lives well away from those who might wish them harm. And if this treasure gives aid or comfort to others who need it, that too will be a blessing.'

The journals were more than Xuelian's last gift to Amais, as and of themselves. They were a legacy, a bequest, something to do in her name . . . and in the name of *jin-shei*, too, which she had invoked as almost her last word to Amais in that room where she had then turned to face what was almost inevitably her own death.

Somehow all the voices of Amais's past had started to

speak the same words to her, pointing her to the same path, one that she had started seeking herself long ago but that she had believed to have been lost and buried under the avalanche of the years of war and conflict and revolution.

We who are your jin-shei . . . will always be with you, spoke Nhia, from the mists of antiquity, from the time when Tai, whose blood now ran in Amais's own veins, was young.

Let not her name be forgotten . . . or your own . . . whispered *baya*-Dan from Amais's childhood.

Let the treasure I leave be used to help begin new lives, Xuelian said, her voice still echoing in this world, barely a day old.

'I have to go,' Amais murmured to herself, her eyes wide and focused somewhere far away, in the distant past, in a time yet to come. 'I have to begin . . .'

But she could not leave without at least thanking Jinlien, and she stayed put in the quiet gloom of the abandoned teaching room, waiting for Jinlien's promised return.

Jinlien did not come that night. But there was a teapot in the teaching room, and a burner that had gathered dust of many years since it had last been used; when Jinlien had brought the sesame buns she had also brought some lamp oil, and a small sachet of green tea, and a few other necessities she had felt it needful for Amais to have. Amais, hungry but reluctant to leave this place without Jinlien's sanction, lest Jinlien get into some kind of trouble over it, made do with the last sesame bun she had hoarded from that morning and brewed herself a pot of weak green tea with little ceremony but a great deal of grateful appreciation. The tiny lamp into which she poured the rest of the lamp oil gave off a flickering light barely more than a candle's worth; it was too dim to read by without strain, and Amais soon gave up, closed the journals, tucked them under her body and lay down on a pallet at the back of the room, covering herself with the single thin blanket she had found lying upon it.

There was no trace of Jinlien the next morning either, and Amais began to feel apprehensive – she was safe here, but isolated, and anything could be going on in the world around her, things that were a danger to herself and to others. She wrestled with the two conflicting urges for an hour or two – *stay put, wait for Jinlien to come and get me/get out of here and find out what's happening* – but when Jinlien still did not appear and she became both hungrier and more apprehensive by the minute it was the latter course of action that prevailed. Amais crept carefully out of her hiding place, closing the door behind her, and made her way almost furtively back into the Temple proper.

There were small knots of Temple people – priests, acolytes, novices – milling about the Temple precincts, apparently aimlessly, resembling nothing so much as an anthill which had been poked with a stick and left in disarray, unable to formulate a response to the incursion. Amais, trying to stay out of sight, snagged a blue Temple cloak that had been dropped beside an empty niche in the Second Circle, and draped it over her shoulders to blend in better – but she could not figure what precisely had transpired to cause this commotion, although something did nag at her, something that should have held more of her attention if she had not been so focused on the Temple people.

An empty niche.

It was a niche that should not have been empty. She was in the Emperors' Corridor, and these niches had been filled with the statues of Syai's old emperors – generations upon generations of them, hundreds of years of history personified in carved stone faces with blue incense smoke curling around them

They were all empty now. Every single one of them. Not a single emperor remained in place.

'What have they done . . . ?' Amais murmured, her eyes wide with shock, and made her way past the looted corridor, through the nearest gate, into the Third Circle.

Some of the niches here had been vandalised, too, the statues of their Gods toppled from the plinths, offerings and incense sticks strewn on the ground. But it was ahead of her, near the gate to the Fourth Circle, that Amais saw something that made her freeze in place, her hand at her throat.

A figure in Temple garb – someone either very short or very young – was bending over the handful of ancient brass burner bowls beside the gate, the ones Amais herself had been allowed to tend with Jinlien once, the ones that had been kept alive for centuries. The person at the burners had a watering can in hand – not entirely unexpected, this was the Third Circle and there were many plants in the gardens here that might have required watering. Except that what was being carefully and meticulously watered – not much, just enough to kill – were the burners themselves, with the embers within being doused with just enough water for the living flame to go out, for the burner to start to go cold.

Amais heard her own voice asking the questions, at that very gate, when she was still almost new to the city – *What would be done to a person who let a burner go cold . . . ?*

She almost moved, almost surged forward to tear the watering can out of the murderer's grasp, when a cry stopped her, froze her again in her tracks. Through the gate, her face stark in anguished grief, came the very person she had come out to seek – Jinlien of the Fourth Circle, keeper of the living fire.

'Stop! Who are you? What are you doing? Stop! In the name of Cahan, *stop*!'

The one holding the watering can, a girl barely out of childhood and still carrying its legacy in the shape of her mouth, the roundness of her cheeks, straightened, met

Jinlien's outrage with a triumphant smile. 'It is a new day, sister,' she said. 'The old must make way.'

Jinlien fell to her knees beside the doused burners with a keening cry. 'What have you done . . . ?'

'The old must make way,' the girl-child repeated.

Before Amais's unbelieving eyes a knife flashed out of a hidden scabbard at the intruder's waist, sank with a soft tearing noise into Jinlien's breast. There was a scuffle of feet at the outer gate, the one Amais herself had but lately stepped through, leading back into the Second Circle, and even as Amais shrank back, ducking under a torn altar cloth from a Third Circle shrine, half a dozen cadres in grey uniforms and with a wide yellow band on their right arms came into the Third Circle. Several of them carried burning torches.

'You won't need those,' the one who had just killed said, straightening, wiping Jinlien's blood off her blade. 'The Tower has fires already burning, always burning. Enough for you to work with.'

'Backup is always better,' one of the newcomers said. 'Lead the way.'

One of the Temple's own, thought Amais, mourning. It had been one of the Temple's own, a novice, by her garb, who had done this – who had committed the sacrilege against the ancient burners, had spilled blood on this sacred ground.

The young one turned, vanished through the gate into the Fourth Circle, and the rest followed. Amais waited for another moment, but nobody else came. Shedding the concealing altar cloth, she raced over to where Jinlien's blood was already pooling by the cooling incense burners, already slowly dying, losing their immortal fire.

'Amais . . .' Jinlien said, her eyes only half open, her breathing shallow, her hand red with her own blood where she held it pressed against her chest. 'Oh, Gods, that I should . . . see this happen . . . go . . . be safe . . . they will return . . .'

Amais dropped to one knee beside her, her eyes full of tears. 'What can I do . . . ?'

Jinlien's eyes flickered towards the burners and then closed with a pain that was far more profound than the merely physical. 'It is already too late,' she said. 'Go. Go now . . .'

She did not open her eyes again. Perhaps she could not bear to, could not die with her last sight being those beautiful ancient things she had so lovingly cared for all of her days in this place fading into nothingness, could not bear the sight of so much that was so unconditionally beautiful being destroyed simply because it existed. The shallow breathing slowed, became quieter, was stilled. The hand that Amais held in her own became limp.

From somewhere else in the Temple Amais could clearly hear the roar of fire, a fire that had taken hold, that was already out of control.

'May your path to Cahan be gentle,' she whispered over Jinlien's lifeless body. In a way this would be like a grand old funeral of ancient times – and Jinlien would cross into Cahan with these incense burners, and they would all live again on the other side, in the gardens of the Gods. It seemed fitting.

Amais bent to place a gentle farewell kiss on Jinlien's brow, before stumbling to her feet and racing back the way she had come. If she had had any intention of finding her way back to the abandoned second-tier teaching room where she had been hiding – where Xuelian's journals still were – she quickly realised that this was no longer possible. There was a fire behind her, and people, possibly Golden Wind, in front of her. Sparing one anguished thought for the loss of those notebooks, touching with grateful fingers the embroidered handkerchief that she had managed to save, the instructions for finding Xuelian's treasure still sharp in her mind, Amais ducked sideways into another doorway, out of the Second

371

Circle, into the back of the Temple and its vegetable plots and chicken coops. There was commotion here, too, but by this stage nobody was paying too much attention to anyone else. Nobody challenged or stopped her; she found the outer wall, an unguarded door, ajar from where someone else had undoubtedly made their escape. She slipped outside, and plunged into the warren of streets behind the Temple.

Eight

No pictures had ever been sanctioned by the Temple of the inside of the Tower, the heart of the Great Temple, the earthly home of the Lord of Heaven – only those who had been there knew what it felt like to walk on that holy ground, to feel the cool smoothness of marble under one's bare feet, to breathe in the air scented with the costliest and rarest of incenses, to see the flames of the holy fire dancing in the stone bowl of the highest altar, always carefully tended, always burning, in respect to the Gods. Those fortunate people sometimes described the experience to others. But for the invaders, the children of the Golden Wind who had been born in war and raised in revolution, such accounts had never been either interesting or necessary. They knew nothing of the intricacies of the layout of this innermost Temple, nothing of its meaning or of its intent – they did not want to know. All they knew was that it was a symbol – perhaps, next to the living Emperor of Syai, the most powerful of symbols. It *was* the old Syai.

Perhaps it might have survived longer – perhaps it might even have survived intact – if the emperor and his family had not been slaughtered, and thus the first real and substantial link in the chain to the past been broken. While the emperor lived, while any who bore that blood breathed, that ancient land lived and breathed with him. Now the emperor was gone, and there had been no retribution. The Golden Wind, maddened by its actions, the lack of censure by anyone at all, and Shou'min Iloh's tacit and, as they saw it, continuing approval, escalated its impulse to devastate and destroy – and the Great Temple stood squarely in their path.

They burst into the Tower, their shoes still sacrilegiously on their feet, their torches in their hands, led by the novice acolyte who had broken with her past and had chosen the now of the Golden Rising over the future of the promise of Cahan. A barked command saw them split up into groups, going from gate to gate, throwing down the nine small altars that guarded the entrances to this place, three to a gate. They smashed the oil lamps on the three inner altars, the oil spilling like blood, the flames licking down the oozing oil, which took the fire across the stone floor, pouring itself across the stone flags until it reached the base of the wooden stair that led to the catwalk which ringed the Tower. It pooled there, the tiny tongues of flame licking at the wood until it started to char, to smoulder – but the invaders had already turned their backs on that, and had converged, all of them, on the central altar and its holy flames.

One of the three Tower priests, the youngest, was up on the catwalk by the great brass bell that hung there, rung every noon by these priests, the holy duty passed from one generation of the Gods' people to another. He could see the fire spreading in the Temple room below. The catwalk was wooden and would burn – was already burning. There was no way out of this for the priest by the bell, no way down, no way of surviving. He looked, and understood. Closing his eyes, he reached for the rope that rang the bell, and pulled it, over and over and over again, a knell, chanting quiet prayers for his soul and the souls of others who would cross to Cahan on this day.

The remaining two Tower priests stood at bay, with quarterstaves in their hands, but they had been frozen into shock by the vandalism that had been happening, brazen and without the least regard to their own presence, in this holiest of shrines. One of them collected himself so far as to call out, his voice surprisingly firm given the expression of blank and bewildered astonishment on his face.

'Stop!' he cried, raising his staff.

One of the Golden Wind shot him, point-blank.

Even as he crumpled, and the other priest dropped his staff, and, covering his face in either terror or shame, ran from the place, the leader of the Golden Wind group was thrusting his sacrilegious torch into the holy fire in the bowl, scattering the embers to the far walls.

'Make him stop,' he commanded, having to raise his voice to a shout above the deep booming echo of the ringing bell.

A couple of his companions emptied out their guns at the priest in the Tower, but the bullets went wide, deflected by the great swinging bell. A few of them finally resorted to other, more primitive methods when the modern weaponry failed, and shoved their own burning torches, this time deliberately, against the wooden railings and stairs of what parts of the catwalk were within their reach.

'It won't take long,' one said to the leader, wiping his hands on the seat of his trousers.

'Down with old customs and traditions!' the leader shouted, brandishing his torch high. 'We will build a monument to the revolution on the ashes of this place! Long live Shou'min Iloh!'

Down with the old . . .

They retreated, then, leaving death and chaos in their wake, pulling back across the quiet serene calm that had been the Fourth Circle, torching altar cloths of ancient silk and the altars themselves, those that had been carved of sandalwood and ebony and cedar. Back through the gardens, some of them lingering there to touch the fire to the helpless fruit trees and ornamental shrubbery. Many of the Temple people had fled before this onslaught, shedding their robes and any other thing that could identify them as ever having been a part of this place – but, curiously, it was these gardens that drew most of those that remained to rally in their defence. The Golden Wind cadres killed without thought the women and the serene old men who had stood their ground in the Temple gardens, protecting some particularly beloved or ancient tree that had featured in generations of Temple teaching tales. But they fell, and their blood spattered the walls of the inner Temple, soaked the raked sands of the meditation gardens, murked up the carp pools. Some of the Golden Wind people had come armed with more than guns or knives – a few of the brawnier among them had brought axes, and used them to hew, indiscriminately and viciously. The axes were there to bring down altars and statues and anything inanimate and old and holy that was too hard to break by hand – but the living limbs of the old willows and the summer-crowned green cherry and plum and peach trees which lent these gardens their ethereal beauty with their delicate white and pale pink blooms in springtime were targets just as tempting, if not more so. Whole limbs of trees were hewed off and left where they fell; deep hacks were made in the trunks of most, ensuring that their chances of survival were almost non-existent even if they managed to retain a spark of life in the inferno that it was intended the Temple should become.

The Golden Wind cadres sang while they did their work. Songs of revolution that told of fire and then of rebirth. They destroyed the things they believed stood in the path of their rising again, washed clean in the blood of the revolution, re-enacting in every word and every deed a belief in one of the oldest legends of their race, the bird of rebirth, the phoenix which immolated itself only to begin again, young and new.

Down with the old . . .

Dozens of bodies littered the colonnade and the upper terrace of the Third Circle – the acolytes and priests who had been devoted to the deities that had once reigned here, the Rulers of the Four Quarters and other Gods of Early Heaven. Their Gods had not protected them, and they had not protected their Gods; the place was strewn with the rubble of broken masonry, shattered idols, scattered implements for the mysteries of the sand paintings and various arcane things that were required – had been required – for worship in this Circle. A coppery smell of fresh-spilled blood lingered in the air, mixed with a crazy cocktail of twenty different kinds of incense all burning together, and the more pungent smell of scented wood altars beginning to really catch the flames.

The Second Circle was always the most populous one, being the cheapest one to buy into with a simple offering to a simple god or spirit, dealing with everyday problems one request at a time. There were more bodies here, some of them Temple people, others simply devotees who had been in the wrong place at the wrong time – women, children, twisted limbs, staring eyes. Here an old woman lay prostrate before a desecrated niche, there a bewildered three-year-old insistently pulled at the sleeve of her dead mother, begging to go home. Whimpers from survivors trying to crawl through the outer gates to any kind of safety at all, wails from the lost and the hurt and the abandoned, moans from the wounded and the dying – all mixed with the sound of singing as the Golden Wind went about its work coldly and methodically. Those that stood in their path – no matter if that was done as a deliberate act or was an appalling accident of ill-fortune – were simply swept away.

The Second Circle niches had been emptied of their Gods and their offerings – all of them – the spirits of Later Heaven as well as those mortal souls who had been granted status there, the generations of emperors, the holy sages. The niche of Nhia, once *jin-shei* to an empress and to a poetess of Syai, the woman who rose from beginnings every bit as humble as the revolution might have demanded to become a power in her land, was only one among many – an axe-scarred hole in the wall. The Golden Wind could spare no thought to making exceptions. Nhia, like all of her holy sage companions, was part of the old, simply by virtue of being enshrined here in this place – therefore she was obsolete, with nothing left to give to the new Syai. The Golden Wind had no time to ponder the wasteland that this sweeping mandate to destroy was making of their history and their culture, leaving their country's past an uneasy, empty void, tearing up their own roots and cheering as the young leaves of a future yet unborn withered on the branch.

And the flames were here, too, licking in from the Third Circle, and from the First as well, where the booths had been indiscriminately put to the torch.

Amais could see it all, sense it all, by the physical senses given by the Gods, with her mind's eye full of vision. Even as she paused in her headlong flight to turn around and look behind her, the Tower of the Lord of Heaven was pouring smoke into the sky, and open flames were licking up high enough above the walls of the Inner Circles for Amais to see them from where she stood.

Fire had a sound – a rumble, a thunder, not so much heard as sensed through the air, through the tremble of the ground beneath one's feet – an animal-like roar, something primal and visceral that stripped the veneer of civilisation from a person just as easily as it melted lacquer off a painted door, laying bare before destroying. What churned in Amais was indescribable, inchoate, all of her outer layers burned away, the raw core of her exposed to the flames. She did not know what to do with this – she could not move, could not think, stood staring at the inferno with the pupils of her eyes dilated with shock, almost obliterating their colour, leaving two huge black holes in her face. She had blood on her clothes and her hands – not hers, Jinlien's; her hair was falling out of its braid, curling wildly around her face and her neck; her face was streaked and smudged with dirt, soot and blood; the roar of the fire obliterated all other sound. She was aware of nothing else, nobody else, only those flames, only the sight and sound of those flames, nothing inside or outside of her except fire. Broken open, scoured clean.

It took a stinging slap across her face to bring her awareness of the world back to the human level, the everyday, the place where other people shared the air that she breathed. One of those other people was speaking to her, asking impatiently, and apparently not for the first or even the second time, her business in that place.

Amais registered the uniform, the yellow armband, the thunderous scowl on her assailant's face – but she was slow to react. Too slow. Through air that felt like molasses, she started to turn, to refocus, to open her mouth to speak, but before she could do any of those things another slap flung her head back, sent her dishevelled hair snapping across her face.

'I said, what are you doing here?' the cadre snarled.

'I was . . .' Amais began, and then heard another voice cut in – a voice vaguely familiar, firm, just sufficiently humble enough to appease but not so humble as to be fawning.

'Please,' that voice said – a man's voice, calm and measured, matching the firm hand that descended on Amais's arm and gave it an imperceptible warning squeeze. 'She is with me.'

'What is she doing out here?' the cadre demanded suspiciously. 'Look at her – she is no bystander. Her clothes and her face betray her.'

'She was in the Temple, with her child . . . She escaped, as you see. But the child . . . the child is still in there, somewhere. Please forgive her, she is a mother grieving.'

'The Party is our mother,' said the cadre, shifting a gun in his free hand. 'Get her out of here, *ximin*. This was the retribution of the Golden Wind – let your wife be proud that her child is now one of the martyrs of the Golden Rising. Long live Shou'min Iloh!'

'Come,' the man whispered into Amais's ear. 'Quickly.'

She had recognised him by then, remembered him – the man with the sword, the one whom she had collided with in Linh-an's deserted streets only a couple of nights before. Xuan, from the house with the blue roof in Siqaluan Street, at the back of the Temple. She bent her head and followed him without question. She could feel, and from the increased pressure of his fingers on her arm she knew he did too, the weight of the cadre's suspicious stare on the two of them as they walked away, until they rounded a corner, slipped out of sight.

'You lie well,' Amais said, when they had done so.

'Saving a life is always a *daoded*,' he replied, 'a good deed rewarded by the Gods. I did not know it was you when I first saw him slap you, but I would have gone to the aid of a woman being mistreated anyway – and then, when I recognised you . . .'

'How did you know it was me?'

He let go of her arm, reached up and brushed her hair lightly. 'The other night . . . the light in the street was enough for me to remember this. Your hair is like no other woman's that I know.'

'Thank you,' Amais said, lifting her eyes to his for the first time. 'I owe you – again.'

'You still have my grandfather's sword,' he reminded her, and offered a wan smile. 'There is already a debt between us. Come.'

'Where?'

'My house. It is not far from here. And if you do then I will not have lied after all – you are, right now, with me, my guest. I don't know what happened but it should be obvious that you cannot wander the streets looking like you do – it is only a matter of time before another of them finds you. At least let me offer you a place to rest and wash up. If there is any other way I can help, and if you are willing to tell me how, I will try. Come.'

Yuan. Amais let the fate take her.

When Xuan's hand dropped back to her arm, to gently guide her around another corner and into a quiet and mostly empty street dominated by a large house with a blue roof, she did not pull away – and somehow, in the space it took to walk down that street to the gate of that house, his hand had slipped down to take hers, holding it gently, without pressure, just a quiet curl of a man's fingers around her own. She did not remember it happening, or recall making a conscious decision to respond to the gesture one way or another, but it felt good, it felt safe, it felt like a wall between her and the fire that had seared her soul.

Sometime in between their turning their backs on the angry Golden Wind cadre and the door of the house with the blue roof closing behind them, the voice of the bell in the Tower of the Lord of Heaven in the Great Temple of Linh-an fell silent at last.

Nine

'You can soak your clothes in cold water, in the basin, there,' Xuan said as he escorted Amais into a bathroom. 'You cannot go out in the street again in those and not be stopped at the first street corner and taken into custody for things you never did. I will have a clean robe brought to you for the meantime. My sister's should fit you.'

'You are very kind,' Amais murmured.

He looked as though he was about to say something, and then reconsidered, contented himself with a small enigmatic smile, and bowed himself out of the room, closing the door behind him.

The place wasn't opulent but by the contemporary standards of Linh-an it was positively sybaritic. There was a tub, and Amais paused for a moment, wondering if she could presume on his hospitality that far – but she did not hesitate too long. There was too much on her, in her, that she wanted to scrub herself clean of. A discreet knock on the door announced the arrival of the robe, but nobody came in to deliver it – this was a household that looked as though it might well have had servants, once, although perhaps it no longer did. The robe had probably been brought by the sister in question, who did not wish to intrude, or by Xuan himself.

The clean water took care of the grime, the soot, the blood, the ashes – all that was left of the ruin of the Temple on the outside of her, on the skin, on the hair. That which remained on the inside . . . needed other cleaning, other healing. That was still to come.

Amais opened the door a crack when she was done, and pulled on the neatly folded cotton robe that had been laid just outside on top of a pair of felt house-slippers. She wrung her wet hair dry as best she could, re-braided it into a damp rope, slipped into the robe and pulled its sash tight around her waist, thrust her feet into the slippers, which fitted as though they were her own. She inspected the basin in which she had, according to instructions, soaked her own clothes. The water was turning a coppery red-brown, and Amais turned away, suddenly aware of whose blood that was, the bile rising to the back of her throat. For a long time she stood there, her forehead between the palms of her hands laid flat against the door, and then she mentally shook herself and told herself sternly that she could hardly repay the kindness that had been shown her by never coming out of her hosts' bathroom again.

The corridor outside the bathroom door was empty as she stepped out, but a doorless arch led off to the right. She followed the rich smells of vegetable soup and sesame cookies through that doorway, across an empty sitting room, and into a kitchen at the back where two women, a young one and an old one, were chopping up a meagre haul of vegetables on a table. They looked up as Amais stepped into the doorway, paused there, suddenly and overwhelmingly unable to utter a single word.

The old woman laid her knife down, wiped her hands, and crossed to where Amais waited.

'My son said you have been through an ordeal,' she said. 'Have you eaten?'

It was the traditional Syai greeting, a variation of the same words with which Vien and her daughters had been greeted when they first set foot back in their homeland. But this time the words appeared to be meant quite literally.

'I can bring nothing to the table,' Amais replied. It was customary, a guest always brought an offering – but she was here as little more than a refugee, empty-handed, a burden and not a gift.

'Who can, these days?' the old woman returned. 'I am Lihong; this is my daughter, Xinqian. My son, Xuan, you have met.'

Amais only then became aware that Xuan had entered through a different door, bearing a bowl in his hands, and stood a few paces away, a slight smile on his face. She dropped her eyes, aware that the colour had risen in her cheeks, that they could all see, and that there was nothing she could do about it.

'Be welcome,' Lihong said, taking Amais's hands and drawing her into the kitchen.

The daughter, Xinqian, glanced up from her work. Her eyes were not friendly, but they were resigned. If there was one person in this house to whom Amais's presence was not agreeable, it was the woman whose clothes Amais now wore, whose shoes were on her feet.

The meal was simple, but a great deal had been done to make the occasion seem cheerful, as though ancient laws of hospitality still prevailed and Amais were really a guest at this family's table. There was even a sprig of greenery arranged artfully in what looked like it had once been a bottle of rice wine. The household had a sense of a vanished grandeur, of people who knew and could understand beauty and grace but from whom it had been torn – but who dared,

384

however covertly and full of symbolism, to express their dreams of seeing it return some day. A vase made of porcelain or fine glass would normally have been in the place of the bottle of rice wine – but although those precious things were gone now, Lihong, the matriarch, did not relinquish the idea of such a vessel being necessary for a festive table.

After they had eaten, Xinqian murmured something about needing to see to her child, and Lihong busied herself with clearing the table, dismissing offers of help. Amais and Xuan were left alone in the sitting room, with only a couple of cheap lanterns with painted rice-paper shades casting light into the shuttered room.

'They were here, weren't they,' Amais said, looking down at her folded hands. 'The Golden Wind.'

'The morning after I gave you the sword,' he said. She looked up at that, a swift glance she quickly hid by dropping her eyes again, but he had seen the fear there, and interpreted it correctly. 'They are safe,' he said, 'your journals. Not even my mother or my sister knows where they are bestowed. But for the rest . . . they took everything, and wrecked what they could not take – and my sister's husband they took with them when they left. I was not here when they came, else I too might have been taken. You must forgive Xinqian for tonight. She is still broken with that loss.'

'Do you know why? Where they took him?'

'No,' he said. 'I have tried to find out, but I haven't had much time – and then, the Temple, and all that . . . It is my mother who has gone out to ask, because she fears what would happen if I were to show up at some overzealous official's desk – but nobody has told her anything, and I think it will be a long time before anybody will. Tragedy has made her selfish, and she will not let me walk the streets and perhaps be seen, recognised, taken – but my sister only sees,

385

right now, that I am here and safe and being kept safe and her husband is gone. I am afraid she resents that, and me.'

'But you walked the streets today,' said Amais.

'Yes, when the bell began to toll,' Xuan replied. 'I could not . . . I could not stay inside like a rat. Not with that echoing across the city.'

'There is nothing you could have done.'

'I know.'

They both glanced at each other at the same moment, caught each other's eye. Xuan looked away first.

'They are all I have now, my mother and my sister and my little niece,' he said, words that connected to nothing that he had just been saying, but everything made sense in this conversation, in this shattered world, where one clung to spars where one could find them.

'I don't even have that much,' Amais told him bleakly. 'My father died long ago, the sea took him, far away from here, in a different land . . . in a different world. My mother is buried in what is by now probably an unmarked grave, and my stepfather is somewhere in the clutches of the Golden Wind. And my little sister . . . *is* in the Golden Wind . . .'

'I can't promise you miracles,' he said. 'I was not able to keep even my own family safe . . . but I will do what I can, if you will let me help you.'

There was bitterness in that last sentence, as well as sincere concern, kindness, hope. Amais suddenly and vividly remembered the feel of his hand around her own.

As she opened her mouth to speak, a flash of light rippled through the shutters followed by a loud crash of thunder. There had been rumblings, distant and muted, for a while – in the background, but easy to ignore. This was suddenly very close, demanding attention. Both of them looked up, startled, as the thunder continued to roll ominously; and then, without warning, as though someone had upended a bucket over the roof, there was a sudden noise of rushing water. Rain.

They both spoke in the same instant.

'It's really coming down . . .'

'Storm was all day in coming. It might help . . .'

Amais suddenly realised something, something that had been niggling at her ever since she had left Iloh's last rally on the Emperor's Square – something had not been 'right' with that rally, something had been missing, and it was only now that she realised what that had been. For the first time since he had stepped onto the podium on the square to speak to the people of the city, Iloh had done so dry. There had been no rain. There had been no rain *then* – and it was now, only now, when the rain would come and put out the fires of the Golden Wind's scouring . . .

Suddenly, incongruously, she laughed. Xuan looked at her in mute astonishment.

'I'm sorry,' she said, and the laughter had turned into a hiccough, and then into a sob, and then back into a wild, fierce chuckle again. 'I had been told a story, by . . . by a friend. It doesn't matter now. But I think . . . I think that he has lost the Mandate of Heaven . . .'

'Who?'

'Iloh,' Amais replied. 'I'm sorry, I know I sound insane. There's a lot to explain, but before I can do that . . .'

She suddenly sat up, her eyes wide, her mouth parted.

Suddenly it all seemed to fall into place for her. All of it, all the things that *baya*-Dan had tried to teach her, the cryptic words that Nhia seemed to have sent to her across the centuries, Jinlien's dying incense burners, Xuelian's lessons on the women's language and the way in which Syai's women had always had a gentle hand in guiding the land's history. Tai's poems. The vow that changed so many lives, when Xinmei stayed in the world and sent her *jin-shei-bao* to the holy crag of Sian Sanqin. The young Amais's certainty, back when she was heartsick at leaving the land of her childhood behind for the strange and unknowable thing that Syai had still been for her – the insight, the firm knowledge, that there would be something for her to do in the land of her ancestors, a task that waited for her hand and no other.

All of it.

In two words.

In a single thought.

Xuan stared at her for a long moment, and then drew a shaky breath, running a long-fingered hand through his hair.

'You have no idea,' he murmured, 'what you look like in this moment. Armies would follow you through fire without question.'

Amais blinked, looked at him; her expression softened, and she actually reached for his hand, folding both of hers around it.

'Please,' she said. 'There is something . . . I have to do. You said you wanted to help me . . .'

He heard her out, and then protested vigorously at the plan she laid before him. She had to concede that he had a point. Going back into the Temple, going back that night, with the remnants of the fires still possibly smouldering in dangerous spots and the wild storm lashing the streets, with roving Golden Wind bands giddy with their recent triumph roaming the city, did seem insane. But that was what her heart was telling her to do, clearly at last, with her path laid out before her – and she was trusting it, just like Nhia had told her to do.

'All right, but I will come with you,' Xuan said at last, having run out of protests and remonstrations, watching them all break on the steel of her resolve.

'You cannot,' she said, 'you can't see this . . .'

'Is this about the journals?' he asked. 'Something in your women's language? But I won't even understand . . .'

'Trust me,' she said. 'Please, trust me. I will come to no harm. You can come with me to the Temple, if you need to, but not inside. What I do there I need to do alone.'

So he acquiesced, in the end, and when night fell they both retraced the steps they had walked earlier that day, back to the Temple. They walked in the driving rain, both of them soaked to the skin in the space of only minutes, with great jagged sheets of lightning tearing at the sky and thunder crashing deafeningly around them. Everything looked different, changed; the shape of the street, the city, was altered. Most of the Temple's great walls were standing, but fire and the cudgels of the Golden Wind had eaten at the rest; there were places where supports were damaged or destroyed and the walls were leaning precariously or had even sagged into near collapse. Some smouldered angrily as embers hidden in deep crevices and unreached by the rain burned still. The familiar silhouette of the Tower was gone from the skyline. Amais and Xuan slipped into the grounds through the same door which Amais had used to escape, still abandoned and ajar, and picked their way across fallen masonry towards the Temple proper and the gardens that Amais had left full of blood and fire only that morning. And then she halted, and turned to Xuan.

'No further,' she said. 'There, that arch is still standing. At least you'll be out of the rain.'

'Amais . . .'

'I will be all right,' she assured him. 'I promise.'

He reached out for her, helplessly, but she slipped out of his arms and walked away with quick, light steps, her way illuminated by the lightning.

It was gone, the great sacred building that she had known – melted into chaos, retaining no trace of the shape or form that she recalled. She realised that she must have crossed the Fourth Circle only when she found herself in the remnants of the gardens of the inner court – and even that, the lightning showed her, was a shattered mess of churned sand and ashes, littered with shapes that might have been fallen trees, piles of masonry, or charred bodies. Amais finally got her bearings when she saw one of the ancient willows, which she knew had been shading one of the entrance gates. It was still standing, but it had obviously burned, and it creaked and groaned now in the driving wind and rain. Underneath it, revealed by another blinding lightning flash, Amais saw a snapped dagger, with its point gone but a couple of fingers' width of the blade remaining in the hilt.

She picked her way across to the tree, knelt beside it with one hand on a miraculously unburned patch of bark, reached out for the broken knife with the other.

She was foreign-born, her blood mixed with that of a foreign people; she knew that, understood that, accepted that. Perhaps it had been that trace of foreignness in her that had both kept her from understanding before this moment what Syai would ask of her, and now, when the hour had come, understanding it with a clarity that only an objective outsider looking in could possibly recognise. Perhaps it had been that foreignness which had allowed her to see beyond the old traditions, to bring an ancient glory out into the light of a new day in a guise entirely fresh and unlooked for. Kneeling there on Syai's earth, her face turned up to the water from heaven, one hand resting on wood scarred by fire and the other on the broken steel of the dagger, she was one with the elements of her ancient kin, as purely and wholly a part of Syai as it was possible for a mortal woman to be. She was spirit, she was its spirit, she was what Xuelian had seen in her eyes and called Syai's soul.

Xuelian had also said something else – had always referred to Syai as 'she'.

And there they were, the mortal woman and her immortal land, both wounded, needing each other.

There had, after all, been only one choice to make.

Amais folded her hand around the hilt of the broken dagger, dug with it into the rain-soft sand at her feet, hollowing out a narrow, shallow trench. She dropped the dagger into it, laid her hand across it so that her palm was on the metal and her fingers dug into the dirt on the sides of the hole, let the currents of the land course through her from her toes to the crown of her head, across her from the fingertip of one little finger to the fingertip of the other – earth, water, fire, metal, wood and spirit.

And spoke the ancient vow into the storm – just two words – softly, because her land didn't need her to shout to be heard.

'*Jin-shei.*'

There were shadows. Deep shadows. The woods were thick
and dense – there was little undergrowth, but the trees grew
close together, sometimes so close that Amais had to slip
between them sideways, scraping the backs of her hands and
her cheek and getting her hair caught and tangled in the low-
growing twigs and branches.

There were trees. Everywhere she looked.

And then she looked harder, and they weren't trees at all.

Every tree, every trunk, – if she peered past the illusion
of bark and bough, she could glimpse what was inside –
faces, fingers, eyes sometimes closed and sometimes open and
glittering and frighteningly aware and staring straight back
at her through the veil of their illusion.

The forest started thinning a little just as she became aware
of what it really was – people, it was all people! Younger trees
started appearing, and saplings, and mere sprouts of soft stems
and one or two leaves trembling on top. And if Amais looked
into those, they contained children – teenage boys with their
hands in fists at their sides, little girls with their hair in braids,
toddlers sucking their thumbs, babies with downy heads curled
up asleep . . . even, in those barely sprouted plants, things that
might have been in the process of becoming babies, tiny trans-
lucent pink things with dark alien eyes floating in a rosy glow
like a halo, their perfectly formed but impossibly small hands
held up near a face wearing an expression of dreamy serenity.

Amais stopped, carefully, watching where she placed her feet so that she would not hurt any living thing that might have curled near them, and simply stared.

'Where am I?' she whispered.

She had not meant to speak out loud; this was a question that swirled in her mind, fluttered around the sleeping people in their trees, trembled for long curious moments at each plant before going on to the next.

'Where it all begins,' a voice said in reply. Amais could not see the speaker, but she recognised the voice – it was that of the little girl with whom she had always shared these dreams.

'But . . . how . . . why?'

'How? That I cannot tell you. That is something that lies between heaven and earth, and it is not for such as us to pick at. Why? Because there are people who need to understand. And you are one of the few who do. Come with me.'

'Where are you?' Amais asked, turning her head, trying to place the direction from which the voice had come. She could see no movement out there, no life except the sleeping people in their trees.

The response to her question was a lilting laugh. 'Oh, I am out there somewhere. So are you. Each of us is planted out here in our time. Just follow.'

'Follow what?'

'Follow the edge of the wood. Come. You need to see. You need to know.'

Amais turned to obey, and trod on something hard and round. She snatched her bare foot back as though the thing had scalded her, with a sinking heart, peering downwards to make sure she had not inadvertently crushed some baby in its sapling cocoon, but all she could see was a tiny round bead on the ground by the side of her foot. She bent to pick it up.

It was the yearwood bead that the little girl had given her, long ago, another dream away. The yearwood bead from which an entire forest had grown.

Amais closed her hand around the bead. 'I think I begin to understand,' she whispered.

'Not yet,' the voice of the little girl said. 'Not yet. Come. Come and see.'

Slowly, carefully, Amais threaded her way through the child-wood at the edge of the forest that was people, her hand tightly clasping the bead that had been, perhaps, the physical incarnation of her own spirit. The trees and the saplings and the tiny little barely budded plants eventually started petering out, the gaps between them bigger and bigger, bare ground showing between. Bare ground that was dust blowing in the breath of breeze that stirred the leaves and raised tiny dust devils on the ground. All too soon the plants were gone, except for sedge grasses with no other life than their own tenacious souls, and the plain that stretched out before Amais was huge, and empty, and parched.

For some reason the sight made her want to cry, and she clung to her own bead all the more tightly – for if she lost it, if she lost herself, in this desert, she would never gain the living lands again.

'Why did you bring me here?' she asked the empty trembling air around her.

'Because everything has an end,' the voice of the little girl said, and it sounded muffled, somehow, as though dust had got into it and started seeping into its cracks and crevices, choking it, damping down its ringing clarity into the mere memory of itself. 'But not every end is an ending. Watch, now – look over there, over to the side. Back on the edge.'

Amais turned an obedient gaze where she was bid, and saw a man walking past a piece of the people-wood. He paced it out, and the plants at his feet were in a grid, planted with precise and meticulous care into rows and columns, regimented, obstinate, applying external order to the primeval chaos. He carried a watering can, and poured exactly the same amount of nourishing water into the roots of every plant, and they all grew almost identical – same height, same form, same shape. The man snipped with a pair of gardening shears at any errant branches, coaxing the plant back into a schooled and educated shape. The plants were flourishing, it could not be said that they lacked care, but several of them had a distinct air of yearning and melancholy, as though they wanted the freedom to cast out branches in whatever direction they wanted and knew that any attempt to do so would be met by the shears.

The man looked awfully familiar – someone Amais knew, or would know – time was fluid here, and it was hard to tell the future from the past. But he kept his head down and his focus on his work, and since she could not see the whole of his face at any given moment it was hard to be certain.

'What is he doing?' she asked instead, watching curiously as the gardener went about his work.

'Taking care of his own,' the voice of the little girl said. 'Look at that in his hand. That is not a watering can that he used to scoop out water from some pond or fountain. Look closely – the can is his hand, the can is himself, he is watering those plants, those people, with what is inside him.'

'And they flourish,' Amais said. 'It is good.'

'They flourish for a moment, for a year, for a decade, for a century,' the voice said. 'And then the time of the gardener is over. Sometimes he finds another who comes in his place, another watering can at the ready, and the plants begin to drink again of a different soul, and they might thrive or they might wither. It is hard to say. But that kind of garden lasts a lifetime. Or a generation. No longer.'

'And what happens then?'

'Sometimes, this,' the voice said, and it was obvious that it meant the desert at their backs where nothing living grew. 'Some people are the living water that feeds others, and they are rich and nourishing, and their folk grows hardy and grows strong. But then they are gone. Other people . . .'

Something rolled against Amais's foot, and she looked down. It was a yearwood bead, much like her own, but weathered, ancient, its carvings almost scoured away by the sands of time. Instinctively she bent to pick it up, and passed it into the palm of the hand which held her own, and began playing with the two beads between her fingers for just an instant. In a moment she became aware she held only one, as she had held before – her own. But it was different – edged with the age of the other one. Before she had a chance to comment, two more beads rolled towards her and came to rest at her feet. She collected them too, in a silence that was full of wonder, and cupped her hands around them all – and soon they were only one again, her own. And while her bead absorbed its fellows, she felt her own mind and spirit bloom with the souls and memories of those whose beads they had been.

And then they came to her, from all directions, and piled at her feet, buried her feet up to their insteps, then their ankles, then higher. Amais crouched down and buried her hands in the beads, and felt them all come to her, into her, felt her own yearwood bead gently take them and wrap them into itself and felt her spirit expand to take all the others that came asking admittance.

'Some people are gardeners for a season,' said the voice that she had followed, and the little girl was finally there, standing a few steps away, her hands tucked into her wide sleeves, wearing a small smile that was almost sad. 'Others are born to be the memory of the land, of its people – not *for a season, but for always. It is not an easy thing to be, but I think you are starting to know what you need to do.'*

The souls of her people, the bones of the land that had made her, came into Amais and found the empty places within her which had been waiting to be filled for so long. She was weeping, although she did not know exactly why, but her hands were open in the mass of beads at her feet, and her soul was open to the voices of the people who had come to her, and her body was rooted through the soles of her feet to the land that was her home.

She was smaller than the tiniest of the embryos in the woods behind her, waiting to be born.

She was bigger than the largest tree in the forest, bigger than the mountains, bigger than the sky.

She was nothing. She was everything. She was love and memory and dream, and life.

The Embers of Heaven

No matter what they put you through, when they
break your body or poison your mind – if you can
hold on to a single warm memory that you treasure,
it can be your passage back to the world of light.
Those memories are the embers of heaven, and from
them life and love can kindle again.

The Song of the Nightingale

I almost expected that Xuan would be gone by the time I finally made my way back to where I had left him – but never, in all the time I knew him, did he prove to be less than faithful once he had pledged his word to something. He did not know what I had gone there to do – he could not know, and I never told him – but he came with me, and he would not leave without me even if his apprehension and all the objections he had voiced to coming here in the first place were plain on his face when I stepped out of the shadows.

'I was worried,' he said. He had flinched, in the moment before he had seen it was me – he had been coiled tight, tense, just waiting for someone to stumble upon our unsanctioned presence and turn us in – but that was all that he said when I returned. That, and then I saw his shoulders relax. Just a little.

It mattered a ridiculous amount to see that small gesture just then, to know that there was one human being left in this world to whom my safety might matter, who would worry about my wellbeing, who would guard and shelter me against danger if he could.

'Was I too long?' I asked. It was a genuine question. I had no idea how long I had spent under that willow tree.

'Long enough,' he replied, after a pause. 'Have you done what you came to do?'

'Yes,' I said. 'We can go.'

I did not turn as we walked away, I did not look back. It was doubtful what I would have been able to see in the night and the storm, but whatever there was, it was not the vision I wanted to take with me of the place that had once been the Great Temple of Linh-an. Not the ruin.

'Xuan . . . I have to go – I have to leave this city as soon as I can do it . . .'

I had not realised that I had been thinking that, not until the words fell into the storm-washed air that still tasted of thunder and of ashes.

He stopped walking and looked at me, his eyes glittering. It had stopped raining by now but we were both soaked; water dripped from our clothes, our hair, and pooled at our wet feet.

'Stay,' he said unexpectedly, reaching out to take my hand.

'I can't,' I said – and for a moment, just a moment, that world-weight reasserted itself on my shoulders and they sagged a little. I had taken it all on, by choice, by oath. I hardly even knew yet what shape the fulfilment of that vow to my land would take, but I did know that I could not fulfil it in this place, not hiding out in cellars and tenements like a mole, too afraid to lift my eyes to the sky.

But I did not pull my hand away.

'I will tell you where the sword is hidden,' I began, and he tossed his head, his wet hair flicking water at my face.

'Damn the sword,' he said with a quiet violence. 'Stay.'

I shook my head. 'I have to go.'

'But where will you go? What will you do?' he asked, his fingers tight around my own. 'I cannot just let you walk away!'

'I have to go,' I repeated. And then I uttered a sentence that I swear I never meant to say. 'You could come with me . . .'

He stared at me for a long moment, and then made an odd gesture with his head, half a nod, half a shake of denial. 'Out of the city?' he whispered. 'But where could I take what's left of my family?'

'I think,' I said, a plan beginning to form in my mind, 'I know a place where we can all go . . .'

He asked me to marry him, the next day, and then he kept asking me, after – but how could we? In the city we would have to go to an official and sign papers with our names on, and I dared not – not if the note of warning left anonymously at my door was right, and they were looking for me – and he dared not – not if the Golden Wind had come to this house already and had missed taking him only because he had not been home. We were already fugitives; we just needed to take the final step to prove it, and flee.

I might have suggested we detour around the Street of Red Lanterns and pick up the sword – or go to the place where he had hidden the journals, and take those – but there was little time left to think of treasures that were, as far as we knew, still safely hidden from harm and which could not be hurt in the way human beings might be.

Xuan's mother readily agreed to leave the city; but his sister balked.

'How will Wulin know where to look for me, when they let him go?' Xinqian said obstinately, clutching her small child to her breast. 'He will come home . . . he will come home. And I must be here to wait for him.'

But Xuan took her aside, and talked to her for a long time. And in the end, she agreed. She was quiet and mutinous and her eyes were full of tears, but she was a mother as well as a wife. She could not know if her husband would *ever return – but the child, the child was her responsibility, her burden. If the child could be salvaged out of the catastrophe, that would mean something.*

There was little to pack. We left towards the middle of the next day, trudging out of the northern gate with our heads and our eyes downcast, praying that nobody would take a closer look at us – for in fact we had no defences, and I didn't even have papers on me that would identify me. We were lucky, or we were in the hands of the Gods – there were four cadres on guard at the gate and every single one of them had his hands full at the time we trudged up. Three women, one of them a grandmother and another carrying a toddler, and a single man in their wake, on foot – we probably didn't seem important enough. And then I led us north and west, towards Hian, the province of Iloh's boyhood, to a farm where I knew I would be welcome.

It didn't quite work out the way I intended in the end. Iloh's father was dead, and Youmei now lived almost on sufferance in a single room in the old farmhouse, with another two families living in the rest of the place and a few new rooms added on to take up the overflow. But Youmei knew me, and the other two families were short on manpower. Xuan was an asset, a strong, young pair of hands, not to mention the added bonus of two healthy young women who could take up the slack on the farm chores. We didn't have papers, but scrounging for identity was something at which the country people had become adept. We acquired new names, new identities . . . as was becoming far too easy in Syai, new pasts.

Xuan said we could marry now, as brand-new people whom the local authorities would have no reason to suspect. He continued to ask, every time I thought he had accepted the fact that I would stay with him anyway, even without the paperwork. The others on the farm had taken it for granted that we were a couple already, and we shared a room, and a bed. We were together – that much had been sealed that night in the Temple, when he followed me into danger, despite his reservations, accepting without question that there were things he had not been told about what I planned to do, because he could not do otherwise. When we had finally gone to sleep that night, back in the house with the blue tiles, under the falling rain, we had done it in each other's arms. It was enough, for me.

Youmei and Xuan's mother struck up an odd friendship, an alliance, two matriarchs who should have ruled over a courtyard full of their grandchildren and great-grandchildren but who had to be content with presiding over an uneasy mix of young people and children who were not of their own blood. They could at least commiserate with each other on the matter while stirring the cooking pots or turning coats or trousers to last another season.

It was safe. For the time being, I even allowed myself to be happy.

In the rest of the country, the Golden Rising crescendoed, and then began to falter. Iloh finally withdrew his support, even the tacit unspoken one – but the damage had already been done. When the army moved in to curb the worst excesses of the Golden Wind, it was far too late. Nobody trusted anybody any more, and people watched one another with hooded eyes. Stolen things remained stolen, and it became routine for people to find their possessions seized by the Golden Wind being sold on the black market or even openly in shops.

The Golden Rising did not burn long, but it burned hot, and its scars were deep – the people had been changed by it, in fundamental ways, and so had the land. The city had its own scars. I knew the Golden Wind had packs of political prisoners, educated people who had a very good idea of what they were being forced to do, at Linh-an's walls – at first just chipping at them with sledgehammers and pickaxes and then, later, with mechanised tools and bulldozers; smashing the massive carved guardian stone lions at the gates. Many of the city's Temples had been turned into small factories during Iloh's ill-fated Iron Bridge campaign, and that had only got worse during the Rising, with beautiful old jewel-box places of quiet worship being turned into a mess of machinery, a stench and a noise, a blot on the landscape, tall chimneys belching black smoke and rising higher than the bell towers. These neighbourhood factories were used as bases for mechanical workshops or produced incongruous goods – like wire, or lightbulbs. I remember thinking at the time that it was a pity someone had so badly misunderstood the idea of 'enlightenment'.

There were parts in the city even before I left it where the fruit trees in the gardens, those that survived the axe and the fire, simply ceased to bear fruit any more, succumbing to first sterility and then to blight and disease. It seemed symptomatic of what had been inflicted upon the people. Some of Linh-an's ancient walls had already been replaced by a cancer-like growth of grim grey high-rises, which rose on the ruins of the ancient courtyard-ringed houses that had once backed against those walls. The city was spilling out into the orchards and the fields, swallowing up the countryside, devouring copses of trees and small lakes – and inside its busy streets the new industries belched out their stinks and their smokes until they covered the sky with an awful patina of a sickly yellowish-grey which smelled faintly of burning oil, and of molten metal, and of many, many people.

I had come to Linh-an with a family, and I was leaving with an entirely different family, someone else's kin – but they were mine, now. They were all I had.

Iloh had remained in the city, of course. But I was not thinking of Iloh, not then. You would think that I would have, there on the farm where he had been born, but I didn't, not in that first year or so in the country. Not since the Gods had smiled at me and let me live, and allowed me to find a measure of happiness.

I never went home again, not to the place I had known as home, not to the couple of rooms that I had shared with Aylun and my mother and my stepfather, all of whom were gone from me. Lixao was in the same limbo as Xinqian's vanished husband but less likely to survive anything harsh or prolonged, Mother was now years dead, and Aylun I knew nothing of after she had left me that heartbreaking note on the night I raced out to salvage what could be saved from the scourge of the Golden Wind. It was all gone, all the memories that had gathered in that place – both those that were ephemeral and clung like cobwebs under the beds and in unswept corners of rooms, and those more permanent, more damning to me if they had ever been discovered and deciphered, the journals I had kept during the Rising, where I spoke freely of my thoughts and feelings. In the journals I had never called Iloh by his title; I sometimes wrote harshly of the Rising, and of what had gone before, and the way that Iloh's dreams were shaping the land and its people. If anyone had wanted to call me counterrevolutionary and hang me for it, the evidence was right there, in those notebooks covered in spidery jin-ashu scrawl.

I suppose I was lucky that few Golden Wind cadres would have bothered to try and get them read by someone who knew how. They were far too busy in those days chasing down actual flesh-and-blood victims – and they had plenty – to bother chasing down the ghosts whose trail was long cold.

But my memories did not vanish with those notebooks; if

anything, it was as though the loss of one sense sharpened another. I had always been the one who watched, who observed, rather than the one deeply involved with the events that had shaped my days. It had always been a struggle for me, between the real and the ideal; sometimes it was very hard to tell the two apart, and sometimes it was more of a question of seeing the differences clearly but trying to reconcile them by looking at the subtle and shadowed things of Syai under the clear, bright, uncompromising light of Elaas. It didn't always work. I knew myself for a flawed recorder, but it had been that very flaw, the slight edge of detachment while in the very crucible of history, that probably made me the kind of witness that history needed.

I found my memories of those times standing out more and more starkly in my thoughts in the day, and in my haunted dreams at night. They etched themselves in my face, and hollowed out my cheeks until my cheekbones stood out and my skin stretched tight against my skull. For a while I grew thin and pale, even my courses stopped, and I thought I might be pregnant, but it was just my body reacting to the things that lay buried in my mind.

It had been Youmei – to whom I had talked freely, of everything except that last photograph I had seen of her daughter in the newspapers and of what that might have meant for her – who gave me the means of surviving this harrowing time.

'You have to write it all down, let it all out, before it eats you alive,' she said as she sat at my bedside. I had blacked out in the courtyard, and they had brought me back in to revive me on the qang, *the same one where I had watched Youmei care for Iloh's father for so many months when I had first come to the farm. 'You're holding everything inside, and you're letting it consume you. It's like a cancer of the spirit, and you have vowed that to a greater thing than*

yourself. You owe it – you owe your health and wellbeing to this land. Do what you have to in order to pay that debt.'

So I started again, from nothing, jotting down the memories and the dreams as they came, and something released inside of me. But it wasn't a journal that I wrote – it was back to my earliest roots that I went, and what emerged from under my pen was a story once more, fiction in terms of its characters and its actual setting, but purest truth in the events I wrote of and the way in which they affected a nation. The language that flowed from my pen was raw and visceral and although such things don't often have much to do with poetry, that is what this was – a harsh poem, cast as story, a history of our times, a truth of the kind that can best be told cloaked in a layer of story grown into legend and growing into myth, like bitter herbs drunk in a tea sweetened with honey. I wrote it in jin-ashu; this was a woman's story, seen through a woman's eyes, and it seemed to be the only language it wanted to be told in.

I did not know, before I started to write it, just how much pain there was to be shared – because the word spread, and people started wandering in, first from the surrounding area and then from further afield, with stories to tell. Some of those found their way into what I was writing; others were simply salt and saffron, seasoning the narrative with the knowledge that they existed and had taken place, without mentioning detail. I could not write much at a sitting because it affected me so powerfully – it was as though I had woken up a thousand voices in my head and they were all clamouring to be heard, and I had only the one voice, the one hand, to let them all through and let them out and let them have their say.

It was the story of revolution and the storms of war – but that was only the public side of it. Woven into it was the secret that had never been told before, the secret I had come to Syai to find, the legend that I had made myself a part of that night in the Temple – the dream of jin-shei, and of what it meant for the land, and the people of that land.

It was initially written for me, for my own eyes – but the women who came to see me and talk to me began asking diffidently if they could copy out this scene or that scene and take it home to treasure it. And those hand-copied fragments began to be read far more widely than I realised. People began asking me to come to their homes, their communities, and talk to them about what I was writing. I said no, at first, but the requests did not stop and somehow I found myself the kernel around which something began to form.

'We should have taught them,' a woman who was a stranger to me said after she listened to me talk to a group in a neighbouring village. 'We, who know. Oh, but sometimes I find myself yearning for the days that the women held it all – in the old days, an emperor ruled Syai, but it was a woman who chose him, and it was that woman whom he asked for advice because he knew he ruled by her word. It was the women who knew everything, and were able to tell each other things that the men never knew, and held the world in the palms of their hands . . .'

'But that was legend,' I said carefully, calmly, but my heart was beating very fast as I listened to her. 'And it isn't as if no blood was spilled in the Imperial days.'

'Blood will always flow,' said the other woman, mother of three children, pragmatic, practical, utterly rooted in Syai and the way its people saw the world. 'That we will never be rid of, not completely. People cannot, it seems, live in complete peace – Cahan does not allow it, outside its own gardens. But that ancient blood was spilled in the name of different things. In the women's country, it would not be the children who would be sent in to do the work of changing the world. Jin-shei would have taken care of it – a sister

410

*would ask it of a sister, and there would be influence brought
to bear. Even Tang – even Iloh – had mothers. And mothers
and their* jin-shei-bao *would have known, would have
understood, would have spread the word in places where
you might have thought it could never reach. All of us listen
to our mothers, when we are young enough to be moulded.'*

Initially it was a community of women I became a part
of, a web of communication, a sharing of knowledge and
experience. Jin-shei – *the kind of* jin-shei *vow that I knew
of from Tai's writings and from* baya-Dan's *stories – was not
quite what was happening here. That had been, in ancient
times, more something shared between individuals than this
sense of belonging to a group with a set of special responsibilities to one another.*

But I had already changed the nature of everything when
I invoked the old oath between myself and my country rather
than another woman, and something began to bind us
together, a new bedrock, a foundation on which a new society might be built, in time. It was, after all, the women's
country – not the one for which I had naively gone searching when I was a passionate sixteen-year-old, but it was here,
after all, and I would have a hand in making it re-emerge
from its centuries of shadow and silence.

So I gave them everything, in that book. I was writing a
book of fiction, but that fiction was woven from the truths
of my own life, my own terrors and triumphs and secrets
and achievements – the way things had been, the way things
had really happened.

I wrote of a poet who had lived more than four hundred
years before, whose blood ran in my own veins, who had
been jin-shei-bao *to an empress of ancient times. I wrote of
my exiled grandmother, waiting for Syai to rise again like a
phoenix from its own ashes, living out her days on the far
side of the world. I wrote of the mother whose bones I had*

411

left lying in a field that had no name. I wrote of my little sister, who wanted nothing more than to serve the people, just like The Golden Words had taught, and ended up taking lives. I wrote of a woman who had loved an emperor once, who could have stood any amount of physical pain inflicted on her frail old body but whose great and generous heart had been broken by the wanton destruction of the last precious legacy of that love at the hands of brutes who could never understand. I wrote of the friend who died in the wreckage of the Great Temple, protecting the things she loved and believed in, and of the way the Temple bell had tolled for her passing as well as its own.

I wrote about things that had been secret for centuries.

There were things I did not write about. Not then. What I had done in the Great Temple on the night of its fall would not let itself be told, not yet. That was for the future.

All of it had become greater than me, somehow. I wove a tale of my own life, but my as yet nameless account had become part of a hundred personal little stories – and I remembered, once, a long time ago, Iloh telling me that only history could judge him. It seemed that he was quite right, and that I would be the one to write that history.

In my life I have loved two men, and it was Iloh who had been the poet – but it was Xuan who named what I was writing. For a long time it was simply nameless – I called it 'the thing' when I called it anything at all. Lihong liked to refer to it as my 'tapestry', and Youmei, who had begun it all, simply dubbed it 'Amais's antidote'. It was Xuan – who could not read it, to whom sections of it were read out loud by Lihong or, sometimes, late at night, by myself – who finally wrapped his head around what it truly was. It was more than just story, more than even just history – it was an elegy, for a thing that needed to be remembered, that did not want to be remembered.

'You were named right, after all,' he said to me one night, lying beside me, his head propped on one hand and his eyes full of tears after I had just finished reading a particularly harrowing part of it. 'You are the nightingale, singing after night has fallen, singing in the twilight of a tragic day from which even the sun has fled and hid his head. That's exactly what this is – the song of the nightingale.'

He wrote that phrase out, the only one in the notebook in which I was writing that was written in firm, bold, masculine hacha-ashu *script*, on the title page.

It seemed that this was payment, after all, of that debt I had taken on in the ruins of the Temple, in the rain.

But it proved to be only a part of that debt. And not, by any means, the greater part of it.

I had nearly two years of this respite – and then, one day, quite suddenly and without warning, an old woman turned up at the door of the farmhouse. At least it seemed to be an old woman, because she moved very slowly and as though she were in great pain. I probably should have recognised her, even so – but perhaps it was more fitting that Youmei did so first, with a gasp, and then a cry, and then, when the visitor lifted her face to us, I too knew her.

It was Yingchi, come home at last – but this was a woman who looked ten years older than when I had had my final glimpse of her, a gargoyle in a blurry newspaper photograph. She seemed to take just as long – maybe even longer – to remember me. It was as though her mind had been ploughed over so comprehensively in the last two years that memories had been buried very deep. Too deep. She came just in time to add her own brand of thin poison into the potion that Song of the Nightingale *was* brewing up to be; but more than that, she was a sudden reminder of that other life which I had somehow managed to completely bury out of sight,

413

clinging to this tiny piece of sunlight that I had found in the centre of the storm, unwilling to look out where the dark clouds were still gathered all around us. Yingchi was a cold wind from reality, blowing into our sheltered little corner of the world. And she brought more news than we really wanted to hear.

'They gathered us up like cattle,' she told us later that night, after supper was over, and we all huddled on the qang to listen to her story. 'I grasped at that like a straw, you know – at least we would be together, at least there would be a friendly face, perhaps, or a voice you knew, something, something of that other life, something to remind you of who you had been, that once you had thoughts and dreams and memories that were your own . . . but it didn't last. They split us all up, after – sent us all over the place. I heard some were sent to the marshes and made to work like coolies at draining them, reclaiming the land – city women, who might have come from farming stock once but who had long forgotten what it was like.'

'What about you?'

'I wound up in a mountain camp,' she said. 'They made us walk there, a hundred miles, maybe more – we walked every step of the way, and the pace was a punishing one – and then, at the end of a long day's march, we had an hour with Shou'min Iloh and his Golden Words before we were allowed to eat anything and collapse for a few hours' sleep . . .'

'Did they know,' I asked her, 'who you really were?'

'What would have been the point?' Yingchi replied.

'It would have brought her nothing but heartache,' Youmei said, nodding her head. 'They would have used her as an example. They would have devoured her.'

'They told us we would be going to a village,' Yingchi continued, 'but there were only caves when we got there, caves and a broken-down old storage shed. So we had to

414

start from the beginning. We had almost no tools, but we made everything we owned – our food bowls, our beds, baskets and tiles, dug our own latrines.'

'But what were you supposed to accomplish there?'

'We cleared the land,' she said, and lifted her hands for our inspection. They were raw, red, nails broken into the quick and showing no sign of wanting to grow again, grimy with earth that was ground into her pores. 'Where there was no soil, we carried it on our backs. There were two hundred women in the camp, and some had duties in the actual encampment – call it a hundred and fifty of us who were the drudges. We carried soil in buckets and baskets until our shoulders were bleeding and our backs felt broken. It took one hundred and fifty women nearly three weeks to carry enough soil to a barren mountain ridge, and reclaim one sixth of an acre. And, down below, they dug spillways and drainage ditches and terraces and made rice paddies.'

'My poor baby,' Youmei murmured.

'And then the ridge we had disturbed came down in a mudslide, and covered the spillways, and we had to start again. But we restored the fields in time, that year, for a crop – we planted and we harvested. In some ways I have never been more savagely proud of anything I did than of those grains of rice at the end of the season. They were born from me as surely as children might have been . . .'

'They let you go?'

She shook her head. 'They quit guarding us. It's different. Some stayed, even – it's home, now, after everything . . . but I wanted to . . . I needed to come back. It's been so long . . . so long . . .'

We left them together, mother and daughter; there was too much there that was for the two of them alone. But, later, when the tears she had brought to shed in her mother's arms were done, Yingchi sought me out.

'Xuelian said to me that she would tell you, also, where the treasure of the House of the Silver Moon lies. Did she?'

'Yes,' I said. 'And what it should be used for. I have not touched it – not yet. There have been no means to use it in the manner that she wished, and . . . and I'm afraid I grew to like my cocoon too much. I am guilty of that. Will you help me? You know these women, you know where to deliver that silver . . .'

'I went back to Linh-an first, to try and find you,' Yingchi said. 'But you were long gone by the time I got there. All I could find out was that your sister was dead . . .'

The words, so bluntly uttered, were a stab in the heart. I made a small sound of pain. She heard, stopped, stared at me.

'I am sorry,' she said, her voice very gentle. 'I thought you must have already heard. Oh, but I did not mean to come back here to bring pain . . .'

The image of Aylun's face swam into my mind, the sweet face of the child she had been before . . . before everything. Before she had so fiercely embraced Iloh's dream, before that had put blood on her hands. The little girl who had once had a different name, in a different land. I spared a moment to wonder if she would have still been alive if she had remained Nika, if she had remained Elena's favourite grand-daughter, if she had never left Elaas.

'How?' I managed to ask. 'Do you know?'

'Suicide,' Yingchi said, almost unwillingly, but now that she had uttered those words out loud there was no real point in withholding other pertinent information. 'Less than six months after . . . after the emperor. You know she was involved with that, she was there that night. Xuelian said you knew.'

'Yes. She told me. Right before they . . . they . . . what became of Xuelian?'

'I don't know,' Yingchi said in a small voice, and tears glittered in her eyes. 'And I would give much to be able to tell you. She . . . meant a great deal to me.'

'And to me,' I whispered. 'I was there, when they took her. One of them broke her emperor's comb, right in front of her eyes; I saw it happen. He might as well have torn the living heart from her breast.'

We shared that, at least – this sorrow, this wound of wanton, vicious death.

And then Yingchi looked at me again, and her expression was more enigmatic. 'She told me, also, about . . . who the father had been to your unborn child, that time I nursed you back in the House,' she said. 'I don't know if you have heard, but Iloh . . . doesn't look well. I was in the city when he gave one of his broadcasts – and I grant you I haven't seen him or spoken to him in person for too many years to be wholly certain of this, but I think I could hear it in his voice.'

That name . . . that name woke things in me, things I thought I had lulled to sleep in the past few years. Xuan was enough . . . should have been enough . . . but Iloh's name alone still had the power to move me. My hands had twisted together into a tight knot, without my even having been aware of it. I relaxed them with a conscious command.

'Hear what?' I asked.

'The hopelessness,' Yingchi said. 'And I think that is the only disease for which I know of no cure.' She hesitated, would not meet my eyes. 'Except . . . maybe . . .'

She wanted me to go back, to try and mend the things that were broken. She did not ask, not directly, but the thing hung there between us, left unspoken, left for me to make up my mind – and I was not sure that I could do this, that I was strong enough to do this, that I could pay the price of taking that healing that Yingchi wanted of me back to the place where pain dwelled. I had not seen Iloh since that last

417

searing time, and I did not know if I ever would again. Not because I didn't want to. More, perhaps, because I wanted to do it far too much – and now there was Xuan, who trusted me, whom I also loved.

But it was Yingchi's coming, Yingchi's words, that precipitated one of what I had learned to recognise as my guidance dreams.

I remembered the place I found myself in that dream – the people-wood, the place where I had seen the spirits of people growing as living trees, but this time, at least at first, I appeared to be quite alone here – that little girl who always accompanied me, the child who had led me in these strange journeys of spirit and mind, was not with me. Or at least she was not in person; it was her voice, however, that hung in a whisper under the trembling leaves of the people trees: 'Follow . . .'

The voice seemed to come from everywhere and nowhere, but after a while I became aware that there was a small figure standing by one of the trees – another child, perhaps, younger than the little girl in my other dreams had been. As soon as it knew that it had been seen, the child turned and slipped away into the shadows under the trees, and my instructions became clear. I ducked under the low branches that had been this new guide's concealment and stepped into the wood.

At first the child I was following appeared to want to escape from me, because it moved fast, and almost stealthily, and once or twice I even thought I had lost it completely – but every time that happened I realised that it had stopped a little way in front, half-turned in my direction, waiting for me. So intent was I on keeping that elusive forest sprite of a child in my sights that I had simply ceased to notice my surroundings – right until the moment I stepped out into a clearing. In the middle of the clearing, a tiny sapling grew –

two pale green leaves, shaped a little like a heart, were all it had had the strength to unfurl. Within it, floating in an ethereal golden-green light – the filtered light of the sun through a forest canopy – I could glimpse the shape of a very young but perfectly formed embryo, its eyes closed, two tiny hands curled into small fists before its face.

Bent over this sapling, carefully watering around its roots, was a man.

A man whom I knew, whom I would know anywhere. The man to whom Yingchi wanted me to return. The man whose child – just like that unborn baby sleeping in its young tree, oh just like it! – I might easily have borne after the last time we had met on the empty country road.

'No,' said a small voice right beside me, 'that child would have been me.'

The man by the sapling straightened. I looked into Iloh's dark eyes, fell into them, my head spinning from a sudden and yet not unexpected shaft of something that was equal parts pain and joy. And then he was gone, vanished, re-absorbed into the fabric of the dream – except that when I turned around to respond to the words that had just been addressed to me, I met those eyes again, in the face of the child I had followed through the woods to this place.

'Who are you?'

'I am you, and I am him. I am what might have been born had you not drank of the bitter herbs.'

Tears sprang to my eyes. 'I am sorry,' I whispered. It was the only thing I could say, the only thing I could think.

'It was not my time,' the child said gravely. It was extremely difficult to pinpoint that sprite's gender – its glossy black hair swung just below its ears, parted in the middle, and its features were formed of equal parts a boy's firmness and a girl's fragile vulnerability. Its mouth was still full and dewy with childhood, but its eyes . . . its eyes were the eyes

419

of the never-born and of the often-born, full of a sad, strange wisdom that touched me deeply in places I had not known existed inside me. Yes, it was mine – I could sense it, I could feel it, I had a mother's urge to reach out and gather it into my arms and croon lullabies into that soft dark hair falling around its face. I had not known that I yearned for a child, but in this moment I knew that yearning in full measure – and the child knew, understood, gazed at me with pity and affection and a quiet knowledge reflected in those eyes.

Iloh's eyes.

'Oh, Cahan,' I whispered, beginning to understand.

'You cannot have them,' my unborn son/daughter said to me, with the weight of prophecy. 'You cannot have children before that child, the one child, the child that this land will need – the child that only you and he can make. It was not to be me – but there . . .' It lifted a hand, pointed to where the embryo hung in its cocoon of light – except that it was no longer asleep, and as I looked into the sapling I met another pair of never-born/often-born eyes, gazing straight into mine. 'There,' the other child said. 'There, my sister waits.'

And I knew, when I woke from that dream, with all those voices still echoing in my mind, that the road ahead would be strewn with hard choices. In order to fulfil the pledge I had made to Syai, I would have to betray someone who loved me and trusted me. Perhaps more than one.

The women's country. She was a woman too, my Syai, but she could not do what needed to be done, not without the living, breathing body of her jin-shei-bao – and the thing that was being asked of me was asked in the name of the vow I had taken in the ruined Temple in the rain.

It was spring when I returned to Linh-an.

Oh, how smoothly I had layered my story for all the people who must never know the real purpose behind my

420

journey, for all the people who knew it all too well! Yingchi said nothing when I explained my reasons for going back; Xuan insisted on coming with me. My heart already bleeding from every treacherous lie I told him wrapped in a tissue-thin layer of truth, I let him come as far as the last train stop before the city. Somehow – and maybe it was those insistent and increasingly demanding voices which I carried that gave me the words I needed – I won the right to go into the city itself alone.

'I have to carry a sword out,' I said to him – for that was my excuse, my reason, my sudden desire to go back. It was to retrieve those treasures that we had once hidden for each other, in a time when there were no reasons for secrets and lies between us, a time when we were innocent strangers to one another. 'They would certainly stop you, if you tried to carry it out – and, if necessary, I know a secret way out of the city and they will never find me.'

'But if it is a secret way then I too could use it and escape undetected,' he had protested. 'You are not safe in Linh-an by yourself, on false papers – remember how you were once eager to leave before they got their hands on you?'

'You, too, and if they get us they get us both,' I said. 'Don't worry. Everything will be fine. I know a safe place where nobody will think of looking for me.'

That much was true. Thank Cahan he didn't think to ask me why I had not chosen to go to that safe place two years before, when we had fled the city to escape the howling furies of the Golden Rising.

He let me go, in the end. I will never forget, till the day I die, the completely open, trusting, honest look with which he bade me farewell when I left for the city the next day – because I carried it with me through what was one of Linh-an's last surviving gates like a wound.

The city had already begun to change, by then – too many

421

of the remembrance arches in the streets, once marble and carved or painted wood, were already gone. That had started back when I was still there – ostensibly they got in the way of modern transport, and slowed the modernisation of the city – but somehow their loss made the streets look grimier, dirtier, more commonplace, more naked. It was certainly reducing the splendour of the Imperial city to the ranks of its less exalted inhabitants – but I could not, in my heart, find approval for it. The heart had gone out of the city, the magic of it all. Like too many things that seemed good ideas at the time, this was turning out to be destruction for destruction's sake, just putting a stamp on the city, claiming it for the plain and workaday Republic from the grandeur and the magnificence of an Empire.

I had been sent here – by a vow, by a dream, in order to conceive a child. I had no idea if any of this wild vision would even succeed. I had not thought it out further than this – I would come to where Iloh was, and then I would see what happened. But what would happen if I did no more than lurk in the teeming city outside the gates of Iloh's guarded compound would be precisely nothing – and then everything would be wasted, all the treachery which the road back to Linh-an had been paved with, all the pain.

So I did the only thing I could think of that might have had an effect, and I did it within an hour of arriving in the city, before I could lose my nerve. I simply marched up to those gates and told one of the guards to tell Shou'min Iloh that Amais was here.

His reaction, initially, was predictable. He snorted in incredulous disdain.

'I should go and disturb Shou'min Iloh just because some chit from the street tells me to?' he said. 'Just who do you think you are? Away with you! Shou'min Iloh is a busy man!'

But I stood my ground, and looked at the two of them. Just looked at them.

One of them cocked his gun and began raising it, but the other reached out and slowly pushed the barrel down again.

'You know we could kill you?' he asked, almost conversationally.

'Yes,' I said.

He shook his head, astonished. 'Who do you think you are?'

'He knows,' I said, 'my name.'

They were beginning to get interested. After another few moments, the one who had addressed me finally snapped to a decision. 'You,' he said to his companion, 'keep an eye on her.'

And he himself turned on his heel and rapped smartly on the gate behind him. It was opened after a short pause by someone whose bewildered face was visible just briefly as the door opened and shut, and then the guard vanished within.

He had left me with the second one, the trigger-happy one, and although I found a small, centred, serene place deep inside myself where everything was well and everything was possible, the message hadn't gotten out to my skin, which crawled uncomfortably every time his fingers curled and uncurled on his gun while he watched me with flat, unfriendly eyes.

It seemed to take an eternity, but it was probably less than ten minutes later that the first guard returned. The expression on his face was pure, unguarded astonishment, and he was accompanied by someone else. I knew this man; not that many years had passed since we had gone to hunt for chickens for Iloh's father's concubine. Those years had brought trouble and disgrace on him, and that showed in the new lines that had been etched in his face, but I knew Tang, and he knew me. He nodded at me in both a tacit recognition of that fact and a coolly impersonal gesture for the benefit of the guards, and said a single word, 'Come.'

And I stepped inside, with the guards still staring after me in what was almost disbelief.

I followed Tang into one of Syai's ancient languid courtyards, flanked by colonnaded open corridors. At the far end, much like Xinmei's house had done, it had another gate which led into an inner fastness, another secret courtyard safe from prying eyes. The corridors in the first courtyard had a multitude of doors opening from them, some of which looked like they were graceless and recent additions. A few were open, and showed glimpses of cramped cubicle-like offices within where the occasional occupant lifted their head and followed my passage through the yard.

'You don't seem to be surprised to see me,' I said.

'Likewise,' he responded, with a small, twisted grin and a sideways glance.

'I thought you were out of his orbit,' I said carefully. 'At a house somewhere in the country. What brings you back?'

'He does. In the spirit of the old saying that you should keep friends close but enemies closer . . .'

'Are you his enemy now?' I asked, startled.

'I am no longer the chosen successor,' Tang said. 'That does make a difference. As for the rest . . . I don't know what I am to him any more. I am here at his pleasure; I can be sent away again just as easily if he changes his mind.' His mouth twisted again, into that bitter little half-smile. 'You know, it is true what they say – a revolutionary leader who wins power can become just as conservative and tyrannical as any old-style official against whom he has fought.'

'Tyrannical?' I said, rousing in defence, however half-hearted.

'Isn't he?' Tang said. 'But me he has in his power. You . . . you and he . . .' He shook his head. 'I have never understood this,' he said after a pause, just as we reached the gate to the inner courtyard and he shook out the proper key from

424

a key-ring he fished out of a pocket. 'Everything he has wanted, he has reached out and taken, and owned. But you – you he allowed to go free – and yet you come back to him, of your own accord.'

'He could not own me,' I said.

'Perhaps that is why he cares,' Tang said, pushing the door ajar. 'I haven't seen his eyes light up in years as they did when they told him your name. When you reach his position, few things are left that are both a treasure and a challenge, and you have always been both to him. Go in, he is waiting for you.'

'Thank you,' I said politely, and entered.

He locked the door behind me without a word.

Iloh himself waited in the courtyard. For a moment, I did not recognise him – he would have been only forty-two years old at the time, but he looked older, with prominent bags under his eyes as if he hadn't slept well for a long time. But the eyes themselves – ah, the eyes were the same, black and brilliant, and hungry.

I stopped, staring at him. He stared right back.

'You haven't changed,' he said at last, breaking the silence.

'Oh yes,' I said quietly, 'I have . . .'

'No,' said Shou'min Iloh in the voice he must have usually reserved for proclamations, because it had the ring of because-I-say-so authority. 'You have not. Oh, I don't mean that you are still the child that you were when I first saw you – you're not that, not by a long way. But you . . . you are still the same. Only you would walk up to this place and assume that your name alone would get you taken straight through to me. Of all the women I have ever known in my life, you remain the only one who doesn't know the meaning of fear.'

I couldn't help it, I laughed. 'I? I am afraid of everything . . .'

'Not of me,' he said. 'That has always been your hold on me. You have never knelt to me. Come.'

I suppose I could have proved him wrong and refused what was fairly obviously a command, and one that he assumed would be obeyed – for he had turned and walked away, and it was obvious he expected me to follow – but this was what I had come here for, after all. So I obeyed, and fell into step – not behind him, beside him. I saw him smile at that, but he didn't speak again until we were out of the open courtyard and into a quiet room which was apparently an inner sanctum – a desk, an office chair, a typewriter, a lamp, an iron bedstead, and not much else. He closed the door behind us.

'You look tired,' I said, and oh, the place where that tenderness came from – the place I still carried within me after all those years – the shores of the ocean of yuan, of the fate that had first delivered me to him. Xuan was my life and the practical sunlit hours of my days – but Iloh had always been the other half of me, the fevered dream of my nights, and nothing had changed there, nothing at all.

This was the man who had broken my family on the wheel of his ideals, who had fuelled the fire of the Rising, who had brought in the army to quell it when it became inconvenient – a man who had never stopped looking for his Iron Bridge, feeding whatever he could into the furnace to create the New Man who would come to live in his dream and make it a glorious reality. But he was the heart of this country, for all that. And hearts, notoriously, do not waste time on practical things. They yearn. They want. They love, beyond hope and beyond reason.

'A few hours' sleep a night suffices,' he said. And then he looked at me, really looked at me, and I nearly cried out with the naked need of that look. 'Where have you been for so long . . . ?' he whispered, and reached out for me.

426

And I understood exactly what I needed to give to my land. My body was the vessel – he was the heartbeat of the life that was to fill it – and that spirit that Xuelian once saw in my eyes, what she called the soul of Syai, that was you, my daughter, waiting to be born.

We talked and argued, for hours, wrapped in each other's arms and minds, as we always did; that was part of what had always drawn us together, the crossing of verbal swords, the occasional flare of pure, frustrated annoyance that we could not make one another yield on anything. We were a matched pair, in that regard – both stubborn, both opinionated, both passionately believing in the things that we held dear. If there was something odd about two lovers planning to change the world, it was only that in this instance at least one of them had the power to actually try.

But Yingchi had been right about one thing – there was something about Iloh that was fey, almost transparent, as though he was already half in another world. I could have asked him about it, because I could have asked him anything – but somehow, maybe it was because of the poetry of the Song of the Nightingale *world in which I'd been living for so long, it came out less direct than I had wanted.*

'After you've lived the kind of life you've lived, after you know what it feels like to hold your hand in the fire, after you've skirted the edge of everything possible . . . is the rest just waiting . . . ?'

His face had changed a little at that, and his eyes looked somewhere through me and into infinity. 'Yes,' he said in reply.

It was a bad moment, because in it I could see his end – and so could he. Iloh was not old – but for a moment both of us remembered that Baba Sung had not been old, either, when he had been called to Cahan. It seemed that great dreamers paid for vision with their lives.

427

He blinked, focused back on me, smiled; we were, for the time being at least, back in the real world. He asked what I was doing these days, and I told him about the Song. He listened intently, and then said,

'I would like to read that, someday.'

'You couldn't,' I replied.

'Jin-ashu, I take it?' he asked, grinning. 'More women's secrets?'

'It has always been far more than that, Iloh!'

He lifted a hand in a gesture of self-defence.

'Truce!' he said. 'Women hold up half the sky – they have always been our equals! I have never said otherwise! But before, in ancient times, they never stepped up to stand beside their menfolk . . .'

'And now you think you have lured them out into the light?' I asked.

'I don't think, I know,' Iloh replied. 'I have seen women – no more than girls, some of them – fighting beside me in the wars. I've seen them stepping up to the machines in the factories . . .'

'All you have done is made them take on the responsibilities of both sexes,' I said.

'They are free to do what they choose,' Iloh responded, 'finally, after decades, centuries, of repression and the utter, unquestioning attitudes that they belonged in the rear, in the dark, always second, always afraid.'

'You have never understood a woman, then,' I flung at him, a challenge. 'In the Empire that was, the emperor was chosen by a woman – it was the daughter of the emperor who inherited the throne, not his son. It was a woman's wisdom that guided. She taught her children things that children now never learn, because in your world they are raised by strangers, in crèches where their mothers deposit them before hurrying off to their important jobs in the factories,

428

in the government. And little by little that wisdom and tradi-
tion dies.'

'But they are now equal,' Iloh said.

Iloh's world. The place where all human beings were equal,
all were brothers and sisters.

I argued bitterly against that too-simplistic idea, as always.
I might have been one of very few people, possibly the only
one, to tell Shou'min Iloh flatly and to his face that he was
talking nonsense. To me, the power that was jin-shei *was*
partly rooted in the fact that it was a choice freely made and
freely accepted, a choice with rights and responsibilities
attached, where Iloh's version of the bonds of brotherhood
existed by default, by the mere virtue of having been born
a human instead of a cow or a dog or growing into a willow
tree. But he held to his own, and finally I gave him a wry
smile.

'You have your dreams, I have mine,' I said. 'And as far
as Song is concerned . . .'

'What?' he asked, when I hesitated.

'You would not like it,' I told him frankly.

Iloh snorted. 'What, you don't trust me to know my own
failings?'

'Not when they're filtered through other eyes,' I said. 'You
are a double-edged sword – you swept through the land and
you woke everyone up, and you made your vision their own
and made them believe that everything was possible – every-
thing, except remembering anything at all of what went
before and calling any of it good. What have you done to
this city?'

'What have I done to the city?' he repeated, honestly
nonplussed.

'That's just it – you don't even notice it. For you, reality
has always been just a stage set – the play was the thing.
But out where the real people live, Iloh, if you savage the

sets, the play itself will falter. You may think you have cured idolatry and superstition, but all you've done is replace it with something else – they began to worship you instead of the old Gods. And you never put a stop to that.'

'It was useful,' he said reluctantly, 'at the time. I did put a stop to it, as it happens . . .'

'You did not do nearly enough,' I said. 'And you did even that when it was far too late to matter. The problem was that some people never stopped believing in the old, and resented you for dismissing and destroying it – and others believed only in the new, and resented those who did not believe in you. It was hardly the best way to mould a new society.'

'It is better to believe in everything than in nothing at all,' Iloh said. 'Nothing is finished, and everything is possible.'

'But believing in everything eventually gets you to the brink of believing nothing at all. And people who don't believe anything have no future, and no past. They live one day at a time. And it is not a comfortable existence.'

'On the contrary,' Iloh said. 'That is the definition of contentment. You get the best out of life every day, you have the desire to enjoy what you hold right now, and no regrets for either failures or consequences.'

'So is that all that this has ever been to you?' I asked, obscurely disappointed in a way I could not quite pin down. 'A passing moment that holds no memory, of happiness or of regret?'

'Oh, but how you do set things on their head,' Iloh murmured, sweeping my hair back from my face with one hand. 'You know that you have been my most profound regret . . .'

It had been too smooth an answer, in a way – but under the circumstances, right then, I had no right to challenge him about it. Coming here was a double betrayal, after all, a betrayal of both the men I cared about so deeply – Xuan, because I was here with Iloh at all; Iloh, because this time it had been more than just yuan, and I had come here with a cold and deliberate plan to conceive his child. And neither man would ever know, could ever know, the truth.

We slept for a while, cocooned in each other. It was our bodies that woke first, and I opened my eyes to his fingers moving in sleepy caresses over my shoulders and back; to my own hand, almost without my being aware of it, gently stroking his side from waist to thigh. The hunger that had been banked for the years that we had been apart had not yet been sated. This time there was no stolen moment, no fear of being surprised by someone who might happen by – we had the time that we wanted, that we needed, nobody would come in and surprise us, he had given orders that everyone in the compound was to stay away from the door that divided us from the world. I did not ask if his wife was in that house, if those orders also applied to her. We talked, and loved, and argued, and slept, and sometimes just lay in each other's arms wrapped in long, deep silences. It was the longest time I had ever spent with him, and in those hours was a hint of life as it might have been had things been very, very different.

But outside this door, things had not changed at all. He was still Iloh, Shou'min Iloh, and whatever that implied. I was still Amais. We were still bound by who we were, what we were.

It was my turn to leave that time, as one of us always did – and in pre-dawn darkness of that night we had spent together I disengaged my limbs from his, knelt beside him for a long moment as he stirred in his sleep but did not wake, and planted a light kiss on the top of his head before I rose and dressed quietly and then let myself out of that enchanted room. In fact, I had no clear idea of what orders had been given – if I would even be allowed out of this place at all. But when I knocked quietly on the door that led from the inner courtyard to the outer, it was opened.

'Were you waiting for me?' I asked Tang in a low voice. 'I wasn't sure myself that I would ever . . .'

'He might have hoped you'd stay. He knew you would go. Those were the orders that were left – when you knocked, the door was to be opened to you.' Tang shook his head. 'Sometimes even I cannot fathom him. He catches himself in his own nets, and trammels himself in hobbles that only he sees as being there. When Yanzi died – that's his first wife – he married Chen, but that was a pragmatic decision, born of necessity. They were a man and a woman out in the wilderness with no hope of imminent return to the mainstream of life, and Iloh is not the kind of man who cares to be alone. It was far too soon after Yanzi, but who was I to argue? But there were always two of him in that skin, the poet and the pragmatist, and then when Chen picked that silly "Songbird" stage name, when she decided she was an actress after all and preferred to fight her wars from the safety of the stage, all Iloh could think of was that prophecy that he was handed when we were all so damned young . . .'

'I remember,' I said, with the sound of Iloh's voice in that ancient family cemetery, on the first night we shared, loud in my memory. I felt curiously dizzy; it was as though I was 'remembering' things that had happened to someone else, a long, long time ago. 'That his life's one great love would be a woman with a songbird's name. And that he would never really have her . . .' There was a question here, and I hesitated about asking it – it was, after all, far too late for the answer to matter. But for some reason I found I had to know. 'When she chose that name . . . did she know about the prophecy?'

Tang shrugged. 'Many knew it by that time – at least the

432

main thrust of it, the part that gave him greatness. Fewer knew about the woman that was foretold. What Chen knew at that time . . . I have no idea. But knowing her, it would not have surprised me. If there was one thing she knew how to do, it was not to allow opportunity to pass her by. It could have been anyone, after Yanzi. Chen made sure Iloh chose her.'

'But the prophecy also said that he would never really have her, the woman that was his destiny,' I murmured.

Tang nodded. 'And how right she was,' he murmured, looking at me in a strange way, 'that blind girl in the tavern. You're his wild bird. But Yanzi died the way she died, and he has never shed the guilt of it. Never. He could not abandon another woman to whom he had committed, and Chen had made sure he was committed by then, to her, to the woman who bore the name of Niaomai. That, and the sense of fulfilment that she gave him by choosing that name of all names – for all that he thinks himself a progressive man full of modern ideas, sometimes Iloh is no more than a son of his people, and that thin sliver of superstition and faith endures, even in him. This was a covenant made between him and his future, long ago – and once he gave his word he cannot bring himself to break that, even if it was the wrong promise, even if it was for you.'

I stared at him with tears standing in my eyes. He looked at me long enough to notice that, and then dropped his gaze down to the keys he jangled in his hand and would not look up again.

'Come on,' he said abruptly. 'The cage door is still open. Don't linger too long.'

He let me out not through the main door but a smaller side gate, leading into the alley behind the compound. I saw the unmistakable shape of a rat scurry out of the way and disappear into a crack between the pavement and the house across the alley. The city smelled faintly of fading night, and antiquity, and the ashes of burned dreams . . . and bright, new-lit flames of nascent hope. The alley gave out onto the wide avenue on which the main gates stood, the place where I had entered Iloh's fastness, and that was well-lighted indeed. Some of that spilled into the dark little alley, a wash of light on the pavement that glittered as though it was damp – had it rained, while I was in there, with Iloh? – like the path a full moon leaves on water, like the moon had often left on the seas of my childhood in Elaas. A path to heaven, my father had once told me. Words formed in my head, strung themselves into sentences, formed into – Cahan help me – a poem. It was as though Kito-Tai had reached out through the centuries and planted it in my mind. It was something that I knew would find its way into the manuscript I had left behind at Iloh's old farm:

> Bright moon, black water –
> A road that is a dream of hope
> Waiting to be born.

To be born . . .

I folded my hands around the warmth that I could feel kindling in my womb. Even the midwives would have said it was too soon to tell, but I knew – I knew that I carried another life within me. I had done what Syai had asked.

The rest of my time in the city is a blur to me now. I went to the place where Xuan had hidden Tai's journals, and found them, safe, and took them. I went to the House of the Silver Moon, which was standing derelict, not yet taken over for a new purpose by a new owner and not yet destroyed – and it was an easy matter to slip into the basement and retrieve Xuan's grandfather's sword. I made a detour to the tunnel of the Seven Jade Springs, the 'secret way' I had spoken of

434

to Xuan, just to see if that was still an option – but I was dismayed at what I found there. The waters had been fouled by the industrial complex that the city was rapidly becoming; what had once been reserved for the holy and the sacred had been freely diverted to other purposes once the holy and the sacred places had been destroyed or subverted, and the channel was slick with algae and weed. The water was at half the level it should have been, and what was there smelled bad and looked worse, with an oily scum on the surface. I decided to brave the gate.

I did not go back to pay my respects to what remained of the Great Temple – I could not bring myself to do it, to see what had become of it. But once again I was in the hand of the Gods, and I walked out of the city without anyone stopping me or asking any questions at all. I had gone in for two treasures, and I came out carrying three – words of four centuries ago, an ancestor's sword wrapped in honour and glory, and the promise of new life stirring within me.

The past and the future, as always.

I called you Xeian when you were born. There are so many meanings to that name. Part of it was a reshaping of the word that means 'heart', because that is what you were, heart and spirit of this land made flesh. But it also means 'shadow', because of the way you would have to be hidden and treasured until your time came, because of the fact that Xuan never knew you were not his own as you yourself never knew that you were not his. All of what I have written of so far has been a secret to you your whole life – but now I will write of times some of which you are old enough to remember.

You were eight years old when the Year of the Black Flux swept the land, and you remember the swathe of destruction *that it left within our own circle. Youmei died of it, and so did Lihong – both the matriarchs of our little tribe, both missed fiercely. But it was the loss of the man you always knew and loved as your father that wounded you most deeply. Lihong was already gone by then, but Youmei was still there, and Youmei had been wise, wiser than I, who always wanted to shelter and protect you. The Black Flux was not an easy sickness, not for the one who had it or for the one who had the care of the patient – it was a dirty, smelly, undignified way to go. And yet you would not be kept away from him – at eight years old you insisted that you too would nurse him, and although I still did the necessary in terms of keeping him clean and comfortable it was you who helped feed him the thin gruel that was the only thing he could keep down; it was you that sat with him for hours and just prattled, like any eight-year-old might, until he fell asleep with a slight smile on his face having forgotten for a moment, in the light of your childish joys and small happinesses, his own suffering. It was you who had been holding his hand when he died. In a way, it was fitting – his sister had gone from the farm by that stage, and his mother was dead, and I, who loved him but who had dealt him one of the worst betrayals of his life, had probably forfeited my right to be his comfort in the end. But you he loved, boundlessly and unconditionally, and you returned that love. It was good that Xuan had that, at least, in the hour that Cahan called.*

You did not know I watched you for a long time, as you sat there without moving, Xuan's hand in your own. When I finally came into the room you lifted your head and looked at me out of those big, eloquent eyes of yours.

'Go away, he is asleep,' you said. 'He doesn't need you.'

You had no idea how much that hurt, but I obeyed you, and I left you with him until you were finally ready to leave him.

You mourned him by yourself, in your own heart – you would barely talk to me about him for years. It was only when you were older that you started wanting to know more about him, and I grew to treasure those occasions when you would come and wordlessly begin helping me with some tedious chore expecting a story of Xuan's life in return.

But I never spoke to you of your real father.

I kept waiting – I don't even know for what myself, now.

Until I had the time – for word had spread, and I travelled ever further to gather in the women of Syai to that groundswell that had been begun. I even went as far as that village carved out of the mountainside where Yingchi had made the fields yield their harvest, fittingly, for that had been a miracle wrought by women's hands.

Until you were ready; until you were older; as though being who you were didn't make you ready enough, and having lived through that tragic Black-Flux year didn't make you as ready as you would ever be to hear hard truths told.

Until the world turned one more time, and one more time, and everything shook itself down into its proper place.

Excuses were easy, and plentiful. But I made all the choices; it was I who delayed, waited for the better time, the blessed hour which never quite came. It was my fault, and I regret it now – I can already see things in you, I know that you have it in you to risk everything for a dream or an idea. You would not be my daughter if you did not, let alone Iloh's . . . Oh, there was so much I could have told you, should have told you. But chances kept coming my way, and I kept on letting them slip through my fingers like they were sand.

You were thirteen when he died, your real father, whom you never mourned at all because you never knew him.

All you knew about that was what you read in the newspapers, what you heard people say in the streets or on the radio or on the one television set with its abysmal reception that lived in the village store. You had no idea of the reality of it . . . or of the fact that your mother knew long before the rest of the world did; that your mother, who lived and worked and ate and slept at your side on a village farm half the country away, was also at Shou'min Iloh's bedside as he died.

I was there.

It could not have been any other way, really. Some part of me had known that when I had gone to him in Linh-an those many years ago, when you were conceived, that was the last time I would see him – but oh, we were always so tightly bound, he and I, and he was not the kind of man to go without having the last word. And it was his turn to leave, after all.

I thought I was dreaming, at first – because that's when it came, late in the evening, and I was almost drowsing after all my chores had been done. It felt strange, because part of me was still there, hearing the farm noises, hearing people talking around me – and half of me was not, was somewhere else, in a room that I did not immediately recognise although I found it oddly familiar. It took a moment, but then I realised I knew that desk, that bed, that rug on the stone-flagged floor – all a little shabbier, older, but unmistakably the furnishings of the place where you had been conceived thirteen years before. And in the bed . . . the man.

I was there, a ghost by the bedside as he slept, his face as familiar to me as though I had shared a pillow with it for twenty years. I watched for a moment, and then I saw his eyelids flutter, once, twice, again; his breathing changed, became sharper, faster, shallower. And then his eyes flew open, as though in a panic. And he looked straight at me.

And saw me.

I could see him try to speak, but his mouth opened and no sound came out. It was as though at this final hour it had all been said, and nothing further remained. But there was one thing that he had said once, and those words were heavy in this room now, at this moment: Only history can judge me, he had told me, and he had had no idea how right he was. Because history had caught up with him and run him over, and he had been broken by it as surely as if he had gone under the treads of one of the bulldozers with which he attempted to remake the landscape of Syai. And I . . . I had been part of that judgement.

Yingchi had taken Song of the Nightingale when I was done, and given it to someone she had known in the city, someone who had a printing press that could print jin-ashu – and the book had been published. At first there were only a handful of copies, but already the women of Syai had done their work, and the book's existence had not been a secret. Those first copies disappeared practically overnight. More were printed up, hundreds of them, and those too vanished into the populace, and then someone transcribed it from jin-ashu into hacha-ashu and printed that version. Thousands of copies, that time.

And it was suddenly everywhere – ironically, much like Iloh's own Golden Words had once been. It fitted the mood of the times, when the Golden Rising and its atrocities could be reviled – if not yet quite openly, then certainly just under the surface, bubbling away like something just coming to a boil. Iloh must have seen it, must have read it – he already knew it existed, I had told him of it, and he would have read it because of me, even had nothing else mattered. But the things that Song of the Nightingale said did matter, and those things were sometimes harsh, accusing. But Iloh had done nothing, said nothing, not in his defence, not to me in accusation. It had almost been a tacit acceptance of the charges.

But now he was suddenly faced with the stark reality that

he would be given no more chances – no chances to do anything new, to undo anything old, to explain or justify any of those choices. No chance, even, of anyone who would listen to such justifications – because by the time someone came, he would no longer be capable of making them.

There was only me, and to me he could talk with his face, with his eyes, with his mind. Yes, I knew him that well – for all that our lives physically touched only three times.

I could not, even now, wholly forgive him – not for Vien's lonely death among strangers, not for demanding everything Aylun had and then asking for more. But sometimes – and even Xuelian could be wrong occasionally – love was enough.

It was not the kind of love that you shared with Xuan, my daughter – not the glow of simplicity and innocence. What Iloh and I had had was always tainted by so many other things, complicated by history, divided loyalties and passion. It was not pure and it had certainly never been simple. We had had to make choices, he and I, and sometimes the wrong choice was leaving one another and sometimes the wrong choice had been choosing one another in the face of a thousand reasons to do otherwise. But we were here at last, at this moment, and all I could choose in the end was just to love him.

'Don't be afraid,' I said. Somehow, it did not seem to be in the least incongruous that someone like me could be telling the most powerful man in my world not to be afraid, nor that I knew that he would be, in this moment.

I spoke in a whisper, Cahan alone knew why – I was a ghost in this place, who could have overheard me? But as I reached for his hand, even though I believed I could not physically touch him, I was surprised that there was a certain amount of physical sense of touch there. It did not feel like skin, more like something hard and cool, like marble – but I could touch him, and it didn't matter. I stroked his fingers *with my own, sitting beside him on the bed, whispering to him like I had done over your sick-bed many a time, Xeian, when you were small – holding the hand of Shou'min Iloh and watching his years reverse themselves, and time turn back like the serpent who is always eating his own tail. I watched it all fall away from him, all that he had accumulated over his life – he lost the title that had first ennobled him and then elevated him and set him apart from everyone else, the loneliness of the Chosen One; he lost the grim desire to return to power after he thought he saw it snatched from him by his friend; he lost the hard revolutionary shell he had acquired in his years as a general, as a revolutionary, as a guerilla, as his friends and the people he loved were sacrificed to the larger goal; he lost the glowing fanaticism of his early idealistic years, when he had believed that everything was possible if only he dreamed it. I finally watched him change back into the boy he must have once been, the boy who loved to read and would shirk his chores to go and hide in the shade of the old willow in the family cemetery with his beloved books.*

I saw his soul leave his body, a pearly breath that came out of his mouth and dissipated into the emptiness of the room. Only then did I go back to my own shell, away in the country, and lie the rest of the night awake, remembering.

There were people who celebrated his passing, and many more who wept at the news. You were thirteen years old. To my shame, today, I do not remember what your reaction was when you heard of the death of the man who was your father.

I never gave you Song of the Nightingale *to read – it was, perhaps, another instinct that was wrong and that in retrospect I find hard to explain. I should have done it, that story was your heritage, too, and it would have been an easy thing to use that as the springboard from which I could start talking to you of everything else that you needed to know about your past. But although I gave Syai the heart and spirit made flesh that the* jin-shei *vow I had made to the land demanded of me, I balked at making you take on that load too young, too soon. The mother in me was always at war with that girl who had chosen to become one with her country and her people. That had been a high ideal, and I had believed then – I still believe – that I could have done nothing else, that this was what I had left Elaas and come back to Syai for. There is a saying in Syai, that predestined enemies will always meet in a narrow alleyway – and my world shrank and shrank until that narrow alleyway was all that there was and I had to look my fate in the eye and either accept it or die. But somehow, somehow, I always thought I had the power to shield you from arriving at that place. That was the mother in me talking, and sometimes that voice is stronger and louder than all the rest.*

That is only natural.

But there were times that Xuelian's words returned to haunt me – and sometimes, perhaps, not even a mother's love is enough . . .

When I first saw you with the book in your hand – a dog-eared second-hand copy of Song of the Nightingale *– I confess to a pang of absolute panic. I had still told you nothing, and it had been years since I had finished that story, and I found myself frantically reviewing it in my head as I saw you bent over it, enthralled, wondering if I had let anything slip in the narrative, if my protective wing would only serve to make you learn a hard truth the hard way – but you were safe from that, then, because that part of my life I had never put openly into the* Song *story. But you and that book had other ramifications.*

You had left it, that time, to go and do something else – and I confess to being unable to resist going over to pick it up and turn it over in my hands. I still found it hard to believe that it was something I had done, something that had come from such depths of anguish and that had served to help heal the pain of others. There were things that I heard said about that book that humbled me, and it almost terrified me to realise how many people found traces of themselves, of their own stories, within that book. Seeing one, picking one up, always gave me a shiver down the spine – and seeing you reading it only made that shiver stronger. But there was nothing out of the ordinary about the copy that you had . . . or so I thought, at first.

Before I started to put it down, a thin, almost transparent, piece of paper fell out of the back of the book, folded over once. It fell open as I bent to retrieve it, and I stood frozen by the two words that were on it, two simple words, but so wholly unexpected and astonishing that they swam in my vision as though I had just taken a swallow of a most potent wine and it had gone straight to my head.

Jin-shei.

Song had been about other things as well – about the bloodshed and the senseless death and destruction, the things that happen when family, neighbours and friends turn on one another and rend each other with tooth and claw because to do otherwise would mean their own failure to survive. But I had written about the bonds that connected people, and of how they had been shredded in the bitter years of Syai's revolutions, thrown into the bonfires, used as kindling in order to make the flames hotter and more capable of forging a new society like the blade of a new sword. The book had not been about jin-shei, not directly, but it had been a lament to its loss – the vanishing of that solid bedrock on which society had once been firmly fixed, and which left Syai teetering unsteadily on crumbling stones that were the side of a mountain about to slide into the abyss and disintegrate into sand and dust, flat, featureless desert, a place where nothing lived or moved.

I had thought I could sense the spirit of jin-shei working its magic in the women whom I had met, who had read Song of the Nightingale, who had made the connection. But the last time I had crossed paths with the actual words, uttered as the vow itself, it had been when I spoke them to Syai in the ruins of the Great Temple, and nobody had even heard them except me, the storm, and the land to which they had been said. Now, here, there was evidence that somewhere that seed had fallen into fertile soil, and although I had never believed that I would see the fruit of it – not in my lifetime, at least – here it was, proof in my hand, that somewhere, somehow, I had managed to find the true path to the ancient women's country and bring a little of it back with me.

Xuan knew nothing of that dream – and Iloh, who did, would have smiled at the way I stood thunderstruck with the paper in my hand. Smiled, because he would have understood in a fundamental way – he had his own dreams and obsessions, after all, and knew how powerful they could be – and because he had always gently mocked me for the struggle that went so radically against his own, to bring back the old and revere it instead of simply razing it to the ground in order to make a place for the new.

And I – I was caught on the horns of a gamut of emotions. I had seen the words written on a piece of paper, which meant that the vow of sisterhood had been exchanged between at least two living women, or at least the intent had been there. But were you, my daughter, one of them? Was this your pledge, given or received, or did someone tuck away a precious slip of paper into a book and then lend it out or let it slip out of their possession without retrieving those two written words of promise? And if it were you . . . ah, my child, but a part of me was overjoyed and another part deeply envious of your experience – because I, of course, had never had a real jin-shei-bao *myself*.

Under my own rules, under the rules of the women's country, I could not ask you, and even if I could, you would not have to tell me. I had already broken those rules, it was true – there was nothing in the sacred sisterhood that defined the thing that I had done, the offering of the jin-shei *bond to the land of one's birth* – but that was something else again, something different, something new. Traditional jin-shei *was still a thing that remained between a sister and a sister, and not even mothers, unless invited, could share it. I ached to talk to you about it, to tell you all that I knew and believed, to tell you what my grandmother once told me* – but I had no right to broach the subject with you, so instead I cheated – I waited until I saw you finish Song, and then I gave to you what I had treasured these many years myself – Kito-Tai's journals.

If there was a place to learn about the power of jin-shei, then it was this wellspring, where I had learned it myself.

And then I realised that I still had things left to learn, and that sometimes mothers can learn from daughters, too.

Jin-shei *was a women's mystery, shrouded in secrecy, buried in centuries of whispers and veils. But there is a time for secrets, and there is a time to bring the secrets out into the light of day and share them among all, built on, wished on, wrought into new dreams for a new day. It's a little bit like those lost and lovely incense burners in the Great Temple, whose embers were carefully tended from the elder days, never allowed to go out, never allowed to die. A living memory of times changing from history into myth and legend, but the scents they served to propagate through the Temple halls were new and fresh every day. I had sworn my own vow to my land, and she was a living thing, Syai, my land, my sister. And I had fulfilled my own part of that vow.*

But the child that I bore had her own vision of secrets

and vows. How could I have even thought it would be any different? You may not have known the whole truth about your true heritage, but you could not help being what you were, Iloh's daughter and mine, Syai's child, born to the instincts of leadership and nurture, of a need to understand, to shape, to make, to do. Even when you were a very little girl you were the one whom the rest of the children followed, yours the decisions, yours the inspiration for games and learning, yours the big dreams that everyone else found hidden treasures in. And that only became stronger as you grew older, more articulate, more self-assured.

I heard you talking to your friends, my daughter, and you told them that you were all Syai's children. And you gave them all that choice, the choice of love – a melding of Iloh's dream and my own. You named it; you gave it life. Some of your ancestors might have been shocked at the thing you did, but all I could do was stand awed at the simplicity and power of your own vision.

'Xion-shei,' you said to the boy who was your friend. 'You are my heart-brother.'

Xion-shei . . .

I am a woman. Jin-shei has been ours, our secret, for so long – but it is time, time to change. We will always have that bond, it will always be something special between a woman and a woman, but jin-shei is no longer a child. Your words, my daughter, were its Xat-Wau ceremony. It comes of age, the ancient vow . . . and becomes something else. Something grand, glorious, huge. Something new.

It has always been the same dream, after all – perhaps that is why Iloh and I argued so fiercely over it. Seeing only our own half of it – until now, until you came, our daughter, to make a whole of it, to knit it together . . . male and female, equal under the arch of heaven. We were both wrong, Iloh, and we were both right.

The past is long dead – Iloh and his years did far too good a job on that. But his own vision was stillborn, lost in war and fire and fury . . . except now we have this new thing that is the old thing reborn – xion-shei – and it may be what will lead this land into the kind of future that even Iloh could hardly have dreamed of.

Long ago, the people of this land helped one another. Then they turned on one another, and the killing years began. When those times ended, there was nothing left but fear . . . nothing, maybe, except that one thing, the oldest thing, the women's country and its vows.

It is like Iloh said to me once, so long ago, on the night that you, my daughter, were conceived.

Nothing is finished. Everything is possible.

'I have dreamt this place before,' Amais said.

She stood on the crumbling steps surrounded by dirty water, with ruined buildings of a shattered city around her, the sky full of a vivid glow as though from distant, unseen pyres, dressed in the elegant garb of a vanished court, holding an impossibly fragile silk-paper parasol in one hand and the trusting hand of a small girl in the other.

She turned to look at the girl, who was gazing at her, in turn, from eyes that were impossibly too old and wise and full of love and pity to belong to a child.

The child smiled.

'Yes, you know me. You have always known me. Why else would you have trusted me to lead you on the path laid out for you in your dreams?'

'Tai,' Amais said, slowly, her voice full of wonder. 'You are Tai. You are the beginning of it all.'

'There is no beginning,' the child said. 'There is no end. It is the same story, only the people within it change shapes and faces. I had a hand in your life in more than one way – I gave you the fire to seek me, because someone had to find me; when you were in danger, I warned you to flee.'

'The note,' Amais said. 'The note telling me they were coming for me. I never knew who sent that.'

'It does not matter whose hand penned it, it was I who wrote it,' said her companion. 'For that, I needed to take no familiar shape. For the rest, for keeping your footsteps on the path, this was the face that you gave me. Tai, the face that you trusted and loved – the face that a guide who wanted to speak to your spirit would wear if she wanted to be heard. But I am more than this.'

For a moment the child wavered and her image flowed into an ever-changing stream of other faces, other shapes, some old and bent or dressed in garb of ancient times and others wandering in, it seemed, from the unknown future. Amais recognised some of them as they appeared and vanished, in the blink of an eye. Her grandmother was there – and Xuelian – and the old priestess from Sian Sanqin – and Jinlien – and Xeian herself, her bright eyes smiling with Iloh's own fiery charm. And then she was Tai again, the grave and serious child that Tai had been, the child who had given all these dreams, whose presence had guided Amais all of her life.

There was something in her that wanted to bow before this beloved ancestress, like others of her kin had worshipped their own ancestors since time immemorial – but she also wanted to simply curl up at her feet as she would do with a favourite grandmother and sigh in contentment and simply be still under a loving hand on her hair. She did neither, in point of fact. Perhaps it was simply that the context of this meeting was the dream, drifting and free, unattached to any stereotype or obligation. In the here and now, on the ruined stairs, wearing their outlandish and wholly inappropriate garb, Amais could look at Tai and see through the patina of protocol and relationships. Here, she was not revered ancestress. Here she could be anything. A guardian angel. A sister.

A friend. A stranger who smiled anonymously as she passed on the street.

Here, she was all the women of the land. Here, she was Syai herself.

And Amais, too, was free to choose her own soul, at last.

I am of two worlds, and that will never change. But I do not have a divided heart. I can be both. I can be that ragged child hunting mussels on the shore in Elaas and I can be the woman who gave her soul to Syai. The two oceans in my spirit have flowed into one another and I now sail on a different sunlit sea, and it has all my worlds in it, and it is richer for it.

I am the daughter of a woman who loved her heritage enough not to lose it for her children, yet not so well as to give them something unbroken and whole to treasure. I am a descendant of travellers who chose to turn their faces to the sun and their sails into the wind and seek new worlds without ever quite having released the old. I am the many-times-great-granddaughter of a poet who once helped to carry the weight of an empire on her slight shoulders, and who did not stumble under the load.

And I am the mother of the child who will take up that load again, and stand at the head of a nation.

I come from strength and from courage and from beauty.

I am one who is two, and two who is one. I am a singer of songs and a teller of tales and a maker of poetry. I am voice and spirit and memory. I am heart-sister to a nation, I am the vessel that carried the legacy of a people; I am the past that was, the present that is unfolding; I will see, through the eyes of my daughter, the history that is to come. I am a footstep in the stone that is the bones of this earth, and some day, centuries from now, they will still see the shape that my foot left there, and they will wonder, and they will remember.

Who knows what Gods will rule, then – and from what heaven? But I will be there, a word in the wind, a whisper in the leaves of the willow trees in the springtime; someday I may even be worthy of being the face that my land will wear to guide another in the path of her destiny.

I am an ending to a story that began long ago, a beginning to a brand new tale that is only just stirring into life. The words that have come from my heart and my pen open the eyes of the tired and the defeated to the triumphs that lie hidden within tragedy; they reveal to the victorious the tragedy that is the serpent in the bosom of every triumph.

I was. I am. I will be.

'Look,' said Tai.

Amais followed her gaze, out to where the sky blazed with red and gold on the horizon, silhouetting ruins that sat silent and empty in the shattered city which surrounded them.

'Yes,' Amais said, 'something is still burning. Maybe the poor quarters are well alight by now. There is probably nobody left to fight the flames and those hovels are made of—'

'No,' Tai said calmly, 'look.'

Amais said nothing, merely allowed her eyes to rest on the improbable sky. She felt both vividly exhilarated and deathly tired, all at once, as though she had lived an entire lifetime in the scope of a few minutes of dream.

Which, in a way, she had.

She was on the verge of asking Tai what it was that she was supposed to be seeing as she stared out over the ruins, but then, inexplicably, her eyes filled with tears – and while her physical vision blurred with them into a mere smear of shape and colour, somehow they opened her inner eye to a glory that lanced at her heart with an exquisite pleasure that was almost as sharp as pain.

The sky was not aflame with the fires of destruction or

devastation. She was facing east, and that which she was staring at was dawn, the rising of the sun, the promise of a brand new day. From the darkness beneath the earth's rim, the orb of the young sun rose slowly over the edge of the night and poured its liquid light into the world, a bright and holy fire, woken by faith and valour from the sleeping embers of heaven.

Historical Note

I write of a land called Syai, and its people.

It is *not* China. But when I wrote my novel *The Secrets of Jin-Shei*, the historical background in which it was rooted was recognisably that of a glittering Imperial China, from which the story drew its inspiration. The follow-up to that book, *The Embers of Heaven*, is more than just historical fantasy – it is a contemporary historical fantasy, one in which my Imperial Syai evolves for four hundred years before I (and my protagonist) return to it. It slips into a parallel history in which it will be easy for the reader to find parallels to what has been happening in our China, the one in this world, the *real* one. There are some characters whose real-life inspirations will not be hard to spot – Shou'min Iloh, Shenxiao, Baba Sung are all based on real historical figures, although I have taken what liberties I needed to make them live in my own story, in my Syai. Even Tang, although he is a bit of a composite of at least three contemporary Chinese political figures, should be familiar. Events such as the Golden Rising and the Iron Bridge should also find a ready parallel in the minds of contemporary readers – and so should the rampaging cadres of the Golden Wind.

But while the parallels are there, and there is a very real history behind all of this, *The Embers of Heaven* remains a historical fantasy about a land called Syai and the events that shaped that land. Conversations between Shou'min Iloh and any other character in this book are pure fiction, for instance, and, as far as I know, the mystical connection between Iloh and a girl called Amais has never actually existed. Readers should realise that I have used the events of which I write as a palimpsest on which I have created my own dramas, my own history, my own country. China pervades this book, and is a fundamental building block of its storyline – but think of *The Embers of Heaven* as a painting rather than a photograph. You will see things that never were, and things that might have been, and you may well not see the things you expect to see. Just remember – there is a veil between the real China and the land called Syai, and by reading this book you have stepped through it and into a world that is mine alone and where actual China, as potent as its presence there is, must be seen as merely a guiding spirit, a Muse, an inspiration. You will find many things very similar, but do not expect to be reading a contemporary history of the facts exactly as they were.

History is complex and complicated, and the history of China more so than most. I know that I have found myself mystified and astounded and sometimes outright awed at some of the things I have found out while doing my research – I have tried to distil the whole potent brew into something that retains the richness and the bittersweet taste of the original concoction while proving to be more easily accessible and understandable for the average Western reader. It may not be a history textbook, but it may well be a starting point for a lasting fascination with China and all things Chinese. I know I have learned a whole lot while writing *The Embers of Heaven*, both in terms of hard facts and in beginning to understand the way a culture very different from mine thinks, feels, functions. I hope that some of that wonder will find its way into the minds of the readers and stay there long after they put down this book.

Alma Alexander

Glossary and Characters

PRONUNCIATION GUIDE
Pronunciation mostly follows the Pinyin system, the most commonly used system for transcribing Chinese words into English, with some exceptions. The less familiar pronunciations appear below, with examples; other letters approximate their English sounds.

C: TS as in 'its', except when before H, in which case it retains the traditional English 'ch' pronunciation as in 'church' – in other words, Cahan is pronounced Tsahan

Q: CH as in 'chair' – Qiying is pronounced Chiying

X: SH as in 'she' – Xuan is pronounced Shuan

Z: DS as in 'buds'

ZH: J as in 'jump' – zhimei is pronounced jimei

A: as in 'father'

AI   or AY: as in 'aisle'

I: usually pronounced as the I in 'machIne'
Exceptions: when it comes after c, s, or z, when it is pronounced like the I in DIvide; when it comes after ch, r, sh or zh, when it becomes pronounced like IR in 'sir'

459

IA: YA as in 'yard'

IAN: YEN

IU: EO as in 'leo', with the emphasis on the o

O: AW as in 'law'

OU: O as in 'joke'

U: usually pronounced as in 'prune'
        Exceptions: pronounced as the u in 'pudding' when
        syllable ends with n (as in Kunan, for instance);
        pronounced like the u in the French 'tu' when it
        comes after j, q, x or y

UI: WAY

A

Amais: descended of Tai and Kito through their daughter,
    Xanshi. Her mother, Vien, married an 'outsider' and
    Amais belongs to two different and distinct cultures
    which are forever uneasily side by side in her. This is
    reflected in her exotic looks, a mixture of Syai and the
    land called Elaas from where her father Nikos is. She is
    a writer, and she makes it her life's work to return the
    women's country to the land of Syai

Aylun: Amais's younger sister, who takes almost entirely
    after her mother in appearance; joins the Golden Wind

B

-ban: endearment suffix, applied to a child by a mother,
    for example (e.g. Tai-*ban*)

-baya: 'grandmother', equivalent to calling someone
'granny'

Baba Sung: the first architect of the Republic which
    replaced the Imperial regime in Syai; Iloh's inspiration

C

Cahan: Heaven
Chanain: first month of summer
Chen: Iloh's second wife
Chuntan: second month of autumn

D

Dan: Vien's mother, descendant of Tai, grandmother to
  Amais and Aylun

E

Early Heaven Cahan, the Spirit Paradise: the home of the
  lower deities of the great pantheon, not the high rulers
  and the greater powers, but deities who originated in
  Cahan and were never mortal
Elaas: land where some of Tai's descendants settled in exile
Elena: Nikos's mother, grandmother to Amais and Aylun

F

First Circle: the commercial circle of the Great Temple
Fourth Circle: one of the inner circles of the Great
  Temple

G

Ganshu: method of fortune telling
Golden Rising: revolution fomented by Iloh in order to
  reclaim power in Syai
Golden Wind: the student movement that sprang from the
  Golden Rising which performed many atrocities during

461

those times (including orchestrating the slaying of the Emperor and his family)

Great Temple: the chief temple of Syai, in the city of Linh-an

H

hacha-ashu: the common tool of writing the spoken language of Syai, once known as the 'male' alphabet in which Syai's women used to be illiterate almost without exception

Hian: province of Syai, birthplace of Iloh

I

Iloh: visionary leader and revolutionary, later head of state and of the People's Party in Syai; Amais's lover, father of her daughter Xeian

J

Jin-ashu: once known as the 'female' alphabet, or the 'women's tongue' – a secret language passed from mother to daughter for generations, an arcane knowledge confined to women and forbidden to males, mostly lost and forgotten or relegated into obsolescence by the time Amais returns to Syai

Jinlien: priestess of the Fourth Circle of the Temple, Amais's friend

Jin-shei: a pledged sisterhood of female friends who are not related by blood. The sworn sisters are much closer to one another than to their own blood kin, and *jin-shei* was a lifetime commitment, binding and holy. If a sister asked anything of another in the name of the sisterhood, the request had to be honoured at all cost. A custom which has mostly followed the women's tongue into oblivion in modern Syai

jin-shei-bao: one of the *jin-shei* sisterhood

jin-shei-kwan: 'House Sisters' – a group of courtesans plying their trade from the same 'tea house' – a custom that is a corrupted version of the ancient bond of *jin-shei* but one with less permanence and less weight – it rarely survives one 'sister' leaving one 'tea house' for another in the course of her working life.

K

Kannaian: second month of summer

Kunan: first month of autumn

L

-*lama*: a term of respectful address, as in 'master', used to a superior or a higher-ranked person or from apprentice to master craftsman

Later Heaven deities and spirits: according to the teachings of the Way, the part of Cahan where the lesser deities, the spirits of those who were once mortal but achieved immortality in Cahan through their actions or attributes while alive, make their home (for instance, the Holy Sages)

Linh-an: capital city of Syai

Lixao: Vien's second husband, stepfather to Amais and Aylun

Lord of Heaven: Highest and most powerful Deity in Cahan, never named

M

-*mai*: a term used from a senior to a junior, as in, for instance, a master to an apprentice

N

Nhia: once Chancellor of Syai in Tai's time, now enshrined as a Holy Sage in the Great Temple
Niaomai: 'Songbird', stage name of Chen, Iloh's second wife
Nika: the name that Elena, Nikos's mother, gives her younger granddaughter; see Aylun
Nikos: father to Amais and Aylun

Q

Qiying: the name Yingchi takes in Xuelian's House

S

sai'an: form of address, 'lady'
Second Circle: the Great Temple Circle dedicated to the Later Heaven Deities and Spirits
sei: form of address, 'lord'
Shenxiao: the Nationalist leader and general, loses civil war to Iloh
Shiqai: warlord who betrayed both the Emperor and Baba Sung, made a power grab for himself as Emperor, died before he could bring his plans to fruition
Sian Sanqin: Temple of Three Thousand Stairs, place of pilgrimage for Amais
Siantain: first month of spring
Sihuai: Iloh's school friend
Sinan: second month of winter

Shou Ximin: First Citizen (Iloh's title), abbreviated into common use as Shou'min

Street of Red Lanterns: the street where Syai's tea houses are, the courtesans' quarter

Syai: the Middle Kingdom, home to Amais's ancestors and to *jin-shei*

T

Tai: classical poet, and ancestress to Amais

Taian: second month of spring

Tang: Iloh's friend from their shared schooldays, constant companion, later heir

Tannuan: first month of winter

Teahouse of the Silver Moon: Xuelian's tea house on the Street of Red Lanterns

Third Circle: the Great Temple circle dedicated to the Lower Deities of the Early Heaven

V

Vien: mother to Amais and Aylun

W

Wangmei: 'stranger of the body', a pure outsider who does not belong in community by virtue of being a foreigner or a stranger to a particular place. It also has connotations of 'vagabond', 'wanderer', even 'outlaw' – because it is such strangers who traditionally commit crimes of robbery and assault (and then frequently move on to new pastures)

Women's Tongue, the: the written version of the Syai

common tongue, passed from mother to daughter, a
secret alphabet nearly extinct in contemporary Syai,
known only to women (see *jin-ashu*)

X

Xanshi: Tai's daughter

Xat-Wau: the coming-of-age ceremony in Syai

Xeian: Amais's and Iloh's daughter, born of the spirit of
Syai

Xeimei: 'stranger of the heart' – one who belongs to the
same community as another but holds a different set
of beliefs or values that makes it difficult or even
impossible to communicate. Often such folk were
simply left alone – but during the times of the Golden
Rising, having 'different' ideas could be very
dangerous

Ximin: 'citizen', title by which people are addressed in the
Republic

Xinmei: Xuelian's sister, woman from whom Amais learns
of *jin-shei* first-hand

Xuan: Amais's 'husband', died in the Black Flux

Xuelian: an old courtesan whose exotic working life
involved being concubine to an Emperor. She now owns
one of the tea houses; a journal keeper, just like Tai
once was, and one of the few who remains who knows
the true and uncorrupted language of *jin-ashu*, the
women's tongue, now considered archaic and almost
lost to the women of Syai

Y

Yanzi: Iloh's first wife, killed by Shenxiao during the early
years of the civil war

Yingchi: Iloh's half-sister, daughter of Youmei
Youmei: concubine to Iloh's father

Z

Zhimei: 'stranger of the soul' – has both commonplace
and mystical meanings. In the common meaning, it
means someone who is of one's own community or
family but does not seem to belong there – it is not as
simple as holding a different set of beliefs, it's a bone-
deep difference, never to be bridged. In theory it is
possible to convince a *xeimei* of the 'error' of his or her
ways – a *zhimei* is removed from that, belongs in a
different world, not just a different set of convictions.
This leads into the more otherworldly meaning, because
zhimei has been used in the context of 'changeling', one
left behind in this world by accident or design but actually part of the spirit world or even the lower heavens –
a spirit or a ghost, whom it is bad luck to tamper with